3/19   3⁰⁰
         JJ

365 Views of *Algorithms of the*

Todd Shimoda

Illustrations by L.J.C. Shimoda

Mt. Fuji

Floating World

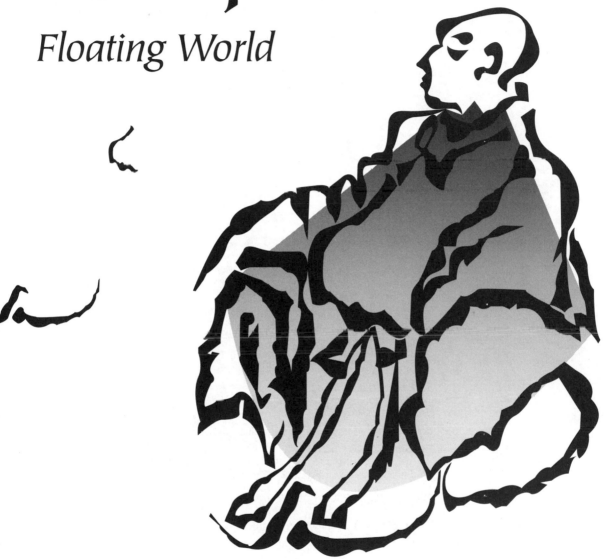

Stone Bridge Press • Berkeley, California

Published by
Stone Bridge Press, P. O. Box 8208, Berkeley, CA 94707
TEL 510-524-8732 • FAX 510-524-8711
E-MAIL sbp@stonebridge.com

For correspondence, updates, and further information
about this and other Stone Bridge Press books, visit
Stone Bridge Press online at **www.stonebridge.com**.

Printed in the United States of America.

10   9   8   7   6   5   4   3   2   1
2002   2001   2000   1999   1998

ISBN 1-880656-35-3

Contents

Author's Note

The primary narrative line of *365 Views of Mt. Fuji* follows the main character, Keizo Yukawa. His story is found in the main text. The stories of the other characters, written in segments, have been placed in the margins. These pieces occur in a non-chronological, but logical, order.

The recommended way to read the book is to read Yukawa's story and the other characters' stories as they occur. Another way is to read the main story line first, then go back and read the other stories.

Keizo Yukawa

Yukawa is the main character of *365 Views of Mt. Fuji*. He is an art curator from Tokyo, about 35 years old. He has had a successful life—attending the right university, landing a prestigious, though dead-end, job at the Tokyo National Art Museum. He has traditional Japanese sensibilities mixed with fashionable, Western tastes. Yukawa is about to embark on a new career that will take him away from Tokyo and his lover, Junko. He hopes his new position as curator of a private museum will give his professional and private life a fresh start.

Junko

Junko, Yukawa's lover, is a Tokyo performance artist, about 30 years old. Known as the Pink Doughnut Girl for her costume of that description, Junko creates outlandish performance pieces that poke fun at society. Many of her jabs hit areas of society in which Yukawa participates. Junko is totally devoted to her persona, yet content being Yukawa's lover.

Ichiro Ono

Ichiro is an industrialist and owner of a robotics empire. He is about 68 years old. He is building a museum in Hakone to display the 365 Views of Mt. Fuji, a series of paintings by the ukiyo-e artist Takenoko. Ichiro is seeking the right curator to assemble the artist's works, and hires Yukawa. Ichiro is stiff, formal, and a traditional Japanese businessman. However, Ichiro has one soft spot: his daughter, Kumi. He is the brother of two siblings, Gun Ono and Akiko Ono.

Gun Ono

Gun is the entertainment king of Atami, a hot springs resort town. About 67 years old, he is the brother of Ichiro. He owns some of the 365 Views of Mt. Fuji, which he creatively displays in his establishment, Club Yoshiwara. Gun feels a true artist reveals his soul in his art and disagrees with his brother's approach to showing the pieces in a sterile museum.

Akiko Ono

Akiko, about 60 years old, is sister to Ichiro and Gun and owns an old-style onsen ryokan (hot springs inn) in Heda. She also owns some of the 365 Views of Mt. Fuji and feels they are best displayed in her ryokan. Akiko is very traditional and, like Ichiro, she has a soft spot for her own daughter, Haruna.

Kumi

Kumi, about 32 years old, is Ichiro's daughter and works at Ono Robotics in Numazu. An expert in artificial intelligence, she attended the University of California at Berkeley. Kumi is devoted to her father's company.

Haruna

Haruna, about 25 years old, is Akiko's daughter and works at her mother's ryokan. She values the simple, traditional life of working at the onsen and has no desire ever to leave its grounds. She meets Yukawa when he comes to inspect Akiko's collection of the 365 Views of Mt. Fuji.

Nekobaba

Nekobaba is an ancient woman who collects trash in an overflowing shopping cart from the streets of Numazu. Yukawa first sees her while haunting the streets of Numazu, looking for excitement.

Takenoko

Takenoko is the mysterious, painter of the 365 Views of Mt. Fuji. An ukiyo-e ("pictures of the floating world") artist, he struggled to eke out a living in Edo (old Tokyo), around 1830–45, but never made a name for himself. Takenoko wandered aimlessly around the Izu Peninsula until he came to Heda, where he began to paint a view of Mt. Fuji every day.

The Last Ukiyo-e Artist

The Last Ukiyo-e Artist is an academic monograph of Takenoko and his works. Its contents are required reading for Yukawa as he begins his new job.

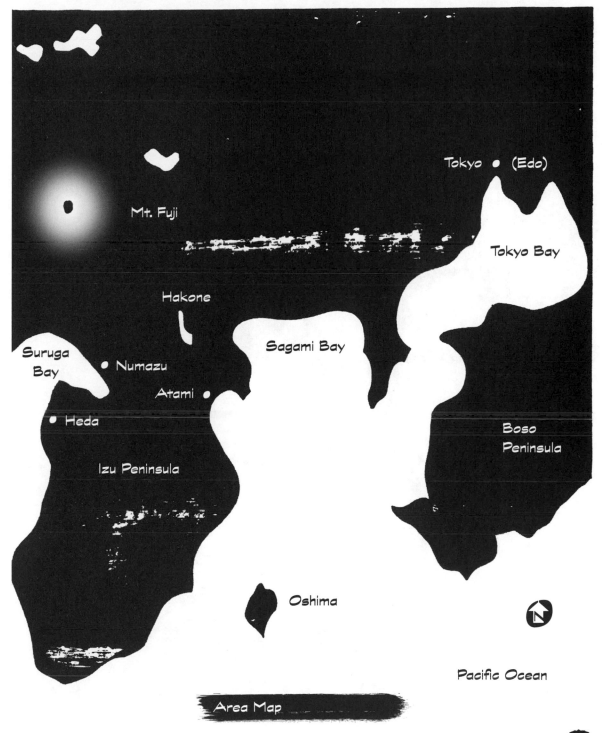

Tokyo • (Edo)

Tokyo Bay

Mt. Fuji

Hakone

Sagami Bay

Suruga
Bay

Numazu

Atami

Heda

Boso
Peninsula

Izu Peninsula

Oshima

Pacific Ocean

Area Map

Multiple Unknown Crimes

A bead of sweat drips from my left armpit, cascades over my ribs, and pools at the waistband of my pants. I hope the moisture doesn't soak through my new suit. I should have worn an undershirt, but I never do—they spoil the line of a well-tailored shirt.

My new suit is a Kenji Fukada design: double-breasted, six buttons, slightly oversized lapels.

I am waiting for the owner of a new, private art museum to interview me for the chief curator's position. The museum is located in Hakone, near Mt. Fuji, a three-and-a-half hour drive from Tokyo. The museum is unfinished: the wallboard is unpainted, the floor is raw concrete, the ceiling tiles are askew, exposing metal joists and electrical conduits. The only furniture is a folding table and two chairs.

I need this job.

Takenoko

The brothel owner—smelling of musty body odor, cloying incense, and the grimy metal of coins—took Takenoko's sketches. The artist fought to keep his stomach from growling.

The brothel owner flipped through the sketches, barely giving them a bored glance. Then he stopped at one of a young courtesan, her body twisted as she inspected the back of her sock where a speck of mud had marred the pure white fabric.

The brothel owner laughed.

Please don't laugh, thought Takenoko. I need this job; I need to work. I'm tired of starving.

Ichiro

Ichiro Ono disliked Yukawa's face; it had the common traits of today's youth: too knowing around the eyes, too self-satisfied around the mouth, too eager to laugh in the throat. Evolution had worked quickly to produce an entire generation of smug know-it-alls.

And Yukawa's suit, with those ridiculous lapels that screamed out for attention, struck Ichiro Ono like a slap on his cheek.

The museum owner strides into the room. He looks to be in his early sixties. He stands with the table between us and introduces himself: "Ichiro Ono. You are Yukawa."

As much as the museum is unfinished, Ichiro Ono is a finished man. Not "finished" as in "done with," but finished as the sculpture of David is finished, with nothing else to chip off or polish. He holds himself precisely—not too stiffly, not too relaxed. He must know what he wants from the rest of his life.

"Yes," I say. "Keizo Yukawa. I am very pleased to meet you."

"Yes. Of course." He sits on one of the folding chairs. I do the same. He stares at me for a long, uncomfortable second, then asks, "What do you know about Takenoko?"

I know very little about Takenoko. Too little, I admit to myself, to be the curator of a museum dedicated to the artist. Should I be honest? Ichiro Ono is very direct, perhaps I should be the same.

But I need this job.

My answer: "Admittedly, there are others more expert in Takenoko and the other ukiyo-e artists than I am. My expertise in art is with the 1930s neo-classical printmakers such as Takahashi and Domoto, as you can see in my curriculum vitae; however, as a trained curator, I am sensitive to all artists and art forms and what they demand in the way of proper presentation and display."

Another bead of sweat drips, cascades, and pools.

Ichiro Ono doesn't blink. He says, "This museum is built to display Takenoko's 365 Views of Mt. Fuji. Only those works." Then he asks, "What do you know about robots?"

Robots?

I know it's a mistake to want something desperately. But it's impossible to stop.

"Certainly I know less about robots than I know about curatorial science," I say, throwing in the word "science" lamely but hopefully.

"Robots are paying for this museum. I am the president of Ono Robotics."

"Ah, an honored and successful firm."

Ichiro Ono says, "You aren't married."

"Well, no." Would my chances be better if I were? "Not yet," I add. Junko despises the institution, all institutions in fact.

I have no feelings about marriage. Take it or leave it. At least that's what I tell people.

Ichiro Ono says, "So far, I have hired three curatorial consultants to help with the design of the museum, but I wasn't impressed enough to hire any of them as full-time curator." He pauses then asks, "What is your philosophy of life?"

Of life? I had rehearsed my answer to the question: "What is your philosophy as a curator?" not my philosophy of life. A trick question? I fight the urge to sweat by breathing deeply before I answer. "My philosophy of life and my philosophy as a curator are the same: to do things correctly."

Ono stares at me. I gaze slightly away from his eyes, around the side of his precise ear.

Ono says, "You have the credentials, especially your assistant curatorship at the Tokyo National Art Museum. But this is a small museum; you'll have to do much of the work yourself."

"That's what I'm most looking forward to."

Junko

While she danced to the Tokyo Tower Boys, Junko ate a pink glazed doughnut. She knew it was making Yukawa angry. So she danced closer to him and offered him a bite. He clamped his lips and turned his face away.

She pushed the doughnut onto his lips. He slapped it away. The pink glazed doughnut flew across the dance floor. Junko danced over to it then began to stomp on it. The pink glaze became violet in the black light strobes. Yukawa grabbed the back of her arm and pulled.

He said, "Is this another one of your performance art pieces?"

"No. It's what I want to do to your ego."

"Because I want to quit my job? To be happy?"

"Because you're selfish."

The Last Ukiyo-e Artist

This book, undertaken in the years 1971 to 1974, explores the largely mysterious life of the artist Takenoko. Many obstacles presented themselves during the research and writing of the book, in particular the lack of records of Takenoko's real name, and consequently his story, and the fact that Takenoko's most revealing body of work—The 365 Views of Mt. Fuji—are widely distributed, although most are owned by the Ono family. The three siblings—two brothers (Ichiro and Gun) and sister (Akiko)—are descendants of the owner of the onsen (hot springs resort) on the west coast of the Izu Peninsula where Takenoko painted the Views. The Ono siblings are seeking to consolidate ownership of the Views back into their family.

I must thank the Ono family for allowing me access to the collection for this unprecedented study. This book would have been impossible, or surely diminished, without such access. My goal in this book is not only to chronicle the artist's life and work, but to put it in the context of the upheaval that was occurring at the time which transformed, at least superficially, the nation of Japan.

Shintaro Hata, 1975

Takenoko is considered to be an ukiyo-e artist. Ukiyo is translated as "the floating world," originally a Buddhist concept referring to the transience of life in this world of suffering. Ukiyo came to represent the fleeting earthly good life of the popular theater, songs, literature (ukiyo-zoshi), erotic pleasures, and art (ukiyo-e).

Ichiro Ono pushes a folder across the desk to me. The thick paper is embossed with both the Ono Robotics logo and the Ono Takenoko Museum logo. "Here is the compensation package I am offering. If you accept, you can stay in the company dormitory at the Ono Robotics plant in Numazu, at least until you find your own place. The dormitory is a convenient drive from here."

I nod. Is he offering me the job? I guess so. Does he want me to say I accept the job? Should I accept the job right away?

Ichiro Ono says, "You can think about it, of course. For a day. We need a capable person on board immediately."

"Sure, I mean yes, thank you. That's a good idea. A day, yes."

Without another word, he gives me a book, then stands up and strides out of the room. The book is *Takenoko: The Last Ukiyo-e Artist.*

4

While a consistent definition of ukiyo-e style or subject matter has never been agreed upon, the term generally refers to the popular art of the Edo period, from 1615 to 1868. This period is named for the capital of feudal Japan during that time, located in Edo, now Tokyo, although the roots of ukiyo-e were put down more in Kyoto and Osaka in the Genroku era (circa 1688 to 1704).

Ukiyo-e had its beginnings primarily as wood-cut illustrations of books with erotic themes, such as those of Saikaku ("Life of an Amorous Man").

As I follow him through the museum, Ichiro Ono says, "In general, your duties, should you accept the job, will be to inspect the collection of Takenoko's 365 Views of Mt. Fuji, determine the condition of each painting, gather the collection together, work with the contractor to finish the interior spaces of the museum, plan the exhibitions, develop budgets, and hire and fire staff. Any questions?"

"I understand clearly, except perhaps what is meant by 'gather' the collection. Excuse my stupidity, could you please enlighten me?"

"I have possession of the majority of the Views. My brother Gun Ono and my sister Akiko Ono have the others … all of the others, I believe."

"I see. You want all of the Views to be here, in the museum, rather than kept in other collections."

Ichiro Ono says, "Well of course."

Takenoko

The brothel owner said to Takenoko, "I can offer you a room in the shack in the alley and one meal a day. In exchange you'll provide the artwork for my advertising posters. You deliver the artwork to the printers. When they are finished, you deliver the posters to the clients and other places where they are displayed."

Takenoko said, "Yes, that is acceptable."

"And," said the brothel owner, "you'll sweep the alley and street in front of the establishment daily."

Bile rose in the back of Takenoko's throat. "Yes."

Ichiro Ono believed that the trouble with those of Yukawa's age—born around the time of the 1964 Tokyo Olympics when everything deemed "unacceptable to Western thinking" was swept under the newly erected elevated freeway structures—is not that they can't appreciate the hard work of their elders, or that they can't concentrate for more than five minutes, or that they reject tradition as if it were as toxic as fugu liver, or that they have no patience and no courage and enjoy whining as a hobby, but that they have no concept of self. That's why they go to such ridiculous extremes in superficial and external displays such as fashion and music and what passes for art.

A concept of self could only flower—and be maintained—from one thing: suffering.

On the way back to Tokyo, I stop at the Fuji International Hotel in Hakone, overlooking Lake Yamanaka. I find the bar attached to the main restaurant (French). Except for two women sipping cognac (executives' wives I guess from their designer afternoon tea dresses), the bar is empty. The bartender is wearing a black silk vest, a crisply starched white shirt, and a too thin, black silk tie. His face wears a continentally grim expression which he must assume is de rigueur for all European bartenders.

I take a seat on a plush barstool. I place the book and folder Ichiro Ono has given me on the copper bartop. I order a scotch and water.

"Your scotch?" asks the bartender, in a voice as stiff as his collar.

"Um? Oh, um …" I peruse the selection of bottles. "Glenfiddich, just a splash of water." The bartender grunts, whether in approval or disgust, I can't tell.

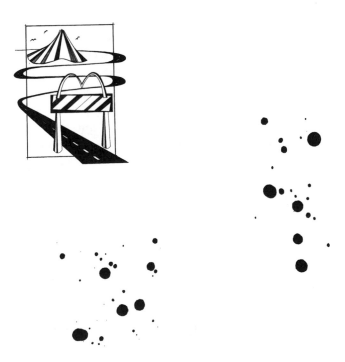

I open the folder and zoom in on the salary. I can live with it; it's ten percent more than I'm making now. The benefits are standard, except an unusual and generous housing allowance.

Is this what I want to do? Does that matter? All I want is to escape the stuffiness of the National Art Museum, escape my assistant curatorship (which is as far as I will rise due to my lack of political acumen), escape the asinine assignments (forest-style calligraphy, Bizen pottery, Heian-era trinkets), escape the chief curator's horribly bad breath.

Do other people worry about what they want from life? Or do they just live it? Junko does and I appreciate that. But then as an abstract performance artist she is expected to be bizarre to the point of irrationality. Rational irrationality.

The bartender places my Glenfiddich and splash on a cardboard coaster. I smile but he doesn't let go of his grim expression. I wonder if he wears it after work or if he has a home face.

I take a sip of the scotch, grateful for the smooth warmth, like a nuzzle on the soft underside of a breast. The scene imprinted on the coaster shows the hotel frontage and Mt. Fuji reflected on Lake Yamanaka.

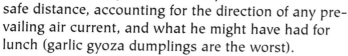

I think of the chief curator. He is only seven years older than I am. He'll be in his position for another twenty-five years if he merely maintains his current level of mediocrity. I would go insane waiting for him to retire. When talking with him, you have to stay a safe distance, accounting for the direction of any prevailing air current, and what he might have had for lunch (garlic gyoza dumplings are the worst).

Junko

Junko adjusted the giant, plasticized, pink glazed doughnut around her waist after she straightened up from giving the homeless man a real pink glazed doughnut. She knew what Yukawa was going to say: "Why give them something so nutritionally worthless as a pink glazed doughnut?"

She would answer, "Nutrition only affects the future. The homeless have a hunger that needs to be satisfied today."

Junko

Junko said, "Dance with me."

Yukawa remained seated with his back against the wall. He squeezed his half-full can of Sapporo lager until the aluminum can popped.

She twisted the desk lamp until it made a circular glare in his eyes. She waited with her arms crossed on her chest. She began to undulate to the acid jazz heavy with synthesized sax.

Yukawa watched. Junko danced over to him. She slipped her silk top off one shoulder; slowly revealing her breast.

The Last Ukiyo-e Artist

Little is known about the life of the ukiyo-e artist known as Takenoko. Historians believe he was born in 1820 in Edo, old Tokyo. His actual name may have been Hideo Shimoseki, and as an artist he changed his name several times, though Takenoko (literally "bamboo shoot") is how he is best known, and (in more than one permutation of "bamboo") the name he used most.

He lived all of his life in Edo, except for the last few years when he traveled around the Izu Peninsula and settled in the small village of Heda located in the northwest corner of the peninsula. There he painted his 365 Views of Mt. Fuji and apparently died shortly after completing the works.

The chief curator knows that I hate him, and knows that I have no other employment opportunities as a curator due to the incestuous fortifications of the national museum and gallery system. "Yukawa!" he shouts in meetings, spewing halitosis-laced spittle. The louder he shouts the more he hates you. "Yukawa will be in charge of the spring flower-arrangement scroll painting display." If he refers to you in the third person to your face, he despises you more than he despises mouthwash.

I open the book that Ichiro Ono gave to me and try to read. I reach the bottom of the page without registering a single word. I take a deep breath, then a sip of my drink, and start over.

After the first sentence, Junko pops into my thoughts. She'll never leave Tokyo. We'll have to split up.

Part of my problem with the chief curator is Junko—he hates abstract performance artists. As Junko began to get a name for herself, it became known that she and I were not only friends, but were living together. A situation that is expected for an abstract performance artist, but improper for an assistant curator of the staid National Art Museum. The chief curator expresses his displeasure of her profession and our living arrangements nearly every Thursday at our weekly meeting.

I keep silent on those occasions. Once I shrugged when I thought he wasn't looking but he caught the slight movement. His jaw muscles tensed and bulged to the size and shape of his beloved gyoza.

I start again, trying to read the book. The author's style is rather breezy, more like you'd read in a biography than a critical analysis.

I wish my life could be more like a light novel.

Junko enters my thoughts again: What does she want from life? Will she always go around dressed in a plasticized, pink glazed doughnut? Will she move on to, say, chocolate eclairs? And where do I fit in with her eternal publicity stunt?

I close the book, finish my drink, pay the bartender, and leave.

In the hotel lobby I find a pay phone. I put in a call to Ichiro Ono to accept the job.

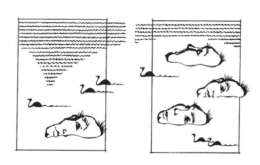

Later, in our apartment, I nearly choke on the painfully direct words when I tell Junko: "I've accepted the curator's job at Hakone."

Junko tugs her hair, streaked and crinkled with dried, pink-tinted hair gel. Her fingers stop at the back of her head and scratch nervously. Then she whips her hand away and stands up. "I don't care." She walks out of the apartment.

Our apartment in Shinjuku is in a twenty-story high-rise, from which we can see the Meiji Shrine park in Harajuku. We have one large room where we sit and roll out our futon to sleep, a small kitchen-dining area, a bathroom, and a small study the size of a car trunk. One wall collects Junko's posters that advertise her shows; the latest posters are in four shades of pink. In the lower right corner of each is her signature icon: a scratch-and-sniff, pink glazed doughnut.

Important to the beginning of this book is a discussion of the end.

That the Edo period was rapidly coming to a close before the arrival of Perry and the black ships is indisputable. The last Tokugawa shogunate was as out of touch with the people and as powerless as an addle-brained, benign king.

The centuries of isolation and unchallenged rule had softened the shogunate and its armies. Now mostly bureaucrats, including a plethora of tax collectors and censors, the ruling elite was increasingly despised.

The shogunate had also been weakened by the string of crop failures, and the strict bureaucratic reforms that followed did little to improve the situation. Continued crises occurred in all aspects of society. In reaction, cults sprung up, as can be seen in the radical communal art movement and mountain-worshiping ascetics.

The few facts about Takenoko, no matter how much circumstantial evidence is offered, are in the end mere guesses.

Takenoko may have served as an apprentice woodblock carver in the large publishing house of Nakamura. This claim is based on an 1869 published history (Nakamura's 200th anniversary) that lists employees who went on to become famous in their own right.

One such entry was: "apprentice Hideo Shimoseki, hired in 1834, became the artist Takeyabu [bamboo grove]." Takeyabu, whose work is regarded as that of the early Takenoko, was only a

I lean back against a pile of pillows and start again on the book. I'm becoming quite taken with the story of Takenoko, even though the author admits many of his "facts" have only the most tenuous evidence. Still, the lifestyle of the more famous artists at the turbulent end of the Edo period—150 years ago—is well documented enough to apply to Takenoko.

Most intriguing, at least so far, is Takenoko's passion for his art, and his sacrifices just to be able to paint and draw.

After I've read for two or three hours I get up to make a cup of tea. Junko comes back just then.

minor artist who painted Yoshiwara [the red-light district of Edo] scenes, particularly of prostitutes and brothels. The history further states that Takeyabu went on to paint a "large volume of work of Mt. Fuji."

Apprentices were usually hired at the age of fourteen. Thus Takenoko's birth date of 1820.

On the tatami mat floor, Junko sprawls out on her stomach. Her arms are drawn up under her chest. Her forehead rests on the tatami and she speaks to the mat. "Why some tiny museum in the middle of nowhere?"

"Look, it's nothing to do with you. It's my problem. I'm selfish. You're right. I'm escaping. The museum, the chief curator."

She raises slightly off the floor. Her hair sweeps the tatami as she shakes her head. "It's me."

"No," I try to speak gently and firmly at the same time. "It's not you."

"But it is me."

It's not her ... I think.

She flings her arms out to the side, flaps them slowly like a great bird on a current of air (I'd seen her perform once as such a bird). After a flap or two she places her hands on the back of her neck. She now looks like a crime suspect being arrested by the police.

"You can come with me," I say softly, knowing that she can't and won't. It would be the end of her career, as short-lived as it is no doubt destined to be.

She says, "I can't come with you. I'm under arrest for multiple unknown crimes."

11.

Takenoko

When she parted the folds of her kimono, Takenoko could see why the other brothel courtesans had nicknamed her "Frog." Her legs had strongly defined muscles, no doubt developed from slogging around rice paddies in the farming district from which she'd arrived only three weeks ago.

Her feet turned outward, as well, adding to the froglike appearance.

She raised one knee in the air; her fingers traced a line from her ankle to the juncture of her muscular thighs. Takenoko took up his brush and started to paint.

"I'll keep the apartment with you," I offer.

Junko flaps her arms gracefully and undulates her body like a fish propelling itself against an ocean current.

I say, "It's not so far away; we can see each other every week."

She draws her feet together and toward her body, then pushes them away like a frog trying to make a distant lily pad.

I almost say, "We can get married," but I swallow the words quickly, as if they were poison pills. I don't like her anymore, at least not right now. And I can conveniently blame her for many of my troubles at the museum. I'll be glad to get away from her, won't I?

Takenoko

Takenoko, the apprentice, looked at his sketches as his teacher leafed through them. When he drew them he had thought they were good. But now, he saw nothing but crude lines, as if he had drawn them with a rock. He wanted to grab the sketches and run away.

He waited, not breathing.

The teacher set aside one of the sketches. He tore the others in half, then in quarters. He placed the bits of paper in the hibachi and they immediately caught flame. The teacher pointed at the remaining sketch, to a single, tiny line that defined a woman's cheekbone.

"That," said the teacher, "is a good line."

At work the next day, I ask my colleague, an assistant curator who specializes in Yayoi artifacts and Edo-period prints, what he knows about Takenoko. My colleague wears his hair longish and his suits are off-the-rack from Seibu Department Store. His face is scarred from a pubescent acne war.

He takes a long time to consider my question before answering.

"Takenoko, late Edo period printmaker and painter, a minor ukiyo-e artist when the style had all but disappeared anyway, most famous for a work called 365 Views of Mt. Fuji, his last."

"Yes." I know all that. "Does his art have merit?"

He considers again. "From a stylistic technique standpoint, he never excelled in any form, but his originality and almost demonic perspective warrants his mention."

Takenoko's late work of landscapes, particularly that of the 365 Views of Mt. Fuji, may not have been very well known at the time the Nakamura history was published. Certainly the quality would have been only rumor at that time. The first scholarly mention of the Views was not until 1878. Indeed, the 365 Views were largely unknown in Tokyo until the early twentieth century, due to the upheaval in politics and society due to the forced opening of the country by Commodore Perry and the disintegration of the shogunate feudal structure.

Also confounding the evidence of Takenoko's early history is the fact that many artists of the time had executed their own large volumes of Mt. Fuji views, especially the artist Takeda [bamboo field] who published "100 Views of Mt. Fuji from All Sides." Only a minor artist, Takeda may have been confused for Takeyabu, or Takenoko as he was later known.

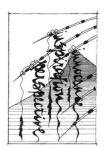 

The chief curator stands between my colleague and me. I hold my breath while he asks me: "Has Yukawa finished that budget analysis for the spring show yet?"

"No, chief curator."

"When will Yukawa finish? When the budget meeting is already over? That'll be too late, doesn't Yukawa think so?"

I can't hold my breath any longer and I let it out. I start to make an excuse for the analysis being late, then, with relief, I remember I'm quitting. "I'll try to get to it later." I smile.

The chief curator turns the color of salted plums.

For lunch I go alone to a little noodle place near Ueno Station. I quiet my nerves with a large Sapporo beer. Not their dry brand or their winter brew or their ice brewed ale, but the plain, old, classic lager.

I rehearse what I'm going to say to the chief curator when I return.

For lunch I order daikon radish pickles, fermented soybeans, and two plates of garlic gyoza dumplings.

Takenoko

Through the pinhole in the upper corner of the yellowed and stained shoji screen, Takenoko could peer into the room. Inside, Frog lay on her back, her muscular legs in the air squeezing the stout man about the waist. She moaned and twisted her head from side to side, her toes curled and uncurled like a baby's fingers grasping at air in search of a breast.

Without taking his eye from the pinhole, Takenoko sketched in hurried brushstrokes.

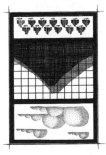

I sit in the chief curator's office, an elegant room with traditional sand-plaster walls and shoji paper partitions. His Japanese mahogany desk gleams softly from ceiling-reflected up-lighting. I can see myself in the front panel of the desk; I look fairly relaxed but my insides gurgle volcanically.

The curator looks up from my letter of resignation. He seems rather calm. Could he be happy?

I stand up and take two steps over to his desk. I touch the wood with a fingertip and it smudges delightfully. Leaning forward, I let go with a deep, rumbling belch.

I go to a tiny but neat bar in a back alley near the station. I chug a glass of beer and belch. The mama-san giggles. I mimic her giggle, which makes her giggle even more.

I had gotten the job at the Tokyo National Art Museum after a twenty-five-month application process, during which I held a succession of menial jobs: copy machine operator, filing clerk, plastic toy model caster, and several restaurant worker positions. When I received word that I had won the job, Junko arranged a surprise party for me in a Shinjuku bar frequented by her performance artist crowd.

We were there for twenty-five hours straight, one hour for each month of the application process.

As the sun sets, several colleagues—ex-colleagues—join me at the bar. We drink beer and sing sophomoric old ballads. Someone brings bags of take-out garlic gyoza, and we have a Chief Curator Breath-Alike contest. I don't really like any of my ex-colleagues, but the evening is mildly amusing.

We stay exactly eight and a half hours, one hour for each of the years I was at the museum.

On the way to the station to take the train home, I lurch through a pedestrian tunnel filled with homeless men sleeping on cardboard and newsprint. Some stink of body odor and urine and feces. One leans up on an elbow and watches me with milky eyes.

Sobered, I hurry past.

Junko waited for Yukawa at the dark corner table. She smoked a cigarette held with her wrist turned just so. She sipped at a lemon vodka. She tried to look sultry but couldn't get the corner of her mouth right; it looked more like a sneer than sultry.

Yukawa arrived with a big smile. He flopped onto the chair with one arm draped across its back.

"Congratulations," Junko said.

"Thank you."

Junko watched his head jerk in surprise as her hand began to tug at the zipper of his pants.

15

Junko said to Yukawa, "Have you ever wondered what your stomach looks like? From the inside, I mean."

Yukawa slowly lowered the magazine he was reading ("Film") and gazed at her. "No."

Junko balled a fist and shook it at him. "What's the matter with you?"

"Nothing."

"Then why haven't you ever wondered what your stomach looks like?"

Yukawa raised the magazine again to hide his face. He sighed loud enough for her to hear.

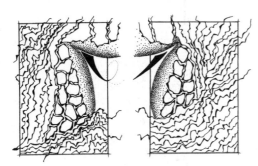

Junko lies in the fetal position, on the tatami, a mini boom box cradled against her stomach. The satirical pop music—Shonen Knife—is muffled by her body. It's as if she wants to absorb the music into her gut.

My clothes are draped over all available chairs, on the dining table, and hanging from door knobs. My closet door is open and stuff has tumbled out. I sort through it, putting things I need into a box.

Junko cries out like a baby.

I sigh and put a book on museum design fundamentals in the box.

"What?" I say to Junko.

She jerks spasmodically. The CD in the mini boom box skips.

I say, "Stop that."

She gets up, turns the volume up full blast, and leaves the apartment. When the door slams I turn off the boom box. The music echoes off the walls and my ears ring.

I grab a beer. While I sip it I read the Takenoko book. I wanted to have it finished before I start the job, but I can't concentrate on it for more than a few minutes.

For the rest of the afternoon I get into a routine of packing, drinking, and reading. Junko has stayed away.

I pick up an album of photos taken at a party Junko and I attended for Saburo Hattori—the venerated performer of Butoh, minimalist organic expressionism. She had talked with him for hours, and after the party she recounted his every word to me.

I can't remember any of the conversation now.

In the first chapter of the book on Takenoko, the author speculates the artist may have been the adopted son of a famous kabuki actor—Takeuchi—who had no son of his own. The actor may have not been married and desired a young male around the house; the real purpose, the author suggests, may have been sexual in nature. Such practice was not unknown in Edo.

The chapter also mentions the Ono family, referring to them as the owners of the majority of the 365 Views. Takenoko painted the Views in Heda, hometown of the Ono family.

I put down the book and fold my suits into the garment bag. I have one gray wool suit, two blue, and the new green-brown double-breasted one I wore to the interview. I wonder if I'll need another suit or two.

The sun has set and the evening has an unusual chill to it. I slip on a sweater and open another beer. The box is nearly full and I've gone through only about a third of the stuff crammed into the closet.

I finish half the beer in a gulp. I tear into the closet and start throwing away my junk:

envelopes stuffed with photos,
design magazines I'd never read,
several pieces of sports equipment I'd tried a few times before giving up (a tennis racket, a squash racket, skates, jogging shoes), and
a few videos, mostly French film noir (they're awful in subtitles).

Takenoko

The brothel owner tossed Takenoko's clothes, brushes, sketches, and paints into the muddy alley. He shouted, "Now you, out!"

Takenoko hurried past the owner. "Stupid! Did I ever tell you that you could watch? Or that you could paint the girls? No, I didn't."

When Takenoko bent over to pick up a sketch of Frog, the owner kicked him in the ribs. Takenoko's blood coursed through his ears like lava. He started to turn, but knowing if he did, he might kill the owner. At least bite off his ear.

Instead, without picking up a thing, he walked away. The owner shouted after him, "Anyway, your art is shit."

I take several loads down to the trash. I keep just one box filled with my favorite books on curatorial science and art history. Other than that box, all that I have left is a suitcase and a garment bag.

Junko can have everything else.

Everything.

I wait just inside the apartment. I'm holding an empty can of Sapporo—the last one from the refrigerator. Junko doesn't like beer; lemon vodka is her drink. The apartment is so quiet I can hear myself breathe. I sound like I'm drowning.

The door opens.

Junko

Zen is the search for intuitive enlightenment.

The circle is the symbol of Zen.

The doughnut is a circle.

The doughnut is intuitive enlightenment.

"You're still here?" Junko says. She flops onto the tatami.

I knew she was going to say that. I also know that she checked to see if my car was in the parking space before coming up.

I say, "I waited so I could say good-bye."

"Why?"

"Good-bye," I say. I stand up.

She starts picking the paint off her fingernails. Flakes of pink polish fall to the tatami.

I leave quietly.

That Takenoko left Edo to travel the Izu Peninsula is fact; exactly when and why are certainly less clear. There is evidence that he held a few jobs as an artist in the Yoshiwara brothels; the occasional work of his survives that is identifiable by location and subject. Whether economic depression or his own personal problems caused him to leave can only be conjectured.

The evidence—mostly as paintings of lower-class prostitutes posing against sea cliffs on the east coast of Izu—has Takenoko leaving Edo in late 1847, surely a desperate measure, as his prospect of finding work was severely limited, infinitely worse than in depressed Edo.

I get halfway down the hallway when she flings the door open and shouts after me:

"You've got no imagination! You're so boring! You're passionless! You're practically worthless!"

As I walk through the parking lot, I feel empty.

But is it me who is empty, or is it my life that is empty?

I sit in my Toyota Sprinter Marino for ten minutes, with my heart pounding fiercely, before I turn the key, start the engine, and put the automatic transmission in reverse. I take an incredible amount of care so I won't ding anyone's car during the last time I'll back out of my space.

By Tokyo Standards

The Ono Robotics headquarters is in Numazu, a city of a quarter of a million, near the northwestern point of the Izu Peninsula and Suruga Bay. The northern coast-line of the bay is where Mt. Fuji rises from sea level and climbs 3,775.6 meters, according to my Handy Map of Mt. Fuji, Hakone, and Izu Peninsula. On the color-coded topographical map, Mt. Fuji resembles a breast. The mountain's crater is an irregularly-shaped nipple. I look over toward the mountain but I can't see it because of the low clouds.

I've been sitting in my car, parked at the Ono plant, for twenty minutes or maybe half an hour. I'd guess about a hundred cars are parked in the lot. Or maybe five hundred, it's hard to tell.

All I know for sure is that my car feels very comfortable.

As I slowly get out of my car, Junko's parting salvo leaps into my consciousness. I can handle, even agree with, everything she accused me of. But the one word I'm having trouble with is "practically," as in "practically worthless." The word implies not total worthlessness. What part of me isn't worthless?

I thread my way through the lot and into the reception area. Just inside is a robot seated in front of a grand piano. His (her? its?) head is a flat piece of plastic, featureless except for a camera lens attached to its forehead. Cables gathered in neat bundles run out of the back of its head and through its fleshless body. More cables run through its arms to the metal fingers. The robot is playing a classical piece that sounds familiar, but the name doesn't come to mind.

I am practically worthless, aren't I?

A woman, about Junko's age plus two or three years walks down the hallway as I wait in the reception area. She is wearing orange coveralls; they are form fitting and she has a well-balanced form. She walks briskly, with her head up and spine straight. Our gazes meet and she smiles, as Western people do when meeting someone for the first time.

She extends her hand as I bow. She doesn't bow, and my face flushes as I straighten up and grasp her

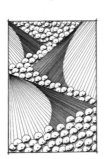

hand. Her grip is firm. I don't know how long to hold her hand, so I give it a good, though probably amateurish, shake. We are still gripping hands. The blood in my neck and ears ignites, and I shake her hand again. Finally she lets go and I drop my hand and bow. She bows a little this time and introduces herself: "I am Kumi Ono."

"Keizo Yukawa," I say, feeling less than practically worthless.

Kumi Ono says, "My father had to go to a meeting today, so he'll meet you at the museum tomorrow. Let me show you around here." She turns precisely and marches away. I follow her through a dim, unadorned corridor until she stops and turns to her left.

Kumi says, "As you can see …"

Through a window I can see into a cavernous room filled with boxes of various sizes—as big as a house or as small as a single room—set up on an irregular grid. A worker in orange coveralls occasionally enters or leaves one of the boxes. A slight humming vibration tickles my inner ear.

"… there's no distinction here between research, design, production, and testing. Each of our employees

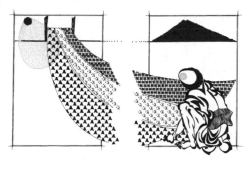

must be capable of upper-level programming as well as checking screws for correct thread angle, although we've eliminated most screws in our newer designs."

"Ah, good idea," I say.

Ichiro

"So, you ask, what is a robot?" said Ichiro Ono. He paused, letting the question float through the board room of the Honda subsidiary. "Actually, you're probably asking what can robots do for us. Or even more precisely—and that is the key word to remember—will robots improve my shrinking profit margin?"

The executives remained impassive except for a slight bend forward from the waist.

Kumi

The artificial intelligence incorporates spreading parallel-distributed processing paths, which are both efficient and inefficient; this of course describes the human intellectual process

<<factory tour function
  [non-technical audience]>>

but then the human brain doesn't have to be incredibly quick except in life-threatening situations where reflexive twitch fibers are automatically activated without cognitive effort.

Kumi says, "Each of the structure modules …"
I assume she means the boxes.
"… houses an individual robotic manufacturing element, not designed for a specific task, but for a range of tasks; for example, that one over there can manufacture any type or size of fastener. All the modules are connected through several layers of underfloor tubes."
"Fascinating," I say, not entirely facetiously.

Next, Kumi Ono takes me through the Ono Robotics museum. I find myself looking at her, not the exhibits. She wears her hair short, all one length and gently curled under the jaw. She would look very good—I think—in a black mini-dress and a gold, double-strand necklace.

In the museum, a class of elementary school kids— holding hands in pairs—are following their teacher. Kumi points to a couple of the exhibits; I only have time to grasp the sketchiest information. The exhibits are mostly about the history of Ono Robotics. The business apparently got its start after the war, at that time making toys.

When we have made our way out of the museum and kids, Kumi shows me the company cafeteria, where I can eat, and the company athletic facilities, where I can play.

Takenoko

The teacher grabbed the apprentice's hand and squeezed it until the bones crushed together. He endured the pain without a grimace.

The teacher let go. The apprentice's hand rose in the air as if drawn upward by an invisible string. The teacher said, "See how light your hand feels now? Draw that way, not as if you're using a lump of charcoal."

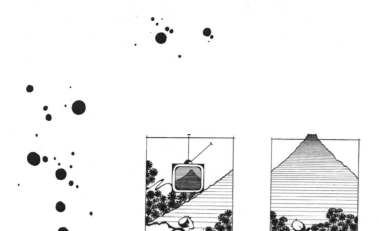

Ichiro Ono spoke to the flat-screen display attached to an optical character reader, "Please show us a brief history of Ono Robotics."

The pleasant female voice (an octave lower than the high-pitched voices heard in train stations) began, "Ono—the name most famous in the world for industrial and domestic robots. Over three hundred thousand ..."

While the display flashed 3-D animated images and video, Ono surveyed each of the executives' faces, watching for what interested them.

People's interests are where they are weakest.

We come to the company dormitory where I'll be staying. The dormitory is in a separate wing. A pale orange ceramic tile covers the walls, giving the wing a rather sterile feeling, like in a hospital. A psychiatric hospital?

Kumi stops in front of a door. Number 432. She opens the door and says, "The dormitory used to be primarily for our younger workers hired from Tokyo or other cities, but now they mostly prefer to live off-site. Most of the residents living here are from companies who have purchased our robots and are training to use them."

"Ah," I say.

We step inside my room.

Takenoko

The next brothel that took in Takenoko was smaller and more run-down than the first. "You sleep here," said the owner.

Takenoko thanked him profusely for the cleared space in the top floor storage room. The owner grunted and left him alone. Takenoko put his rolled bundle of belongings on the wood slat floor between piles of spare bedding.

The room had one sliding panel window. Takenoko pushed it to one side. He took a deep gulp of fresh air, then looked out.

On the horizon, Mt. Fuji poked into the clear air. Takenoko shut the window. The only views important to him were of suffering.

Kumi

Father: "Starting the process is easy, the hard part is knowing when to stop."

Yes, the activation of "intelligence" or "thinking" (literally casting neural nets) could easily be triggered. But what parameters define closure?

<<agreement/encouragement string
    [nod: vocalize]>>

The metal door clangs shut behind us.

Kumi guides me through the room, hardly necessary as it is so tiny—an area for sleeping and a compartmentalized bathroom. There is a low kotatsu table, a TV on a stand, several floor pillows, a cabinet for storing futon and bedding, an open clothes stand, and one window.

She doesn't apologize for the accommodations.

I go to the window and twist the rod that controls the blinds. They open and the room is much lighter even though the sky is still quite overcast.

Kumi hands me a plastic card, about the size of a credit card, but a bit thicker. "This is your access card. It works like a bank cash machine card. You'll have to enter a three-digit PIN the first time you use it."

"Thank you," I say. I'm dizzy after our quick tour.

As Kumi walks to the door, she says, "When you've settled in please come to my office to fill out the necessary paperwork. You are essentially an employee of Ono Robotics." She turns the knob.

"Yes, I will. Where is your office?"

She starts to open the door, then stops. "You saw it."

I did? "Oh, right," I say.

I wait until I'm sure Kumi is gone before I open the door to my room and walk out into the corridor. The orange-tinted tile makes me ill. I hurry out the dormitory wing door, and walk around to the front parking lot. I find my car and settle snugly into the five-way adjustable seat.

After a couple of minutes of just sitting there, I drive around to the dorm. I park near the door and unload my bags. I have to use my access card to get back in. I use my room number for the PIN. The door opens and I hurry through the corridor and into my room.

I take a good part of two hours unpacking my bags and box. Each decision of where to put something seems to take an eternity. I'm filled with a numbing self-doubt.

Have I taken too many steps backward?

Takenoko

The apprentice's hand trembled with pain. Self-doubt burrowed into him like a worm into an apple.

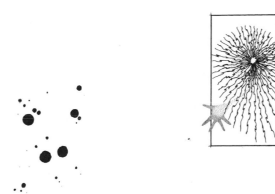

Being surrounded by utter strangeness gives me a feeling of being disconnected not only from my past but from the present. Forget the future. I find myself deliberating over each thought and action.

When I've finally unpacked and hung up my suits, I start to read the book on Takenoko, then I wonder how long I should wait to see Kumi. Perhaps I've taken too long already and should hurry to her office.

Where is her office?

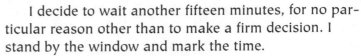

Kumi

Reduce the power of the time factor in the equation. The fastest isn't always the best, and the quickest paths often lead to the incorrect solution.

Father rubbed the cupped palms of his hands together, like a sushi chef forming a ball of vinegared rice. Expression of pleasure. "Still, with our clients, quicker is usually better."

Something slipped, distantly, in the intellect, as far away as the last wheel of the end car of a long, long train slowly derailing.

I decide to wait another fifteen minutes, for no particular reason other than to make a firm decision. I stand by the window and mark the time.

I haven't missed Junko yet, in fact I still feel glad to get away from her. I wonder if she feels the same about me.

At least outwardly, Kumi Ono is exactly opposite of Junko. I suppose I should find that refreshing, but it obviously has made me nervous and self-questioning.

As I stand by the window, down to five minutes before leaving to see Kumi, the clouds break and Mt. Fuji comes into view.

My first view of Mt. Fuji in my new life.

Will there be 364 others?

I wander through the Ono Robotics buildings toward the reception area. The school kids are mercifully gone, and I encounter only the occasional worker in orange coveralls. Will Kumi issue me a pair of Ono Robotics orange coveralls?

I'll have to refuse.

I ask an employee studying the screen of a portable computer where I can find Kumi's office. He cocks his head in confusion, thinks, then says, "This is her office."

"Where?"

"The whole building. None of us has an office, per se."

"Okay," I say slowly to the man. I want to pick him up by his orange coveralls and shake him. "Do you know where I can find her right at this moment?"

He scratches the back of his head. "Check the main floor."

"Thank you." I throw him a smile that feels more like a sneer. I assume the main floor is the room with all those boxes—what did she call them … modules?

I find the cavernous room and walk onto the polished and gleaming gray concrete floor. Multi-colored, reflective tape marks paths on the floor.

For no particular reason, I follow the blue one.

After following the blue path with no success I switch to the red. Turning a corner at one of the more giant boxes, I run into Kumi standing at a computer terminal.

"Hello," I say.

She looks up. "Yes. Hello. Here," she says and hands me a file folder barely giving me a glance. "Please fill out the forms."

I look around for a desk or table, but don't see one. I don't recall seeing a desk or table anywhere in the factory. Perhaps an efficiency expert told them how much time employees waste sitting down and standing up.

So, I fold the file cover back and start filling in the forms while standing. I notice the vibrating hum in my ear has become louder.

The spreading neural net activated the modules of intelligence. The underlying hum of the machinery wavered, then stabilized. The wavering cry of a woman having sex, sometime between foreplay and the onset of orgasm.

As predicted, the factory is becoming an organism.

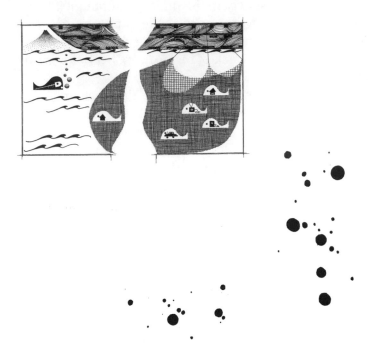

Father rubbed his rounded forehead. Father: "The question has been and always will be: is a robot a mechanism attached to a computer—the traditional Japanese approach—or a computer attached to a mechanism—the American approach?

"But the question is becoming moot with increasing inorganic and organic intelligence applied to both computer and mechanism. It's like asking if a human is a brain attached to a body or a body attached to a brain."

When finished with the paperwork, I stand patiently near Kumi. She punches at the computer keys. I ask, "What are you working on?"

She doesn't say anything for several seconds. "My research into artificial intelligence for robotics."

"Ah," I say, nodding stupidly. I hand her the paperwork. She accepts the folder and glances through the forms.

She says, "Do you know about AI—artificial intelligence? Particularly for self-replicating machines capable of pattern recognition?"

"As much as I need to know. Nothing." I laugh, trying for a natural, intelligent sound.

She smiles a little, though even that seems forced.

Standing close to her, I ask Kumi about Numazu—where to shop, where to eat. Those kinds of mundane things that occupy my brain instead of AI-whatever.

"Well …" Her face twists in confusion. A difficult question, I wonder? "I'm not real good at those kinds of recommendations." She turns away and studies the computer screen.

Her response gives me some degree of confidence. "Well, then, perhaps you could help me explore some this evening? You could help me get my bearings at least."

She says, "Sorry, I'll be working on this research until late."

Takenoko

Takenoko showed her the sketch of her face, neck, and shoulders. He had softened the unattractive angularity of her cheekbones, thinned her too-full lips, rounded her square chin, and tightened her sagging eyelids. He preferred the woman's raw appearance, but …

She smiled. Confidence and disappointment collided in his chest.

When she was gone he added a small line below her ear—just the suggestion of a wrinkle, or a sagging of flesh.

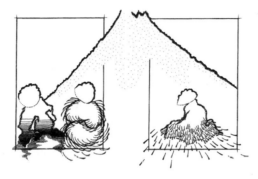

My confidence evaporates. I try to congeal it by saying, "Yes, well, I'm sure you're in the middle of something very important. AI and all that. I'll leave you alone."

"Yes, and thank you for filling out the forms."

"My pleasure."

"Yes, well, good luck and welcome." She shakes my hand.

As I walk from the Ono plant, a fresh breeze floats off Suruga Bay, a pleasant change from the stuffy, polluted air of Tokyo. So far the breeze is the only thing that's been pleasant about my new home.

I walk on the top of the concrete embankment that curves along the shoreline. The narrow strip of sand is littered with plastic soda bottles, beer cans, plastic bags, and tangled fishing line.

The people I encounter acknowledge me with a bow and a quick smile. The women are dressed in baggy, primary-color polyester pants and quilted coats, the men in too-short polyester pants and windbreakers, and the youth in jeans, T-shirts, and cheap tennis shoes.

Takenoko

From his space in the storage room, Takenoko could hear the courtesans playing the samisen, the grunts of the coupling couples, drunken laughter, the rushing about of the apprentice courtesans.

He felt comfortable in the tiny space. He sketched in the moonlight.

I look back toward the city, rather, the town. A five- or six-story office building seems to be the highest point in the skyline. To my left, the Ono plant imposes on the view of the lower elevations of Mt. Fuji.

The fog reappears, blocking the sun, chilling the breeze. I wish I had worn my Ryu Murano overcoat.

The sounds are few: cars and delivery trucks traveling along the side streets, laughter from kids on the beach, a boat chugging toward the piers down the shore.

The breeze now seems provincial and downright unfriendly.

I feel weird. Empty.

I head away from the water and along a footpath that leads to a street. On the corner is a coffee shop in a white building trimmed in blue. A ship's anchor made out of plywood sheets—the seams visible—is stuck onto the side of the building.

Inside, the air is warm and moist. I'm the only customer and I sit at a table near a window. The waitress—a high school girl, I guess—hands me a menu without a word. She waits while I look at it. She inspects her nails. I order coffee and a slice of chocolate layer cake. She leaves still surveying her problem nails.

I take out the book on Takenoko and put it on the table. I open it to read, but I am thinking about Kumi Ono.

The first prints attributed to Takenoko, who was signing them Take-ishi [bamboo stone], were of lower-class prostitutes of the Yoshiwara district. His particular style, that of incorporating a small detail incongruous with the relatively conservative construction and common "beautiful woman" ideals, is unmistakable. The small detail, of course, would later become less small, and lend the composition the air of a story.

Yoshiwara, at the time Takenoko arrived on the scene, had just begun rebuilding after a disastrous fire. Of course, the less prosperous establishments (and usually unlicensed ones) tacked together shacks, and those more prosperous establishments had to conform to the increasing morally reactionary shogunate. The rules didn't mean the brothels were no longer offering sexual services, but that they had to put up fronts of respectability (e.g., "serve tea").

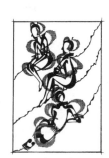

"Is that him?" Junko asked her friend Goto, who acted in underground theater. His most famous work was the one-act play "Suspension Bridge" in which he played the title role.

Goto nodded once and sipped wine. They were at the opening for Ko Naka-mura's installation of anthropomorphized television sets.

"He looks rather stuffy," Junko said.

Goto whispered, "Yukawa's got a keen eye. He's got a sense about him. He'll go far. If you want to meet him, I'll talk to him."

Junko stared at Yukawa and wet her upper lip with white wine.

Kumi Ono's differences from Junko appeal to me, but does Kumi herself appeal to me? I try to imagine going out with Kumi. What would we talk about? AI? What would I say? What can I talk about?

Junko and I usually talk about her performance ideas, about fashion and art and music. It now seems superficial when put in the context of Kumi Ono.

But our conversations—Junko's and mine—had energy, if nothing else. I smile inwardly at the thought, and I have the sudden urge to talk to her. She would get a laugh out of Ono Robotics, the dress of the locals, the sullen waitress.

I get up from the table and go over to the pay phone near the front door. The waitress delivers my coffee. She looks at me, and I smile lamely and pick up the receiver and point at it. She stares at me blankly.

I plunk in a coin and start to dial. The waitress retreats behind the counter; she stares at me from around the coffee machine. I realize she will be able to hear my conversation no matter how softly I speak.

I dial a few numbers, not enough to complete the call. After I count the time it would take for five rings, I hang up the phone, retrieve the coin, and give the waitress a shrug.

I return to the table and stare at a page of the book. I take a sip of the burned, bitter coffee. My cake arrives. I thank the waitress, and she nods.

The cake is tired and bland.

The bad coffee revives me a little. I get into the book, a chapter on Takenoko's life on the Izu Peninsula.

When I've finished the coffee and cake, I suddenly feel unburdened, energized, ready to get wrapped up in my work at the museum. My own museum! It's the first time I've felt truly excited about it.

I'm glad I didn't call Junko.

Takenoko most likely left Edo in a certain amount of pain, both physically and emotionally. Physically, he must have been suffering from malnutrition due to the famine exacerbated by his lack of employment. Emotionally, he must have been drained by the fact that his art was improving (although becoming perhaps less accepted) just at the time when disposable income dried up.

It is not known what Takenoko was expecting to find on the Izu Peninsula, which was considered terrifyingly wild by Edo denizens. A few popular spots existed for the well-heeled to visit, but they wouldn't have been Takenoko's attractors. What did draw him there, other than the differences from Edo, may remain a mystery.

I head out of the coffee shop and walk briskly toward the center of town. The buildings are rather unremarkable, like most of those in Japan: utilitarian, two or three stories, mostly a business on the ground floor with living units upstairs.

I pass a few single-family homes located in a more expensive residential area. The houses have a small garden, each with a dog tied to a post. They bark at me in turn as I walk past.

The main downtown area has two department stores, the train station, and a covered pedestrian mall lined with shops: videos, electronics, CDs, clothing (nothing I would buy), and fast-food restaurants. I wander around for hours, soaking up the little bits of neon and the empty sidewalks (by Tokyo standards).

Takenoko

The narrow alley (he could stretch out his elbows and touch the walls of the buildings along each side) closed in on Takenoko like a collapsing trench. The frozen air crushed him from above. He escaped through the side door of a shack brothel.

Three men in the front were tossing dice, coins were piled in front of them. They barely hesitated as they glanced at Takenoko. The smell of fermenting rice was strong as a week-old corpse. The men continued with their game. Takenoko slid to the floor against the wall. When his cold fingers could move, he started sketching.

After I've wasted a couple of hours, I stop in at a grill and have a few slices of barbecued eel and grilled eggplant. I drink a beer. The food's not bad.

It's dark when I start to head back to my room at Ono Robotics. I don't know the fastest way, but then I'm in no hurry, and it would be hard to miss the factory.

Nearing the factory I pass a neighborhood police box. A young officer is standing outside, smoking a cig-

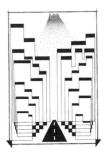

arette. When he sees me, he flicks the cigarette to the ground and stamps on it as if it were a cockroach. I nod at him as I pass. He just stares at me. I'm someone new to his beat.

A few blocks further, on a deserted, narrow lane which runs along the train right-of-way, I suddenly see a huge pile of moving trash. It's higher than the top of my head.

Nekobaba

Blue

Yellow   Green

Red   Purple

Black   White

Light   Dark

I stop walking and wait in the space between two buildings. I watch the trash come toward me.

When the trash across the street is even with me, I can see it's heaped into a shopping cart and being

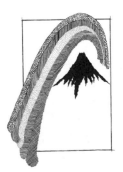

pushed by an old woman. She is hunchbacked horribly. A true *nekobaba*, the word coming from the description of a cat arching its back.

Her hair is white and stringy, her eyes swollen nearly shut with folds of loose skin. Dirt streaks her face like a coal miner's after his shift. She wears layers of rags of all colors and origin.

She stops to pick up something from the gutter. She holds a piece of foil or other shiny metal up to the light. It glitters.

She places it under a drooping old blanket or tarp that seems to be holding down the trash heap. I can see other pieces of the trash that stick out from under the blanket: metal tubes from appliances, aluminum cans, glass bottles, paper scraps, a bent bike tire rim.

I wonder how a life could come to this?

It'll do, this glittery thing, she thought to herself as much as to her long-dead mother.

Although it's not exactly a glitter that penetrates or dazzles, it will fit. Yes, she thought as she put the bit of glitter under the canvas tarp near the other glittery bits, I know exactly where it should go.

And if you don't like it there—right there—then suggest another place, as long as it doesn't clash with the things that don't glitter, or things that glitter with more, or at least different, brilliance.

I know, Mother!

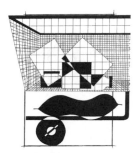

She moves ahead a couple of steps then stoops again. She retrieves a plastic carton of some kind. She rubs at it with her palm and finds a place for it under the tarp.

I follow her for several blocks; she's heading roughly in my direction anyway. She collects several other items. Twice she picks something up, inspects it, then puts it back down, carefully leaving it in the same position she'd found it.

Curious as to what criteria she uses for acceptance or rejection, I cross the street and run back to the things she left. One is a plastic knob, the other is an empty cigarette package.

The nekobaba continues her stroll along the gutter. After inspecting the items she rejected—I can't decide from the two anything about her criteria—I decide I look silly following her.

I turn down another street and briskly walk away.

The apprentice said quietly yet firmly, "I'll work harder."

The teacher grasped the apprentice's bamboo brush and snapped it in two. "Harder? Yes, you'll work harder. But will that do any good when you don't listen to your teacher?"

Back in my room at Ono Robotics, I sit with my legs under the kotatsu with the electric heating element on low. I am reading the book on Takenoko and have taken a few notes that might be useful in my work at the museum.

There's a knock on the door. For some reason it sets my heart pounding. I hesitate for a moment before I get up and open it.

"Hello," Kumi Ono says.

"Hello." I smile.

The soft knock on the door to his storage room lodging sounded magical. Takenoko said, "Come in."

She, the one who obviously had started to dye her hair, came into the room quickly, gliding on her hands and knees. She shut the door behind her and stayed on her hands and knees. Takenoko sat up and leaned forward to bow.

"Don't mock me," she said.

Takenoko hesitated, then leaned back against the wall. She sat up and rested on her heels. She said, "It's slow tonight."

"Oh."

"I'm bored."

We are sitting around the kotatsu. She has brought a bag of rice crackers and two large bottles of beer (Asahi Dry). She is still in her orange coveralls. They'd look better if they were just a touch baggy.

"I didn't see you in the company cafeteria. For dinner," she says.

"No," I say. "I went for a walk."

"Oh." She pours beer into my glass. I start to reach for the bottle to fill hers but she fills her own. "I want to apologize for not showing you around the town, as you suggested. My mind was on something else."

"IA, or AI." I smile again. She doesn't smile back right away. Then she does, a quick lifting and dropping of the corners of her mouth.

Problematic associations of elegance and functionality can be overcome with if-then rules, certainly themselves an inelegant solution.

<<non-verbal communicative function [smile]>>

Can aesthetics (an aesthetic "sense") generate a human-machine interface that accomplishes this melding?

<<mindlessness string [small talk]>>

She points to the book. "Homework?"

"Yes, sort of." I take a big swallow of beer. "To tell you the truth, I don't know much about Takenoko. In fact, I have yet to see one of his works in person."

"You'll see plenty of them tomorrow." Then she adds, as if she thinks I don't understand her, "When you start at the museum, I mean."

"Yes, I suppose I will. Have you seen them? The 365 Views?"

Kumi opens a bag of rice crackers and spills some onto the table. "No." She picks one up and studies the brown, soy sauce glaze. "I'd be interested in your opinion of the aesthetics of the 365 Views, and of your aesthetic parameters in general."

Father: "The only way you can see the 365 Views is to achieve a concept of self."

In general or specific?

Father: "Of course, I mean your own self."

There's no self now?

"No."

My aesthetic parameters? What does she mean by that? Feeling inadequate, I ask, "You haven't seen them? The Views I mean, not my parameters."

The tip of her tongue flicks out from between her lips and pulls a cracker in her mouth. "I was never

asked to see them. Father keeps them to himself." She takes a swallow of beer. Her eyes seem focused beyond the walls of the room. "But also, well, Father has his ways."

I wonder if I should ask what his "ways" are, but then maybe I don't want to know.

I feel too groggy to talk. I just want to listen. "I'll tell you about my aesthetics if you tell me about AI," I venture bravely.

Yukawa has a look of sexual desire: slack-jawed, dreamy yet probing, surveying. With that look, Yukawa cannot articulate an answer to the question of aesthetic evolution.

<<mindlessness string [drone]>>

Kumi talks, while I eat and drink. I catch a recognizable word here and there, though with decreasing frequency. I lean against a stack of pillows piled into a corner of the room. It's very comfortable.

I wonder if I should feel guilty for having a woman in my room only one day after I left Junko.

I am looking to see if Kumi is wearing a wedding ring—she isn't—when I can't keep myself from drifting off to sleep.

I wake up. It feels like I've been asleep for about an hour or so, but I don't know for sure. I check my watch; it's been three hours.

Kumi is gone, and the kotatsu has been cleaned. Only my book is there, marked with the notes I had stuck between the pages.

I get up slowly. My neck has a bad crick in it from laying at a severe angle on the stack of pillows. And my rear has fallen asleep. I stretch and notice a large, thin package by the door. I crawl over to it.

I turn it over and find the end of the paper wrapping. I peel away a corner. Inside is a painting, a landscape of Mt. Fuji. If I'm not mistaken, it's one of Takenoko's 365 Views of Mt. Fuji.

A Private Office

It's only a few hours from dawn but I'm no longer tired. I peel away the layers of wrapping from the painting. Inside, the painting is between two sheets of ordinary cardboard—not the correct way of storing a painting, particularly one using the fragile paints of the Edo period. The chemical reaction can be quite acidic, and will debilitate the colors.

This View of Mt. Fuji shows the peak in spring, judging from the snow level and the green spring vegetation in the foreground. In the lower right corner, a praying mantis sits on a rock, its head cocked as if contemplating the peak.

Kumi

Kevin opened the curtain. The apartment in the Berkeley hills overlooked San Francisco Bay. Kevin stood naked in front of the window.

Kevin: "Look at this sunrise, Kumi. The Golden Gate Bridge is pink-orange. Beautiful."

Naked backside so unfamiliar, suddenly a stranger.

Under the covers,

comfortingly dark.

When he crested the hill and came out of the grove of trees, Takenoko stopped at the sight of Mt. Fuji. The sun—just over the horizon—bathed the mountain in pinks and yellows. Just touching the tip of the peak, a wisp of a cloud parted around the rock and snow.

Takenoko took one step forward, then a slight movement caught his eye and made him stop. There, on a rock facing Mt. Fuji, sat a praying mantis. It turned its head slowly toward Takenoko. The insect's bulging eyes stared dully into his.

The teacher said, "You must repress your imagination. Your work is pure fantasy; no one wants to see your fantasies."

Takenoko didn't humbly bow and tell the teacher he was right.

The teacher waited. Takenoko's face burned, but he didn't relent. The teacher threw the drawing at him. "You think you don't need a teacher, do you? You don't want criticism, do you? Get out."

According to the book on Takenoko, the painting presently in my possession is No. 82. Hata, the author, makes the point that the scene is from the same vantage as several of the paintings, from a ridge near Heda, the village where Takenoko stayed during the year he completed the 365 Views.

Hata explains that many of the early Views (Takenoko started his work the day after the New Year) are executed from actual settings. Many of the later Views, however, appear to be pure fantasy, both in setting and construction.

I read for a solid hour, only looking up from the book to study View No. 82 in relation to the author's research. I am fascinated, I admit, by the rich descriptions of the Views and speculations of symbolism.

Had I read this book before I was interviewed I might have been a little more enthusiastic about the subject of the museum, rather than looking at it merely as an escape.

The author's musings on the presence of the praying mantis—which, he says, appears in many of the Views—is particularly interesting.

Takenoko

Takenoko dipped his brush in the blue paint. He spread it quickly across the paper.

The prostitute watched him paint as she untied her obi. "You can escape when you paint, can't you?"

Yes, he supposed he could. "What about you? Do you escape when you are with a customer?"

She laughed.

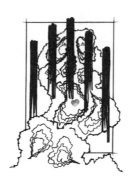

The Last Ukiyo-e Artist

After musing upon the meaning Takenoko wished to impart (the word "symbolize" is intentionally avoided) with the recurring praying mantis, this author must conclude that the key is found in the contrast the artistic treatment provides to other nature studies of the time. That is, the Japanese ideal of nature is presented as "beauty," never ugliness. One certainly cannot say that a praying mantis is beautiful, according to human perceptions.

Clearly then, Takenoko is rebelling against tradition (once again) by adding a speck of mud to the courtesan's white socks.

45

I place an ashtray on the book to keep it open at the page that shows View No. 82. I study the small, black-and-white photo. Only a fifth or so of the Views in the book are in color. The cost would have been prohibitive, no doubt, to print all of them in color. The market for a book on Takenoko must be very small.

The View that showed up in my room looks genuine, even down to the seal of the artist, but I would prefer to have it verified by an expert. But who would be that expert? And how would I explain how I came to possess View No. 82?

Suddenly, I have a very bad thought. I would be in a difficult situation if I am caught with this painting in my possession. It would be like a company accountant caught with wads of cash as he left the office. On his first day.

As the sky starts to lighten with the rising sun, it brings a rising panic. What am I going to do? What would the accountant do? Would he say, "By the way, Mr. Company President, I just happen to have found a few million yen in my pockets as I was leaving"? The accountant's first day would be his last.

Ichiro strikes me as the sort who fires people if they come back from lunch with a speck of soy sauce on their orange coveralls. If I get fired from the Takenoko museum, I couldn't go back to the National Museum. I can't go anywhere. My career, my life, would be over.

I must suspect Kumi Ono, of course.

She had the opportunity, though I can still think of no reason why she would do it. She hadn't given me any reason to suspect she harbored ill will toward me. The only people who hate me right now are Junko and the chief curator, and I don't think they know where I am. Exactly where, anyway.

The sun rises over the horizon, but no enlightenment comes with it.

I decide to do nothing for now. Except have my breakfast. The company cafeteria of Ono Robotics is, of course, robotic. I push the menu activation button on the computer screen, I push some more buttons—from the Japanese breakfast menu—and a voice tells me to move to the pick-up window.

When I get there, I can see conveyor belts and mechanical arms in motion. In a few seconds, my meal is delivered to me on a tray by a robot similar in appearance (though not in function) to the piano player. It doesn't spill a drop.

Kevin pulled down the covers. Light flooded in. Kevin: "Cold? I can turn on the heat."

The covers pulled back. Comforting darkness returns. Muffled footsteps. Puttering about. Musky human smells under the cover, clouding already twisted thought patterns

crowding out reason.

Takenoko forced himself to slowly eat the boiled millet. On top of the bitter grain were a few slices of pickled radish.

Across the street, the great artist Hokusai stopped a merchant. The artist showed him some prints.

Imagine!

Hokusai, forced to peddle his work on the street!

Takenoko

Takenoko ran a thin finger over the ridges and valleys of his ribs.

>Eating
>>Painting
>Filling a stomach
>>Filling a belly

I take a seat at an empty table; there are plenty of empty seats, actually. Only about fifteen or so orange coverall-clad workers are eating.

They all look like single males—no doubt graduates from the best universities. A few are staring at me, probably jealous of my gray and ivory-pinstripe Okuda suit.

From my tray, I remove the half-dozen dishes and cup of coffee and place them on the table.

While I eat, I try to read some more of the book. But I can't concentrate.

Kumi

Under the comforter, the splashing of water in the shower muffled—the shower so quick, bulky frame already clean. Next, a bowl of granola.

To the crunching, crunching, chewing, chewing, the fight to clear the twisted patterns, to return to normal functioning.

...

<<function: ?>>

My Japanese-style breakfast of rice, miso soup, fish, roasted seaweed, and egg is quite good. I might not mind living at the Ono plant if the food is consistently this good. The thought strikes me as absurd; surely I wasn't serious?

I wonder if I should tell Ichiro Ono about the painting. I've never found honesty to be the right course. It's

a dead-end. If you lie you can go all sorts of places. Anyway, if I did tell Ichiro today, it wouldn't be getting off on the right foot. He'd see me as a troublemaker. Maybe I should hang onto the painting for a few days, until I can establish myself. Or find out why the painting showed up in my room.

Did Kumi leave the painting for me? She said she'd never seen one, though. I was having a good time with her; I recall, with fondness, her enthusiasm for her work. I can only remember a little of what she said, but I might find the subject fascinating, given enough time and tutoring. But if her father finds out about the painting in my room, I may get fired before I get the chance.

48

And then there's that crazy, old lady trash collector. The nekobaba.

What's the madness behind her system for accepting or rejecting street trash? As I think more and more about it it starts to drive me crazy. I get up from the table and stack my dishes onto the tray. When I lift the tray up, tiny nozzles spray the table with a cleaning solution, and a thin rubber squeegee slides from one side of the table to the next.

I find an opening in the wall where the dirty dishes go. Of course, a robot takes the tray and says, "Thank you."

I start to say, "You're welcome," but I stop myself before I do.

Back in my room, View No. 82 is still there near the door. I left it exactly where I had first found it; if someone happened upon it, I could say that I don't know anything about it.

I tidy up my room; it doesn't take long.

I stare at the painting. I have an idea.

I find my empty garment bag, lay it flat on the floor, and unzip it. Then I carefully place the painting in the bag and zip it up. Carrying the bag carefully, I walk out of my room.

In the parking lot, I open the trunk of my car. I gingerly place the bag in the trunk. I make sure the spare and jack are secure so they won't roll over the bag.

After closing the trunk lid and taking a deep breath, I check around to see if anyone has seen me.

I feel like I have just hidden a body of someone I hadn't killed but the circumstantial evidence against me is overwhelming.

Nekobaba

Purple should never be placed near or cover flat objects.

Round objects should never be blue or green.

Bright metallic colors should never be used with red, yellow, blue; dull metallic colors can.

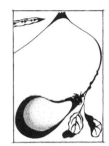

Tender bamboo shoots marked the four corners of the altar. On the altar, the priest arranged ceremonial rice cakes, bottles of sake, branches of tea leaves, and pyramids of fruit and vegetables. The altar had been constructed on the plot of land where the first building of the new factory would be built.

After the priest prayed and the gods had descended from heaven to bless the ground, Ichiro Ono poured sake on each corner of the plot of smooth ground. No one could tell the ground had once been the remains of a bombed-out submarine factory.

The drive to the museum site at Hakone relaxes me, maybe it's the familiarity of my car, maybe it's the breakfast sitting happily in my stomach, maybe it's Mt. Fuji keeping an eye on me the entire way.

Maybe it's being far from orange coveralls.

The parking lot of the museum has been paved recently, the blacktop gleams and the white lines sparkle. I park and get out of my car. I feel good about life.

I have forgotten about View No. 82 in my trunk until I reach for the door handle to the museum and see Ichiro Ono on the other side of the glass door. When I see the stern expression on his face, panic attacks me like tropical dysentery.

My new employer says, "I'll show you to your office."

We walk down the unfinished hallways. A power saw buzzes somewhere. Ono doesn't say anything; the silence jabs at my nerves.

I speak up perkily, "It's a nice drive here. Very scenic."

He remains silent to that comment as well; I wonder if I've said or done something wrong.

Maybe he knows about the painting.

In my office, Ichiro demonstrates the phone system, which also controls the lighting, heating, air, intercom, fax machine, computer on my desk, and the security system.

Security system?

I say, "Security system?"

Ono says, "Watch." He speaks into the phone. "Security." A deep voice says over the speakerphone, "Security here."

Ono says to the voice, "Just testing." Then to me, "Voice recognition of course."

"Of course," I say.

As Ono explains the system of alarms and video monitors, I think about the View in my garment bag locked in my trunk. I suddenly realize that the painting is a test. Ichiro himself sent the painting to me, to see what I would do. And I've flunked. Miserably. I should have called him at home the minute I found it.

Too late now.

What comes to mind, instead of a way to get out of the situation, is that the painting's praying mantis is sexual symbolism.

So, if the praying mantis is sexual symbolism—the female mantis eats its mate after consummation (I wonder if that is really true)—then the message might refer to Kumi.

Why? Because she and I are marriage compatible, at least from age and social standing (though her family is of course incredibly richer than mine, my family does have some old samurai blue blood). Then was the "message" from Kumi, or was it from someone else about Kumi?

Perhaps it was Ichiro Ono.

Kumi

Kevin: "Am I your first American?"

American what? First American lover?

Well, yes.

First lover.

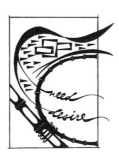 

51

I try to stop thinking of Kumi Ono, at least for now, as her father is sitting in front of me. Ichiro is staring at me, waiting for an answer to a question I hadn't heard.

"I'm sorry," I say, my voice squeaks like a teen-ager's. "I didn't catch what you just said. Must be the construction noise."

Ono listens for the noise, none is audible in the office. "I asked if Kumi was helpful."

Helpful? What does he mean by helpful?

Ichiro

He liked to tease Kumi by making up grand philosophical statements that really meant nothing. She always took him seriously. He enjoyed listening to her analyze them.

It was at such times he felt most intimate with her.

"Oh, yes. Kumi helped me get settled." That sounds too intimate so I add, "I mean, she gave me a tour of the plant and showed me the dormitory and the cafeteria."

Ichiro Ono gives me a long look (which gives me the shivers), then says, "Kumi is very competent."

"Oh, yes. Very competent. Very intelligent. She talked in depth about artificial intelligence."

Ono laughs, loudly.

Ono says, "I apologize for the poor accommodations at the company dormitory. The room must be very small and uncomfortable for you. It's barely big enough for one."

For one? Not big enough for two is what he is implying. "No, everything's just fine. Thank you for letting me stay there. And the company cafeteria is very good."

"Did you find the plant of any interest?"

"Oh, why yes. Incredibly. Very complex."

Ono's brow furrows as if I've said something stupid. "Well, of course, it's simple in its complexity. You should feel free to explore the plant and the grounds. And Numazu itself isn't such a bad town; it's not without its charms and characters."

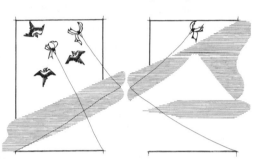

Ono says, "You've read the book on Takenoko by now, what do you think of him?"

"Fascinating," I say.

"The Edo ukiyo world provided him rich fuel for his imagination, don't you agree?"

"Absolutely."

Ono says, "I'm confident you'll be able to present the artist in the manner he deserves."

Kumi

Kevin's studio loft:
    Bare concrete walls
      Japanese paper floor lamps
        Futon
         Cat
          Jade plant
           Kites
            Computer
             Bowl of pastel condoms

Ichiro

Ichiro Ono said to Kumi, "Live life small."

Kumi said, "Small?"

Ichiro nodded. "Small, as opposed to big."

"But you own one of the biggest companies in Japan."

"It got that way by thinking small. Or small thinking."

"You mean, small as in nano-technology?"

Ichiro laughed.

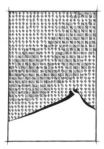

While contemplating Kumi's analyzing, Ichiro recalled that his ex-wife would not perform such mental exercises. In fact, she was quite boring. She had no concept of self; she had never suffered.

That's why he'd tossed her out of the house.

When I don't say anything, Ono asks, "What are your ideas for displaying the Views?"

"Well…," I stall as I don't have any yet. "I have several ideas, but I would like to spend a little more time with the Views themselves, as well as become more acquainted with the space itself, on the ground, so to speak. Perhaps studying the ideas of the previous curators you—"

"No. Start fresh," Ono says. "I want your ideas. That's why I hired you."

"Oh, of course. I didn't mean … I mean, yes, fresh, that's a good idea. Yes, could you show me where the Views are being stored? I'd like to start an inventory and to catalog their condition."

Ichiro gets another funny look on his face, this time as if he's bored. I need an idea.

Ono says, "I was going to get to that, of course." He sounds very irritated. I make a mental note never to speak to him in that tone of voice again. Whatever that tone was.

Ono unrolls a set of architectural plans. "Here's the floor plan; you can start by checking these. The contractor is working here." He points to the main gallery space. Then he points to another room. "Here is the storage room where the Views are kept. You can start to inventory my part of the collection."

He looks at me. When I nod, he says, "You also need to meet with my brother and sister as soon as possible."

Without another word, Ichiro stands up and leaves me in my new office. I wish I had something to wash down the lump in my throat.

I feel like I've been through another test, and I don't know if I've passed or failed.

Worse, I don't even know the subject matter.

From my briefcase, I take my book on Takenoko and find the room where the Views—Ichiro Ono's collection—are stored. The room has a locked metal door; I turn around and a security guard standing there startles me. I want to take a deep gulp of air; instead I consciously breathe slowly.

He points to a security camera located high in the corner of the corridor. He uses a card key to open the door. He holds the door open and gives me the key.

"Thank you," I say. He nods, but doesn't say a word.

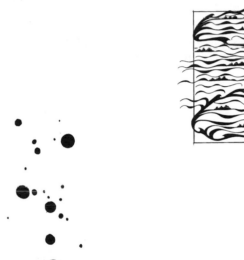

Takenoko sighed when the prostitute left. He slid the door closed. Being alone in this lonely room, in the nearly deserted village, quieted the noises inside his head. It also quieted his conflicting, tortured emotions.

It grew so quiet, finally, that he could hear the waves of the winter sea run along the black sand beach.

The storage room has a digital temperature and humidity gauge, two long layout tables, a desk with a telephone and computer, several pairs of white gloves in plastic wrappers, and six rows of stacked flat files.

In one corner of the ceiling is a security camera.

I open the first drawer of the nearest file. Inside is a computer printout listing the contents: Views ranging in number from 32 to 65. At first glance, the Views appear to be stored correctly, using pH neutral, unbleached paper.

The bamboo stuck out of the ground at odd, intersecting angles, as if randomly thrown from the sky.

To Takenoko, the grove brought back fond memories of the splayed legs of the clumsy but enthusiastic Frog.

That seemed a lifetime ago.

The apprentice asked, "How can I tell a good line from a bad one?"

The teacher said, "You must feel it, not see it."

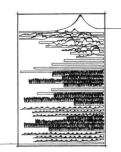

I put on the white gloves and remove the top View, No. 32. The scene takes in Mt. Fuji through a bamboo  grove, the plants growing at all angles. The peak itself is painted without hard edges and outlines—a major break from the norm of the time. The technique slightly blurs the peak and relegates it to the background.

The colors are in good condition; the paper is pinhole-tattered at both upper corners, but not enough to mar the value of painting.

I return the painting to the drawer and examine—at least cursorily—a few more, all in good to excellent condition. Then I notice that the computer printout doesn't seem to match the Views actually in the drawers.

I quickly leaf through the rest of the file drawers. The inventory is off on ten occasions; that is, paintings that are listed aren't in the file, and a few paintings I find in the files are not listed.

Is this another test?

A wave of acid indigestion burns my stomach.

I leave the storage room and head toward the front of the museum. On the way, I notice the placement of the security cameras; they seem to cover all corners of the museum. I don't recall seeing one in my office, however.

I hurry out of the museum and go to my car. I get the garment bag out of the trunk, along with a box of office sundries I'd packed: reference books, a calendar, a calculator, a pen and pencil set.

I hold the box under my arm and drape the garment bag carefully over my back.

At the front door, the security guard stands stiffly, with his hand on the door pull.

The guard opens the door for me. "Need help?" he asks.

"No, no. Thank you."

I hurry past him, and boldly stride back into the museum, through the door to the corridor that leads to my office.

Of course, Ichiro Ono is waiting there.

Ichiro stares at my box and garment bag. I try to act nonchalantly about them, quickly putting the box on the floor behind my desk and laying the bag on top of it without bending the painting inside.

As I sit down trying to not gulp in air, Ichiro turns the computer screen so both of us can see it. "I've entered the day and time of the meetings I've arranged with my brother and sister into your e-mail appointment calendar. Just press F1 to see it." He presses the button and a weekly appointment calendar opens.

I say, "Yes, I see, very efficient." He gives a look like I'm a third grader asking if the world is flat. I say, "Is there some way I should approach them?"

Ichiro thinks for a moment, then says, "You're the professional. But to smooth the way with my brother—he can be difficult—I've asked Kumi to go with you when you meet him."

Ichiro

What does Yukawa see? thought Ichiro Ono.

His eyes are constantly flitting up, down, side to side, constantly blinking. Fear?

Definitely, he has no concept of self.

57

Ichiro

Ichiro said to Kumi, "Artificial intelligence in robotics ... is it a manufacturing problem? Or a design problem? Or a marketing problem?"

Kumi pondered his question. Ichiro watched her.

She looked at him, and said confidently, "A marketing problem with a manufacturing subproblem."

He smiled lovingly.

Kumi

Help.

But there won't be any.

I'm not sure what he means by my being the professional, but I quickly reason that if I have to ask then I'm not the professional he wants me to be. So I don't ask. I hope Kumi will be able to help me with Ichiro's brother, her uncle. I find myself looking forward to seeing her again.

Ichiro says, "The contractor has a question or two for you now. And I have a meeting to attend." With that, he leaves.

I track down the contractor in the main gallery space. He has the blocky head of a steer. He shows me where his crew is working and asks about a wall location.

"I haven't had time to study the floor plans yet," I admit.

He mumbles something I can't hear over the power saw.

"What?" I say.

"Never mind," he says and walks away—in disgust? I want to shout after him: "Hey, I'm a professional."

I leave the gallery space and return to the storage room. I put on the gloves and take out one of the Views. I go back into the main gallery space, near the contractor and his crew.

Holding the View at arm's length, I stand before a blank wall. I move it around to a few different placements. I nod and shake my head, professionally. Then I go into my office.

I close the door. I realize this is the first time in my career I've had a private office with a door to close. I place the View on my desk. I take out View No. 82 from my garment bag and slide the painting under the one on my desk. I walk out of the office and back to the storage room.

Without looking at the security camera in the storage room, I slip both Views back into the drawer.

I sit at the desk in the storage room and try to look busy—and nonchalant—by checking out the floor plans. The space seems well laid out, with good flow. But it's hard to concentrate; my mind keeps wandering back to View No. 82.

I wonder if the security guard saw me. If he did, he's probably telling Ichiro Ono right now.

Takenoko

From the back door of the inn, along the hill following the creek, and up to the ridge point, Takenoko had begun to beat a narrow track—wide as one bare foot—into the grasses and earth.

The track had appeared so gradually, he never noticed it.

I spend the rest of the day getting things organized. I make notes on the floor plans, on technical preservation of the Views, on how to display them properly, and even begin to set up a spreadsheet on the computer that categorizes attributes such as condition, scene, colors, and symbolism. I use the book on Takenoko to establish most of these categories.

By mid-afternoon, I start to feel comfortable with my new position, as if I made the right choice and that everything is going to work out just fine.

And I'm a little hungry. I wonder where I can eat lunch around the museum. I'm also a little tired, probably from getting so little sleep last night. A nap would be nice, but I have to meet Kumi in a couple of hours to leave for her uncle's.

I wonder if I should ask her about View No. 82.

Genius
or Madness

Kumi and I don't leave Numazu until after six p.m. I think it's rather late to go calling on someone. But I don't ask Kumi if she feels the same way. During the drive, she remains quiet, probably working out some arti-ficial-whatever equation. I don't ask her what she's thinking. My mind has gotten very foggy, maybe from the lack of sleep combined with the stress of the first day on the job.

I'm driving at the speed limit, which seems slow along the winding highway to Atami. Having Kumi next to me in my car reminds me of the first time Junko and I went for a drive. The difference is that Junko never stopped chatting.

I can't recall a word she said.

Takenoko

The winding path, diverging from the main Tokaido road, brought Takenoko quickly down to the sea. The day was breath-less; he could have used the still, flat sea as a canvas.

He sat on the cool sand. In the moist grains he traced the line of the rocky cliffs falling into—or rising out of—the sea.

The lines were rough, jagged, not the smooth line of a thigh or breast. There was power in the jaggedness.

On the first drive-date, Junko spent most of the time chatting, nervously chatting, she knew, but couldn't stop. (She had the right to chat all she wanted to, if she felt like it, and if she felt like it that must mean it was a natural condition and, if anything, she was a natural personality, that is, she didn't restrain herself to fit into society's model personality, but of course, her chatting could also have been the result of the two "pink doughnuts" she'd popped an hour ago ...)

She wanted to set the trends, not follow them.

I wonder how I should approach Ichiro Ono's brother, Gun. I'm supposed to catalog his collection of the Views, I know, but I have this feeling of conflict—perhaps from my interview with Ichiro Ono. The way he said "gather" the Views from his siblings. Something about the word itself? Or the way he said it, with the slightest hesitation before the word came out?

I don't want to worry about it now. I've just gotten over the hurdle of dealing with View No. 82. No need to replace one worry with another.

I glance at Kumi; she seems very uptight, not at all the confident person I met yesterday at the plant.

"Well," I say cheerfully, "Quite a scenic drive."

Kumi gives me a quick glance, then stares out her side window for a few moments. "Quite scenic."

I continue my cheery small talk: "What's your uncle like? Is he like your father?"

Kumi doesn't say a word for several long moments. Then she slowly turns her head, stopping to stare straight ahead out the windshield. After another moment she says, "I haven't seen him for many years."

Scenic?

Random, asymmetric, fractal-like, natural images:

  Rocks   Coastline
                  Trees
        Clouds
              Shadows

Deliberate, symmetric, two and three dimensional images:

  Curved roads
        Geometric signs
             Aerodynamic automobiles

Scenic?

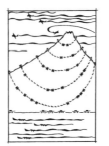

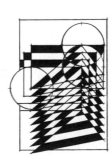
Father: "You must never think like your uncle Gun. Especially, you must not adopt his aesthetics."

Aesthetics?

"His thinking is not compatible with yours."

63

In the darkest corner of the Berkeley campus, deep in the fragrant Eucalyptus Grove, Kevin stopped, pulled and hugged, kissed.

Long fingers slipped between jeans and smooth abdomen. Rubbed slowly. In. Rubbed fast. Wet.

Passersby, on the opposite sidewalk, laughed, but surely couldn't see. Kevin didn't stop.

"Your father has quite a strong personality," I try.

"Yes, very strong." I look down to her hands; she has held them in her lap, one on top of the other, since we left. She is wearing a rather dowdy, two-piece, dark-blue suit—cut jacket and knee-length skirt. A horrible length: a skirt should be above or below the knee, never at the knee.

She doesn't seem too comfortable in the suit, probably preferring her orange coveralls. She'd look better in a pair of jeans.

I want to ask her about finding the View in my room, confide in her, though I must suspect her of putting it there. So I don't ask her.

I don't want to spoil our delightful repartee.

"Sorry I fell asleep last night," I say.

Kumi says, "No need to apologize. I was the one who put you to sleep, talking about my work."

"Oh, no. It really is fascinating. I just haven't gotten much sleep the past few days. Packing and moving. Quitting a job and starting a new one." Breaking up with a girlfriend.

She nods.

I say, "By the way, when I was walking around Numazu, I saw an old woman. She was pushing a shopping cart—at least I assume it was a shopping cart—piled high with trash. It was quite a sight.

"The strange thing is that she was picking up pieces of trash from the gutters, nothing so unusual about that, but she was being very selective about what she picked up. She'd study each piece of trash before putting it in her cart or putting it back in the gutter. That's very unusual, I thought.

"Do you know anything about her?"

Kumi says, "No. I've never seen such a person."

We reach the outskirts of Atami—the Pacific coastal city is built on the steep rise from Sagami Bay at the northeast corner of Izu Peninsula. Kumi directs me around the narrow streets lined with hot spring inns and larger tourist hotels.

I ask, "What does your uncle do?"

"Entertainment. He owns a club."

"What kind of club?"

She hesitates before saying, "I've never been inside." She points to a street.

I turn down the street. "I sense some conflict between your father and your uncle. Is there something I should know about?"

Kumi says, without hesitating this time, "I'm not aware of any conflict."

The fishing village clung to the side of the steep slope, as a child clings to its mother's legs the first time she sends it off to school. Steps hewn into the stone—or, less deliberately, the result of generations of fishermen trudging up and down—marked a path up from the sandy cove.

Takenoko gathered up his bag of art supplies and climbed those steps. His hunger had long since evolved from pain to dull ache, but now the smell of fish grilling on an open fire renewed the prickling pangs like the opening of a festering wound.

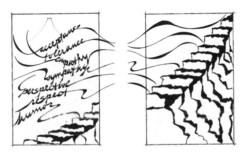

Kumi directs me to a lane deep in a crowded neighborhood. The lines of the buildings cross at obtuse angles, creating a lack of realness. I feel a twinge of sensitivity coming from my underarms, the beginning of the nervous sweat I felt in my interview with Ichiro Ono.

As I slowly drive on the narrow lane, Kumi squirms in her seat, whether nervously or restlessly (certainly not sexually) I can't tell. She does squirm charmingly. A smile creeps up on me and I fight it back. I never thought Junko did anything that could be considered charming.

Charming's a nice change.

At the top of the steps, or rather where they petered out, Takenoko followed his nose to the grilled fish. A shack stuck onto the end of a lane seemed to be the source of the aroma. Wisps of smoke were floating straight up from a hole in the roof.

Whether the shack was actually leaning considerably, or the steepness of the hillside created the illusion, it appeared to be sliding down to the sea. The siding boards were split and bowed, some inward, some outward. Even the shabbiest, back-alley unlicensed brothel in Yoshiwara had many redeeming qualities compared to the shack.

The shack had no door, just a tattered cloth. The place was a traveler's brothel. A desperate traveler he would have to be to search out such a desperate place.

Takenoko squatted on a rock, took out a sheaf of paper and charcoal stick, and began sketching.

We stop in front of a long, cedar-sided building, which takes up about a quarter of the block. At one end, an L section digs back into the hillside and rises an extra floor. The view of the bay, with its symmetrical blue-green and white wave lines, and the Izu coastline, with its steep, random lines so much in contrast, is postcard material.

I park off the side of the lane as well as possible. We get out and Kumi walks ahead of me to the front door. The door is framed with an eclectic facade of Greek pillars, stained glass, and Shinto shrine architectural elements.

Kumi opens the door and holds it for us. I hurry up to her and smile. She turns away and gazes out to the bay.

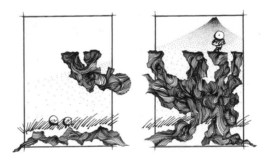

66

Inside the club, we are wrapped in red, from the velvet-covered walls, to the carpeted floor, to the painted ceiling. The dim interior is hushed and smells of perfume and cologne, cigarettes, stale food, and spilled drinks.

Kumi stops just inside and looks up and down the corridor. At one end is a maître d's lectern, above which rises a pin light on a long, flexible neck.

Kumi walks toward that end of corridor. Then, after a few steps, she stops, pivots, and heads the opposite direction. I follow her.

She finds the door marked "Office" and raps twice. A voice says, "Come in."

Takenoko

"Hey," shouted a man as he stormed out of the shack. "What're you doing?"

Takenoko held up his sketch. The man, smudged with charcoal and dressed in a threadbare kimono, could have been old enough to be Takenoko's father, or his son. He couldn't tell.

The man, undoubtedly the shack owner, examined the sketch as if checking a suspicious coin. He grunted. Takenoko said, "You can have it for a bit of fish."

The man opened his mouth—only one front tooth remained and it was black as charcoal. He laughed so loudly, he farted.

When the man choked back the laugh, he said, "I don't know who is more sad, you or me."

After the end of class, Gun Ono ran from the school yard. He ran hard, but they caught him. The three of them formed a triangle, Gun trapped in the middle.

One of the boys grabbed his book backpack. Gun lunged for it, but the other two pinned back his arms. The boy dumped the contents on the ground.

Four books
Pencils
An empty "bento" lunch box
Sketch pad

"See?" said the boy to the other two. He picked up one of the books: "Comrade Loves of the Samurai" by Saikaku. Then he picked up the sketch pad and opened it up. The sketch was of two nude, male youths, all sinewy and languid, looking into each other's eyes with affection.

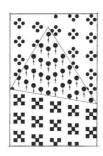

The office is cluttered with piles of magazines, photo albums, a couple of overstuffed chairs and a sofa, filing cabinets, erotic statuettes in classical poses, and a huge desk covered with more stacks of magazines and papers, as well as empty wine and cocktail glasses, tea mugs, and appetizer-sized plates empty except for unidentifiable crumbs. The paneled walls are a collage of snapshots. The photos are of people, usually two or three with their arms draped across each other, their faces washed-out from the flash.

The man behind the desk is hunched over a set of photos. His hands seem cramped, slightly misshapen. His perfectly white hair brushes onto his shoulders. When he looks up, I see an immediate resemblance to Ichiro Ono, though Gun is much softer, fuller, certainly not as polished, or not as chiseled.

"Kumi," he says, smiling an affectionate, concerned-uncle smile. His voice is as gentle as the cool jazz playing from an invisible source.

Gun Ono says to me, "You must be Yukawa."

"Yes. It's a pleasure to meet you."

Gun is wearing a linen blouse-shirt. He says, "I'm going to let you know where I stand right up front. My brother doesn't know a thing about showmanship." He casts Kumi an apologetic smirk. "Your father sent me a copy of the architectural drawings. Sorry, Kumi, but that museum of his would be better suited as a mausoleum."

Kumi blinks once but otherwise seems unaffected.

Returning his gaze to me, Gun goes on, "I'll be honest; I'm not happy about the museum location or its design or Ichiro's bullying. He's driving me crazy." He laughs (almost crazily, I think) and leans slightly forward. "But then the line between creative genius and madness is the thinnest, blurriest line."

What? Genius and madness?

Gun says, "But, for the sake of the family," another glance at Kumi, "I agreed to see you. But that doesn't mean I'm going to cooperate with Ichiro. Far from it, I want you to convince him to change his approach."

My new life is collapsing into ruins. My sweat glands begin to swell, becoming heavy as a new mother's breasts.

Gun says, "But I hate to start on such a negative note. It's not often my niece comes to see me. In fact, it's the first time since, well, a long time." He beams at her, then says to me, "Anyway, my collection of Views is stored in a special little gallery. I'll show it to you, later, after we have dinner and get to know each other. And you can see our show."

Kumi shifts from foot to foot and says, "That would be wonderful, Uncle."

Takenoko

Takenoko peered through a crack in the wall at the table of bureaucrats from Edo. They clapped to the samisen chords plucked by one of the inn's courtesans. Another courtesan danced, her loose kimono getting looser.

The dancer went into wild contortions, shouting song lyrics rather than singing. She tripped on the leg of a pudgy man and fell to the tatami.

Her legs spread apart, and the kimono opened. All eyes went to the juncture of her naked legs. She raised and bent her knees to give them a better view.

Gun

Gun ran. Hot and wet and sticky blood filled one ear and trickled down his neck. The other ear was filled with taunts and yells: "Freak. Girl. Bride." Their spittle burned his cheek.

He stumbled down the hill, to the beach. He ran along the edge of the water, kicking up spray.

They weren't chasing him any longer, but he kept running.

The Last Ukiyo-e Artist

Then (in Takenoko's Edo days) as now, the city of Atami with its spectacular view of the Izu coastline and onsen [hot springs] resorts, attracted well-off, vacationing urbanites. Less than an hour on the Shinkansen [bullet train] from Tokyo, Atami is just off the old Tokaido road from Edo to Kyoto.

It has been speculated that Takenoko stopped at a pleasure house in Atami that is currently (at the time of this writing) called Club Yoshiwara, and is owned by Gun Ono.

Gun is saying wetly (he sprays saliva as punctuation marks), "I hate robots; they're more human than we want to admit. They work like drones, very precise, with no imagination. Striving for some version of perfection." He drinks heartily from a champagne glass. "Nothing is more overrated than perfection. Perfection cannot change, it simply disappears. Imperfection, on the other hand, drives change."

We are in a private dining room, overlooking a small theatre at the opposite end of the club from his office. The club is filled with noises now: clatter and shouts from the kitchen, voices from behind the stage, the clink of glasses and china. We are having coq au vin, asparagus, and champagne. Not exactly the classic combination, but it works somehow.

"What about art?" I say. The champagne has relaxed me.

Gun looks at me, with almost a twinkle in his eye (am I passing his test?). He asks Kumi, "What about art? Can robots make art?"

Kumi says, "Certainly a robot can be programmed to use brushes to apply paints to a surface according to  some rules of aesthetics, that is, realistic representations of images or perhaps even abstract representations of mood."

Gun beams. He points the lip of his glass at me. "Now, would that be art?"

"Well," I begin slowly, thickly, "I would have to see it."

Gun shakes his head. Wrong answer? I hurriedly sip some champagne.

"A true artist," Gun says, "will eventually go mad."

There is a tension in my chest, from anger, frustration, lack of sleep. What kind of twisted logic ...?

Gun goes on: "You see, a true artist explores his—or her—soul. Not just explores it, but rips it out and holds it up to be examined. By himself, at first. Then he creates a visual image of what he sees. All the horror, the pain, the guilt, the shame, the forbidden and unspeakable thoughts. How many times, do you think, can a man rip out his soul and stare into it, before he goes mad?"

Kumi squirms. I squirm along with her.

The gun butt ripped Gun's scalp and nearly tore his ear off his head. He screamed in agony, and rolled on the floor. A booted foot kicked him in the ribs, then in the stomach.

His second lieutenant fell onto him, their faces close, noses almost touching. Their blood mingled.

Gun has been silent for several uncomfortable seconds looking from me to Kumi. I pick up my champagne glass and swirl the bubbles into a spiral pattern. "I see what you're saying."

Kumi says, "If that's the definition of art, then I don't think robotic intelligence will ever be capable of such abstraction."

Gun slouches, disappointed I think. "Ichiro will never be able to properly show the works of Takenoko, because he doesn't understand Takenoko. He only understands that there is some paint on paper and you put it on a wall so people can be impressed by your cultural wealth."

Gun leaves us, saying he has to play host. The club is filling up with customers, mostly in groups of several men each; there are only a few women. Most are wearing lightweight yukata kimono and wooden geta sandals. Their dress tells me they have come from nearby hot springs onsen, undoubtedly businessmen on company-sponsored get-aways. They are boisterous, already well on the way to being drunk.

Kumi eats in silence, absentmindedly. I don't interrupt her thoughts.

We, and the other guests, are being served by women in geisha costume. As our server removes a plate I notice her wrist is quite thick. I follow the arm, up to the neck, which is thick as well with a prominent Adam's apple. She smiles with overdone femininity.

Our geisha is a man.

I don't know if Kumi has noticed. She is picking at her dinner. The lights in the club dim.

On the stage, a spotlight shines a circle of light on the red velvet curtain. Gun steps between the break in the curtain and into the circle of light.

"Welcome to Club Yoshiwara. Please, continue to enjoy your dinner. But now, for your pleasure, we have our little show to put on."

The curtain opens, whisking away Gun with it. Our geisha waiter stands alone on stage. Off stage, a pounding drum begins to beat, and then assorted traditional instruments—koto, samisen, shakuhachi—begin playing.

To hoots and whistles, he begins to unwind the obi sash of his kimono.

The show lasts an hour, a wild hour of a bawdy, irreverent combination of burlesque and kabuki. Solo "geisha" stripped down to bulging G-strings; "geisha" couples performed stylized couplings; transsexuals competed in a breast size contest (the audience judged the contest, using their hands to measure); and a chorus line of all the geisha danced in the rousing finale.

I hadn't looked at Kumi during the show, at least not directly. Out of the corner of my eye, though, she seemed to be watching impassively.

As the house lights come up, Gun returns to our table. "Fun show," he says. "Good crowd. Very good crowd."

I nod.

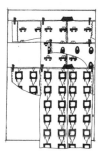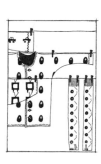

Gun

The club (it had no name) was in a back alley off a back lane. It opened after curfew, long after curfew. The one-room club—a tea shop that had survived the Tokyo fire bombings—was set with four rickety tables with nine chairs. Another table—a more stable one—served as the bar. There was a single lamp with a dim, flickering bulb. A phonograph played the same scratched jazz record over and over. It was the only record Gun could find.

From the black markets, Gun had accumulated two bottles of sake, five bottles of "shochu" grain alcohol, a pint of whiskey, thirty-six cigarettes, and a carton of American ration crackers.

The first-night crowd consisted of his second lieutenant and two other young army officers who danced to the record, over and over.

Gun asked the American officer, a second lieutenant in the Army, this question: "Are many other American soldiers homosexual?"

The officer chuckled. "I was an Asian art history major before I joined officer's training, as an interpreter. So I don't really consider myself a soldier." He lit a cigarette, took a puff, and then handed it to Gun.

The second lieutenant went on, "Sure, there are a few. We keep underground, though. Otherwise, we'll get a dishonorable discharge, along with a stint in a military prison. So the few of us form a tightknit club."

Gun said, "A club! Yes, a club. Do you think there are enough to support a club? A small, intimate, confidential club, of course."

After we finish our drinks, Gun leads us through the club, past his office. "The club began a few years after the war, you see, under my ownership. The building itself has a history of over two hundred years."

I say, "Interesting."

Gun says, "What did you think, Kumi? What do you think of your uncle's show?"

"The audience enjoyed it very much."

Gun laughs.

We go through an unmarked door and enter a living room only slightly less cluttered than Gun's office. A young man, his longish hair parted in the middle and wearing a yukata and white socks, shuffles into the living room. He greets us with a bow and a yawn.

Gun says, "Show them to their rooms, Tabo."

Rooms?

Gun reads my mind. "Well you must stay. We'll be up late talking about art, and about Takenoko's Views, won't we?"

My room is adjacent to Kumi's. It's small but comfortable. The floor is covered with well-worn, velvety tatami mats. Tabo hums lightly to himself and communicates by pointing and yawning.

Tabo brings us back to the living room, where Gun has set out brandy and snifters. He's warming one of the snifters in his cupped hands. Kumi and I sit on the sofa and sink into its pillowy down.

Gun laughs and says, "Careful, that sofa is a Living National Treasure."

Kumi and I sip brandy, while Gun gulps his. He says, "You see what I mean, don't you? About showmanship? The audience will never forget that show. Their hearts are filled with laughter, gladness, surprise."

I doubt if they will remember much the next morning; their hangovers will erase any gladness.

Gun asks, "And what will Ichiro's tomb—I mean, his museum—do for those who visit?"

Kumi speaks up. "They will be able to view the paintings of Takenoko in an elegant setting."

Gun smiles, a tad condescendingly. "Yes, but will they understand what the paintings mean? Will they understand the soul of Takenoko?"

Suddenly, all I can think about is wanting to be alone. Away from Gun. Away from Kumi. Away from that Tabo person lurking somewhere over my shoulder (I can hear his humming and fussing with things).

I want to be with Junko. With her single-minded way of poking a stick into society's ribs.

But I don't really want to be with Junko. I need to make my new life work. I put my snifter onto the table and stand up. I ask Gun, "May we see your collection of Views?"

Gun cupped the head of his second lieutenant in his hands. The American Asian art historian turned officer and interpreter smiled.

The boot came down hard onto Gun's hands; the bones crunched.

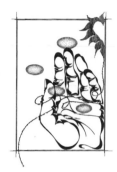

Gun

Gun closed his eyes and imagined:
 All shapes and sizes,
 they come in.
 Symmetry is unnatural, not sensual.
Boring.

Gun's private gallery is in a small circular room, about the size of a two-car garage, if garages were round. The low lighting comes from pinholes in the ceiling, like starlight. The walls are covered with paintings, as his office walls had been covered with photos. There is also sculpture on pedestals. But it's too dark to make out anything other than general shapes.

Kumi and I sit in the middle of the room on a round sofa, facing opposite walls. Soothing electronic music

floats in the air like a sea breeze. A spotlight comes on, illuminating a painting.

Then, from behind me, two hands slip over my neck, fingertips caressing and massaging the tense muscles.

Gun

His neck—the curator's—is just slightly too delicate and rather shapeless in a symmetrical way, and could be snapped rather easily, thought Gun.

 At least then his neck would no longer be symmetrical.

A spotlight brightens the painting in front of me. The fingers gently massage my temples. The painting is one of Takenoko's 365 Views of Mt. Fuji, if I'm not mistaken. The painting moves toward me, somehow, Tabo must be behind the free-standing frame. The painting stops a few feet in front of me.

A low voice, near my left ear, whispers, "View No. 228, one of my favorites." It's Gun speaking. "This

view clearly shows the departure from Takenoko's earlier obsession with the peripheral scene. His focus is once again the mountain itself, though in an increasingly violent depiction."

The hands undo the top buttons of my shirt.

I wonder if Kumi is getting the same treatment. The massage and guided tour (non-tour?) of the paintings continues for a half dozen paintings; not all of them are Takenoko's Views.

Just as I'm getting used to the bizarre, almost silly, presentation (in fact I'm anticipating the next painting and the next muscle to be worked on), the show ends. The hands are gone, and the lights come up slowly, as gently as my masseur's touch.

After a quiet moment I look behind me. Kumi and Gun are standing together, looking at a painting. I join them. Gun smiles at me. My shirt hangs open.

Gun says, "Well? Do you see what I mean?"

As I button up my shirt, I say, "Very intriguing." I don't want to argue with him about how impractical it would be on a large scale.

Gun turns to Kumi and repeats, "Intriguing."

Kumi says, "Intriguing."

Gun laughs.

Kumi

<<Human-human interface
   [conflict]>>

Thoughts grasped, like trying to catch air.

<<Human-human interface
   [detach]>>

Emotions grasped, breathing fire.

Kumi

What if no senses existed—no vision, no smell, no touch, no hearing, no taste. Would human sexual arousal exist? Or is there an innate sexual desire?

If such innate desire exists it could never manifest itself without sensory perception.

Or: If an intelligent robot—say, a bio-logical-simulation procreating robot—were endowed with a range of senses and the ability to judge them, would humanlike sexual arousal in the robot manifest itself?

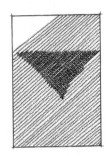

In my room for the night, I'm under a thin silk sheet, the room is slightly too warm. I'm really very exhausted, but my mind is racing around crazily, like a cat infested with biting fleas.

There's a quiet rap on my door. I immediately think of Kumi, and I find myself unexpectedly aroused.

Maybe it was the show, or the massage, certainly Kumi hadn't given me one whiff of sensuality.

"Come in," I whisper in a voice that rasps weirdly.

A head of white hair peeks in the open door.

Takenoko

The pudgy bureaucrat had the girl—she couldn't have been more than fifteen and was dressed in courtesan apprentice clothes—down on the ground behind the well house. She screamed once and pushed at him; the man pinned her arms down with his hands and bit her neck. She whimpered.

Takenoko rushed toward them. He pushed the man off her, then stood there stupidly, staring at the girl. She just looked confused, certainly not grateful.

"What?" cried the man. He got up and stepped up to Takenoko. He stood quivering, then as if swatting a fly, slapped Takenoko on the face. Takenoko instinctively raised his hand to hit back. The bureaucrat turned red and glared at him. Takenoko lowered his hand.

The girl got up and slapped Takenoko, too.

"What did you really think of the presentation?" Gun asks. He has seated himself close to my futon.

"As I said, intriguing. Really." I'm irritated at him for not being Kumi.

Gun says, "We don't need another sterile museum where one walks around with one's hands clasped behind one's back, spending four and a half seconds at each piece."

"No."

Gun sidles a little closer. "Did you like the massage?"

"Yes, but …"

"Ah, 'but.'" He pats my arm and leaves.

I don't sleep well. Every creak of the house startles me and keeps me from drifting off. I can hear Kumi and Gun talking quietly in her room. Their muffled voices are soothing and should put me to sleep, but I can't stop thinking.

The dawn light finally rouses me completely. Gun and Kumi are still talking. I get up, put on my clothes, and slowly open the door. I peer outside; no one else is around. I go back inside the room and retrieve the book on Takenoko and my notes.

Then I'm off in search of Gun's collection of Views.

I walk as lightly as I can, but the floor of the old house creaks with each step. I find the gallery and go inside.

Kumi

Uncle Gun: "I haven't seen you since you returned from school in California. Of course, your father is hiding you from me. He has always hidden you from me. He would hide the world from me."

Why? Something to do with aesthetics?

"Aesthetics?" Gun laughed. "My aesthetics? He's afraid of my aesthetics, what, corrupting you? How perverse is your father?"

<<Causality theorem [normative]>>

"Then why would he let you come with that boring curator he's hired?"

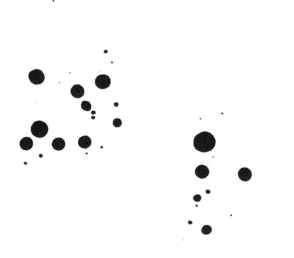

79.

The crowd had grown steadily, and after two months the bar was always filled by midnight. The record collection was now up to twenty, and someone had donated a radio.

To celebrate the second month anniversary, Gun "found" a case of American bourbon. He poured a round of free drinks and sat down with his second lieutenant.

Gun jumped to his feet when the door burst open with such force the hinges ripped off. Into the bar stormed three, four, five, then six American soldiers with rifles and black armbands of the military police.

Several of his customers ran to the back of the bar and threw themselves against the flimsy wood. They crashed through but fell on top of each other. Gun raised his arms to stop the MPs. A rifle butt struck him behind the ear, and his legs no longer supported his body.

I find a door behind one of the free-standing frames. I try the handle, but it's locked.

A voice behind me makes me jump. "Key."

It's Tabo. He isn't humming, and his eyes are puffy and heavy with sleep or lack of it. He yawns, puts the key in the lock, and opens the door. He leaves without another word.

In addition to his collection of Views, Gun also has a large collection of prints from other ukiyo-e artists, in particular those who specialized in kabuki actors and erotic themes.

I catalog the collection of Views for about an hour; Gun has stored them quite correctly. His collected work is comprised mostly of the latter numbers, the last quarter of the year.

These Views are quite different from those in Ichiro's collection. Takenoko's style definitely grew more fantastical, and in some cases bordering on the grotesque, during the year he painted Mt. Fuji.

I can only get a few of the Views cataloged. I'll need to come back and spend a long day, at least. That thought doesn't exactly please me.

I take one quick survey of Gun's collection of erotic prints. One is of a woman (reminding me of the "geisha" in Gun's show) swooning in ecstasy, with the back of a hand pressed against her lips, the other hand grasping the back of her lover's hair, pulling him tightly to her.

I close up the collection vault.

"I'm bored, too," said Takenoko.

She leaned forward and slid her legs out from under her. The white skin of her thighs flashed in the dim light. She said in a matter-of-fact tone of voice, "If you fuck me, I'll let you draw me." Then she laughed.

The erotic print stirs up a fullness in my abdomen. Kumi comes to mind.

Kumi. Not Junko.

I find Kumi in the kitchen, seated at a table. She is drinking coffee, a plate of toast in front of her. Gun isn't there; I'm glad.

Tabo is humming away, dropping more bread into the toaster. He smiles at me and points to a chair. I sit down, and Kumi nods at me. "Good morning."

She seems somehow different, a sharp edge or two has been beveled. She seems more like Gun than her father.

Kumi

<<Pleasantry sequence [morning]>>

Critical thinking: no emotions, abandon unbalanced irrationality. Would the image stay the same if the eyes were closed, or if the light is gone?

Please return.

Kumi

Don't ask Father about aesthetics.
Answer to humor. Or be wrong.

<<Primary function [shut down]>>

We don't say much on the way back to Numazu. I want to ask her about her uncle, if she knows he's gay, or at least bisexual. Not that he's shy about his personality and lifestyle. Not that it matters.

Anyway, I'm too tired to ask Kumi about her uncle. She is quiet, probably back in her AI-mode.

The return trip seems to take only a few minutes, instead of an hour. I drop Kumi off at the front door of Ono Robotics, and I pull around to the dormitory.

When I get to my room, a tube-shaped package leans against the door. I hope it's not another one of the Views …

But it is.

The Grand Conspiracy

The latest View that's been dumped on me is wrapped differently from the other I'd received. This might, or might not, mean that a different person delivered this one, View No. 39.

The scene is set on a beach, where a group of four fishermen are trudging along, their nets empty. Three of them have their heads down, the other is looking up at the looming Mt. Fuji. He seems startled, as if he'd seen the mountain for the first time, even though he must have seen it almost every day of his life.

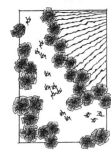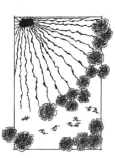

Perhaps he sees something unusual. I study the painting closely, but don't notice anything out of the ordinary. I'll have to check the book to see what it says about this View. When I get a chance.

Takenoko

Takenoko watched the bureaucrat leave with the apprentice courtesan. She glanced back at Takenoko as they turned the corner.

Her face was sharp with hate, and her words were another slap: "You're crazy."

He picked up his brushes and paints and sketches, and walked to the path leading away from the village.

I roll the View up and put it back in the cardboard tube. I put the tube behind my clothes hanging in the open stand, and then I drape my Rengo-Hon raincoat over the tube. Good enough for now.

Next, I take a quick bath and change into a fresh suit. It's nearly noon; I have to be in Heda, to see Akiko Ono, by two p.m. Checking my Handy Map, I calculate the drive is a little less than an hour.

I could take a quick nap for an hour, but I may not wake up, or wake up groggy. I could eat but I'm not really hungry. I could sit in my room and read, but I'm too restless. And I hate my room.

Might as well leave now, enjoy the drive.

Takenoko

The cliff dropped off to the sea. Takenoko had no choice but to skirt the ravine, and climb over the bramble-covered hill. The sun grilled the top of his head.

He finally came to the village. Another village where he knew no one. Another village where he had less respect than a stray dog.

Another village, where he had to start over from nothing. For the hundredth time.

Now let's see, he wondered, where is this village's brothel?

In my car, alone, driving on the quiet, winding coastline road, I feel at peace, at home. As if my car is my last connection to myself. To my soul?

I wonder: does Gun Ono really believe that true artists go mad from looking at their souls? But he said

it was more than just looking; he said they rip them out and hold their souls up for intimate inspection. Something like that. I do recall his proverb: "The line separating creative genius and madness is the thinnest, blurriest line."

On which side of the line is he?

I'm glad I don't have to see Ichiro Ono today. He makes me nervous and I don't want to report what happened with his brother. I'm not sure how successful I was in dealing with Gun. I don't think I made the situation worse, but then I didn't come away with a commitment to "gather" Gun's collection for the museum. I hope I'm going to have more success with the sister. I need a success. Maybe she'll just hand me her collection and I can leave.

I don't know why gathering the Views should be my responsibility. That job seems like something Ichiro could have done better than a stranger. Maybe not, though. Gun wasn't happy with the museum idea. Maybe Ichiro is afraid of his brother and is using me as a go-between.

Like it or not, Ichiro did specifically mention "gathering" in the interview, a duty to which I agreed. Great. Maybe I should forget trying to start my new life. Turn the car and drive back to Tokyo.

But there's nothing there for me.

On the Izu Peninsula coastal highway, I pass a marine life park, a floating hotel ship named the Scandinavia, several fresh seafood stands with their racks of filets drying in the sun, and a scuba diving shop.

I have to give it my best shot. I can't give up now. I pull over at a tiny market, where I buy a canned coffee, a pack of shredded dried squid, and a vitamin drink.

Sitting on a rock retaining wall, I eat and enjoy the view of Suruga Bay. A lone fishing boat is cruising into my view, bouncing sensually in the light waves.

Takenoko

Takenoko sat under a tree and stared at the village. There's nothing there for me. There's nothing for me anywhere.

The Last Ukiyo-e Artist

Other evidence does point to the route that Takenoko took, before arriving in the village of Heda on the northwestern corner of Izu Peninsula. Such evidence includes works that are found in a handful of venerable resorts such as the Ito Jozen Hotel. The hotel's private gallery has six of Takenoko's paintings of fishing village poverty.

The striking feature of the work is the increasing energy shown, from the boldness of stroke to the less-refined line, as well as the inclusion of nature in the works. The Izu Peninsula released something inside the artist.

Takenoko

Takenoko scraped the skin off his knee clambering over the rocks. He plopped onto a flat rock and caught his breath. Below, the village seemed overwhelmed by the green thickets of bamboo.

A fly buzzed around his knee. He sat still and watched it land near the bloody raw skin. It hopped over to the wound, and bent over, as if to get a better look. Satisfied, it rubbed its front legs together.

Takenoko tried to rub the back of the fly, as if it were a cat. As if it were the only living thing he'd ever encountered.

The fly buzzed off as Takenoko's finger brushed against its wings. He followed the insect's flight until it crossed the horizon and disappeared.

At that point, Mt. Fuji began its rise as a gentle slope at the edge of the sea.

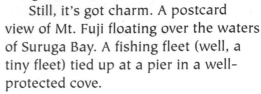

I arrive in the village of Heda about half an hour early. Small-town Numazu is a metropolis compared to the tiny Heda. I can take in the whole village in a blink.

Still, it's got charm. A postcard view of Mt. Fuji floating over the waters of Suruga Bay. A fishing fleet (well, a tiny fleet) tied up at a pier in a well-protected cove.

The village runs up from the sea into a triangular gorge that quickly gets too steep for building sites. I drive around the village, trying to kill some time. It takes five minutes.

The ryokan traditional inn owned by Akiko Ono is called Heda Onsen. Right now I could use a stay at such a hot springs inn, soaking in the mineral waters, sipping sake from a floating tray, being served traditional Japanese meals by a kimono-clad onsen attendant, getting a massage.

I follow the map given to me by Ichiro Ono and find the inn. I drive up to the front entrance.

The inn is on the north side of the gorge, tucked into a scooped-out pocket in the hillside. Surrounded with pines, maples, and bamboo, the cedar-sided building has a wooden porch polished by footsteps and time to a gleaming patina.

I park on a wide spot in a graveled driveway, and listen to the ping-ping of the cooling engine. I roll down the window; the warm air is moist and fragrant. I sigh deeply, not sure why, other than it feels good.

I get out of the car, heavy with reluctance. From the back seat I take out my briefcase with the book about Takenoko and my notes. Then, I put them back, optimistically hoping Akiko Ono will give me her collection of Views to take back with me.

Walking up to the entry, I stop and look around. Nothing is modern. I could be in the Japan of the shogun, in the time of ukiyo-e. I could be a wandering samurai.

Well, maybe not.

The door opens, and out comes a young woman, too young to be Akiko Ono, I think. She's maybe twenty-five, and has her long hair tied back. She isn't wearing makeup, but is wearing a kimono.

"Hello, hello, hello," she says, sounding quite apologetic for some reason.

"Hello," I say. "I'm Keizo Yukawa. Is Akiko Ono here? I'm—"

"Yes. I'm Haruna, her daughter. Come with me. Do you have a bag?"

"No. Well, yes. I mean, I can get it later."

She laughs, in a lilting voice, though also a little odd sounding, but compared with what?

87

Haruna took off her tabi socks. The cool sea foam breaking on the beach curled over her feet. The boy's words echoed in her mind.

She reached down to the beach and placed her open palm on the damp sand. The smooth glistening surface sand turned to rough grit as she curled her fingers under, like a claw, digging into the beach.

She pulled up a handful of the sand, let the water drip from it, then packed it into her ears.

As we walk toward the inn, Haruna asks, "Is this your first time in Heda?"

"Oh, yes. It's a beautiful town."

She stops, turns and gazes down the valley, out to the sea. "Is it?"

"Well, yes, of course." It really is.

She stands gazing with her head tilted slightly for several long moments. I want to touch her to see if she's awake. Then she turns to me and smiles pleasantly. "Yes, it is, isn't it? Thank you."

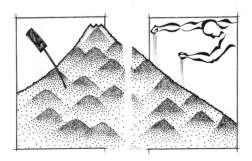

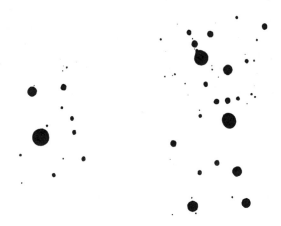

Haruna drops her gaze to the wood porch and we start to make our way to the inn. I notice a movement inside, a figure nearly invisible in the shadows of a window.

A woman watches us.

We take a step into the entryway—the cobblestone floor is like a dry river bed. Haruna slips off her outdoor thongs and slides her feet into a pair of indoor slippers. She places a pair of slippers near my feet. I take off my shoes and slide into the cozy slippers. I'm instantly relaxed, as if it's Friday evening before a week-long holiday.

Haruna calls out, "Mother!"

I follow Haruna into the building. Just off the entryway, to the left, is a dining room, with several low tables marked off by painted screens. To the right, an open screen reveals a traditional garden of rocks, moss, bonsai, and a pond.

Without a sound, a woman suddenly appears at my side.

"I'm Akiko Ono," she says. She bows formally.

I return her bow. "Keizo Yukawa. Pleased to meet you."

She rises and nods to Haruna, who leaves us.

Akiko points to a small room just off the garden. We sit on the tatami floor, a low table between us.

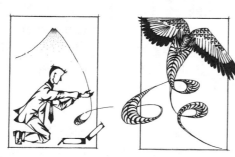

Akiko doesn't resemble her brothers—her forehead isn't as high, her chin is much thinner. Her black hair is too black; perhaps she colors it. Her jaw is set tightly, giving her a stern expression, reminding me of Ichiro more than Gun.

"So," she says. "My brother is too cowardly to come here himself."

"Excuse me, who are you?"

Takenoko drew his attention from the mountain to the voice. A woman, dressed in a rustic kimono, clutched a basket of dried seaweed in one hand and a basket of dried fish in the other.

Suddenly self-conscious, Takenoko brushed the grime from the rags he called clothes. He didn't say anything.

"I suppose you're hungry," she said.

Oh, yes.

One was tall, dressed formally in a well-tailored suit. He'd come for an overnight stay with another businessman, both from Tokyo. The other was jolly and red-cheeked as if he'd been drinking.

The tall one will have me, Akiko thought. And this time Mother won't be watching.

89

Mother grabbed Akiko by the back of her hair, ripping it out of the tortoise-shell comb that held it on top of her head. Akiko yelped. Mother yanked her hard, and she lost her balance and twisted her legs under her. Mother held her off the tatami mat floor with her hair.

Akiko whimpered. Mother began to drag her toward the paper shoji door. Akiko dug in her heels and clutched at the tatami, but Mother pulled harder. Akiko gave up struggling, and started pushing herself forward to lessen the pain.

Mother opened the shoji door. She pushed Akiko's legs out onto the lower floor of the corridor. Akiko was on her stomach. Mother jerked the hem of her kimono over her waist, exposing her buttocks. Mother bent over and, with a closed fan, spanked her hard.

Akiko could hear the guests laughing.

Cowardly? Ichiro Ono? I laugh nervously. What am I supposed to say?

"My brother, Ichiro, is trying to force his museum on us. Not that Gun is helping, he has his own … ideas."

I nod understandingly, still not knowing what to say.

Akiko glares at me, as if I'm a child about to be punished. "He hasn't been here for years. What does

Ichiro know about Takenoko and what he went through to paint the 365 Views? All Ichiro knows is robots. He doesn't know anything about people. How long have you known my brother?"

"Well, not very long. I was just hired."

"Aha."

Akiko gets up from the tatami. I rise out of my sitting position, but she waves me back. She glides over to the paper shoji screen and gently runs a corner of a tissue along the lip of the frame.

She returns and sits down. "You see, Ichiro, being the oldest male, believes he has control over our family."

"I take it you and your other brother, Gun, don't necessarily agree with Ichiro's decisions?"

Akiko looks back over her shoulder. "Where is Haruna?"

Akiko says, "A curator, huh?"

"Me? Yes, I'm a curator. Formally with the NAM—National Art Museum—in Tokyo."

She says, "Ichiro can afford the best."

I'm tempted to take that as a compliment, but I have a feeling there's some other meaning behind the statement.

Haruna comes in the room with a tea tray. "I'm sorry. Excuse me. Sorry, I'm so slow."

She drops to her knees and places the tray on our table. She pulls back the long sleeve of her kimono and pours our tea with practiced and efficient motions.

Akiko says, "Haruna, will you show our guest around the inn after tea?"

Haruna gives me a pleasantly warm smile that, for an unnerving moment, is terrifyingly knowing at the same time. "Yes, Mother. Of course."

Warm is round.
  Circles, oranges.
  Clouds rising from tea cups.

After tea and small talk, I follow Haruna outside. She pushes open the door to the hot springs bath. We step onto a covered walkway then into the washing area. Randomly placed, smooth black pebbles dot the floor. Hot and cold taps are at squatting distance above the floor, and wooden stools and plastic buckets are scattered about.

The hot springs bath itself is the size of a small swimming pool. It's screened from view with bamboo. A stream meanders between the bath and the washing area. A small, slightly arched stone bridge connects the two areas.

The trickling water in the stream and the inviting bath soothes me a little. Haruna is staring at the stream when I turn to her.

Haruna plunged her head into the stream, the cold, cold water like a slap from a closed fan. The sand flowed out of her ears into the stream.

She tilted her head, until one ear was clean, then tilted her head so the other ear could be completely emptied as well.

The warm sun—the warmth was round and smooth—bathed her cold face in brightness for a moment. She stripped off her kimono, neatly folding it and placing it on a pad of moss. She stepped into the stream, and sat down in it. She shivered. Her hands cupped together, forming a bowl, and she filled the bowl with water.

She splashed the water on her neck and breasts.

91

Takenoko

The woman took off quickly up the path, and down into the ravine. Takenoko kept up, remaining a step behind, but his feet ached with each step.

"You can't come inside. You'll have to eat out back."

"Of course. Out back." He wondered, out back of what? Takenoko almost smiled, but his feet sent slicing pain through his legs.

The woman said, "My name is Ono. I run an onsen ryokan up ahead."

"I'm Takenoko." He didn't say he was an artist.

I say, "This is one of the most beautiful onsen I've ever seen."

Haruna says, "Thank you. Would you like to take a bath?"

"Wouldn't I though. But I should do my work first."

Haruna nods. "Later, then. We've had many famous guests stay here."

"I'm sure you have." I don't really care who they might be. For some reason I've lost all my energy. I really would just like to slip into that bath.

Haruna begins reciting a history of the inn.

Takenoko

The Ono woman said, "My inn is hundreds of years old."

Takenoko crunched the grilled fish between his anxious teeth. He nodded.

"My husband is a fisherman. Now he fishes at the bottom of the sea."

What? Takenoko paused.

She explained, "He died in a storm."

"Heda Onsen," Haruna tells me, "is hundreds of years old."

"Really."

We stop at the path to the garden. Haruna points out the interesting features: a view of a thatched roof, a nice detail in a wood panel, a trickling stream of water. She's like a girl showing off her doll collection.

My tired brain gets tangled with Haruna's descriptive tour. And my lack of progress in my "gathering" mission.

A headache blossoms and flowers.

We have gone through the garden and out a gate, and are now walking up a path behind the inn. My guide hasn't said anything for a few moments, and my head is beginning to clear.

We come to a clearing in the muggy woods and stop. The sun has heated up the day and I'm getting a little warm in my suit. I wish I had on a light kimono like Haruna. I ask her, "Do you work at the onsen for your mother?"

"Work? Well, I live here and help her." Haruna points through the clearing.

Mt. Fuji fills the space between the trees.

Takenoko

The sound of wooden geta on the stone walk made Takenoko turn from his meal. A young woman was coming up the walk.

The Ono woman said, "That's my daughter, Natsuko."

She stopped next to her mother. She looked at Takenoko out of the corner of her eye. The pure whiteness of her eye surrounding a deep black iris made Takenoko inhale audibly.

The woman said sharply to Natsuko, "Leave us."

As we stare at Mt. Fuji, a peacefulness fills me up. Everything is going to be all right. Is it the view of Fuji, or being so far from trouble and stress, or being with Haruna?

Haruna leads us back to the inn. She says, "I like living in here and helping in the onsen."

"It's a very idyllic lifestyle," I say.

"Idyllic … I like simple."

"Well, idyllic often implies simple."

Haruna is staring at the sky.

Haruna

The teacher yelled at Haruna, "Don't you understand? What's wrong with you? Why are you so simple-minded?"

The class laughed. The word "simple-minded" flicked off their tongues.

93

We walk back through the garden. From this angle it has quite a different feel, as all good Japanese gardens do. I ask Haruna, "You have a very interesting family. They're not typical, that's for sure. I mean interesting in a good way, of course."

Haruna doesn't say anything, so I quickly add, "Your two uncles are very inter—" how many times have I said "interesting" already? "They're intriguing and, um, thought provoking." I don't mention Kumi, her cousin.

I ask her, "Does your father work in the inn as well?"

Haruna just shakes her head.

I catch a glimpse of Akiko, watching us from the garden-viewing room.

Akiko

Ichiro, Gun, and Akiko were sitting in the private room of the tea house. The shoji doors were closed tightly. Her brothers spoke in low, grim voices as Akiko poured tea.

"She has made us suffer all our lives," Ichiro said.

Gun fiddled with his tea cup. "The grand conspiracy," he said quietly.

Akiko put down the tea pot. "What? We aren't a conspiracy. You're always so dramatic."

Gun said, "Well, we aren't a house-wives' card club."

Haruna leads me to her mother. Haruna bows politely then leaves.

Akiko has a grim expression as she asks, "Did you enjoy the tour?"

"You have a very lovely ryokan," I say. I want to add her name to the statement—her last name as required by etiquette—when I realize

her last name is Ono. That means she kept her family name when she got married, or she returned to using it after her husband died. Or she might have gotten a divorce before he died. Not that it mattered.

Akiko says, "I'd like to show my collection of Takenoko's Views. In their best and most natural setting."

She takes off and I step quickly after her.

Akiko first shows me one of the rooms, a traditional ryokan setting: tatami mats, floor lamps, a lacquered table, and a tokonoma—the wall alcove in which a flower arrangement is placed and a painting or calligraphy scroll is hung.

In this tokonoma is one of Takenoko's Views of Mt. Fuji.

Akiko says, "Most of my Views are from the early paintings. This one is my favorite. I love the snow, it's so realistic."

In each of the rooms, some twenty in all, a View is hanging in the tokonoma. Most of the Views appear to be from the lower to middle numbers, but I need my notes to be sure. Akiko tells me there are other Views in storage.

"You do see what I mean, don't you?" Akiko says.

"Well …"

"Ichiro is wrong. The Views belong here, where they were painted. They're beautiful here. In that museum of Ichiro's, they would be like insects under a glass case. Dead."

Seeing the Views, I'm anxious to begin cataloging them. It would give me a break from Akiko, for one reason. Before I can suggest that, Akiko says, "You do understand what I'm saying." She peers at me as if I'm one of her analogous insects.

"Well, you want some of Takenoko's Views of Mt. Fuji to stay here."

"Some? What do you mean by some?"

"Well …" I don't know what I mean. "You have several rooms with tokonoma and want the Views to be enjoyed by your guests." I'm not sure if that makes sense.

Akiko sighs and walks away.

Takenoko

As she posed on the futon, the Ono woman said to Takenoko, "You must never paint my daughter."

Takenoko paused with his brush in front of the paper. "Why?"

She pointed a finger at him. "Just don't. Do you understand?"

Her words were so cold, he shivered. "Yes."

I catch up with Akiko. "I'm sorry. I didn't mean to say anything wrong." Which is true.

She whirls around. "I know Ichiro hired you, and you're just doing your job. I'm asking you to see my point of view."

So I can make her brother see her point of view?

She says, her voice somewhat less shrill, "Ichiro mentioned you need to study the paintings?"

"Catalog. Just jot down some notes on your collection and its condition."

She squints at me suspiciously, but says, "You may do that."

Akiko leaves me alone to do my cataloging. I've retrieved my briefcase from my car. I take out my notes and the book. The task of filling in the number and condition of each painting is a sedative for my nerves, though my mind keeps wandering.

The Views in Akiko's collection are primarily the winter and early spring views. They are in fairly good condition, although there has been some fading, depending on how the light enters the rooms. And the edges are curling, probably from the humidity.

They would be much better protected in the museum.

The old rooms of the ryokan do show off the Views quite nicely, I have to admit. By nicely, I mean they do seem to belong here, just as Akiko said.

I sigh. Things aren't getting any easier with this "gathering" business. I wonder how Ichiro expects me to resolve the conflict between his siblings. I certainly don't have any control over these people. All I know is that if there aren't any paintings, there isn't a museum, and I don't have a job.

As I go from room to room, I catch Akiko watching me from the shadows of the old inn.

After I've cataloged several of the Views, Haruna finds me. She says, "You will be staying for dinner, won't you?"

I check my watch; it's already early evening. I realize I'm very hungry, and my back aches from standing awkwardly to peer at the Views. "Yes. I would like to eat. I don't think I can finish today."

"Then you'll stay. Come with me."

She takes me to one of the rooms just off the outdoor bath. She hands me a towel and a yukata. The lightweight kimono is white with a blue cross-hatch pattern.

After I wash off, I slip into the steaming outdoor bath. I can't help but let out an "ahhh." That "ahhh" feels so good I let out another one.

Luckily, no one else is in the bath. It's early in the week, as well as between peak vacation seasons, so the inn shouldn't have many guests, if any.

I lie back against a smooth curve of tile and let my arms float. My thoughts begin to float as well, to Haruna.

I hear someone else approaching the bath. The clip-clop of wooden geta sandals. The clip-clopping ends with the rush of water from a tap. I open one eye. It's Haruna.

She slips out of her yukata. Both my eyes open wide and my head turns slightly to get a better view. She lathers a sponge and quickly soaps herself. She dumps a bucket of water over her body. The suds flow away.

She gets up. I close my eyes—but not completely—and sink down into the water. Clutching a small towel that barely covers her navel, she pads over to the bath and slips in without a making a ripple.

Haruna

Water has the perfect shape, no shape at all, yet every shape:

> round
> flat
> straight
> crooked

"I like a bath this time of day," Haruna says.

"Yes," I say. My voice wavers nervously. I've been in mixed baths at hot springs resorts, of course, but usually there are more than two people. And the two people usually aren't me and a woman I've just had lustful thoughts about.

Haruna says, "The light is soft, yet full of color."

I glance up to the sky. I hear a rustle in the bamboo. I look in that direction, but see no one. And there isn't any wind.

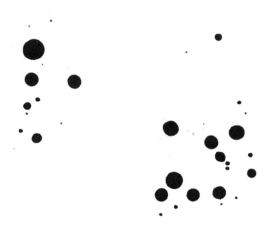

After ten minutes of soaking, Haruna rises and climbs out of the bath. I follow her progress with interest. She says over her shoulder, "I'll be serving your dinner in about half an hour."

"Oh, okay. Thanks. I've enjoyed your company." She smiles.

I wait until she's gone, then I climb out. I dry off and put on my yukata. Back in the inn, I find the room where I've left my clothes and change back into them. While I'm trying to do something with my hair, Haruna enters the room and starts setting the table for dinner.

I ask her, "You'll be joining me, won't you?"

"No, Mother will."

I don't pay much attention to Akiko during dinner. I mostly watch her daughter place the typical, multi-course ryokan-style dinner in front of us. Akiko is a healthy eater, not the demure elegant lady picking at tiny bits of food with the tips of her tapered chopsticks.

Akiko asks me how the cataloging went, and when I tell her it will take me another day at least, she nods. "You will pass along my message to Ichiro, won't you?"

I'm not exactly sure what message she means, but I tell her I will.

Haruna pours green tea. She smiles at me. I smile back, a conspirator's smile.

Akiko gazes from her daughter to me.

Akiko

Akiko accepted the term, "conspiracy." The grand conspiracy. By accepting it, she became a conspirator. And by being a conspirator, she must perform the duties of one.

She prepared herself and her mother.

When dinner is finished, Akiko leaves and I lean back against a pile of pillows. A tray of sake is at my side; Haruna pours for me, and I pour for her. We take a sip from our cups.

I feel as if my body is suspended in one of those isolation tanks. My mind drifts on a cloud of exhaustion and sake, propelled by the lust I'd experienced in the bath.

I reach out and stroke the back of Haruna's arm. She leans into my caress. I push myself off the pillows and lean toward her. She bends at the waist, toward me, her eyes disconcertingly open. I close my eyes and we kiss.

After hours, how many I don't know, Haruna is stroking my naked body with the tips of her fingers. I'm so tired, I drift in and out of sleep. But Haruna is there when I return, always awake, smiling gently.

She bends over my face and offers her breast to my mouth. Her fingertips stroke lower, the muscles in my abdomen contract and release. Contract and release. Her fingers travel still lower.

Again she has aroused me.

What's the catch?

I lean up and hold her. Over her shoulder I see that the door to our room is open a crack.

Passions
of Others

I open my eyes to full sunlight streaming in my room at Heda Onsen. I sit up and check my watch. A couple of minutes past seven. I remember Haruna leaving my room, finally, at dawn.

Next to my futon is a fresh yukata and a folded towel. My body cries out for the hot, hot water of the outdoor bath. I throw off the futon cover, put on the yukata, and walk out of the room. I don't run into Haruna or Akiko on the way to the bath. In the wash area, I rinse off quickly, then sink into the steaming bath.

"Ahh."

Haruna watched the stream flow over the rock. She touched the rock. It was so smooth she began to cry softly.

Her tears flow to the sea.

Haruna listened to her mother. "The other children have fathers in their homes. Some don't, like you."

Haruna wonders.

Her mother goes on, "You can say anything you want: He went on a long trip, he works in a far-off country, he's exploring the world, he drowned at sea as a fisherman."

When I'm thoroughly relaxed, my limbs as loose as an octopus's tentacles, I climb out and dry off. The fresh yukata wraps me in reassuring comfort. I stroll back to the inn.

In my room, Haruna is setting up a breakfast on the low table. "Good morning," we say at the same time. She smiles.

While I eat, Haruna drinks tea and watches me eat. A feeling of guilt about last night enters my thoughts; it's just that she seems so innocent. I swallow the guilt with a mouthful of rice and raw egg.

A question, or rather an unanswered question, comes to mind after I've satisfied most of my hunger. "What does your father do?"

Haruna refills my tea cup. She says in a hushed voice, "He died, drowned, during a storm. He was fishing."

"Oh, I'm sorry," I say.

Breakfast over, Haruna clears away the dishes and leaves. We haven't said a word about last night. We haven't said much. I start getting dressed. Just as I slip on my suit coat, Akiko is at the door, asking if she can come in. "Yes, come in," I say. My voice sounds confident.

She gives me a long, uncomfortable gaze. To quiet my nerves, I say, "Thank you for the wonderful hospitality."

She nods. "Did you finish cataloging? You were up very late."

"Well, no. Actually, I need to return. It might take another couple of days."

"When you see Ichiro, you'll tell him what we discussed." She hadn't phrased it as a question; it sounded like I owe her that much. I wonder, am I supposed to owe her a favor for sleeping with her daughter?

I hurry out of Heda Onsen. I don't see Haruna, but I don't think I should look for her. I throw my notes onto the passenger seat of my car and get in. I take a deep breath and start the engine. As I start to drive away, I unintentionally spin the wheels and spray a few bits of gravel.

The winding road from Heda gives me something to concentrate on, instead of dwelling on the strange night at the onsen. That pleasant full-feeling I'd achieved with Haruna— bath, food, sex—is replaced with depression, or paranoia, or both. I've got a dull headache from lack of sleep or too much sake. Or both.

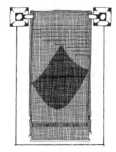

Mt. Fuji fills the view most of the way back to Numazu. But I don't care.

Akiko

Akiko's mother asked her, "Do you know what a debt is?"

Akiko shook her head. "I don't know exactly."

"A debt is something you owe someone else."

"Like money?"

Her mother yanked Akiko's hair. "Money has nothing to do with it."

Takenoko

The Ono woman gave Takenoko the food on a wooden plate. A grilled whole fish and some pickled radish. He devoured it while she watched his every move. Finished, he wiped his mouth with his hand.

"Thank you. I will forever be in your debt."

The woman nodded.

103

By the time I reach Numazu and pull into the Ono Robotics dormitory parking lot, the feelings have crystallized into dread. The dread of finding another of the Views delivered to my room.

I park and pull out my notes and book, and carry my dread up to room 432. I open the door and look around. Nothing seems out of place. I check behind my raincoat—that one is still there. But no other.

The dread lightens, for a moment. As I change into a clean suit and am wondering what to do about the View I have, a thought hits me. I run down to my car, throw open the door, and push the front seat forward.

There, on the floor, is a package tube.

Of course, there's no way to tell when the package was delivered. It could have been in Heda, in Atami, or just now.

Back in my room, I close the door and lean against it. The tube is unmarked and opens easily. I pull out another View. Without examining it, I insert it back in the tube and place it under the raincoat next to its brother. Or sister?

A change in my mood—from feeling sick to feeling angry—propels me through the factory. I want to ask Kumi a question or two.

On the main factory floor I wander among the box-like structures. It's the weirdest factory I've ever seen. Not that I've ever actually been in any factory. But everyone's seen them on TV: sparks flying from robot welders, workers mindlessly performing the same repetitive task over and over, the assembly line crawling ever forward.

In the Ono factory, I can only see a few workers and, except for the slight hum, the noise level is that of a temple at three a.m.

Curious, I duck into the opening of one of the box-like structures. In the box, a corridor wraps back on itself. I follow it around. The deep, vibrating hum becomes deeper and louder. The corridor ends in a glassed-in control room. A bank of controls— computer screens and levers and knobs and keyboards—lines the wall. I peer through the glass and down.

Far below me is a slowly moving assembly line.

It's an assembly line without people. Robot arms pick up half-assembled products of gleaming polished metal and move them to another branch of the line. Another part is added and the product continues along its creation path.

The robot arms move with the smooth practiced flow of an experienced—and bored—human worker.

Kumi, in her form-fitting orange coveralls, is standing at the computer terminal where I found her the other day. Fingers flying over the keyboard with intense concentration, Kumi makes my anger vanish, as if she were an old elementary school chum bringing back fond memories.

"Hello," I say, beaming.

She looks up. "Oh."

So much for my old chum. I say, "I'm back from Heda. Your aunt is very hospitable." I don't mention Haruna.

105

Oh, escaped the sound. Again: Oh.

Kevin grunted, moaned, breath held then released, then panted. "You, you, you."

Oh.

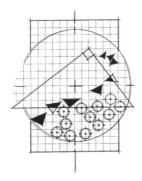

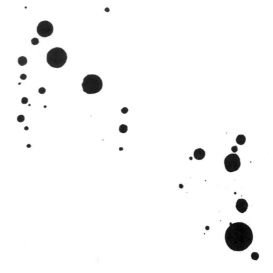

Kevin finally stopped, sagged, laughed. "Did you enjoy that, my inscrutable geisha girl?"

Push away, pull up jeans, get away.

Kevin laughed. "What's the matter?"

Kumi asks, "Was my aunt helpful?"

"Well, about as much as your uncle," I say honestly.

Kumi hesitates, as if she's considering my comparison. I add, "The onsen is quite pleasant."

"Pleasant," she repeats. "Enjoyment. Could that be considered an aesthetic, or an emotion? And is it a function of the object or the person experiencing it?"

What?

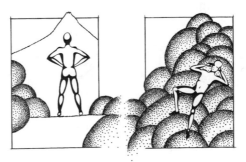

"Interesting question," I say, quickly regretting my phrasing. She'll probably be asking me the same question about "interesting" as she did about "pleasant." I jump in before she can: "Well, I better get up to the museum to meet with your father."

She nods and looks at her watch. "He's expecting you."

He is? I don't like the way she said that. For some reason I blurt out, "Would you like to go to dinner with me tonight? I mean, I'd like to continue our discussion." I'm not sure what discussion that is. Certainly I'd like to learn more about her aunt and uncle. And her cousin.

As if she were expecting the suggestion, Kumi says, "Yes."

I'm not sure if that's the answer I want.

<<social intercourse
    [respond: affirmative]>>

Social activity—more often than not—puts people at ease, but that activity makes artificially intelligent machines very "nervous." That is, the spread of activation emphasizes experiential patterns rather than cognitive ones.

As I pull into the museum parking lot, I remember the two Views I left in my room. I should have brought them with me, so I could sneak them into the storage room. But it's too late to go back.

Inside the museum, the contractor confronts me. His hair is plastered to his scalp, his eyes are red, and his breath reminds me of the chief curator. The contractor says, "So you're here."

I spend the next hour going over the finish plans with the contractor. I don't really have many answers. I tell him that I haven't had much time to think about the space planning. He mumbles and shakes his head, then walks away.

The stiff, wooden chair was made with knobby dowels. The knobs dug into Ichiro Ono's back. If he got too comfortable or the pain lessened, he pressed himself into the dowels until the pain was renewed.

He said to Akiko, "No, we aren't going to kill her. But we must do what we must."

Gun sucked in a breath. "Come on Ichiro, don't be so abstract. What are we going to do?"

"I'm the oldest son; she's my responsibility."

Ah, thought Ichiro, Yukawa is suffering. He doesn't seem pleased, however, with his suffering. He doesn't realize that he's developing a concept of self. He doesn't realize I'm helping him build his concept of self.

Ichiro Ono recalled his own suffering with delight.

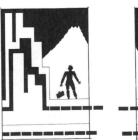

I run into Ichiro on the way to my office. He follows me in and sits down. Before I can reach my chair, he says, "Well?"

I know what he wants—to find out how I made out with Gun and Akiko—but I don't want to get into that, not right away. Instead I say, "The contractor needs several decisions made so he can proceed with the work."

"Yes? So, make them."

"But some of the decisions involve how we are going to display the Views. Whether thematically, or chronologically, or in other groupings. We need to decide on the number to show at a time. And other such decisions. I haven't had time to make those decisions. These types of decisions involve your input as well." I stop, realizing I'm droning. Ichiro doesn't look pleased.

Does he ever look pleased?

Ichiro says, "I don't have time to micro-manage. I hire the best people to do that for me."

I'm starting to sweat. I want to leave; I want Ichiro to leave. "Yes. Certainly. I can definitely make those decisions. Of course. I will make those decisions. I just thought that, well ..." I don't know what I thought, "All right, I will make those decisions. Yes, certainly."

Ichiro now looks considerably less than pleased.

Ichiro taps the fingertips of one hand against those of the other. "You were successful with my brother and sister?"

I wish there was a sword in the room so I could cut open my stomach. "They are very strong minded," I say.

"So they aren't going to contribute their collections?" His voice rises with each word.

"Well, they, um, want to make sure that the museum is the proper place for the Views."

"And you've assured them that it is quite proper."

"Yes, yes. Of course. I assured them. I think it's just a matter of them getting comfortable with the idea." Ichiro himself looks quite uncomfortable.

Ichiro said to his mother, "You'll have less to worry about."

She continued to stare at the top of the table. Her shoulders moved up and down, very small movements, in time with her breathing.

Ichiro said, "You won't suffer. I know that's what you're worried about. All old people worry about suffering. That's all they worry about. What I say is, why live just to worry about suffering? Especially since you've lived so long anyway, what's there to worry about at all? I mean why continue to live just to be not dead?"

His wife had the most delicate fingertips, not flat ugly pads, or concave octopus suckers, as some have. Her fingertips used to excite him, sexually, but over the years that had changed to mere fascination. He could stare at them for hours.

Yes, he would miss those fingertips.

He was glad he had made castings of them, to use when molding life-like robot fingers.

Ichiro says, "What's your strategy?"

My strategy? I need a strategy? "Ahh, a strategy. Perhaps you can help me formulate one."

Ichiro says, "Do you know how many employees I have? Am I supposed to help them form their strategies and schedule their time? Am I supposed to help them over every hurdle? Surely as an experienced curator you've dealt with uncooperative and difficult donors before?"

"Oh, well, certainly." Not really.

I clear my throat, cough nervously. I try desperately to come up with some sort of strategy. "My strategy," I begin slowly, then it comes to me, "is to reach some sort of compromise—"

Ichiro's face puffs up like an angry, red blowfish. "Compromise? What kind of strategy is that? Compromise means half-failure, and half-failure is utter failure."

He pushes out of his chair. "You'll have to do better than that." He turns sharply like an infantry soldier on parade and marches out of my office.

Ichiro

Ichiro said, "We must not look on this as a failure, Mother. Nor should we blame anyone. Most of all, you shouldn't blame yourself."

She turned her head toward him. She stared at him, without saying a word.

He contemplated her, and briefly wondered what she was thinking. But that was useless because it didn't matter.

At least he's gone. I sit at my desk with my hands gripping the edges. Gradually, I relax and start to breathe again.

I decide—yes, I can make a decision—to calm my nerves before I try to do anything. Cataloging a few more of the Views should be calming. I pick up my briefcase and go into the storage room.

The storage room is cool, dry, and quiet. I can hear my heart pounding, the blood rushing in my ears like waves of the sea.

I pick up my notes where I last left them, and find the View they refer to. I open the reference book and read.

My heart painfully bangs against my ribcage. I try to focus on the words, hoping they'll calm me down. Then a sentence does catch my attention. It's about Takenoko's troubles with the established art publishers. They wouldn't use his work (the author speculates) because of his morbid fasci-

nation with imperfection. The author clarifies that he is not referring to randomness as idealized in Japanese gardens and other nature-based art, but ugly imperfections.

Takenoko

From the storage hut where the Ono woman let him sleep for the night, Takenoko could just hear the waves of the ocean. They lulled him into a peacefulness he hadn't felt for a long time. A full stomach helped.

He could stay here for a long time, he thought.

Besides, he had no place to go. Not back to Edo, he'd starve there. He'd face rejection there.

But what could he do here in this little village of fishermen, their poor families, and an onsen ryokan?

The Last Ukiyo-e Artist

That Takenoko had many troubles during his sojourn in Izu, before reaching Heda, can be seen in the increasingly desperate measures he went to for subsistence. The sketches of idealized courtesans for advertisements, for example, surely must have driven him mad.

And his more artful works, particularly of the rural prostitutes, show a certain desperation in their expressions. A desperation of being perhaps their last hope: that Takenoko's drawings might find their way back to Edo, where they might result in the girls being "discovered" and summoned to the capital.

Takenoko likely never made it back to Edo.

In the eyes of several historians, particularly Howard Friedrikson ("The End of Feudal Japan"), it is agreed that at the end of the 1840s Japan's shogunate bureaucracy—the "bakufu" and its fatuous edicts—was as respected as the currency it kept devaluating to support itself. Commodore Perry's arrival in the early 1850s didn't mark the end of the shogunate as much as it marked the beginning of the new emperor-based military-power regime.

The result, for the arts, was a temporary release from official censorship, which had been an irritation more than a deterrent. Takenoko's best work was not that which found favor under the censor's approval. However, the new power regime would prove to be much more effective in squashing outlaw artists. Takenoko wouldn't have flourished under the repression, and perhaps he saved his soul as an artist by staying in Heda to complete his last works.

Then Ichiro's words roar through my head:
    strategy
    micro-manage
    failure

No, no, I won't let him get to me again. I'll make decisions. I'll form a strategy. I'll have many strategies, one for each situation. I'll be able to pull them out of my pocket like loose change.

All I want is to be a quiet curator in a quiet museum.

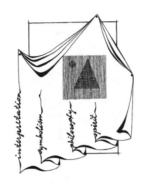

I need someone to help me. Kumi? She knows who these people are. They're her family. And she's logical (to a fault), and she doesn't have her own agenda, other than her constant queries about aesthetics.

She must help me.

I'll approach her for help at dinner. I'll use my charm to get her on my side. Right. Maybe I'll try a good vintage champagne. French, of course.

See, I can come up with a strategy.

When I think of Kumi, I see her in those tight orange coveralls, working on her computer. It's a pleasant memory that intrudes.

Pleasant. That word reminds me of her questions about aesthetics. What do I know about aesthetics?

I know it isn't orange coveralls.

Another memory pops into my head: Haruna. It too is a pleasant memory.

I haven't felt so lustful for years. Not since I was in college, the second and third years especially. Then I had the time and energy to follow where it led me.

Now the feeling is one of confusion, and it's getting in the way.

The storage room suddenly closes in on me. I'd never felt claustrophobia before, but do now. It takes my breath away.

I close up the storage room. In my office, I pick up a set of blueprints. I wander around the museum, checking the plans against the work. I begin to think about my curatorial duties: how I would arrange an exhibit, what the general public would find interesting and educational.

I jot down a few points to bring up with the contractor. It's my museum again.

Takenoko

Takenoko choked on the words.

"What is it?" said the Ono woman.

"I'd like to stay," he blurted out.

"Stay here? Why?"

He didn't want to tell her that he was afraid of leaving. "I'll paint for you," he said. "A picture a day. Of whatever you want."

"You want me to feed you, I suppose."

"That's all I need. I can get paints, brushes ..."

The Ono woman said, "You can paint me, I suppose. If you make me beautiful."

By the time I get through the majority of the unfinished museum, the contractor has already left for the day. Tomorrow I'll have a list of decisions for him. That'll show him.

I come to a side room, dominated by a large plate glass window. In it, Mt. Fuji is perfectly framed. I sit on a cherry wood bench in front of the window. A lump in my throat inexplicably thickens; never before has Mt. Fuji caused the least reaction in me.

The museum, with its wonderful view of the mountain, is an impressive structure. A swelling of pride puffs up my chest.

Is this why Takenoko painted his Views?

Ichiro

The room became quiet. It had been decided; Ichiro would handle it.

Akiko said quietly, "Thank you."

Gun nodded to his brother.

Ichiro finds me on the bench. I hurriedly open the blueprints and scrawl something in the margin. I say officiously, "I've made several notes for the contractor."

Ichiro says quietly, almost friendly, "No, you're not fired."

What?

Ichiro says, "I want you to keep seeing Gun and Akiko. You can make your own arrangements; my  involvement might exacerbate the situation. I think you may have a good strategy."

What?

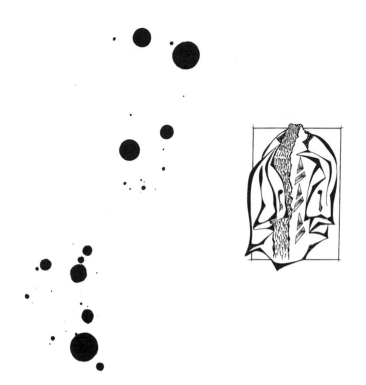

"Gun and Akiko and I ... we, have discussed many options. We decided that as oldest I will take care of you. And I will. Yes, I will."

She shook her head slowly.

"But I will." Ichiro's voice sounded almost shrill. "So, the time is now. Get your things together. I'll help you."

She shook her head. Not as if she were refusing to go, it seemed to Ichiro, but that she didn't understand. He touched the back of her arm. Her skin was cold, her bone thin. He pulled her up.

She resisted at first, then let him guide her.

Ichiro sits next to me and gazes out the window. "This view is worth the price of admission, don't you think?"

"Yes. A nice touch. The public will be taking many pictures from this point."

Ichiro grunts. He says, "A compromise, but not really a compromise. That's our strategy."

"I see." Although I don't.

Ichiro adds, with great enthusiasm: "Exactly. You'll be our compromise."

Ichiro made the first toast. "Thank you for attending this celebration. I must admit I am very happy today. Happy for our company, for our employees, for my family, for our customers.

"I am enthusiastically looking forward to finishing the building—the first in our new complex, which signifies the evolution of the next generation of industrial robots.

"We will always strive to stay one step ahead of the others, even if it means sacrifice. But today we celebrate. Tomorrow we will sacrifice.

"To Ono Robotics! Banzai!"

There can be no reconciliation. Never.
There is, actually, no such thing. For to
reconcile means to forget the past. To
forget the past is to forget one's self,
because that's what we are, the past.
We certainly aren't the future, although
we can project ourselves into the future,
at least what we imagine the future to
be. And the present means nothing, a
point in time with no dimension. As soon
as you think about the present it's gone.

Ichiro says, "Of course, I'll leave the details up to you. But you can bring my message of reconciliation to my brother and sister."

"All right." I pause, waiting for him to tell me what the message is.

Instead, he slaps his knees and stands up. "Good. That will work." He leaves.

I stare helplessly at the view of Mt. Fuji.

Ichiro pokes his head back in the viewing room. "By the way, Yukawa, when you finish your inspection of the Views I should like to review your findings. I hope that all the Views are in good condition."

"Yes, certainly." Including the ones in my room?

"When do you think you'll be finished?"

"Another week, I imagine." Ichiro starts to turn red, so I quickly say, "I mean, definitely. A week."

Kumi and I find a casual, trendy restaurant on the third floor of a building near the Ono Robotics factory. The first floor is a beauty salon that smells of chemical perm solutions, the second floor is a travel agency whose posters boast of sun and sand and sex.

At a quiet corner table, Kumi sips her wine; I have a gulp or two. She isn't exactly chatty, but I'm getting used to that. I say, "You work very hard, in fact, you seem to run the company. Will you own the company some day?"

She starts to say something, then hesitates, "I suppose. I don't have a brother."

"But would that matter? I mean, if you have the ability and a brother didn't?"

She says, "I won't ever have a family of my own."

I ask, "You'll never get married?"

"No, I don't believe so. I'm too busy with my work." With her chopstick she tears apart a slice of grilled eggplant. "I wouldn't make a good Japanese wife."

"Oh?"

"I like to work too much. And I went to graduate school in California for four years. I couldn't be a proper Japanese wife after living in America."

Of course I'd heard of that myth before, but didn't think anyone really believed it.

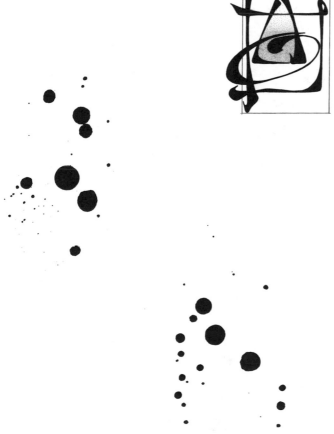

The daughter, Natsuko, watched Takenoko while he added brush strokes to the painting of her mother. "Very nice," she said.

Takenoko said, "Thank you."

Natsuko put the "bento" lunch box on the table. She sat down. He put down his brush and started to eat. She watched him for a moment, then asked, "Why aren't you married?"

He shrugged. "Why aren't you?"

She laughed. "There's nobody in this village I want to marry." She turned her face in profile and said, "Will you paint me?"

"I'd like to, sometime," he said. He didn't tell her that her mother had forbidden it.

Gun: "Aesthetics is the twin of emotion. Without emotion there is no aesthetic. Without aesthetics there are no emotions. I know your father would disagree, not that he would agree with anything I say."

(Father: "Building a robot with aesthetic sense is insane. But if it can be done, then I will expose myself to ridicule by naming it after myself.")

Gun: "Don't you feel anything when you see a beautiful painting?"

<<internal reaction
   [describe function (normality)]>>

I guess you could say I'm not a good stable marriage prospect either. I'd lived with a woman. I'd just quit a prestigious job.

Kumi asks, "What aesthetic rules did you learn when you studied to be a curator?"

I want to sigh, but say patiently, "Well, there were many kinds of rules. Line, color, symmetry and asymmetry, mood, texture."

She nods, then asks, "Can a person have an aesthetic sense without subjective, or emotional, involvement?"

"Is this about your uncle's theory? That a true artist will go mad?"

Kumi stops, literally freezes. After a long moment, she picks up her glass and takes a sip of wine.

I say, "I think he's a little off-base with his theory. Sure, there may be a higher percentage of artists who suffer some mental disorder, but is it the art that made them insane, or did they start out that way and were drawn to art? So to speak." I chuckle at my witty pun.

Kumi stands up. "Excuse me. I'm sorry. I have to … I just remembered something I forgot to do. Back in the plant. I'm sorry. I had a nice time."

As she rushes off, I stare after her, then slowly shake my head. I pour myself the rest of the wine.

After another dazed half hour, I finish eating and pay the tab. I'm walking down the steps, when a taxi driver pulls up in front of the building. "Yukawa? Keizo Yukawa?" he shouts.

"Yes?" He hands me a packaged tube and drives off before I can stop him to ask who ordered the delivery.

Kumi

Of course. A separate emotional storage base with its own set of algorithms must be incorporated. The emotional base can conflict with or enhance the knowledge base. The perceptual data stream can go into both, or either, of the bases.

Return to plant …

<<sudden departure function [apologize]>>

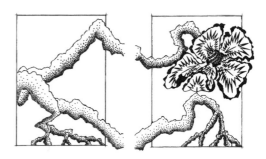

I peek inside the tube, enough to see that it indeed holds another View. Three of them are now in my possession. Panic squeezes my throat like someone is choking me. How many more am I going to accumulate? What am I going to do with these? Why am I getting them?

I hurry away from the restaurant and walk briskly toward Ono Robotics. On the way, in a dark and quiet neighborhood, I stop at a vending machine of a corner liquor store and buy a large can of Sapporo beer.

A block away, the mountain of trash rolls along the gutter. Pushing the shopping cart is the old woman. I stop when she does. She leaves the cart and, with her upper body stooped nearly parallel to the ground, walks up a narrow alley between rows of houses.

I sneak up to her cart.

Nekobaba

Hopes are treasures, nothing else.
And colors are treasures.

Darkness hides the contents of the trash heap, but not the odor. It's musty, moldering, dusty, and wet. I hold back the urge to gag.

Maybe I should add the View I'd most recently acquired to her collection.

She is heading toward me, so I scurry off like a rat down a sewer grate. Then she stops and picks up some bit of treasure. She rummages around the heap until she puts it in just the right place. She resumes her travels, pushing the cart so slowly it doesn't seem to be moving at times.

The shopping cart wheels squeak and groan under the weight of the trash and the unevenness of the gutter. I open my beer; the "pop" is drowned out by the noise of the cart. I take a sip and follow her.

We continue our crawl for several minutes, in the general direction of the sea. She hasn't stopped to pick up anything; maybe she's already culled everything in this area.

At a concrete embankment, she comes to a large, square culvert opening and pushes her cart inside. I finish my beer, put the can in the gutter, and run across the road. Inside the culvert, the darkness is absolute. I can hear the cart moving, becoming quieter. Then nothing.

The bottom of the culvert is damp, there's no flowing water, but it's mucky and I worry about getting my shoes muddy. But curiosity drives me ahead. I start walking slowly, then more quickly. I give up keeping my shoes clean. I come quickly to the end of the culvert. It ends at the sea, and at the lowest end of the fenced grounds of Ono Robotics.

The nekobaba has disappeared.

Something, Someone Dangerous

Back in my room, I put away the latest addition to my collection of Takenoko's Views. I'm not in the mood to open the package.

But I can't sleep either. For one thing, the Ono family has overwhelmed me. I feel like an anthropologist trying to figure out the social customs of a mysterious, long-extinct race of people.

I splash cold water on my face, then stare at myself in the mirror. Since I last remember looking at myself, my face has aged five years: dark smudges under my eyes, wrinkles on my forehead, puffy pouches of fat, and loose skin along my jaw.

What do they say? When you reach thirty-five your body starts dying.

Takenoko

Takenoko finished the first painting of Mt. Fuji by moonlight and the glow of embers. He stepped back and took a quick survey of his work. It wasn't bad, he decided, though he did feel rushed. He would have spent a little more time on it, if he hadn't had to finish in one day.

A warmth spread in his chest. He cleaned his brushes feeling energized. When he finished, he was too awake to fall asleep. He picked up his sketch paper.

He roughed out a few lines, but they looked much like the painting he had just finished. His warmth went cold.

121

Takenoko

The next morning, Takenoko jerked awake at the first, gray light. It was cold in his hut, his breath visible in clouds of steam. He wrapped himself in his blanket and stepped over to the painting.

Overnight it had become horrible. Awful.

He grabbed the painting and threw it. The painting floated slowly, until it drifted against the wall. It stuck there for a moment before sliding to the floor.

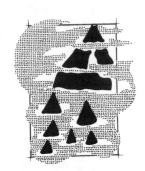

The Last Ukiyo-e Artist

When offering to explain the symbolism of an artist's work, particularly work as slippery as Takenoko's, there is always a danger of putting words into the artist's mouth, and preventing the viewer from arriving at her or his own interpretation.

On the other hand, this author is merely theorizing, that is, proposing a hypothesis based on evidence. The symbolism hypothesis thus proposed offers a starting point, which can certainly be refuted or revised based on new evidence or reinterpretations of the old. In other words, the reader may take them or leave them.

I lie down on my company-issue futon, trying to sleep. In the quiet I can just hear that persistent hum. Perhaps I feel it more than hear it. Whatever, the hum keeps me awake. I flick on the floor lamp and open my book on Takenoko.

At various points in the book the author is stretching his deductive abilities, I feel, especially when he

proposes reasons for Takenoko's actions, or gives theories on symbolisms imbedded in the paintings, for instance, the recurring praying mantis.

Still, I'm struck by a similarity between the artist and myself. For one thing, we both fled Tokyo, or Edo as it was known then.

One difference between us is Takenoko's passion for his art. A passion for something, for anything, has eluded me. I used to be passionate for my career, but the chief curator extinguished that flame. I used to feel that art is the zenith of the human race. Now that seems rather silly.

Do I need a passion to live? I don't have any reason to live, other than, well, not dying. No wife, no kids, no cause, no friends.

I'm really nothing except an observer of life and lives.

Of the passions of others.

The hum from the robotics plant intrudes into my self-pity. Who do I complain to? About the hum, not my self-pity. Kumi, I guess. Maybe she's still working, although it's pretty late. Does she live in the plant dormitory? Surely she wouldn't live in the company dorms; surely she could afford a nice place of her own. Maybe she still lives at home.

The damn hum. Wasn't there a hum, a louder hum, in the culvert that swallowed up the nekobaba? Yes. I toss the book aside and throw on a pair of jeans and a sweatshirt.

I go to my car and get the flashlight from my glove box. I walk across the grounds and enter the culvert.

Takenoko

The praying mantis turned away from Takenoko. He followed the insect's gaze.

It was focused on Mt. Fuji.

Takenoko looked from the praying mantis to Mt. Fuji, and back again. A peacefulness came over him, as if he were seeing something intrinsically good. Or a sign that something good might happen.

After gazing at the mountain for several moments, he noticed the praying mantis had left. Takenoko sat on the rock and sketched Natsuko from memory.

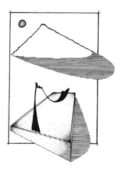

The culvert's dank air hangs on me like a wool blanket. The muck on the bottom of the culvert sucks at the soles of my Run-Man sneakers. The circular spot of light reveals some muddy trash (which must not have interested the nekobaba), a few scribbles of graffiti (somebody loves somebody), and several grates recessed into the walls of the culvert.

The deep hum is definitely louder near the grates. I shine the light through the bars; I can't see anything before the light fades away. I push on the grate, but it doesn't budge.

I try the other grates, none open. Still, the nekobaba must have gone through one of them. But which one? And how do they open?

As I near the other end of the culvert, I recall seeing a map, or site layout of the plant. Yes, it was in the Ono Robotics museum. And I also recall that the plant was built over an old wartime factory. Submarines or something. That might be a clue on how to get inside.

I reach the end of the culvert. The air becomes fresher, sweeter; a breeze floats in from the sea. I climb to the top of the culvert, and sit on the concrete wall. I take in deep breaths for several minutes while I play my light over the sea and up to the stars. I shine it toward Mt. Fuji, barely visible as a dark outline on a darker sky.

I feel like some goofy kid.

"Excuse me?" a voice says.

Startled, I turn around. My flashlight shines on the face of the young officer of the neighborhood police box. His name badge reads: Officer Tani.

Officer Tani says, "What exactly are you doing?"

I stand up and turn off the flashlight. I chuckle nervously. "Well, I, um, couldn't sleep, and I thought I'd take a walk. Yes, a walk."

He flicks open a small notebook, and pulls a flashlight from his belt. Holding the light under his arm, he shines it on the notebook. He writes something in it. "Name?"

"Tani—I mean Yukawa. My name is Yukawa. Keizo."

He shines the light in my eyes. "Have you been drinking?"

"No, I mean yes. A couple of beers, but I'm not drunk."

He shines his light to the gutter near the entrance to the culvert. The beer can I'd left earlier reflects the light. Tani asks, "Is that yours?"

I swallow the lump in my throat. "No. I don't think, I mean, no. But I'll throw it away if you want."

Officer Tani picks up the can. "Still cool," he says. He pours out the remaining drops of beer and sets the can onto the ground. He writes something in his notebook. Then he says, "You're new around here. Where do you live?"

"Actually, I'm the new curator of the Takenoko museum in Hakone. Have you heard of it? No? Well, it's owned by Ichiro Ono, surely you've heard of him. I'm staying in the Ono Robotics dorm. Until I get a place of my own."

He looks out to the sea. "Who were you signaling out there?"

"What? Signaling? Oh, with my flashlight. No, I wasn't signaling anyone. I was just, um, playing."

He stares at me for several seconds. "I'll believe you for now. But stop acting so suspicious. Perhaps you should go home."

"Yes, sir." I walk away but can feel him watching me. I hurry back to my room. Acting suspicious? I was acting suspicious?

Takenoko had been staring at the blank canvas since dawn, his paints still unmixed. A knock on the door interrupted his paralysis.

Natsuko opened the door. She gave him the box lunch. "How's your painting today?" She smiled.

Takenoko noticed that one side of her smile had a dimple and the other didn't.

I sleep late, into the midmorning, but don't feel at all rested. I feel as if I've been trying to run from danger, but am paralyzed with fear.

I get up, shower, and shave. In the mirror I look a little better (less suspicious?), except for those dark smudges under my eyes. They must be permanent now.

I get dressed and go down to the company cafeteria. It's empty. After I eat an egg salad sandwich, I stop in the company museum. No school group bothers me while I look for the map.

I find it in a glass case. Next to it is a grainy black-and-white war photo of the bombed factory. It's a submarine factory, built mostly underground, according to the map.

I poke around the museum some more, looking for other information on the culvert and grates. After a few minutes, I feel like I'm acting suspicious. I don't want to do that. I go back up to my room.

I call Gun Ono to see if I can drop by to catalog his collection. He sounds pleased to hear from me, and says to come over anytime. I tell him I'll be there in a couple of hours.

I putter around my room, mindlessly, then leave.

During the drive to Atami, I find the scenery quite beautiful, dreamlike as on a traditional landscape scroll. I never have appreciated landscapes; they're too easy, too rooted and static, not psychological enough. I prefer urban scenes.

Gun Ono greets me at the door. "Welcome, Curator Yukawa."

I follow him inside. He's wearing white silk pajamas. He says, "Excuse my dress; I don't get dressed before mid-afternoon. A bit of decadence that's become habit." He smiles. "That's a dangerous situation, don't you think?"

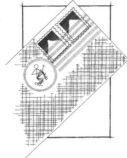

"Yes. Very dangerous." We sit across from each other on the sofas.

"So," Gun says, "What did my brother say?"

"Well, he has agreed to compromise."

Gun chuckles, then laughs loudly.

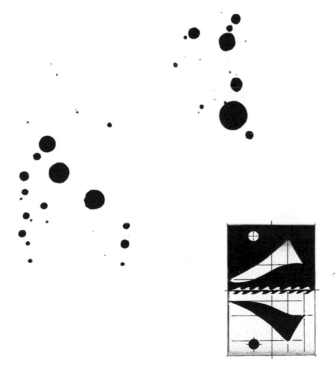

The letter arrived nearly a year after the military police hauled away the second lieutenant.

"I don't know if you'll get this letter, Gun, I certainly hope so. And if it reaches you, I hope it finds you well and in good spirits.

"Well, I survived the trial and the six months in prison. I survived the humiliation, the taunting, the names, the hate, the blame for all that is considered decadent. Anyway, as soon as I got out, I left for Paris, and that's where I am now. I love it here, though I'd rather be in Japan with you, but I can't go back there, with the Occupation forces still in control of all aspects of life. How are you coping?

"Paris is full of life, renewed vigor. Every night is a celebration. A celebration of life. I only wish you were here. Can you make it somehow? I'll help all I can."

Takenoko

Takenoko said, "I must ask you to reconsider."

The Ono woman didn't take her eyes off the painting. "Reconsider?" she said.

"About me painting your daughter."

"What? Why her? Can't you paint me again?"

Takenoko didn't say that the Ono woman wasn't beautiful enough, or ugly enough, or that she was too symmetrical. He walked out of his hut, toward the ridge behind the inn.

127.

Gun

"I still can't believe you're here, in Paris, with me," said the second lieutenant. The ex-second lieutenant, now Richard, shook his head over and over.

"I can't believe it either," said Gun.

The curtain opened. Richard said, "You won't believe this show. It's hilarious."

After the show was over, Gun knew what he wanted to do with the rest of his life.

Gun recovers and says, "Are you sure that's what he said?" I start to say it is, but he goes on: "My brother has never compromised in his life. It's not in his nature to compromise. It would be like a dog flying. Did he actually say the word?"

"Yes," I answer emphatically.

Gun shakes his head, his white locks swishing above his shoulders. "Sorry, I just find it incredible. So tell me, what's the compromise?"

I don't know, of course.

"Well," I say slowly, "the compromise he proposes depends on the results of my inspections and cataloging of all the Views."

Gun locks his fingers together as if in prayer, except he has a smirk on his face. "I see."

"Yes. And he wants you and Akiko to meet with us as soon as I'm finished. Then the details can be worked out."

Gun says, "Akiko hates Ichiro."

Wonderful.

Takenoko

The morning light slowly evolved from gray to red to orange to yellow. The light filtered through the bamboo grove and into the hut. Then Natsuko was standing in the doorway.

"Let's go look at Mt. Fuji," she said.

Natsuko hurried up the trail, Takenoko followed in much less of a hurry. Who cared about Mt. Fuji?

When he got to the top of the ridge, Natsuko had already seated herself on a flat rock. The flat rock on which he'd seen the praying mantis.

Gun shows me to his private gallery. "I'm sure that you noticed that Akiko doesn't preserve her collection.

Some of them are fading from being exposed to direct light. And the temperature and humidity swings in the onsen are excessive."

I agree.

Gun says, "Of course, Ichiro is the other extreme. Precision control over everything and everyone. But you already know how I feel about his style. Or lack of it."

Gun opens the storage vault. "There you are; I'll leave you to your cataloging. Later, I'd like to point out a few interesting ideas I have about the Views."

Alone in Gun's vault, I open my briefcase and pull out my notes and book. I start cataloging.

But my mind wanders. Concentrating doesn't help me to focus on the paintings. Concentration hurts.

I should have brought the three Views from my room. What if someone finds them there?

I open the book on Takenoko. I close the book on Takenoko.

What am I doing? I don't know where to start.

I leaf through Gun's collection of Views, trying to get a general impression of the works. I notice the change in details and style as the year progresses. Takenoko paints with increasing power. Certainly with more confidence. He paints the mountain not as mere landscape but as mood.

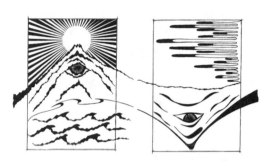

There, I'm actually concentrating, my mind is slowing down. The Views draw me inside each scene. I spend more and more time on them. The notes I take are insightful, complete.

I take a deep breath. I feel like myself, for once.

For the most part, each of the Views has a narrative, that is, it tells a story, usually with the foreground figures. Mt. Fuji becomes the background, providing a contrast, and often functions as voyeur.

Takenoko

Takenoko asked Natsuko, "What do you see when you look at Mt. Fuji?" He wondered if she saw it as a symbol of mystical power, or as a symmetrically perfect mountain.

Natsuko hugged her knees to her chest. She rested her chin on her forearms. "I don't know. I don't really see anything, yet I see everything. It's different every day."

He was struck by the profoundness of her statement. He wondered if he could capture the mountain in a different form every day for a year. His mood switched instantly from depression to elation.

All the well-known artists have painted their 100 views of this or that city, or 100 women of Yoshiwara, or 50 famous kabuki actors. What a triumph he would achieve if he could paint a different view of Mt. Fuji every day for one year. At least the mountain wouldn't complain he hadn't painted it beautiful enough.

As I focus on a View, I realize I'm starting to like these works. I hadn't admitted it to myself when I took the job that I don't care about Takenoko's work; I might have panned it as trivial. But I didn't care, I just needed a job.

What else about my life, my feelings, have I failed to admit?

The Last Ukiyo-e Artist

While the technical quality of the Views can be called uneven, although that is understandable as the artist's style is evolving on the fly, just the sheer mental effort required to come up with 365 ideas—and undeniably different ideas—is a noteworthy achievement.

But why Mt. Fuji? Why one painting a day for a year? Takenoko never kept a diary, as far as we know, or sent letters that have ever been found, so we don't have a direct connection with the artist. He might have been desperate to make a name for himself. He might have been mocking the established artists. This author's speculation is that something occurred in Heda.

Perhaps an epiphany.

After studying the structure of a couple of the Views in detail, I find it amazing that Takenoko could paint one of the Views each day for a year. Just to come up with that many ideas is a feat. I wonder if he sketched them out first, or if he went straight to the brush?

My back gives me a twinge and I straighten up before it cramps. I decide to take a break. Just then, Gun comes into the vault.

"Tea?" says Gun.

"Yes, please."

We go into the living room, where his houseboy—Tabo? yes, Tabo—is serving tea. He says, "Milk or lemon?"

"Lemon," I say. I sit down and take a sip of the English tea. Tabo offers some biscuits as well. I take one. It's slightly sweet.

Gun asks, "How are you progressing?"

I answer, "Slowly, I'm sorry to say. Even if I spend a few minutes on each, the time adds up quickly, with 365 of them."

Gun nods. Tabo leaves; out of the corner of my eye, I catch him yawning. Gun asks me, "Is this how they do things at the National Museum?"

I say, "They would laugh if they saw what I have been doing for the last few days."

Gun smirks. "So your recent career move wasn't a step up?"

"It will work out in the end," I say, not knowing where that ridiculous statement came from.

Gun says, "Have you come across the View with the four fishermen yet?"

I almost choke on a bite of the biscuit. Isn't that one I have in my dorm room? Or is it the one I snuck into the museum? I'm not sure. I cover with a swallow of tea. I take too much of a mouthful and it burns. I suck in some air. "The four fishermen ... it, um, sounds familiar. I'm not sure, sorry, I've seen so many, um, why?"

Gun says, "It's quite revealing, I think."

Takenoko

The Ono woman said, "I thought you were going to paint me every day? When do you want me to pose again?"

Takenoko said, "I've changed my mind. I'm painting a different Mt. Fuji every day for a year."

"What? Mt. Fuji? Why? Aren't I a better subject than a mountain? Or don't you have enough talent to paint me?"

Takenoko didn't answer.

The Ono woman turned on her heel. "Well, I'm not going to feed you if you're not going to paint me."

Gun

Yukawa, with his lack of humor and self-absorption and monotone voice, reminded Gun of the serious student in Paris. Richard's serious student, the one who was destined to kill himself.

Gun says, "It reveals much of what Takenoko feels is wrong with his society, with ours as well. I think it says that I'm right about Ichiro's museum being all wrong. Do you see?"

"Well, um—"

Gun's voice is intense, penetrating. "Those people who will go to the museum won't learn anything. They'll pass by the Views, spending three or four seconds looking at each. Of course, their minds will be on what they will eat in the museum cafeteria, or the souvenirs they will buy in the museum gift shop, or if they should have that affair with their co-worker."

After a pause, he goes on: "It's just like the fishermen in the painting: they don't see the one thing that is so very important."

Takenoko

Takenoko's back ached from painting. His legs alternated between numb and throbbing. His eyelids dropped heavily from lack of sleep. His fingers sometimes shivered in the cold and he had to warm them up before he could continue. His stomach growled; he hadn't eaten since the day before yesterday.

He didn't know how he could possibly finish today. It was only the second day of his quest.

There was a knock on the door. Natsuko came in and placed near him two rice balls wrapped in roasted seaweed.

I say, "Certainly some people won't get anything out of the museum experience, but others will feel something."

Gun's voice rises another notch. "No, absolutely not. They won't feel a thing. Nothing. Except maybe their stomachs growling or their feet aching."

I say, rather meekly, "But certainly some will be inspired by the art."

Gun laughs. "No, no, no. Those who are capable of being inspired—a handful out of millions—don't go to museums to become inspired. They don't go to museums to be inspired anymore than people go to cemeteries to learn how to live."

132

This argument isn't getting us anywhere; maybe I should excuse myself to continue cataloging.

Gun rages on: "People will do what you tell them to do. That's not inspiration. They are told they should go to a museum to become cultural. That's as ridiculous as someone believing that going into a bank to be around money will make him rich."

I'm restless now.

Gun smiles. "I see I've made you uncomfortable. You'll get used to my ranting."

After a few hours, I finish cataloging for the day. Gun insists I have dinner and drinks in his private booth. I don't really want to, but then I don't want to go back to my dorm room either.

I'm joined in the booth by four of Gun's friends from Tokyo. All are male, my age or a few years older, quite fashionably dressed. After introducing us (I quickly forget their names), Gun excuses himself. At first I'm not pleased, feeling none too social (the odd man out?), but his friends are very cordial and we're soon chatting away. They are quite knowledgeable about the Tokyo art scene: the popular artists, which galleries are in, what shows are at the museums.

After a couple of drinks, I give them the inside scoop on the National Art Museum (the chief curator's lack of taste and his outrageous halitosis), and when I tell them how I quit my associate curator's position they howl with laughter.

Takenoko

Takenoko finished eating a rice ball wrapped in roasted seaweed. Natsuko had watched him eat, as she sat on the floor at the edge of the hut.

He wanted her to leave; he didn't like the way he had been painting lately. It reminded him of his apprenticeship.

But at the same time, he felt good with her. He turned back to his painting without saying a word.

The food—smoked salmon salad, pheasant baked in parchment with baby leeks—is quite excellent, we all agree. In fact, we all seem to agree on everything.

We've gone through several bottles of French wine—crisp white Bordeaux, smooth Pouilly-Fuissé. I

haven't felt so relaxed since, since I can't remember when. Certainly not since I'd left Tokyo. Even with Haruna I'd been on edge, I now realize.

Gun joins us, and we congratulate him on the wonderful meal. He bows and orders cognac—Remy Martin—all around.

What good taste.

Gun

Gun sat with his jaw clenched. Ichiro's and Akiko's jaws were also clenched.

Ichiro unclenched his jaw to say, "I know you've suffered. I've suffered too. Akiko suffers. But we have to pull together before we can go our separate ways. We all need the money that the Views can get us, but if we split it up my share wouldn't be enough to help me. Haven't I offered to remove Mother as an obstacle?"

Gun unclenched his jaw. "But we can't wait for you to make your fortune before you toss us some crumbs."

Ichiro said, "But they wouldn't be just crumbs."

Akiko unclenched her jaw. "There might not be anything left at all."

Gun says, "The trouble with art today, is that there seems to be no middle ground between the traditional or the post-modern, at least nothing with any feeling to it."

"I agree," says one of his friends. "It's either flash or rehash."

We laugh until our eyes stream with tears.

Gun says, "It's all a matter of letting go. No one lets go anymore. I'm not talking about tipsy salary workers singing at karaoke bars, but really letting loose all their passion, living with all their hearts."

I add, "All their souls."

Gun nods. "Yes, all their souls. Even if it's a violent, dark soul. Even if it means spraying bullets into a crowd with an Uzi automatic."

I don't know if I'd go that far.

Gun

The gangster—he made no pretensions he wasn't—said, "We wish you the best, of course, but if we aren't paid on time, we can become very violent."

Gun's heart beat faster, stronger. "Oh? What happens when you become violent?"

The gangster looked surprised. "You want to know? Maybe you want me to show you."

"Yes." He felt intensely alive, as he did when he spent time studying Takenoko's Views. He missed them. He'd get them back someday.

The gangster shook his head. "You're a strange man."

Gun, ever the host, refills our cognac snifters. "We bottle up our emotions. Why bother? Sooner or later they'll come out, like the genie in the bottle. And the longer the emotions have been bottled the more monstrous we become. Just like the evil genie."

Gun looks at me while he continues, "We must use our emotions to fight insanity. We must live off our emotions, as surely as we eat and breathe."

I can hear what he is saying, even understand, but I find myself repelled, like a toe testing bath water that's too hot.

As I take a long draw of the aromatic cognac, I sense something dangerous about Gun.

But is it a danger to me or to himself?

Whether it was the lack of sleep, the lack of food, or his nearing the completion of the second painting on the second day of his quest, Takenoko found his mood soaring. Natsuko spent most of the day with him, watching silently, as she did on the hill looking at Mt. Fuji.

He started to wash his brushes, when Natsuko started to reach for them. "Let me help," she said.

"No. I must take each step myself."

The talk at our table lightens up after Gun's pronouncement on souls and emotions and Uzis. The conversation returns to the vapidness of pop music, the hideous fashions of certain designers, the Americanization trend, the insanity of avant-garde performance artists (I don't say a word about Junko, making me feel guilty, a traitor, which brings my mood down).

But after another cognac and watching the evening's show I'm back up, soaring to euphoric heights. The show seems completely different from the time I saw it with Kumi. The show is hilarious, a riot, and we can't stop laughing.

After the show and the rest of the audience is gone, we're swimming in our sea of cognac and cigarette smoke and laughter and conversation when Gun rejoins us.

"Let's go to Tokyo," he says.

Without a word of discussion, we gather up our suit coats, straighten our ties, and follow him out to the cars. I get into Gun's Celsior, in the back seat with one of his friends. Tabo drives the others in the Nissan they had driven down from Tokyo.

Gun says over his shoulder, "How does Japanese society view homosexuals, Yukawa?"

"Well," I begin seriously, my tongue thick with cognac and smoked salmon, "as with any lifestyle outside the normal, most Japanese tend to simply ignore it, they don't want to confront it."

Gun's friend in the back seat says, "Right. And as long as it remains in the background, like a hobby, it's okay."

Gun snorts, "Yes. They can't believe it's what you actually are. People may ski a few times a year, but they aren't skiers. Men love men, but they aren't really different, it's only a hobby."

Gun

Gun often recalled those heady days, those first months getting the club running. Of hours that stretched into the dawn and beyond. Of putting together the show. Of combing the underground clubs in Tokyo and Yokohama for the best talent. Of finding many lovers who loved with abandon, with passion.

After an hour and a half drive, we arrive at a club in Yokohama. We take up a couple of tables in the club. The only light comes from thin, red neon tubes. In one corner, men dance with men.

We refresh ourselves with a drink, washing away the lethargy built up from the drive. Soon we're back to our glib selves.

Gun says, "You see, everyone has a male and a female side, and one side can manifest itself strongly or weakly regardless of anatomically evident sexuality."

I say, "Just like madness and genius—there's a fine line dividing the two?"

Gun gives me a big, friendly smile.

Gun

Gun had no time for lethargy, he only had energy. And more energy. The memories of his past became distant, as if they were someone else's memories.

Sure, his debts piled up. He owed his brother, his sister, the gangster, countless crafts people. But they would get paid.

One way or another.

137

We hop on over to a club in Shinjuku. We pass by the apartment building where I used to live. It's only been a few days, but I feel as if I've crammed another whole lifetime into those days.

Does Junko still live there?

I don't want to find out. I'm practically worthless anyway, why would she want to hear from me?

I need another drink.

Two or three or four more clubs later, I'm in the back seat of Gun's car. Tabo is driving. Gun is sitting in the passenger seat, still being the philosopher.

Before I pass out, I wish I could be with Junko.

Or Haruna.

Or Kumi.

Praying
Mantis Eyes

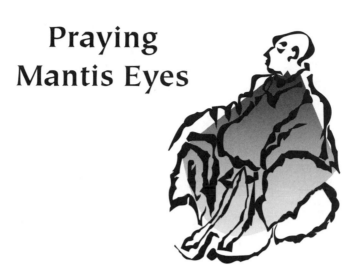

The sun has risen—the windows are rectangles of light behind the blinds in my room at Gun's place. I didn't sleep well; time passed with a succession of dizzy spells.

I'm in the same room where I slept the night Kumi and I stayed here. Was that just two days ago? My stomach rolls and my head pounds and my mouth is dry.

The door opens a crack and Gun sticks his head into the room. "I heard you stirring and thought you might need this." He comes in the room carrying a tall glass filled with a clear fizzy liquid.

He kneels down by my futon. I take the glass and drink gratefully. Gassy bubbles pop painfully in my mouth.

Takenoko

Takenoko twisted on his hard mat, under his thin blanket. Sleep, awake. Never asleep, never awake. Always tired, often euphoric, energized. Always painting, always thinking about painting.

He threw off the blanket and jumped up. He went out of the hut and walked to the inn. Except for the light from one window, the inn was dark. Low voices came from some of the rooms.

He sat in the garden near the rooms, watching, listening.

139

Gun folds his legs under himself. "Did you have a good time last night?"

"Yes." My voice cracks and sounds two octaves below normal.

Gun nodded. "Everyone did. They liked you."

We all got along a little too friendly, too easily. Had Gun picked those four just to make me … make me what? Laugh? Relax? Soften me up? For what?

I push myself up to a sitting position. "I better be going."

Takenoko

Takenoko awoke not knowing what day it was, or even if it was day or night. It doesn't matter, he thought, it's just another day of painting Mt. Fuji. He took a step out the door. The sun was rising, not setting.

He had to blink his eyes; the colors were all wrong. The sun's rays weren't the yellow-white they should be, but almost blue. He blinked and then held his eyes shut tightly for several heartbeats.

When he opened them again, the yellow-white was there, but so was the blue, although the blue had coagulated into spots in the periphery of his vision. He looked at his hand; he could see the blue blood flowing through his veins.

Gun says, "What? So soon? Aren't you going to finish cataloging my collection today?"

"Oh, um, I promised Akiko that I'd come back to Heda today."

Gun stands up and folds his arms across his chest. "No. It's early, you should have some breakfast. Have a bath. Relax. I'll call Akiko and tell her you'll be late."

"I really should go to Heda; Ichiro has a strict deadline set up for me. I'll come back here soon though. Tomorrow. I'll call and set up another time."

Gun says, "Don't let Ichiro intimidate you. He does that to get his way."

"Thanks. I won't let him." Sure, I won't let him.

The gangster smoothed his greased hair with his hand. "Look, are you sure you want to see this?"

Gun nodded. "Are you going to intimidate him? Threaten him?"

The gangster patted his hair like it was an unruly child. "I'm not going to do anything. I just watch. They do everything." He nodded toward the shadowy street corner, where two young men, probably still in their teens, were huddled together, smoking cigarettes.

When they were finished smoking, the young thugs went through the door. A shout of surprise came from inside, then a steady whine. The gangster went in; Gun followed.

The thugs held the scrawny man by his arms. The scrawny man was drooling from the corner of his mouth. The gangster nodded. One of the thugs moved in front of the scrawny man, and with a flick of his wrist, thrust a thumb in and out of the scrawny man's eyeball. The eyeball popped out of its socket and dangled on his cheek.

Gun sees me to the door. When he opens his mouth to say something, I thank him again and hurry out the door to my car. I start it and look back. He's there, arms still folded across his chest. He suddenly looks old. I wave and drive off.

When the club is out of sight I pull over to the side of the road. I check the back seat for a package. Nothing there. I pop open the trunk. No View in there either.

I drive away slowly, my head pounding, my stomach still queasy. But at least I'm alone.

I take the back roads through the mountains that form the spine of Izu Peninsula. The winding road doesn't sit well with my hangover, but after a few minutes, Gun's fizzy medicine starts to settle my stomach. I soon feel well enough to stop for some breakfast at a roadside cafe. I devour toast, juice, coffee, then get back on the road.

Along the way, the road is marked with several signs that announce an officially designated National Scenic View. Each has been rated on a scale of 1 to 7. I drive by one that has achieved a rating of 7. It has also been designated a National Beautiful Viewing Treasure.

The signs irk me. Why can't people figure out their own scale of beauty? Why does the government have to tell them where to stop? Why can't they find their own scenic views?

I'm starting to sound like Gun.

So, I wonder, what really happened last night? Gun must be trying to get me on his side in the battle over the Views. If such a battle is going on.

Whatever the reason, I'm glad to be away from Gun. But I don't know if I'm glad to be headed back to Heda. And Haruna.

Last night I would have been glad to be with her. But now I don't feel anything, except a lack of sleep.

I can't resist the officially designated Scenic Views. The next one has a rating of 6. I pull into the turnoff and park at the end of the cul-de-sac.

The parking spots are laid out so you don't even have to get out of your car to enjoy the view. How thoughtful. I tilt back my seat and settle into it.

I drift off to sleep taking in the view of a steep and wooded gorge. Nice, but I'd give the scene only a 5.

I don't get to sleep too long because a car soon pulls up next to mine. In the car sit two elderly couples, probably retirees on a sightseeing jaunt. They give me a friendly wave that I find irritating enough to ignore.

No telling what they think of me, or what I was doing there. It's none of their business, besides I wasn't doing anything but sleeping. But what irritated me is that I know what kind of people they are. They are the ones who spend three or four seconds mindlessly looking at each painting in a museum. They are the ones who stop at officially designated Scenic Views. They are Gun's average, uninspired people.

I start my car, back out of the space, and pull in behind the car of uninspired retirees. When I'm just a hair from their bumper I lay on my horn. Four startled faces stare at me. I give them a big friendly wave, back up, and drive off.

143

Takenoko

Takenoko sensed the movement before he saw it. The movement was Natsuko stepping around the rock outcropping. Takenoko ignored her and went on sketching Mt. Fuji.

Natsuko sat next to him, on the ground. She didn't move or breathe for a long while. Takenoko stopped sketching.

"Am I disturbing you?" she asked.

No. Yes. He had to paint her. He turned to her, with a fresh sheet of paper, and held the charcoal stick over the paper.

"Do it," she said.

He turned away, and began sketching the mountain.

I drive the rest of the way to Heda without stopping. The village is its placid self. I'm feeling better. I'm not sure why I ran out of Gun's in such a hurry. I'm not sure why I honked at the retirees.

No one greets me when I walk into Heda Onsen. I walk through the quiet inn, until I see a movement. In

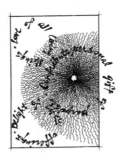

one of the rooms, Haruna is cleaning with a feather duster.

I watch her. She moves smoothly through the room. She obviously knows where dust collects and how to remove it. Some spots require a quick flick of the wrist, some require a more thorough swishing. She must have made the same movements thousands of times.

I wonder if she wants more out of life, or if she's perfectly happy.

Haruna

You aren't sure of life.

You don't know the shape of life.

Once you find the shape of life, it's very simple to live within it.

How can you protect yourself if you don't know the shape?

I step into the room. "Hello, Haruna."

She stops her feather duster in mid-stroke. "Hello." She smiles.

"I'm back. It's good to see you again."

"Yes, me too."

"How are you?"

"Fine. And you?"

"Fine." Why does intimacy make one so uncomfortable?

Haruna and I are sitting in the room with a view of the garden. She pours tea from an antique pot; it's probably Oribe, as evidenced by the iron glaze. I say, "When I arrived in Heda today, a kind of peaceful feeling came over me."

She tilts her head, and looks up at me out of the corner of her eyes. I want her right now. I wonder if we're alone. Where's Akiko?

She stares intently into her tea cup as if all the answers are in it. "Yes," she says, blind to my lust (or perhaps not), "life is usually very peaceful in Heda."

"But, I would go crazy living in such a small town."

She continues staring into the cup. She shakes her head once and says, "No, you wouldn't."

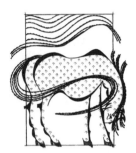

I ask Haruna, "Where's your mother?"

"Shopping."

"Oh." Should I ask how much longer she'll be gone? Too obvious? Instead, I say, "I spent yesterday at your uncle's club. Have you ever been to it?"

"No."

I could have guessed that would be her answer. She hasn't mentioned ever having been anywhere outside Heda. Simple is best—isn't that what she said? Simple ... the word aggravates me somehow, as if she were ignoring the problems of the world, letting someone else deal with them.

Haruna

Haruna thought: The past has its own shape, a horrible shape, the shape of darkness. The shape can't be described, really, what's the shape of pain? Well, it's a twisted shape, but not of a single strand like a rope wound in a ball; it's more like a mass of eels in a basket, withering, trying to escape.

The present has a nice shape, rounder, calmer, a single white cloud in a summer sky. The present keeps a nice shape, if it doesn't get disturbed.

My mood swings to one of irritation, as I felt with the tourists at the Scenic View. Haruna's innocence seems contrived, no longer attractive.

"But," I say to her, "aren't you just turning a blind eye to the world's problems by hiding here in an out-

of-the-way ryokan, in a tiny isolated village?"

She begins picking up our tea cups. "I like simple."

"But simple for simple's sake doesn't accomplish anything," I say wildly.

She thinks. Then shrugs.

As Haruna picks up the tea tray, Akiko Ono calls out from the front of the inn, "I'm home. Come help me, Haruna."

I instantly regret goading Haruna.

Akiko

Akiko cried out, "Mother?"

Only silence came from her mother's empty room. Akiko ran through the inn, pausing only to peer into each room.

When she reached the end of the hall, she ran to the garden. It was empty. The bath was empty.

Mother was gone.

"So," Akiko says to me, "you're back already." Haruna trots off, loaded down with several bags of food: produce, tofu, meat.

"Already. Yes. Oh, sorry I didn't call first. I was in Atami, and I just drove over from there."

Akiko gestures to the sitting room, where Haruna and I had been. "How's my brother?"

"Gun? He's fine."

Akiko laughs, though it sounds more like a cackle. What's so funny?

We sit at the low table. Akiko asks me, "What about your family? Do you have any brothers and sisters? Where do your parents live? What does your father do?"

The tone of her questions is not just inquisitive but demanding. I don't know if I want to answer, but I do. "I have a sister. She and my parents live in Shikoku. My father is a teacher."

"A teacher," she repeats. "A professor?"

"High school," I say quickly. I don't like the line of questioning and I try to change it. "And your parents? Where are they? How about your husband?" Then I remember Haruna said he died in a fishing accident.

Akiko smiles mischievously. "I'm sorry, did my questions offend you?"

Akiko wanted to slap Haruna, but she resisted. Earlier, she had wanted to slap the school principal, but she had resisted that urge as well. The space above the principal's upper lip was dotted with sweat as he told her that perhaps it would be better if Haruna didn't return to school. For her own good, he insisted. She's dropping further behind every day, he added quickly, and she needs special attention.

Akiko said to her daughter, "Haruna."
"Yes?"

"If you don't return to school and try harder, you will have to stay with me at home. You will have to work for me. You'll have to work very hard. Do you understand?"

"Yes. I'll work very hard."

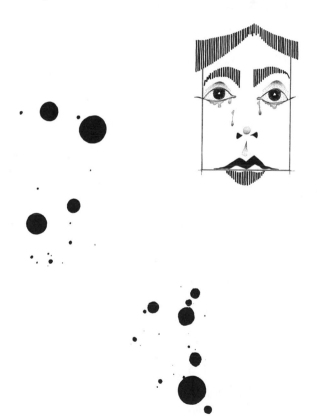

The businessman—vice-president of a major corporation—pressed the bills into her hand. They were warm from his pocket. "Okay?" he said again.

Akiko nodded.

"You understand what I want?"

Akiko nodded, but she was thinking that her mother, Haruna's grandmother, was to blame for Haruna getting expelled from school. And she blamed her mother for this:

She led the vice-president into the storage room. While he stood over her, she kneeled down next to the wall. She quietly pushed aside the cardboard box. Leaning against the wall, she put an eye against a pinhole. A young couple in the room was making love on the futon. She heard the vice-president fumble with his yukata, then moan, as he watched her watching.

Akiko's smile disappears after a moment or two. When it's gone, she says, "It's just me and Haruna."

"She works hard."

Akiko gazes directly, deeply, into my eyes; the gaze makes me very uncomfortable, but I can't break away. She finally says, "Haruna is a good daughter."

I say to Akiko, "Your brother, Ichiro, has told me that he's prepared to compromise on the Views. He would like your cooperation."

Akiko takes out a silk handkerchief and wipes a corner of it along the joint between the glass and wood frame of the table. "He'd like my cooperation? I've done nothing but cooperate. You're here, aren't you?"

"Yes, well …"

"What about Gun? Is he going to cooperate?" She said "cooperate" as if it meant committing murder.

I say, "Gun seems to be coming around to, um, working with us."

Akiko says, "You don't really understand him, any of us, do you?"

I wanted to shout at her: what's there to understand? Do you think you're so special or something? But I don't shout. I don't say anything.

I stand up. "Well, all I can do is pass along Ichiro's offer. He will be prepared to provide details of the compromise when I have finished cataloging all of the Views." I sound very officious.

Akiko reaches over the table and wipes a smudge on the glass. "What exactly do you do when you catalog?"

I relax a bit. "I'm noting the condition of each painting, the types of paints and paper used, as well as the themes."

"And you'll be able to tell if any are missing?"

I try to remain calm. "Missing? Missing. Are any missing?"

"No, not that I know of." Akiko folds her handkerchief.

Gun said, "It's not just about the money we can share by selling the Views."

Akiko said, "No, it's not. That's what I'm saying. I've been taking care of her for so long, while you two have been out making your fortunes. Meanwhile, she's chasing guests away with her behavior."

Gun and Ichiro didn't say anything.

"She's damaging the inn. I can't take care of her and the inn at the same time. And what if she starts damaging the Views?"

Ichiro snorted. "Yes, well, we can't have that. The paintings are our future."

The hours dissolved into one another. The ideas flowed now, a constant stream.

Ideas. More ideas. Ideas on top of other ideas.

Takenoko painted that day's view while he mentally created the next view. And the next view after that. His fingers did the painting on their own.

I retreat into one of the rooms where I begin cataloging. The room is quiet, the whole inn is quiet. The quiet makes me sleepy.

I feel beat up, more than tired, now that I think about it. My body feels bruised. My psyche is bruised. This job has become a pain. I just want to lounge in the hot springs bath until I dissolve. Ahh ...

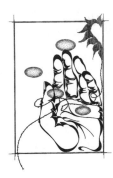

Natsuko's head seemed different—there was a bulge at the outside corners of her eyes. And the chin ... the chin ... what, narrower? Yes narrower.

Takenoko shook his head.

"What?" said Natsuko. "What is it?"

He felt like he was dreaming. Time slowed then sped up, bent around itself, but he knew he was awake. He had never seen the daughter and the praying mantis together. Were they one and the same?

He shook his head again. "Nothing."

I put all thoughts of the bath out of my mind. No use torturing myself; I focus on the View in front of me.

The painting's condition is better than most in the ryokan, probably because this room doesn't get much

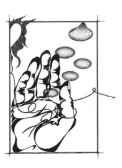

light. Of the colors, the blues have faded most, perhaps because of the quality of the original paint, which may have been diluted.

The View shows Mt. Fuji through a rainstorm, probably in early spring— the snow level is still low on the mountain. A fat bird perches in a bamboo grove with its head cocked toward Fuji.

I feel drawn into the painting's narrative. I don't care about the painting's condition, or where it hangs, or who has control over it. But I do want to know what the bird is thinking.

Perhaps the bird is admiring the mountain's beauty through the slanting spring shower. Do birds and animals admire anything? Do they have a sense of aesthetics? Ah, Kumi, there's a question for you. I suddenly want to be with her, and her cool intellect.

In the book, I find the description of this View: the author believes that Takenoko is merely using the bird's gaze to draw the viewer's focus to the mountain, which is nearly invisible, or certainly less visible, in the rain. I sit down to read more from the book.

After an hour, my legs are asleep. I stretch and yawn. I need to get some fresh air, and that might help me start over. I bring the book on Takenoko with me.

In many ways the village of Heda remains much the way it was over a hundred years ago. The main occupation is fishing; the fleet fishes Suruga Bay off the western Izu coast, sometimes going down as far south as the Izu Islands. Fishing has always been a dangerous trade, and the fleet in Heda suffered losses from storms or other tragedies on the sea.

The other main occupation is tourism. A small number of onsen ryokan can be found along the ridges of the small triangular shaped valley, where natural hot springs water bubbles to the surface. These onsen have been known from literature as far back as the thirteenth century.

With little doubt, the peacefulness of the present day Heda was there during Takenoko's stay. That peacefulness might have been attractive enough to keep the world-weary artist from leaving.

Akiko is sitting at a desk near the front of the inn; an accounts ledger is open on the desktop. "Finished?" she asks.

"No. That first View took awhile. I need to clear my head. I'm going for short walk."

"Don't get lost," she says, cheerfully. Or mockingly. I can't tell which.

I walk down the hill to the village. I run into a few older village residents. They give me a quick nod as if they know me. I walk onto the harbor's breakwater causeway. Across the bay, Mt. Fuji is obscured by haze.

The air is cool and fresh. As I inhale deeply, it does clear my mind.

I find a coffee shop on the road that passes quickly through town. The interior consists of a counter with eight seats, and two tiny tables along the front windows. I'm the only customer.

I sit at the counter. A middle-aged woman, probably the owner and sole employee, showers me with "welcome"s. I order a cup of coffee and a slice of cheesecake. "Yes, sir. Yes, sir. Yes, sir." She probably doesn't get many customers wearing designer suits.

As she prepares my order, I pick up a brochure for a local scuba diving shop. A young couple in wetsuits smile happily at me.

"Here's your cheesecake, sir. Sorry it's not so good."

She has an endearing quality about her, despite her fawning.

I take a bite of the cheesecake and make a smacking noise with my tongue and roof of my mouth. That seems to satisfy her. "Are you passing through town?" she asks, as if anyone like me would stop for any other reason.

"Actually," I answer candidly, "I'm doing some work at the Ono ryokan. Heda Onsen."

Her eyes open wide. "Oh, really?" She leans forward and whispers, "They're a strange family, aren't they?"

I say, "Yes, they are different. Do you know them very well?"

She grins. One of her front teeth is gold. "I know everyone in this town quite well."

"What kind of work do you do for them?" she asks, her full attention on me, a fellow gossiper.

"I'm actually employed by Ichiro Ono as the curator for the Takenoko museum." She squints at me and shakes her head. I say, "You know the artist that painted the 365 Views of Mt. Fuji." I show her the book cover.

She stares at it. "Oh," she says, obviously uninterested. She refills my coffee, even though I've only taken a couple of sips. "Has Akiko Ono told you the story about the fishing boat accident that killed her husband?"

I nod.

"Well," she says slowly, "it's not true. A lie."

The coffee shop owner says, "Akiko has never been married. No one knows who Haruna's father is. Well, except Akiko. Supposedly." She waits for the information, and insinuation, to sink in. Normally, I dislike gossiping and gossipy types, but how can I resist?

"Really?" I say encouragingly.

"Yes. And the same for Akiko's mother."

"The same?"

She nods and adds a drop of coffee to my full cup. "She never married, but had three children."

"Did Akiko's mother run the onsen?"

"Yes. A long time ago."

"No, the sunlight is all wrong," Takenoko said to himself. He adjusted the paper window shade. The light filtered through the paper.

He applied the blue-green paint to the sea. He formed waves using darker and lighter shades of hue, not with black outlines as the traditional technique had been for centuries. He no longer had time for outlining, not if he was going to finish one painting each day.

He could hear the laughter from his teachers, from the critics. No outlines? What kind of madness are you painting?

I pay for my coffee and cheesecake. The gossip must be free of charge. The coffee shop owner has a twinkle in her eye as she gives me my change. "Good luck with your museum."

"Thanks."

I head back toward the onsen. Halfway there, I realize I don't want to go back. The sun and warmth

feel too good. I wander up the lane toward the inn, then turn off in the general direction of the ridge behind the onsen.

When I get to the top, I find a nice spot where I can lean with my back against a rock facing the sun. I take off my suit coat, undo my collar, and roll up my sleeves. I start to read the book, but am immediately sleepy. I close my eyes.

The praying mantis turned its head back toward Mt. Fuji. Takenoko slowly lowered himself onto his hands and knees, then crawled toward the insect.

When he got within a body length, he stopped. The mantis turned briefly to look at the artist, then turned back. Takenoko crawled forward. He bent low.

There, in the insect's bulging, black, glistening eye, was a distorted reflection of Mt. Fuji.

When I wake up, my neck has a crick along the spine. I open my eyes slowly, adjusting to the bright sun. Then I see a slight movement to my right. My head swivels in that direction.

On a nearby rock is a praying mantis, its small forelegs folded in front of its green upper body. Its

head, overwhelmed by bulging eyes, turns in my direction.

"Hello," I say. I half expect it to say "hello" in return.

But it doesn't. It just looks at me.

I wonder if the praying mantis is a descendant of the one in Takenoko's paintings.

Or maybe the same one?

Maybe I've gone back in time. I check my Seiko. I was asleep only about ten minutes, and the month and day are still the same, of course; the year doesn't show.

What am I thinking? Of course I didn't go back in time.

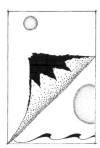 

"Hello," calls a familiar voice.

I look up from my Seiko. Haruna is standing near the rock where the praying mantis is sitting. Was sitting, as it has vanished.

"Hello," I say. I straighten my shirt and roll down the sleeves. I stand up.

"Enjoying the sun?" she asks. She looks elegant in her powder blue kimono. I never liked kimono, but she wears them quite naturally, unlike most women her age. I couldn't imagine her in anything else.

"Yes. It's very relaxing." I brush off my suit coat and fold it over my arm. "Did you see the praying mantis sitting there on the rock?"

"Praying mantis?"

In the dark, Takenoko was lying still. The door creaked open.

"Are you asleep?" whispered the Ono woman.

He didn't answer for a moment, then he said, "No."

She came in and squatted near him. After a long silence she said, "I enjoyed posing for you."

Another long silence.

"I liked the way you looked at me." She crawled under the thin blanket.

Haruna

Why was the man standing over mother like that? And what was she doing on the floor in the storage room?

Her mother saw her, and inhaled sharply. The man turned around. Cursing, he fumbled with his yukata.

Her mother whispered sharply, "Haruna. Go back to your room."

She looked once at her mother, then the man, before leaving, shutting the door quietly but firmly.

"Never mind," I say.

She smiles that simple smile of hers. "Okay."

"Well," I say as I take a couple of steps in the direction of the inn, "I suppose I should get back to work."

"Are you worried about something?"

"Worried?" I repeat. "Worried about what?"

"I don't know."

Takenoko

Takenoko looked over the edge of the cliff, a cliff like so many along the Izu coastline. The waves rolled into the rocks, breaking up and around them. I could, he thought, throw myself off. No one would care.

So why do it?

We walk back to the inn, where she leaves me to do my cataloging. The going is rough. I fight off sleepiness, indifference, and a mixture of curiosity and anger. Curious and angry at being lied to about the fishing boat accident. But, should I be angry at Haruna? She might not know the truth. That seems unlikely. If the coffee shop owner knows the truth, the whole village, and a good percentage of the rest of Japan, knows. She would have told them personally.

I have to admit that Akiko never did actually tell me the fishing boat accident story herself, although she didn't deny it when I mentioned it. But maybe it isn't a lie at all. Maybe Haruna's father did die in a fishing boat accident.

"Hello." It's Haruna again. I find myself glad to see her.

Haruna asks, "Are you hungry yet?"

"Not starving, no." Actually, the cheesecake sits like a lump in my gut.

"Okay. I'll serve the other guests first. Please have a bath, if you want. You may change in this room."

I do just that. The bath is heaven, except Haruna's company would have been a nice addition. I soak until I feel like jelly, and when I return to my room, Haruna is placing dishes of food on the table.

When she's finished, she pours me a glass of beer. I gulp half of it. "That hits the spot," I say.

After I've eaten, I ask Haruna, "Have you ever been to Tokyo?"

She shakes her head, but says, "Once, on a school field trip. I didn't like it."

"Too big? Too crowded?"

Haruna doesn't say anything for several moments. "I felt out of place, out of my time. I don't know, too much in the present. Something like that."

I feel sorry for her, and I reach over to her hand and give it a squeeze. She looks grateful.

Haruna takes back her hand. I ask her, "What's wrong?"

"Nothing," she says very softly. I can't help myself; I move around the table and put my arm around her. In a moment we're on the floor, getting all tangled up in her kimono.

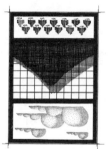

We're getting untangled when I hear a creaking at the door to the room. I stop and listen. Haruna pulls me close. I push away and crawl across the room. I fling open the door.

Akiko is there. She turns and walks away, down the corridor, silently sliding in her white slipper socks.

I hurry after Akiko. She moves quickly, and opens the door to the garden. She slips into a pair of outdoor thongs and walks into the garden.

I follow her. The evening air has become humid, sultry. It might as well be raining it's so damp.

Akiko is sitting on a bench made from a flat rock slab balanced on two cross sections of a tree stump. I stand in front of her, a couple of steps away. She says, "Yes?"

I'm unsure why I chased her. She may have been passing the room innocently and heard us. I say, "Did you want something?"

Akiko smiles. It's a knowing, smug, I-know-you're-doing-it-with-my-daughter smile. But the smile is also motherly, affectionate. She says, "No, I don't want anything."

"Oh," I mumble, not knowing what else to say. Then I remember the story—the truth?—I heard in the coffee shop.

I start to confront her about it, to ask her if it is the truth. I want to know if Haruna knows the truth.

I wonder, though, if it's better that Haruna doesn't know the truth.

Akiko

The three siblings sat in silence. The tea had gone cold; the sweet, pounded-rice cakes had become crusty.

Akiko said, "All I want is peace in my head, and in my heart. All I want is my life to be free from torment."

Ichiro and Gun nodded once, twice.

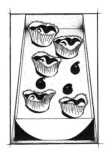

Only
Mt. Fuji

When I return to my room after confronting Akiko (or rather not confronting her), Haruna is gone, my dinner dishes cleared, and the futon laid out. I drop onto the futon and let out a big sigh.

I pick up the book on Takenoko and start to read. But my mind wanders: to Akiko watching us, to the gossipy coffee shop owner, to Haruna and her kimono.

I can hear other guests' muffled laughter and, I think, singing. I put down the book. I stick my head outside my room, and find the direction of all the revelry. I follow the noise until I reach the room. I peek inside.

Haruna is performing a stylized dance to the singing and clapping of two elderly couples. The couples I had seen at the Scenic View.

Takenoko

Takenoko found the night softer, more comfortable, more sensual than the day. He roamed at night, wandering the grounds of the inn, peeking into windows.

The terror of painting, of picking up the brush in the morning, vanished at night. There were no colors at night, no shapes. Just formless, colorless shadows.

Takenoko

In the morning, Takenoko wanted to scream.

Instead, he just whimpered.

He was alone with his brush.

The morning comes quickly; I read most of the night. There's a knock on my door. Haruna comes in with a breakfast tray. My eyes feel puffy, thick, bloodshot.

"Did you sleep well?" Haruna asks.

"No. Too much singing and dancing going on around here." I laugh at my weak joke; Haruna looks confused.

A wild thought strikes me. "How would you like to go to Tokyo with me today? I can show you that it's not such a cold place."

Haruna looks surprised, or afraid. "Oh, no. No."

Haruna

Doesn't he know? Haruna wondered. I can't leave the ryokan.

The shapes would change, be all wrong.

His shape is changing.

I quickly finish my breakfast and leave the inn. Haruna is busy with the other guests (I feel a bit jealous) and Akiko is nowhere to be found (not that I look very hard). I decide I should go back to the museum to check in with Ichiro and the construction progress. As I drive out of Heda, for some reason I feel like I've failed, or made a fool of myself. Or both?

I drive quickly to Numazu and pull into the parking lot of the dormitory. I remember to check the car and trunk—there's no View in my car.

I hurry up to my room. On the door is a note to see the person in room 427, down the hall. I go there and find another note: "To Yukawa: A delivery service left two packages for you inside. I left the door unlocked."

I open the door. Leaning against the wall just inside are two packages, one flat, one tube.

In my room, I take a shower, shave, and change into a fresh suit. In the mirror my eyes have dark circles under them and my skin looks mottled.

I gather up all the Views I have now and head out to my car. I think about stopping to see Kumi before I go to the office, but I wouldn't know what to say.

On the way to the office, I daydream about Haruna dancing for the two elderly couples. They seemed to be having a good time. Then Akiko storms into the daydream and pulls Haruna away by the wrist.

I turn into the parking lot of the museum. My museum. The security guard is marching in front of the building, keeping a wary eye out for art thieves and gate crashers.

I leave the Views in the car.

Takenoko

Takenoko arched his back. The Ono woman was a lusty lover. As good as any of the brothel courtesans. She pulled Takenoko tightly to her again and again. He felt as if he were drifting at sea.

She finally stopped and rolled onto her side. They were both panting.

She reached out to some of his sketches lying on the floor. "What?" She found the sketches of Natsuko.

She sat upright, pulling her kimono around her shoulders. "What's this?" she demanded, shoving a sketch under his nose.

"Just a sketch."

"You promised you wouldn't—"

Takenoko protested, "It's just a sketch. I didn't paint her." She tore the sketch into pieces.

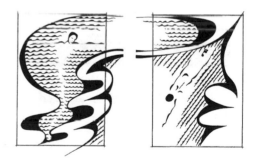

The guard gives me a professional nod and holds the door open for me. "Good morning," I say.

"Good morning, sir."

Now that's the way to be treated first thing in the morning. With respect.

My office (my office!) hasn't been touched during the two days I've been away. I'll have to say something to the contractor about that. He should make my office a priority. I sit at my desk. The computer screen comes on automatically and displays: You have two messages. Would you like to read them? Press Y for yes, N for no.

I choose Y and the messages scroll up, one at a time. They're both from Ichiro, wondering where I've been and how my negotiations have gone, and telling me to see the contractor, who has several questions. The computer asks if I want to reply to the messages or delete. I savagely hit the delete button.

I sit at my desk, twisting left and right, left and right, in my swivel chair. Why did Akiko have to interrupt us last night? The lust lurks in my gut like a heavy, undigested meal.

Was Akiko watching?

I call the security guard looking for Ichiro. He tells me Ichiro will be arriving at the museum after lunch. I  go back out to my car to do something about my collection of Views. If I wait long enough I'll have enough of them to open my own museum.

Sitting in my car, I wonder how to get the Views past the guard. I can say I got them from Gun and Akiko, as part of the compromise. No—what if the guard tells Ichiro who then calls to thank them?

There I go, worrying about the guard again. It's my museum. I gather up the Views and walk right up to the front door. The guard holds open the door.

I smile and say confidently, "Nice day."

Takenoko

The Ono woman crumpled up pieces of the sketch. Her fingers squeezed so hard the knuckles turned white.

Takenoko rubbed her hands.

She gave out a little cry, as if no one had ever shown her tenderness before. "I'll tell you why," she said. "She's so very beautiful, but she's a mirror. I see in her my own failings."

162

In the storage room, I study the two latest Views I'd received. One of them shows Mt. Fuji through a bird-of-paradise. The flower is presented very realistically, while the background, including the mountain, is slightly out-of-focus, almost like a photograph. A very stunning painting, actually, so different from the usual technique of the time. In the book, the author speculates that Takenoko may have seen an early photograph at some point, but that seems unlikely.

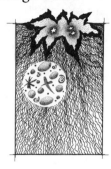

The second one shows a group of men dressed in extremely poor clothing, bent low as they climb toward the slope of Mt. Fuji. The author believes they are part of a cult of mountain worshipers, ascetics who believe Mt. Fuji is a god.

I can't detect a pattern in the Views I've received. They're all quite different—the praying mantis, the rain, the fishermen, the flower, and the ascetics. They represent different seasons, themes, and styles.

I put them into the appropriately numbered storage drawers.

I start cataloging the others, but quickly get bored. The Views blur together into one massive Mt. Fuji. I rub my eyes. I stretch and yawn.

I need a vacation.

In some ways, my old life in Tokyo was easier than my new life. I had a prestigious job, one that came with an elegant business card. Sure, I didn't like my job. Well, I could have liked my job, I suppose, if it weren't for the chief curator. If it weren't for the ridiculous assignments he gave me. If it weren't for his halitosis.

And Junko was all right.

All right? That sounds a little weak.

But what's so good about my life now? Well, I'm in charge of my own museum—I have to keep repeating that. It has to be worth the headaches, because I don't really have much choice. This is it, my life.

Maybe things will settle down, when the museum is finished, and all the Views are together. When I don't have to see Gun or Akiko again. I won't mind seeing Haruna again, but not at the onsen (although their outdoor bath is outstanding). Akiko makes me too nervous.

Takenoko

Takenoko grabbed the Ono woman's hand. She glanced up at him. Takenoko said, "No one knows what beauty looks like, just as no one knows what is success or failure, good or bad."

She let the pieces of the sketch fall to the floor. "You're a fool."

What about Kumi? I'd miss seeing her in those orange coveralls. But, I could still see her—she seems to be more independent from the family, certainly more than Haruna.

And, when things settle down, will I ever see Junko again? That seems unlikely. I haven't even called her,

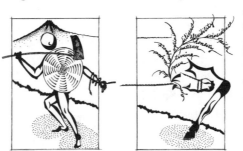

as I promised I would. Or did I promise her?

Junko, Junko. Oddly, for a brief moment, I can't remember what she looks like.

The contractor sticks his steer-like head into the storage room. "Hey, there you are. Where ya been?"

His eyes are red, again, maybe they always are. His nose is quite red as well, as if he's got a head cold. And with his head, it would be quite a cold. "Well? You got some answers for me?"

I want to yell something like "I've got more answers than you've got questions, fool." But I don't.

The contractor follows me to my office, where I have my set of plans. I show him my notes and that, yes indeed, I have some answers.

The contractor points to the entryway on the drawings. "What's this?"

"I moved the ticket booth away from the door. You don't want people to bunch up at the front entry. Besides, who wants to see a ticket booth the first thing when they walk in? You want to give them a little time to get in the right mood."

"Mood? Mood, huh. Mood." He clucks and shakes his big head. "Okay, but that'll mean some rewiring."

"And tone it down, too," I say. "The booth, I mean, it's too big. Unfriendly. Like a train station."

Cluck, cluck, goes the steer-head.

Takenoko

Takenoko ran back to his hut, where he had left a few drops of tea in his morning cup. He picked it up and ran carefully back to the rock. The praying mantis was still there, staring at the mountain.

The insect looked at Takenoko. The artist's mood changed instantly from darkness to lightness. Takenoko leaned closer, and tilted the tea cup. A drop spilled into an indentation in the rock.

The insect—the same shade of green as the tea—bent its head and took a sip.

It was a strange mist, for a day so deep in winter. It drifted down from the sky, as a summer mist does, rather than floating up from the ground as a winter mist does.

It was the first day that Mt. Fuji had been completely obscured. Takenoko stood on the ridge, his arms hanging limply at his sides. The mist was beautiful, alive. But how was he supposed to paint the mountain if he couldn't see it? Was he supposed to imagine it?

He had always worked from live models before. He sat down on the damp ground in disgust.

He stared and stared at the mist, then he remembered what a teacher had said, "You feel a good line, you don't see it."

Could he feel Mt. Fuji?

I walk around the museum with the contractor, going over the plans. I feel confident, and make decisions left and right. Up and down. Top and bottom. The contractor doesn't cluck after awhile, although he does shake his head and mutter about "change orders," which mean more work for him and more money from Ichiro.

"He's a strange one, isn't he?" says the contractor. "Ichiro Ono?"

"Yep. He'll change his mind in a heartbeat. He'll drive me to an early grave."

That and the steer-head's drinking and smoking, I think.

 166

"I know what you mean," I say. If I agree with the contractor, he might be more friendly toward me. And I could use a friend. "Just between you and me, I think he's a bit loony."

The contractor guffaws. If there was ever a perfect example of a guffaw, his was it.

What I had said in jest hits me: maybe Ichiro is loony. What if he isn't opening a museum at all? Why start a museum without all the paintings in hand? What if he's just building the museum to build something? Isn't there a house like that in California? A fortune teller convinced a rich widow she had to keep building onto her house to keep away ghosts. There are staircases that go nowhere, hundreds of rooms. I remember seeing it on a TV travel show.

"If," the Ono woman said to Takenoko, "you paint, or even sketch, my daughter again, I will turn you over to the village fishermen who will beat you. They have very strong hands from hauling in their nets. After they beat you, they will take you out to sea and chop you into pieces for bait."

She paused then added, "Chop you to pieces slowly."

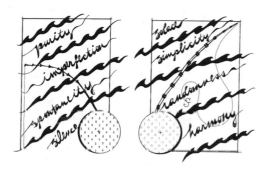

Certainly a few of the Views are cries for recognition on Takenoko's part: weird and unnatural colors, shocking distortions of reality, or parodies of technical mastery of recognized artists. But these "cries" do not detract from the vast majority of Views, which are heartfelt and nonevidential; the artist himself is off the stage, well in the wings, maybe even outside the theater, to stretch the analogy.

One will make comparisons to van Gogh and other artists not appreciated in their time, although Takenoko did start out making a living from his art, albeit from painting what are essentially advertising brochures. Still, in Japan, artists not appreciated in their time never get appreciated at any other time. No such sentimentality or critical re-evaluation exists. Artists only get one chance to make it or break it.

I start to ask the contractor if he'd ever heard about that house in California, but I don't want to be *that* chummy with him. Walking around with him, though, I suddenly see the sterility of the museum. It's nothing spectacular, not much different from other small museums. The only thing different is the big window with a view of Mt. Fuji.

The museum is uninspired. Slick and modern, for sure, but are the Views slick and modern?

Perhaps Gun and Akiko have a point about the museum not being such a good setting for the Views.

The Views are unique, I've come to appreciate that. Their uniqueness cries out for an appropriate setting. An inspired setting.

But how can I convince Ichiro of that, especially since the work has progressed this far? Am I working for the wrong side?

I'm about to tell the contractor to stop work, that I'm going to completely redesign the whole museum, when Ichiro finds us.

"Well," he says, looking around, "not much is getting done around here, I see."

I draw myself up, but his cold gaze on me makes me slump. "Sorry. I've been gone for a couple of days. Meeting with your brother and sister."

Ichiro looks over the shoulder of the contractor at the plans. "What's with all these changes?"

The contractor, my new friend, my ally, my chum, points at me.

In my office, Ichiro sits across from me with his hands on the desktop and gripping the edge as if I was going to steal the desk out from under him.

"Did they accept our compromise?" he demands to know without so much as a "How have you been?"

"Well," I begin slowly, "I stalled them."

"Stalled them? What does that mean?"

My knees go weak. I resolve not to let my voice crack as I answer him. 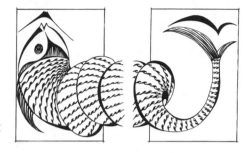 "I told them that once I finish cataloging the Views, we would like to have a meeting to arrive at the compromise."

"A meeting? I don't want to have a meeting. I haven't seen them for over twenty years."

Takenoko

The night sky was moonless, starless. The low clouds, now just shadows, absorbed all sounds. Takenoko peered through one of the many cracks in the wall of the hut. He could see the path from the inn to the hut. The path Natsuko had worn deeper.

He put his ear to the crack. The muffled world sounded dangerous. A band of fishermen could sneak up easily to his hut.

What would it be like to be chopped to pieces in front of your own eyes? What would it be like to see the pieces, your pieces, flung into the sea to attract fish?

Ichiro

With his head down, Ichiro stood in front of the guests. They're already laughing. At him. His mother stripped off his yukata.

"There, you see what I mean? Have you ever seen such a scrawny child? And such a scrawny child from such a voluptuous woman as me?" She shook her body, jiggling her breasts until one popped out of her loose kimono. "See what I mean?" She shoved the loose breast into the face of a guest.

Then she leaned over Ichiro. "What's this? A pubic hair? Come look everyone, the boy is becoming a man!"

They pointed and laughed.

Ichiro sat in his car, just outside Heda. He had waited until now to come up with a plan, a strategy. And it did come to him.

Mother wouldn't care. It's not as if she knew where she was anyway. She existed in her own world, and her physical environment wouldn't matter.

She had lost her battle.

"But, but," I sputter before I get control of myself (I think I'm hyperventilating), "We don't have to have a meeting. I mean, I just stalled them, until we ... until I could come up with a firm strategy. At least we have their cooperation for now. I think I'm making real progress with them. That's my strategy." I hope I've said "strategy" enough for him.

Ichiro leaned back in the chair and pressed his fingertips together. "An adequate strategy."

Really?

Ichiro says, "Now I'd like to see the results of your cataloging."

"The results of my cataloging?" I repeat meekly. "Well, I'm not quite finished yet. I'm doing a very thorough job, and it's taken quite a lot of effort, far more effort than I originally envisioned. But I think a thorough job is better than an unthorough one." Unthorough? What am I talking about?

Ichiro nodded. "That's right, you're the one with the philosophy."

"The philosophy?"

"Your philosophy of life is the same as your philosophy of work, to do things right."

Oh, that philosophy. Do employers really believe anything you say in job interviews? Don't they just want to hear the "right" answers? Right, but not necessarily true.

Ichiro says, dreamily, "My sister and brother—you've met them—have very distinct philosophies, wouldn't you say?"

"Oh, yes. Very distinct."

"Akiko works very hard. I don't know if that's a philosophy or not, but if it isn't, what is it?"

I nod.

"And Gun, well, Gun knows me better than myself. Now that's a frightening thought, don't you think? To have someone know you better than yourself?"

I nod, but he doesn't notice. Or doesn't care.

He says, "Akiko has helped me. Gun helped me once very much. With an employee who stole company secrets."

I try not to gulp air. I whisper, "Stole company secrets?"

Ichiro waves his hands. "Nothing for you to worry about, Yukawa. It's in the past. Now, what about all these changes? Are they good changes?"

"Oh yes. I believe—"

"No need to justify your decisions to me. I hire the best people to make them."

Or steal them.

Ichiro says, "Dinner tonight at my house?"

"Dinner? Well, yes, of course."

"Good."

When Ichiro has been gone for five minutes, I finally breathe again. My adrenaline rush slows. His words stop echoing in my bare, unfinished office, and in my tired, addled brain.

I take another breath. Be calm, I tell myself.

I'm calm, but alone, vulnerable. I'm balanced on a knife edge; one slip and I'm sliced clear through.

I don't have any allies. Even the simple-minded contractor betrayed me.

Ichiro pushed the folder across the table to Gun. "This is the information about the employee gathered by your private detective."

Gun opened the folder, then shut it quickly, without reading anything. "Perhaps it's better that I don't know."

Ichiro nodded. "So you'll make the arrangements?"

"Yes. To what level do you want the problem taken care of?"

Ichiro pressed together his fingertips. "The damage has been done. He can't undo it. He won't be forgiven."

Gun nodded.

I spend the rest of the afternoon cataloging, trying to get into it, but it's slow. The storage room is a prison cell. At the end of the afternoon, I add up all the Views I've cataloged. It comes to about twenty percent of the total. It's going to take me forever to finish.

I drive to Ichiro's home; he left me directions on my computer mail system. His house isn't too far from the museum. Of course, it's quite a mansion, especially the wrap-around deck with a view of Mt. Fuji. I'd give it a 6.5 on the National Scenic View rating scale.

A pleasant surprise greets me at the door. Kumi. "Welcome," she says. She's wearing an orange (Ono Robotics orange) sun dress. The color isn't exactly fashionable, but she looks good in the dress.

Kumi

Kevin: "I don't know what to say. You hardly respond anyway. 'What's wrong?' I ask. 'Nothing,' you say. Or you don't say anything."

Nothing.

"See what I mean? Nothing. And don't tell me you don't understand my English, I know you do."

Understand.

"Maybe you should move back into your own apartment."

Own.

Kumi takes me into the house, a sleek Western-style home. The furnishings are high quality, comfortable, and match the house's sleekness without being minimalist. The art is also Western; none of Takenoko's Views hang on the walls.

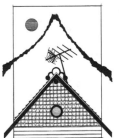

"Do you live here?" I ask Kumi.

"No. I have my own apartment in Numazu. But I come here a lot."

"I can understand that. It's beautiful."

And filled with robots, it turns out. Kumi demonstrates the automatic lighting system that responds to human presence and levels of natural light, the continuous dust and odor removal system, the infrared-sensing heating and cooling system, the robotic vacuum cleaner.

"Wow," I say.

Ichiro joins us in a large room overlooking the view of Mt. Fuji. He smells freshly bathed and perfumed. By a robot? Or does he have to do that himself?

Over cocktails we exchange pleasantries. Ichiro is more relaxed here, or around Kumi. Kumi is her quiet self.

We're called to dinner by a maid. She's dressed in a maid's plain black uniform with a collar frill. Not even Ichiro would dress his wife in a maid's outfit, would he? I wonder if he's divorced or a widower.

The dining area looks out over Mt. Fuji. Dinner is Japanese, fashionably rustic Japanese. The conversation dwells mostly on the reason why robots are so accepted by the work force, instead of being seen as a threat to their employment.

I get the feeling that Ichiro would prefer to see an entire workforce of robots, rather than one of people, but I'm not really following the conversation too closely. I spend most of my time trying to catch glimpses of Kumi.

"In fact," says Ichiro as he slices a yellow beet neatly in half, "robots are viewed as sexy things, right?" He looks from me to Kumi and back to me.

I say, "I suppose you could say that. They are perfect Japanese, after all. They work hard without complaining."

Ichiro laughed. Kumi smiled at her father's laughter. He seems to appreciate her smile and gives her back a big smile.

Ah, nothing like a nice, happy, family meal. Minus the wife and mother.

We finish up with a salad of a myriad of greens and sautéed burdock root. Kumi and Ichiro are deep into a discussion of human versus machine intelligence, and I feel perfectly happy to be left out of the conversation. I have to admit, sipping sake, a feeling of belonging has come over me.

In Tokyo, Junko had been the one who supplied my life with friends, culture, conversation topics, get-togethers. Now here I am, all on my own, having gotten here all on my own, enjoying a stunning dinner in a stunning setting with one of the richest men in Japan.

And his lovely and eligible (I assume) daughter.

Ichiro

"What's intelligence?" asked Ichiro. "What's a mind?"

Kumi said, "It's the sum of neurons and their connections that form distinct patterns."

"Patterns."

"Patterns that form memories, or trigger hormone secretions."

"What about visualizing the future, or imagination? Or fantasy?"

"Recreations or recombinations of patterns."

"I think it's more than that."

As the conversation drags on however, I'm still left out of the loop. I scrape my salad plate clean. The maid picks up the plate, before I lick it.

Through a few pots of roasted tea, I'm still out of the loop, and getting more and more irritated. I wish I were back in Heda, having a nice bath with Haruna.

"Well," says Ichiro to me, "should I call a taxi for you two?"

"I can drive," I say.

"Then would you mind giving Kumi a ride back to her apartment?"

"No. Not at all."

Riding back to Numazu in my car, I ask Kumi, "Is it difficult working for your father?"

"Difficult?"

"Well, I mean, you know." Actually, I'm not sure what I mean. "Always having to discuss work?"

"Oh, I see. I must apologize for so much technical discussion during dinner. Once we get going it's hard for us to stop."

"You don't have to apologize. I find it fascinating."

"You're just saying that to be polite, aren't you?"

"Oh, no." I try to look innocent, but can't, and I must look goofy, because she gives me a confused look. Then she asks, "Would you like to come up to my apartment?"

Kevin: "Being polite means nothing more than being a liar."

Liar.

"So why don't you stop lying? Stop being so fucking polite."

Slip.

We drive past the Ono Robotics plant, through the dark residential area. Kumi points out the street up ahead I need to turn onto. Out of the corner of my eye, I see a mountain of trash moving down a side street. The nekobaba.

A brilliant idea pops into my head: I'll leave a trail of things, trash, in the gutter, then see which ones she takes and which ones she leaves. That might tell me how she decides which pieces are suitable.

What a great idea.

I still need to find out more information on those grates in the culvert, and where they lead.

Takenoko crept up to the inn, up to the window of Natsuko's room. He couldn't see in through the darkness, but he could imagine.

He imagined her asleep, curled around herself, her face peaceful, her breath even.

He imagined slipping into her room, stealing up to her without waking her. He imagined sketching her, painting her.

I ask Kumi, "Did you see that old woman back there, pushing the shopping cart full of trash? Remember, I asked you about her the other day?"

Kumi gives me a blank stare, then shakes her head.

Kumi's apartment is in a newer building of five floors. It's a nice-sized apartment, not a rabbit-hutch, and has a separate bedroom. She's furnished the place rather starkly, nothing on the walls, minimal functional furniture. I get the impression she doesn't spend much time here. There is, of course, a view of Mt. Fuji out the window.

I sit on the couch, while Kumi makes coffee. "Nice apartment," I say.

"Thank you," she says. I smile. She smiles.

Halfway through our coffee, I'm feeling relaxed enough to ask, "Are you happy with your life? I don't mean to be too personal, it's just that, well, it's a hobby of mine."

"Hobby?"

"I'm fascinated with people's lives, and if they are happy. Most, well, almost all of the people I meet seem to be happy. I wonder why, what makes them happy? My life is okay, but I wouldn't say I jump up for joy every morning."

Kumi says, "I'm very happy with my work. My personal life is not perfect."

"Oh?" I say.

She says, "Do you find me attractive?"

Well, of course, but what does her question mean?

Evidence of sexual attraction itself will offer a clue to aesthetic rules.

"Well, yes. You're very attractive." My face feels flushed.

I feel as if Haruna's watching me. As if Ichiro, Akiko, and Gun are watching me. I look up.

It's only Mt. Fuji.

177

Another
Trick Question

I'm in Kumi's apartment, I'm sure of that, but my body and mind feel disconnected. If I wanted to I could probably float away from my body.

Kumi is facing the window. I can almost hear her brain gears meshing, purring. Probably working on her artificial-whatever.

As if she hears me thinking about her, she twists around. She gazes at me. I can't tell what she's thinking.

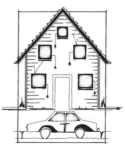

Despite the coffee, and my lust, I'm barely awake. I fight to keep my eyes open. Don't the Onos ever sleep? I must be getting old.

Kumi

Working, working, the computer flashes, the hands of the clock icon whirl, whirl, hurry, hurry, show, show now
   Next, next function
   Call, get, read
   Move [out], get [away], call [home]
   Escape, return
   Yes [Y] return
   Home
   [H]

Takenoko

Takenoko wanted to sleep. His body cried out for sleep. But his mind raced along, planning the next painting.

He wished he could tear off his head, so his body could rest.

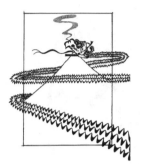

Kumi asks, "Have you had many lovers?"

"Me?" I say. "Ha. Me … no." What is this? A survey on sexual behavior?

"What sort of lover do you like?"

"What sort?" As in breathing? Warm to the touch?

"Are you attracted to certain physical types or personality types?"

I haven't ever thought about it. Maybe it's a trick question. "Well, your type, of course. Am I your type?"

She turns away.

Takenoko

Takenoko and Natsuko were on the ridge. He was painting; she was watching. The air was crisp, cold, the clearest it had been since Takenoko had begun painting the views. Takenoko stared at the mountain, his brush poised over the painting for several long moments.

Natsuko asked, "What do you see?"

He shrugged, and went back to his work.

Natsuko said, "If you stare at one point on the mountain long enough, it begins to move."

The mountain moved all the time for Takenoko. More than once it had gotten up and danced.

We're walking along the beach, a few blocks from her apartment. The sun is still below the horizon, but the eastern sky is orange. Ono Robotics orange.

Kumi says, "I've only had one lover."

I've only had one lover this week. Her cousin.

She says, "In California, when I was in school. An American."

We stroll on the damp sand. The air is heavy with moisture. She points to Mt. Fuji; the sun is lighting the peak. She asks, "What do you see?"

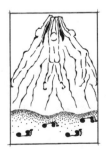

A mountain? Another trick question?

"It's beautiful," I say of Mt. Fuji at dawn. "There's a nice view of Mt. Fuji in Heda, on a ridge above your aunt's ryokan. I think that's where Takenoko painted many of the Views."

"Why do you think Mt. Fuji is beautiful?"

I feel a grain of irritation working its way under my already battered psyche. I try my best to ignore it. "Well, okay, let's see ... its shape, of course, and the contrasting colors are nice. The mountain seems really close right now, like you could touch it. That must be because of the way the light hits it." It's hard to describe why something has beauty.

She stops walking. "So your perceptual inputs automatically determine a sense of beauty or non-beauty, that is, even before cognitive processing?"

The grain of irritation grows to a boulder.

We reach the end of the beach, at a point where a concrete-banked river reaches the sea. We turn around and head back. Before she can ask me another crazy question I ask her, "Do you regret what you've done with your life so far?" I don't know why I ask that question, it just popped into my head. Do I regret my decision to take this job?

Kumi says, "Regret ... regret what? Specifically?"

"I don't know," I snap at her, then add more softly, "you know, regret leaving your lover in California. Regret working for your father."

"Regret ... I don't know. I've never thought about regret."

Natsuko asked, "You said you'd paint me, remember?"

Takenoko scrubbed his face with his hands. "I want to."

"When?"

"I have to finish the Mt. Fuji paintings."

As we near Kumi's apartment, I casually say, "It's a real tragedy about your cousin's father."

She looks confused.

"You know, the fishing boat accident, his drowning at sea?"

"Oh? I don't know much about their family."

That seems odd to me. "What about your mother?" I ask rudely, too directly.

"She died when I was very young."

Don't tell me— she drowned in a fishing boat accident.

One more finished.

The pile had grown to thirty. The first month. Finished. One twelfth.

Thirty done.

Are they thirty good paintings? Takenoko asked himself that question every day. Many times a day.

But he no longer worried about it.

I don't go up to Kumi's apartment; I'm sure she has to get ready for work, put on her orange coveralls and think artificial-thoughts. We say a perfunctory good-bye.

I drive back to Ono Robotics and haul myself up to my dorm room. I flop onto my futon and close my eyes. I realize then that I hadn't received another View. I had forgotten to check my car, though. I can't do it now, I just want some sleep.

I do sleep. A hard, furious, one hour of sleep. I wake up groggy, with a dull headache on the left side of my head. I roll onto the floor, stand up, and go into the bathroom for a hot shower.

When I towel off and start looking in my closet for a fresh suit, I notice a tube package by the door.

I open the door and check the hallway. It's empty, of course.

The latest View to be delivered shows a hand in the foreground, possibly the artist's, and Mt. Fuji in the background, off-center to the right. The hand seems to be scooping up the mountain, or caressing it.

Touching it?

Hadn't I just said that to Kumi a few hours ago?

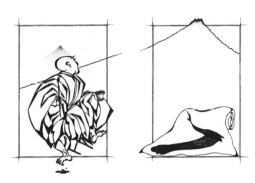

I sit against a wall, the concrete blocks are cold. My hair and face are still damp from the shower. The View is on the floor in front of me.

I have to talk to someone about them. Why do they keep showing up? Who's doing it? Could I talk to Kumi? But she seems a likely suspect, actually. This latest View relates to our conversation. And she does work right here in the plant. But she didn't have any Views in her apartment, none that I could see, although I didn't poke around in her drawers or closets.

My room is depressing, everything is depressing. I think about Junko. Could I talk to her? No. That makes me depressed, too.

Takenoko

Takenoko stared at his hand as it painted. Not as he painted, no, as it painted. The hand knew when to make a precise, subtle stroke, or when to make a bold, mad swipe of color.

The more he tried to control it, the more it exerted its own power.

Takenoko

The Ono woman stretched out next to Takenoko. He touched her shoulder. She pulled away, and got out of the bed. She straightened her kimono, and retied her obi.

She went over to his stack of finished paintings. She studied the top painting, then quickly glanced at the rest.

The Ono woman said, "Aren't you tired of painting Mt. Fuji?"

183

Maybe I'm on some TV show, like Hidden Camera, or Practical Jokes and Laughs. The whole thing has been set up, the chief curator and my ex-colleagues at the National Art Museum are behind it. Junko, too.

I pick up the phone and dial the chief curator's number. A secretary answers. I hang up. I dial my ex-colleague, the expert in ukiyo-e prints. I imagine him sitting in his chair, at his tidy desk, trying to look busy for the boss, but really just wondering where to eat for lunch. He answers after one ring and I say in a disguised voice, "You're not very funny."

"Pardon? Hello? Who is this?"

"You'll pay." I hang up.

I'm tired of my room. Tired of Ono Robotics. I'm tired of the Views showing up without an explanation. It's got to stop. I'm tired of everything.

All I want is to be the curator of a small private museum. I want to earn my paycheck, and maybe even a little respect in the community of art museum curators. Even though it is an incestuous, back-stabbing, egomaniacal world.

All I want is a nice apartment I can go home to after work, cook up a simple yet tasty meal, and have a glass of wine or a beer while listening to soothing jazz or classical music. Occasionally, I'll have a few friends over for a sit-down dinner, filled with lively and stimulating conversation. They'll go home before they are too drunk, or the conversation lags, or someone steps on someone else's toes.

Is that too much to ask?

It's well past noon when I finish fantasizing about my perfect life. I roll up the View and replace it in its package. I put it back where I found it.

After that, I'm hungry, so I walk down to the company cafeteria. I order soup and a sandwich, and find an empty table. I eat quickly, barely perceiving the food's flavor. It's adequate as usual. The robotic table washer does its thing.

I leave the cafeteria and go into the museum. I find the display case that contains blueprint plans for the plant and also some old faded plans of the submarine factory. One view shows a cross-section of the sub factory; most of it was underground. Apparently, there were huge caverns in which they built the subs. When a sub was finished, they slid it directly to the sea through a huge culvert.

I poke around the museum, but don't see any other pertinent information, such as how to get the grates open. I walk outside the plant and stroll through the grounds toward the sea. I try to visualize where the sub factory had been.

I walk down to the edge of the grounds, through a small traditional garden. An old gardener is bent over, yanking out a weed.

"Hello," I say.

He gives me a grunt in reply. It's a friendly grunt though.

"Nice day," I say. "Um, by the way, I was down by that big culvert the other day," I point to it, "and I noticed several grated tunnels. They wouldn't lead to the old sub factory, would they?"

He shrugs. "You don't want to go messing around there."

I thank the gardener, who grunts in return. I wander down the grounds, where the slope gets steeper and is protected from the sea with large boulders, and huge, blunt-tipped, concrete stars.

When I get to the edge of the grounds I come to the culvert entrance. I look back and see the gardener watching me. I give him a shoulder shrug, meaning: "well, who can resist trouble?"

I decide that exploring the culvert would be better at night. So I walk back up the slope and off the grounds. I start wandering the streets of Numazu.

It's mid-afternoon, too late to go to work. Or to Atami or Heda to do more cataloging. I feel guilty, like I'm truant from school. But I could use a day off. I'll get back into it full swing tomorrow.

"Hello, Yukawa." It's Officer Tani. I've wandered up to his neighborhood police box.

"Hello." I say. I feel my cheeks redden.

"Out for a walk?"

"That's right. A walk, yes. I've got a headache. Trying to get rid of it."

"Sorry to hear that. Having a bad day? Something troubling you? Something I can help you with, maybe?"

My cheeks are hot. Beads of sweat break out along my hairline. I mop at them with a handkerchief. Maybe  I could confide in him about the Views. But what could he do to help? He'd no doubt tell Ichiro Ono, or ask why I haven't told him.

"Trouble? Oh, no. No trouble."

Takenoko

The boy watched his father struggle to balance the load of charcoal on his back. His father bent low, his forehead nearly touching the ground. With the load finally balanced, he took a step into the street. The sun beating on him made the load heavier.

The boy wanted to help carry the load, but his father only let him pick up any pieces that might fall.

When they rounded the corner, his father ran into a samurai dressed in ceremonial finery. One of the worn bags of charcoal split open and spilled onto the white, white socks of the samurai.

"Arrrr!" The samurai screamed and pulled out his sword. The boy's father dropped to his knees, and tried to sweep the black soot off the samurai's socks. He smudged them worse.

Officer Tani doesn't move, doesn't speak, doesn't blink. He doesn't seem to be breathing. But he's thinking, oh yes, he's thinking. Be cool, I tell myself. He's waiting for me to crack.

But I don't have anything to be guilty about. Maybe I should be up front with Ichiro. I didn't do anything; I didn't steal the Views.

But I've already acted suspiciously, hiding the Views, sneaking them into the museum. What was I thinking? Certainly Ichiro knows which Views he owns. Sooner or later he'll find out.

I smile at Officer Tani.

Officer Tani asks, "So, what exactly do you do in your profession?"

Ah, an easy, non-criminal question. "Being an art museum curator? Well, basically, we put together exhibitions of an artist's work. We have to learn about the artist and his or her works, and display them properly in the correct environment."

Officer Tani nods. "That sounds very complicated."

"Oh no. Not really. Police work is complicated." I smile.

Tani doesn't smile back, obviously not impressed with my compliment.

Takenoko

The boy's father offered the back of his bare, sunburned neck to the samurai. The sword glinted in the sun.

The boy picked up a lump of charcoal and tossed it at the samurai, hitting him on the cheek.

The samurai turned. As he wiped the soot from his face, he pointed his sword at the boy. Then he laughed.

The samurai kicked his father in the ribs. His father grunted as the air rushed from his lungs. The samurai stepped over the charcoal maker, put away his sword, and strolled off.

Officer Tani asks, "Where's your home prefecture?"

Another question I can answer. "Okayama."

"Immediate past residence?"

Now it sounds like he's grilling me. "Tokyo. Shinjuku. Shinjuku Towers."

"Apartment number?"

I clear my throat. "Do you mind if I ask why you want to know this?" I ask meekly.

"For our records. Just in case."

Tani writes the information in his book. "Thank you for your cooperation, Yukawa."

I nod. "Sure," I say, trying to sound friendly. "By the way, you must have seen an old lady around here pushing a shopping cart full of trash."

Tani squints his youthful eyes. "Why do you ask?"

"Oh, no reason. I just wonder if she's all right. She seems quite old."

Tani slaps his book closed. "She's none of your business."

I need to settle my nerves after the encounter with Officer Tani, so I find a tiny mama-san bar near Numazu Station. It's late afternoon when I arrive and I'm the only customer. She serves sake, beer, and several kinds of omelets. Strange combination. If I were hungry I'd try an omelet. But all I want is a beer.

She serves me a Sapporo and a bowl of boiled soybeans in their pods. I hate boiled soybeans, but to be polite I pop open a couple into my mouth and wash them down with beer. Besides, a few of the bland beans won't hurt me. They're quite nutritious. Soybeans and Sapporo, a complete meal.

After a couple of long draws of beer have settled my nerves, I get a little angry at that Officer Tani. What's his problem anyway? A small-town cop trying to push around the Tokyo newcomer wearing a designer suit?

"Where are you from?" asks the mama-san. Her eyes are mere slits in a wrinkled face. Then I wonder why she wants to know where I'm from. Maybe she's an undercover cop working for Tani, trying to see if I slip up.

"I was born in Okayama," I say, not mentioning Tokyo on purpose.

"But you're from Tokyo now," she says, pointing at my suit.

"Well, I have lived there for several years. Actually, I work here now. Well, in Hakone. But I live in Numazu, at least temporarily."

She looks confused. I sound confused. I am confused.

Takenoko

Takenoko painted while Natsuko talked. Or rather, his hand kept the brush moving.

Natsuko said, "Mama says you're crazy."

I try to straighten out the mess. "I work at the new Takenoko Art Museum in Hakone run by Ichiro Ono of Ono Robotics."

She raises her painted-on eyebrows up to her scalp; the movement unfolds her wrinkles and opens her eyes a bit. "Ono Robotics. Strange company. A lot of their workers used to come here, but most got laid off. Automation replaced them, they said."

"Really," I say. "The plant does seem highly automated. Quite empty sometimes, for as big as it is."

The mama-san refills my glass. "Have you seen the old lady nekobaba around there?"

I choke on a boiled soybean.

Nekobaba

Children
  Colors
  The colors, the children.
  Where are they?

At last. "Why yes. I have seen her. What's her story?"

Mama-san grins. The action pushes her wrinkles together, completely hiding her eyes. "Which story do you want?"

"There's more than one?"

"Well, let's see, there's the story that she's the retarded daughter of the past emperor, or maybe the past emperor's brother. Some say she's the illegitimate daughter of the past emperor. Anyway, the past emperor's retainer secreted her away from the palace grounds and paid a farmer to take care of her. When the farmer and his wife died, mysteriously, the nekobaba wandered off."

"Interesting," I say. But unlikely.

Nekobaba

The embers glowed in the iron pit. The flakes of paper instantly burned when they dropped from her hand.

"What are you doing, Mother?" asked Akiko.

Another paper flake ignited.

"Don't you think that's dangerous?"

Another puff of smoke. So white. The embers so red.

"Or," says the mama-san, "there's the story that she's a writer who went insane. She spent several years locked in a house writing a book, then the house burned down just as she finished writing."

"I like that one."

The mama-san opens another beer for me. "How about this: she was a worker trapped in the sub factory

 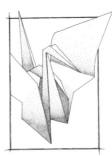

when it got bombed and survived by eating the leather seats."

I like the writer story best.

"Or," mama-san goes on, "she was an aborted fetus, still alive when she was flushed down the sewer. She was rescued and raised by a sympathetic rat."

Don't like that one so much.

I stick around mama-san's bar until dark, when the place fills up with construction workers, rail maintenance workers, and other blue-collar types. They're friendly enough, but my suit and I don't fit in, so I leave.

I go in search of the nekobaba. Time to put my plan into action.

The night is sultry. Not that I'm feeling sultry. The beer makes me feel heavy, slow. But as I walk briskly up and down streets, my energy picks up. I stick to the darker streets, hoping to avoid running into Officer Tani.

As I walk, I pick up bits of trash: a Red Stripe cigarette pack, a Lemon Suds soda can, a Fuji film box, a couple of bottle caps, a yellow Bic lighter, a Pink Skin condom wrapper.

As I spot items of trash, I find myself getting excited, a little rush of joy.

I'm leaning over the gutter, trying to decide if I should pick up another cigarette package (Peace brand), when I feel someone looking at me. I straighten up. A young couple, arm-in-arm, hurries off. "Boo," I say to their backs.

Then I see the nekobaba. She's poking between two buildings, her shopping cart parked at the curb. I watch her for a few minutes, but I can't see much in the darkness.

I walk ahead a block. On the sidewalk, I place my little collection of trash, a neat row of irresistible treasures. I wait across the street.

Finally, the nekobaba comes out from between the buildings, puts her latest acquisition into the shopping cart, then rolls ahead. She stops at a storm sewer grate. With a straightened coat hanger she fishes a bit of trash out of the storm drain and puts it inside the cart.

Nekobaba

She poked at Akiko with the stick end of the twig broom. Poked her in the buttocks, poked her in the stomach, poked her in the arm, poked her in the legs.

At first, Akiko laughed, then she whimpered, then she cried. "Stop mother, stop. Please stop."

But she poked some more.

191

She snatched at the boy's hair.

"Ouch," cried Ichiro. Gun watched, hung his head. Akiko ran out of the room.

"Ouch? Ouch, ouch, ouch."

Ichiro pulled away, a clump of hair stayed in his mother's hand. She held it out to Gun. "Are you next?"

"Yes, Mother," answered Gun.

She almost rolls her cart over the row of treasures I'd lined up for her. I start to yell "Stop" but she puts on the brakes. She leans over and studies each item in the row. She studies them again. Up and down the row.

Then she reaches down, and snatches up one, then two, then three items. She walks back to her cart and stows them under the plastic tarp. Then she rolls forward. When she's ahead of me, I rush across the street, and kneel on the sidewalk.

She selected the Red Stripe cigarette pack, the green Fuji film box, and the Pink Skin condom wrapper.

"I don't understand," said Gun.

What's there to understand?

"Why are we in trouble?"

Who is in trouble? Why is Gun's skin so pale, almost the transparent white of a ghost? She pulls him close, rubs her cheek against his. Maybe some of her color will rub onto his face.

Color is life.

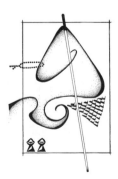

My experiment worked, I suppose. The results: she selected all the paper or cardboard items and left the metal objects. Does she only want paper items? No, I had seen metal objects in her cart.

So, I really don't know if I have gained any evidence in my quest of understanding her selection process. I'm starting to sound like Kumi.

I continue to follow the nekobaba, just because I don't know what else to do.

The nekobaba heads back to the culvert. I have to keep well in the shadows, as I'm nearing the police box of Officer Tani. When I'm directly across the street from the box, I can see inside. An officer, not Tani, is hunched over the desk, filling out paperwork. Or maybe selecting lottery numbers. Who knows what police officers do when not chasing crooks, other than harassing innocent citizens. Innocent curators.

The nekobaba disappears into the culvert. I try to stay close but not too close. Then, suddenly, she's gone. I run ahead. I don't know which grate she went into, but I can hear the cart wheels clacking on the concrete floor of the culvert.

I pull on the nearest grate; the metal is slimy and it doesn't budge. I feel around the perimeter, and find a long bolt. Several bolts. I can't get them to turn. I need my flashlight and some tools.

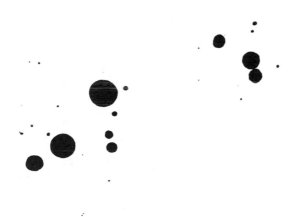

I hurry out of the culvert and up the slope to the dormitory parking lot. When I get to my car, I notice a familiar car parked next to mine.

It's Gun's car. Gun and Tabo are inside. Gun rolls down the window and says, "Why, hello. What a coincidence."

What's the matter with Yukawa? Can't he talk intelligently? He's so lacking in any sign of life, of any passion, of any genius.

Gun needed someone to talk to. But there really wasn't anyone.

"We're a very spatially oriented species," said Richard.

"Spatially oriented?" repeated Gun.

"Yes. Place is important, vital, for mood, for creativity."

"Paris is a good space."

"A very good space."

Gun tipped the champagne bottle and refilled their glasses. "Most spaces go better with champagne."

"Well, yes, of course."

"Gun," I say. "And Tabo." Tabo nods once and yawns.

Gun says, "Yukawa. We need to talk. Can I come up to your room?"

"Well ..." Isn't there a View in my room? And who knows how many have shown up since I've been gone.

"Um, what do you want to talk about?"

"The Views, of course. And Ichiro's museum. The compromise."

"Oh, really?"

I say, "Okay. Sure. But not in my room. It's too small and depressing. I hate the place."

Gun nods. "I can understand that. Environment is everything. How about dinner? Any good restaurants in Numazu?"

"Well, I've only tried a couple of places. Casual places."

"Hop in. I know a good place in Hakone."

I climb in the back. Gun joins me, while Tabo drives. I say, "The Fuji International Hotel?"

"Why, yes. How did you know?"

"I was there once. It seems like your kind of place."

Tabo drives like a grand prix racer, and we get to Fuji International Hotel before I get settled into the plush back seat. Gun chats mindlessly: a new artist popular in Tokyo, a show he saw in Paris, his last good meal (also in Paris).

Tabo stays in the car, while we go into the hotel. It's late, and we have no trouble getting a seat in the Continental Room. The way the maître d' fusses over Gun, we probably wouldn't have had trouble getting a seat if the restaurant had a three-hour waiting list.

We order drinks—single-malt Scotch, neat. After downing those, we're well into appetizers—glazed baby hen thighs—and a bottle of white Burgundy, when Gun says, "I want to control the Takenoko museum."

"Well," I say slowly, as I slide tender meat off a tiny bone, "it doesn't seem likely to me that Ichiro would relinquish control of the museum to you. Not that I pretend to know him that well after only a few days."

Gun sucks on a thigh, and pulls the bone out of his mouth. "Ichiro will get tired of the museum after it's open. Just as he got tired of his robot factory. He turned that over to his managers as soon as he could. Now Kumi is running the show. The same will happen with the museum, so why don't I take over now? We can keep him in some ceremonial position—executive board chairman, perhaps."

When Ichiro had left, Gun said to Akiko, "You know this is more than a favor he's doing for us."

"More than a favor?"

"This is a debt that will hang around our necks until we die."

"Still," I say.

"Look, you don't know him, as you correctly admit." Gun sucked another baby hen thigh and washed it down with a gulp of Burgundy. "Besides, Ichiro owes me a favor. Yes, I know it's a family matter, and you shouldn't mix business with family, but I'm sure he'll see reason."

I'm not.

Gun says, "And wouldn't you rather work for me instead of that robot builder brother of mine?"

Well ...

Gun touches my forearm. "No need to answer."

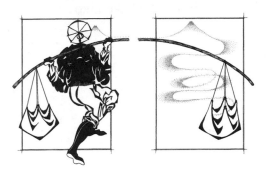

Gun says, "Look Yukawa, I think I can be honest with you ..."

I hate it when people say that, because they're usually about to tell you a big lie.

Gun continues, "I have a certain need to diversify my business accounts."

It didn't sound like something Gun would say. But he said it, I'm quite sure. "Oh?" I say. The waiter brings the sauerbraten and Médoc red wine that Gun had ordered for both of us.

When the waiter's gone, Gun says, "Let's just say I have had certain business partners in the past who believe they are partners in the present."

We don't say a lot after that, Gun just tells me to pass along his message to Ichiro. I say I will, although I'm not sure exactly what I'm going to say. Ichiro won't like it, despite what Gun believes.

We round off the meal with coffee and chocolates. And then cognac. He chatters and I nod and smile and utter nonsense syllables.

We leave and climb back in the car. A yawning Tabo drives us back to Numazu.

They drop me off in front of the dormitory. I wave good-bye and turn to go inside.

At the corner of the building, I see a vaguely familiar figure standing and watching.

Is it Officer Tani?

A Long
Time

I walk up to my room and check around the door for a package. None.

I wonder if it was Officer Tani whom I saw. Talk about someone getting on your nerves. Then I remember I was going to get my flashlight and tools when Gun showed up. I better not explore the culvert now, not with Tani watching me. I'm tired anyway.

I get out of my suit and collapse on my futon. Of course, the instant I do, I'm wide awake. I get back up and find a quarter-liter of Suntory whiskey the previous occupant had left in a cupboard.

I toast to myself, suddenly wishing Kumi were here, or I were at her apartment. I think she's warming up to me. Couple more dates and …

After a couple of whiskey shots, I drift off, almost like I'm in a rowboat without oars in a lazy current. It's not sleep, but it'll do.

My floating trip ends at dawn, when my whiskey-and-sauerbraten breath clubs me between the eyes. I jump up and head into the bathroom. At the idea of entering my mouth, the toothbrush rebels. I have to force it in. I shower, shave, and select my last clean suit to wear. I need to get to the cleaners.

I need to see Kumi.

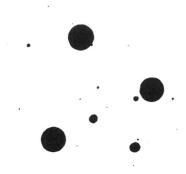

Kumi

The flight attendant punched the pillow a couple of times, then placed the pillow carefully. "Is that better?"

The function ... which function?

<<societal politeness
  [verbal appreciation]>>

Two hemispheres of the brain in constant conflict, searching for the correct pattern of activation.

Pattern.

Home pattern.

Kumi is hunched over the computer keyboard. She looks pleasantly familiar in her orange coveralls; her hair is tied up in a loose bun. I say, "Good morning."

She punches a few more keys before looking up. In that second or two, my confidence and good mood vanish. "Oh, good morning," she says.

"Already hard at it?"

She stares at me blankly.

I sputter, "I had a good time the other night."

She nods once; her gaze drifts to the computer screen. I could become jealous of that machine.

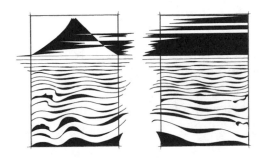

I say, "Sorry I didn't have a chance to see you yesterday. I slept in, then had a few errands to run, then Gun tracked me down for a long dinner meeting."

"Okay," she says, and goes back to her keyboard.

"Maybe you can help me," I say loudly. I'm not going to be outdone by a machine.

She pauses. I say, "Well, there seems to be quite a conflict brewing between your father and Gun, and Akiko to some extent, about the paintings, and the museum."

She stares, uninterested.

Exasperated, I say, "It's like a war starting. Who knows where it will end up. Aren't you even a little concerned?"

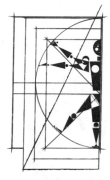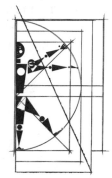

Kumi

Two halves: left, right. Analytical. Imaginative.

The two halves make human intelligence. Two balanced halves.

Left + right = more than the whole.

Unbalanced, asymmetry, the conflict rages.

Kumi finally speaks: "What?"

Is that all she can say? "Yes, it's true. In fact, I think there's been some monkey business with the Views. Some of them may be missing."

Kumi actually looks concerned. "Oh?"

"Well, yes. I'm doing the cataloging, you know, and sometimes the list doesn't match the Views in the collection. As curator I should know what's in the collection. I'm ultimately responsible for them. I don't want to get in trouble. But I hate to bring it up to your father, since I just started in this job. Do know what I mean? I was hoping you could help me, tell me how to deal with this problem."

Blank stare.

Kumi

Father: "You must speak to me. Tell me what's bothering you. What's wrong?"

It's school, the boring, slow, stupid classes. The other kids are stupid, always laughing, squealing, playing. The kids tease, push, hit, make up mean names.

Father: "Speak to me, Kumi."

"Look," I say. "Never mind. Just forget what I said.
I'm just feeling a little tired. I'll deal with the problem;
that's what I get paid for, right?" I chuckle.

Kumi says, "I'm sorry, can we talk later?"

Ahh, a sign of life. "Yes, yes. That'll be perfect.
Thanks, I really appreciate it." I look at my watch. "I'm
heading off to Heda this morning, right now, to do
some more cataloging at your aunt's ryokan. I'd really
like to finish her collection, so I might be late. I'll catch
up with you when I get back."

She nods and turns back to her keyboard.

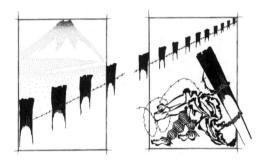

After breakfast in the company cafeteria (the food
is starting to taste like it's cooked by a robot—always
exactly the same, never any surprises), I drive to Heda.
When I pull into the village, I park next to the curved
breakwater that protects the tiny harbor. The view of
Mt. Fuji is partially obscured by a low cloud, dark and
flat on the bottom, white and fluffy on top.

I realize I just came to Heda to get away from Kumi,
from Gun, from Ichiro. I don't really want to catalog. I
wouldn't mind seeing Haruna, but I don't want to see
Akiko.

I walk back to my car, and drive toward the ryokan, but instead of turning down the driveway, I continue past. I drive to the end of the lane, which peters out at a stand of bamboo.

I park there and walk up the slope, toward the ridge behind Heda Onsen. The muggy air and the exertion make me perspire. But the climb is short, and when I get to the clearing, a cool breeze is coming off the sea.

I sit on a rock and watch the cloud moving across Mt. Fuji.

For the first several Views, Takenoko employed many of the techniques he used in his portrait work combined with what he had seen of the works of the great landscape artists. No doubt his training was under a portrait artist and not a landscape artist (see the chapter on his apprenticeship).

As an example, his early clouds were less based on realism than on the ideal shape of a woman. That is, comparing the lines from his figures and the early clouds, a similarity is immediately evident. Later Views show his abandonment of the figure-based line for one more based on impressionistic or even expressionistic principles.

203.

Standing on the flat rock, the praying mantis stared at Takenoko. "Good morning," Takenoko said to it.

The praying mantis cocked its head toward the artist.

Takenoko said, "Do you mind if I paint you? I'd like to add you to this painting of Mt. Fuji. It's not a particularly exciting scene, just the mountain and some plants in the foreground, but with you in it, well, it would become very interesting, I feel."

The insect turned its gaze to Mt. Fuji, and held perfectly still.

Then I see a movement out of the corner of my eye. I turn to see a praying mantis on a nearby rock. As I watch it, it cocks its head toward me. The insect gives me the once over.

I think about picking up a rock and dropping it on the praying mantis. The thought gives me a chill. Could I be capable of such unnecessary killing? But that's not what gave me the chill. No, it's more a feeling of dread, as if the insect would kill me first. Or its ghost would haunt me forever.

What am I thinking about? I've never had such weird thoughts before. I've always been a straightfor-

ward thinker. Thoughts such as what's on TV, where's the best clothing store in Aoyama, what kind of coffee brewer should I buy? Pure vanilla thoughts, bland as rice cake, boring.

Hadn't Junko told me that? So she's right.

The praying mantis turns its head back toward Mt. Fuji, and I do the same. The cloud has moved, but also grown, as if the mountain is creating the cloud to hide itself. When I look back to the rock after a few moments, the praying mantis is gone.

I relax a little, then my mood darkens. It's a kind of guilt. What am I doing wasting the morning hiking and looking at mountains and insects like a retired salaryman? Maybe a cup of coffee would get me going. I could stop in the local coffee shop and get some more information—gossip—on the Ono family.

Even that doesn't excite me.

Then Haruna shows up.

"Hello," I say. My voice sounds too happy, like a middle school kid in love.

"Hello." Her voice sounds sort of happy. Maybe I'm just hoping it does.

"How are you? Busy?"

"No, not so busy today." She's dressed in a light green kimono.

"That's a nice color on you."

"Thanks." She blushes.

I find that charming; who blushes anymore? "I'm sorry I rushed out the other night. I heard a noise, and thought someone was coming in."

She says, "I'm sorry." She stares at the sky.

Haruna traces some shape in the sky. I follow her finger; she's following the outline of the cloud. "Nice cloud," I say.

"I like its shape."

A warm lust lightens my mood. I want to fool around on the hill, under the sun, in the cool breeze, in the open air, for everyone to see if they weren't so busy with their little lives.

"I better go," says Haruna. "Are you coming to the ryokan?"

I sigh.

Haruna

When Haruna walked past the cave the boys jumped out. She ran, but didn't get far. They knocked her down; she fell hard on the pebbles.

The boys tore off her backpack. They turned her over. She kept her eyes shut tight, her limbs rigid.

"Your mama's a whore!" one shouted, then the rest shouted it over and over.

"What color?" one shouted. They had her paint set from her backpack.

"Red!" They poured the red paint over her face. "Make her up real good."

Takenoko

The Ono woman said to Takenoko, "I've seen you looking at her."

Her. Natsuko. "I don't look at her."

"You look at her. You're painting her in your mind."

He couldn't deny it. "I'm sorry."

The Ono woman stood over him. "Stop it. Stop painting her even in your mind. Stop looking at her." She paused, then added, "Or, I'll get the village fishermen to make you stop. And I'll discipline Natsuko."

He was turning his shape inside out. Haruna once had her shape turned inside out. Like an orange peel, the inside is so different from the outside. Not only the color, but the shape, the texture.

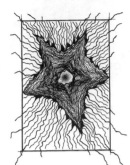

"No," I say, sounding like a sad old man. "I'll just sit here for a few more minutes. I'm clearing my mind."

"Okay."

As she walks away, I say, "I'll talk to you later."

"Okay," she says, without turning around.

When she's gone I look to the rock where I'd seen the praying mantis; the insect hasn't come back.

The scene came alive—the old poet, contemplating the mountain. Or maybe contemplating a past love affair. Who can tell?

Takenoko didn't know. He didn't look at the paintings anymore. He had neither time nor desire. Takenoko felt nothing, nothing for his paintings, nothing for life, nothing for the mountain. The lines and shapes and colors were pieces of him.

Like the old poet.

The cloud obscuring Mt. Fuji evaporates in the sun, finally leaving a clear view of the mountain. I sit on the hill, on my rather comfortable rock—comfortable as a rock can get—and stare at the conical mountain. The slope steepens as it nears the peak. I remember reading in the Takenoko book that the actual angles of the slopes (something between 30 and 40 degrees I think) are rarely duplicated precisely in the Views. The angles are drawn to fit the painting.

After a few minutes, the blue of the mountain nearly matches the blue of the sky, making the mountain all but disappear. The whole scene is rather cold and lifeless. How could Takenoko have painted so many different views of it? And make each scene so alive? Takenoko wasn't

There is nothing you need

That you don't have

Or can't do.

practically worthless.

206

I give up staring at the lifeless scene. I can't dredge up any imaginative ways of painting it, if I had a mind to paint it. I don't have a mind to do anything, except, well, make love with Haruna.

I'd better stop daydreaming and get to work.

I head down the path to the inn. Halfway there I notice the burned remains of a small building, the size of a shack. There really isn't much left, just the square outline of the foundation stones and a few charred boards. The ground vines and tall grass have grown over much of it.

The Last Ukiyo-e Artist

One wonders what would have happened if Takenoko had survived to show his 365 Views in Edo, soon-to-be Tokyo. Would he have been laughed out of town? Or, with the change in mood and government, would Takenoko's imaginative new style have taken the art world by storm?

Probably, the former.

In the long history of Japanese art, which is based on the apprentice and master system, change comes very slowly. And change is, of course, looked down upon by the established art world as an aberration. Change comes about by small increments, generations of students each taking tentative steps away from the master.

Takenoko ran from the established art world at full tilt.

The teacher rapped the apprentice on the knuckles with a bamboo stave. "Were you daydreaming?"

The apprentice's head dropped.

"Stand up! Go to the front of the room. Were you dreaming of being a famous artist? Were you pretending you were a giant bamboo in a grove? You're nothing but a bamboo shoot. That's what we'll call you from now on—Takenoko." The other boys giggled.

The teacher said, "Tell us what you were daydreaming about, Takenoko."

In front of the room, the apprentice Takenoko said, "I was thinking about the shape of the teacher's head; it's sort of narrow, like a fish head."

The boys howled with laughter.

I walk past the outdoor bath; the steam rises off the water. My lustiness returns at the memory of the bath I took with Haruna.

I continue on, reluctantly, through the garden, and enter the inn. I realize then that I don't have my brief-case with my notes and the book. The thought drags me down—another stone thrown at me by life as I drown.

I drop my downtrodden self onto the sofa in the sitting room. I can hear the sounds of a vacuum cleaner in a distant corner of the inn. It sounds soothing for some reason. I'd always hated the sound before. When I was a kid I always went outside when my mother was vacuuming. And she vacuumed a lot.

Finally, I push myself up, and head out to find my car. On the way out, I run into Haruna lugging the vacuum. She's wearing a brown kimono.

I'm afraid to ask her if she's changed her kimono. What if she says "no"? She did have time to change, of course, and brown is a more appropriate color to be cleaning in. Maybe the brown looks light green in the sun.

"Hello," she says. The tone of her "hello" is more like a hello that you'd say when you haven't seen someone for a couple of days, not half an hour. Or is it my imagination? Or my feeble mind?

"Hello," I say, my voice cracking slightly.

"I didn't hear your car."

"Ah, no. I parked down the road a bit. I, um, needed a walk. But, I left my briefcase there, so I have to go back."

She smiles, as she'd smile at a senile grandfather who'd forgotten her name.

Haruna carefully formed the shape of the word, its tone.

His shape would change as he questioned his reality. He must begin by seeing his shape differently.

I get back to my car, and think about driving away. I'd been doing that a lot lately. I drive back to the inn. I park and go back inside. I manage to avoid Haruna.

I find the room with the View I'd last cataloged, and then I go to the next room down the corridor. I pull out my notes and begin.

My mind isn't focused, and after several minutes, I realize I haven't looked at the painting. I concentrate on the View, then it hits me. I've already cataloged this one. But it was at Gun's.

I think it was at Gun's. Maybe I made a mistake. Maybe it's just similar. Surely with 365 paintings some may look alike.

Akiko cringed at the expression on her mother's face. It was strange, not as if she were angry, or sad, or hateful, or disappointed. The expression made her feel she was no longer a daughter.

Her mother watched from the door that was open just a crack. Her mother's expression never changed until the man was done.

Before I can straighten out my notes, or my own mind, Akiko comes into the room.

"So, you're back," she says. She wears a hard expression, something between a frown and a grimace.

"Yes. Hard at it."

"How's your progress?"

"Well, slow, I'm afraid."

"I do have a ryokan to run, you know."

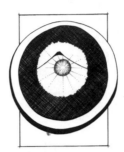

"Do I have to remind you?" Akiko's mother pulled her by the wrist. When Akiko slowed, her mother jerked her hard. Her mother tore off Akiko's kimono and threw the one with gold and silver threads at her.

"Put it on. Hurry." Her mother left.

Akiko changed, slowly at first, then quickly. She ran into the guests' room, where her mother was playing the samisen, and the guests were clapping.

Akiko began her dance.

"Yes," I say. "I'll do what I can. Maybe you can help."

But she doesn't look like she wants to help. I ask anyway, "This painting, has it always been in this room?"

Akiko steps up to it and studies it. "I like this one a lot. The mountain has a lot of power and it seems to rise out of the fishing nets stretched along the beach."

"Yes, it's very powerful all right. But—"

"It reminds me of my husband, dying at sea. I've often wondered what happens to men who die at sea. I think they eventually come back to us. In the fish and crabs and lobsters we eat."

Akiko stares at me and says, "I see a lot of death and depression and darkness in the Views, don't you?"

I study the View, mostly to avoid Akiko's stare. "Yes, some of them are very dark." I say that, but actually my first impression of the Views has been one of lightness as opposed to darkness. Life, not death.

Akiko says, "But we all feel dark on some days, don't we?"

Some more than others.

The moon had set when they finished. The night sky was fired with stars.

Ichiro said, "When it's finished, we will avoid seeing each other, won't we?"

Gun and Akiko didn't say a word. By then, silence had come to mean agreement.

"By the way, Yukawa," Akiko says, "I need to hear the details of the so-called compromise my brother is offering."

"To tell you the truth, I don't really know any of the details."

"Do you think I'm stupid? I know my brother told you his plans."

"He hasn't, honestly."

Akiko smirks. "Oh, I see. Honestly."

Akiko said to Ichiro, "Then we'll trust you with the details?"

Ichiro said, "It's better to have just one of us knowing the details."

Gun said, "I disagree. If one knows, we all should know. We should be in this all the way."

Akiko said, "I don't want to know. I'll side with Ichiro on this."

Gun shrugged.

I change the subject by asking her, "What about your brother, Gun? How do you think he'll react to a compromise?"

"Gun." That's all she says for a few moments.

I say, "Gun seems to be more aggressively pursuing control of the museum."

"That sounds like Gun. He's always been quite pushy."

"What kind of conditions do you want in a compromise?"

Akiko turns and stares out the window. Suruga Bay glimmers. "We pile up many debts in our lives, don't we?"

Hadn't Ichiro mentioned debts? Gun too? I ask Akiko, "You mean family debts? Financial debts?"

She doesn't say anything. I get tired of waiting for an answer. "I better get back to work."

She says, "Family debts. Financial debts. Debts of the heart, the soul. Debts upon debts. And you never really pay them off, even if you repay a hundredfold, the debts are still there, piling up, crushing you."

Ichiro

"The steps to achieve the productivity efficiencies you desire are as follows." Ichiro pressed the button on the remote. The list appeared:

One: Have a concept of self

There's a rap on the door. Akiko and I turn around. Ichiro Ono steps into the room.

Akiko inhales sharply.

Ichiro says, "Hello, Sister." He gives me a curt nod. I give him one back.

Akiko says, "It's been a long time."

"A long time."

I'm feeling out of place, so I start to step out of the room.

"Wait, Yukawa," says Ichiro. "This involves you, too."

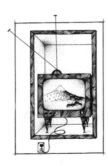 

Ichiro says, "We're at a critical point in the Takenoko museum, and I think I should put some personal effort into the process to ensure its success."

Akiko and I don't say a word.

Not looking at either of us, and with his chin jutting out like a ship captain's, Ichiro goes on, "As you know, the museum is in its final phase—"

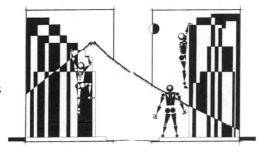

Akiko interrupts him, "What do you want?"

Ichiro clenches then unclenches his jaw. He does it again. Then he folds his arms across his chest. "You always were the direct one, Akiko. All right, Sister, I want to talk to you about your collection of Views."

"What do you want?" Akiko repeats.

"Well," Ichiro clears his throat, "I believe the Views are at risk here in the onsen. The lighting, and humidity, and temperature swings are damaging to them. I'm sure Yukawa would agree with me." They both look at me.

I hesitate, gathering my thoughts, then say, "Well, technically speaking, certain environmental conditions do adversely affect

art works; it's a matter of degree, of course, and the types of paints and canvas used, among other parameters."

Ichiro nods at me. Akiko, unimpressed, sneers.

Ichiro

The speech continued. "Robots must be more than mechanical arms. More than just brawn, or mindless components that will perform repetitive tasks without complaining. Robots supply an aesthetic to a system. A synergism of man and manmade.

"It's an aesthetic of endeavor and achievement. Of will. Of self.

"If we forget that aesthetic, we will die as a company. And as men."

Ichiro

Ichiro asks, "Will his throat be slit?"

Gun laughed. "His throat slit? Is that what you want? Aren't you the one who didn't want me and Akiko to know the details about what you did with Mother?" He laughed some more.

Ichiro didn't laugh. "I thought we were never to bring that up again."

Gun stopped laughing and said, "I thought we were supposed to avoid seeing each other again."

Ichiro said, "This is an unusual circumstance."

"And after the emergency circumstance is over, will we go back to avoiding each other?"

Ichiro nodded once. "Of course."

Ichiro says, "But that's not the only reason why the Views would be better in the museum. Another primary reason is the issue of viewership. Certainly only a small number of guests see your collection, Akiko, compared to the numbers that would pass through the museum. To be precise, we anticipate a daily average of nearly a thousand." Ichiro looks at me. I haven't made an estimate, but it sounds high.

"Um," I say, not sure if he wants me to verify the number.

He doesn't. He says, "And think of the prestige of being a part of it."

Haruna comes in the room, breaking the tense negotiations. "I've served tea in the sitting room."

Ichiro says, "Is this Haruna?"

Akiko nods. Ichiro bows. Haruna bows. "I'm your uncle Ichiro, remember me? It's been a long time. You've turned out to be quite a lovely young woman."

We walk into the sitting room. I wish I could get away. We sit around the table, and are served profes-sionally by Haruna. Ichiro remarks on her skill. Akiko says nothing, until Haruna leaves.

"Now," says Akiko, "I have some demands."

"Oh?" says Ichiro.

Akiko says, "I don't think you have the final say in this matter. You only have control of a third of the collection."

Ichiro holds up a hand, "I believe it's a little more than a third." He looks at me.

I say, "Well, I haven't completed the cataloging yet." I add quickly, "But perhaps you two would be better off if I weren't here."

Akiko and Ichiro nod at each other.

I get away from them as fast as I can. I hide in one of the rooms, where I can start cataloging, at least pretend to be.

I wonder why Ichiro showed up? Just the other day (yesterday? time has blurred) he said he hadn't seen his brother or sister for twenty years and had no intention of meeting them. But then I also recall the contractor saying that Ichiro changes his mind often.

Whatever the reason, I'm glad to see Ichiro dealing directly with Akiko. Now if he'd only do the same with Gun.

"Hello," says Haruna.

"Hello," I say. "So, we have an unexpected visitor."

She sits on the floor next to my notes. "Yes, Uncle Ichiro."

I sit down next to her. "Why haven't you seen him for so long? Over twenty years ... you must have been just a little girl."

She doesn't answer. Maybe she doesn't know. Maybe it's a painful subject. So, I ask, "Do you agree with your mother about the Views?"

She squints, as if staring into the sun, at the View hanging in this room. "I would miss them. Their shapes."

I want to kiss the back of her neck.

The pain of colors, the euphoria of colors, seared Takenoko's days, tortured his nights. Blues were cold ice pellets in his blood. Reds were hot charcoal embers behind his eyes. Blacks were blindness, loss of knowing himself. Whites were death, nothing.

Greens were life, infinite life, life without him. Purples were food, drink, lust, wanting. Yellows were another day, another painting, another ...

We sit in silence, but it's a good silence. A comfortable silence. I have no idea what she's thinking. She probably doesn't care what I'm thinking. Besides, I'm only trying to figure out what she's thinking.

We sit like that for I don't know how long. Again, time is blurred. The sun is just setting when we slip out

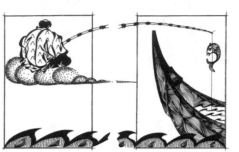

of the inn without disturbing Akiko and Ichiro.

We rinse off before stepping into the bath. One other couple—guests at the inn—is soaking in the opposite corner of the bath.

The hot, hot water sears flesh, liquefies muscles, boils bones.

Haruna turns me sideways on the ledge and twists herself behind me. She begins massaging my shoulders and neck. Then further down my back.

She pulls her legs up and around my waist. Using her feet and calves, she massages my legs. With her breasts, she massages my back.

Finally, the two guests leave. They might have been disgusted by my moaning. Now I twist and face Haruna. She slides against my body. I return the massage, except I can't do that thing she did with her legs.

Instead, I massage her legs with my hands. My massage technique is amateurish, and my hands soon drift up to the junction of her thighs.

While we make love in the bath, I wonder: is Akiko watching? Is Ichiro watching?

I'm repulsed by the idea. I want get out of the bath and find them. I'll let them know how impolite it is to spy on their daughter and niece.

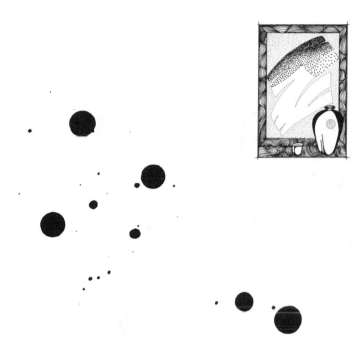

Takenoko

Takenoko snuck up to the inn. His steps made no sound on the moist ground. Through the window, he could see the guests singing, drinking, laughing, drinking. Natsuko was pouring drinks.

A guest, an older man, white hair growing out his ears, reached up under her kimono. Natsuko giggled, smiled.

He had to paint that perfect smile with the dimple on one cheek and not the other.

Ichiro

The other boys stripped off their shorts and shirts and jumped into the surf. Ichiro took off his shoes and socks and kicked at the sand.

"Come on, Ichiro." He looked up, the boys were watching him from the water. Their arms already had well-defined muscles. A wave rolled up to the boys and knocked a couple down to the sandy shallows.

"It's too cold," Ichiro said, hoping they didn't hear him. "I have to get home."

"He's too scared," one yelled.

Ichiro picked up his socks and shoes and walked away.

They were stupid louts, fishermen's sons. Nothing more.

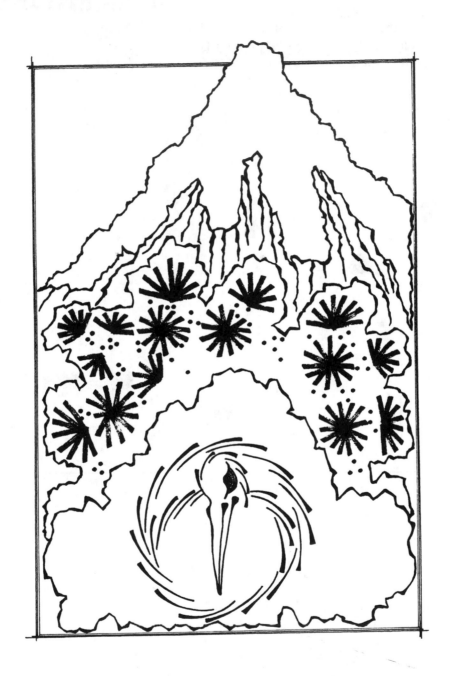

Analogy
within Analogy

The dinner with Akiko and Ichiro had just begun (Haruna serving as if nothing had happened) when Ichiro says to me, "No wonder you're not getting much done."

What does he mean? Does he mean the bath, or the sex, or both? True, I haven't been getting much done, but how does he know that? I haven't shown him my lack of prog- ress, unless he checked my notes when I was in the bath. On the other hand, he simply may be referring to 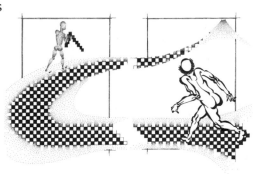 the relaxing atmosphere of the ryokan. I have to go with that: "Oh yes, they've treated me very well here. Akiko has been filling me in on some of the history and color that go with the Views. It's an important part of my research." I pause, then say, "And the food's pretty good, too, don't you think?"

Ichiro's eyes narrowed suspiciously (lately all his looks have been suspicious ones). He says, "Delicious."

Ichiro wondered why he hadn't thought of running away before. The ryokan had nothing for him; it wasn't really a home. His mother wasn't really a mother, not like the other kids had mothers.

And fathers.

He recalled no pleasant memories of the inn, of his fourteen years there. Why not leave? Gun and Akiko were old enough to take care of themselves.

What would he do? He had heard that the submarine factory in Numazu was taking on boys as young as he was.

219

Akiko said to Haruna, "If all you do is work in the onsen you'll have only half a life."

Haruna raised her head. She blinked her red, moist eyes. "But it will be the happy half, the half with the good shape."

Akiko stroked her daughter's hair. "That may be good, that may be bad. But you have to find your own way. If you want to try, then you can."

Ichiro said, "The direction I'm going to take on this action must come from within me."

Gun said quietly yet firmly, "You can't push us around because you're the oldest son. We aren't a traditional family. We have equal say, equal responsibility, and equal benefit."

Akiko sat in silence.

Ichiro said, "I'm not pushing you around. I only feel I have more responsibility. I left you alone with her."

Before Ichiro can say anything else, I ask Akiko, "Has the inn always been like this, or have you had to remodel?"

Akiko says, "It was in quite poor condition after the war, as you can imagine. It wasn't bombed, of course, but it had been neglected. And it needed modernizing. Private baths and such." She gestures to the tea pot. Haruna picks it up and goes off to refill it, even though it must still be more than half full.

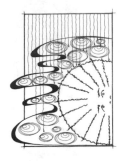

When she's gone, Akiko says, "Ichiro and I have been discussing certain things."

"Oh?" I say. "Certain things?"

Ichiro says, "Yes. Options."

Akiko says, "About the Views."

Ichiro says, "We're thinking in the direction of a creative partnership."

They both stare at me. Are they waiting for me to say something? What do they mean by a creative partnership? I don't want to ask, they act as if I'm supposed to know. I suddenly feel like a fake, a fraud, as if I'd never really been a curator, or studied art history. As if I'd been a janitor at the National Art Museum, not a curator, and now they are catching on to me. The stuff of a bad dream. A nightmare. I want to wake up.

I nod and make approving noises in the back of my throat. "Ah, a creative partnership. Could work, could work. Yes. Of course, there are many kinds of creative partnerships and many details to work out, logistically speaking."

Akiko and Ichiro continue to stare at me. I pick up a slice of raw tuna belly and dip it in the hot radish and soy sauce mix. I get too much of the sauce on the tuna, and when I put it in my mouth it flares up in my sinuses. I fight back tears.

Ichiro says, "Yukawa, don't bring up details; that will ruin the good feeling of cooperation we've spent all afternoon to achieve. We'll leave the details to you, the expert. That's why I pay you the big salary. Besides, we have to wait until you've finished cataloging."

"Right," I say. "Sorry to bring up details. I guess that's the kind of curator I am. Detail oriented. But you're right, they can get in the way." I pick up another slice of tuna belly, this time passing on the sauce.

I don't bring up Gun and his offer—demand?—to control the museum. That might further darken the wonderful mood of cooperation the brother and sister have worked so hard to achieve. I don't want to be accused of that. Nope, I'm no mood wrecker.

We work on our dinner mostly in silence, except for a few compliments on the food. Akiko says that she personally does most of the cooking. It's traditional Japanese food, as is expected at a first-class ryokan. The food is a welcome change from the impersonal robotic food at the Ono plant and from the rich continental food that Gun and I ate the other night.

Haruna brings in the tea pot, refills our cups, and tidies up the table before leaving. I feel strange watching her go about her duties as a servant and not as a daughter, a niece, a lover. Am I feeling sorry for her or for me?

Haruna

The shape refilled itself.

The shape ground the kids torturing her to nothing.

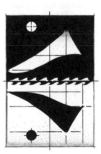

After hours of slow, painful, mindless small talk, I start to drift off to sleep. My head jerks upright when it falls to one side. My eyes open briefly, then shut heavily.

Ichiro stands up, and says he must be going. I stand up groggily. Akiko and I follow him to the front. I mumble that I should stay here and get an early start. Ichiro says, "Yes. Get a good night's sleep so you'll be fresh."

I say I will. Akiko follows Ichiro out to his car. When they're gone, Haruna shows me to my room. She lays out my futon while I get undressed. We finish at the same time, and I drop onto the bed. She turns out the light. After a moment, she slips under the covers.

I'm instantly asleep. But during the night I wake up several times, and feel, not see, Haruna watching me sleep.

Takenoko

Takenoko walked through the bamboo grove to the ridge clearing. The night air smelled earthy, as if all the floral, light, busy scents during the day fell back into the ground.

In the center of the clearing he stopped. He stood still, waiting, watching for something. He didn't know what it would be. Would it be inside him, or outside?

He waited for a long time. Nothing came.

Then he saw the flashes in the sky—bursts of light, with long trails of fire that disappeared in no time at all.

When I wake up—seven a.m. by my Seiko—Haruna is gone, and Akiko is entering my room with a breakfast tray.

She says, "You wanted an early start."

I sit up and reach for my yukata. I pull it around my shoulders.

Akiko says, "Haruna is serving other guests."

"Oh."

She pours a cup of roasted green tea. I was just starting to enjoy the earthy, charred aroma, when Akiko asks, "What exactly are your motives?"

What a way to start the morning. "My motives?" I say.

Akiko paddles steaming rice into an eggshell-white bowl. "Your motives."

I sit very still. I'm not sure if I should feel angry, paranoid, frightened, or what. I decide to fight it out: "I have no motives." That sounds a little stupid.

She clucks her tongue. "We all have motives. We wouldn't be alive, if we didn't have motives. You have motives."

"Well, of course, I have motives, if you put it that way. I need to make a living so I can eat, have a place to sleep."

"And have a woman to sleep with."

I could have guessed that was coming.

His tongue probed inside her mouth. Akiko pushed him away. She took a few steps toward the door, then looked at him over her shoulder. He got up and followed her.

She led him into the garden. The night fog clung to them like a warm blanket. The trickling splash of water in the pond was the only sound; even the cicadas were silent.

In the rooms around the garden, Akiko could feel the guests gathering, watching.

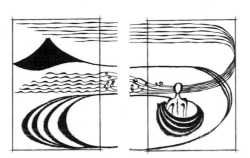

223

Yukawa's voice, his actions, the way he stood, the way he ate, the way he dressed, the way he breathed, everything about him belied his foremost trait. The trait of balance.

Akiko knew he would be perfect.

I don't touch my breakfast. That'll show her. I say, "I have no motives for sleeping with women. It just happens."

Akiko stands near the door—blocking it? "I see. It just happens. My, aren't you the ladies' man."

"No, that's not it. I'm just trying to do my job, a good job. I just want to do things right."

"You knew Ichiro was going to show up yesterday, didn't you? It had been arranged."

 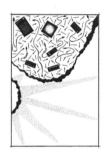

What? "No, no. I had no idea."

Akiko turns her back to me. Before walking away she says, "There's a conspiracy going on here, and I don't like it."

Takenoko

Natsuko brought him:

    a basket of dried squid

    a jug of water

    a jar of sake

    brushes, paints, and paper

"Where did you get them?" Takenoko asked.

She just smiled.

When Akiko is gone, I get dressed, gather up my notes, and head out of the inn. I'm in no mood for cataloging, or seeing Akiko again. I get into my car, and wait for someone to come out and stop me. Preferably Haruna. But no one does.

I drive to Numazu in a fury. Like a teenager, I screech my tires on the tight curves. I pull into the dormitory parking lot, and wave to the shadow sitting in a white Toyota Mark II. It's obviously an unmarked police car; only police drive white Mark IIs.

I hurry up to my room, barely noticing the package leaning against the door.

I take a quick shower and put on the cleanest suit I have. I need to get to the cleaners. The slightly wrinkled suit makes me feel like a slob.

I open the package just enough to see it's another View. I close up the package.

Talk about motives ... what are the motives of the person sending me the Views? Or persons: there could be more than one.

I hide the package under my raincoat and go back to my car. I want to go to Hakone, to the museum, and sit in my private office with the door closed.

The unmarked police car hasn't moved. Why am I being watched? What are their motives?

Motives. Motives. Motives.

I get into my car, tossing the raincoat, and package, casually in the back seat. Why am I feeling so paranoid? The more I worry about it, the more paranoid, the more guilty, I feel. I must be guilty of something; the police don't watch someone who isn't guilty.

I start up the car, and drive nonchalantly, innocently, through the gate and pass the Mark II.

It starts to follow me.

Spring arrived with a sudden warm breeze that penetrated Takenoko's hut. The warmth loosened his stiff wrists and aching shoulders. The warmth made his fingers tingle.

He hoped the warmth would dissolve the pain that slowed his painting during the winter. He hoped the change in seasons would rid him of the hopelessness of completing the 365 Views.

But the warmth only made him lethargic, and desperate to get away from his brushes for even an afternoon.

I drive to the museum in Hakone at precisely three kilometers per hour under the speed limit. Not too fast, not too slow. Nothing suspicious. I don't turn my head to look in the rearview mirror, just move my eyes, like a cat watching a mouse.

Except I'm the mouse, aren't I?

Just a few minutes away from the museum, the white Mark II slows down, and takes a turnoff.

What's going on?

Takenoko watched the paint fill up the paper. There is no longer an I, he thought. Someone is painting, someone thinks of what to paint next, someone sketches the scene, someone eats, someone breathes.

Someone is no longer me. Whatever used to be an I is now just a shell.

Walking up to the museum, I carry my briefcase and the package under my raincoat. The security guard isn't at the front, so I have to use my card key. The front area is empty, but I can hear a power saw in a distant corner of the museum. I walk into my office. It feels good. I feel good. It's my office. I resolve to stick to my job, forget all the other nonsense going on around me. I must remember that I'm the chief curator.

I put down the briefcase and package on my desk. That's right, my desk. I drape my raincoat and suit coat over my extra chair so they won't wrinkle more than they already are.

The contractor sticks his large head into the room. He sneezes, then says, "If you've got time, boss, could I get some answers?"

I walk around the museum with the contractor, answering his questions as best I can. When we're finished, I say to him, "I found out what you mean by Ichiro Ono changing his mind."

"Oh?" he says, wiping his nose. "I never said that." I don't care if he is lying.

When I get back into my office, I shut the door and collapse in my chair.

I open the latest package. This View is odd, in a comforting sort of way. It's not as disturbing as many of the others. A boat on the sea is being tossed by a wind storm. The man in the boat is admiring Mt. Fuji, while he furiously oars to keep his boat from being swamped by the waves.

I wonder if the man is using Mt. Fuji as a landmark to keep on course, or if he's using the mountain for strength. Or if he's looking at the mountain for the last time.

Rivers of rain tore through the slats of the hut.

Takenoko opened the door, and leaned into the wind. He forced one foot in front of the next, until he reached the clearing on the ridge.

The wind churned the sea into froth, scattering the tops of waves in an explosion of white and blue spray.

His clothes were soaked. He took them off and let the rain pelt his skin. He opened his mouth and screamed, but the wind drowned out the sound.

If I were in the mood for making analogies, I'd say the man in the boat could be me, struggling against the storm of life. If I were in that kind of mood.

But would I be staring at Mt. Fuji? I wouldn't use it as a landmark to steer by. Actually, the mountain may itself be an analogy. An analogy within an analogy. What kind of landmark would I use to steer my life … my job? Maybe so, but if it's so important, I would have said "my career" rather than "job."

Or would my life landmark be a person? Not Junko. She is well out of my life, out in such a short time that I wonder what was there in the first place.

Haruna? Kumi? I don't really know either of them.

Assuming that Takenoko did indeed complete the 365 Views in exactly one year, then one could compare it to a strenuous feat of athleticism, such as running a marathon every day for a year. The toll would not only be mental, but physical as well.

Such sustained mental activity requires a great deal of energy. Without adequate rest and revitalization, the body and mind would begin to break down.

Perhaps he would only have been able to complete the Views in a setting such as Heda, so distant from the distractions from a much more rowdy Edo.

What about an analogy of Mt. Fuji as strength? Just off the top of my head, there's no one I'd look to as a mountain of strength. One assumes that a son's mountain of strength should be his father. My father was just a father who went to his job, came home late, didn't complain, rarely yelled or disciplined. He didn't have a hobby, except to go on a Sunday walk. That's not a father to look up to, though not down on either.

I concentrate, think hard about my life, family, and friends. There are faces, events, incidents. There is no inspiration, no strength, no direction.

Okay, what if Mt. Fuji is the last sight I see before my life is swamped by waves and I drown? I suppose it would be an adequate last sight. But I doubt I would be calm enough to be resigned to my fate. I would probably be panicking, screaming in fear.

What would I want to see for my last sight? What would be my last thought? A happy one? Or a sad one, filled with regret? Has there been a pivotal point in my life?

I can't think of any.

I leaf through the book on Takenoko and find the discussion of the View I'd most recently received.

Reading it, I'm amazed to see that my thoughts on the theme match the author's. He too speculates that the man in the boat, with a load of reeds, may be taking his last trip. 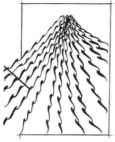 The man probably had to haul his load of reeds every day in order to survive.

I realize that I'm getting into my new job, and into Takenoko's work. Maybe everything is going to be fine.

There's a knock on the door, and Ichiro comes in.

Ichiro stands by the chair where I've draped my raincoat and suit coat. I say, "Excuse me," and pick up the coats and drape them over the back of my chair. We sit down, me on the edge of my seat.

Ichiro says, "You need a coat closet."

"Good idea. I'll get a coat rack."

With his voice full of impatient irritation, Ichiro says, "Tell the contractor to build you a proper closet."

I look around the office, as if I'm sizing it up for closet space. "Ah, good idea."

"What did you think of the meeting yesterday?"

Takenoko

The waves tossed the boat like a leaf. Each wave bounced it violently up into the air. The man steering the boat wrapped his arms tightly around the rudder pole, as much to keep him in the boat as the boat on course.

What a strange life, thought Takenoko. Why didn't he wait until the storm had blown over?

What a strange life ... why don't I give up painting the 365 Views?

Ichiro

The wail of the air raid siren cut through the air. The workers moved without any undue concern. The foreman ran the opposite direction. One of the workers, about the same age as Ichiro gestured for him to follow.

They filed down a metal stairway, reaching the bottom of a concrete-lined tube. They crammed into a shelter the size of a closet. The harsh light came from a bare, low-wattage bulb.

The air in the room quickly became stale. Ichiro fought to breathe. One of the workers said, "The foremen have their own shelter. Stocked with sake and warm rice balls."

"Warm women, too," said another.

Ichiro gazed up as the bombs exploded.

The foreman sized him up. "You ever worked before?"

"Yes, sir," said Ichiro.

The foreman spit on the ground near Ichiro's feet. "Then pick that up."

The other workers laughed.

Ichiro bent over. With the flat of his hand he slopped up the viscous liquid. "Finished, sir. What do you want done with it?"

"The meeting yesterday at Heda?" I stall for time while I try to come up with something to say. "Excellent strategy. You got right to the heart of the matter. Your presence instantly changed your sister's attitude from reluctance toward cooperation. I believe it went very well."

Ichiro nods. "Yes, I thought it went very well, too. I take it you've finished cataloging there?"

"Well, no. I needed to catch up on my notes here. And check in with the contractor."

Ichiro tilts his head. I follow his gaze to the View on my desk.

Ichiro says, "Why do you have this View in here?"

"What? Oh, this View? Well, I'm going to see how it looks on the wall in the east viewing room. The contractor had some lighting and painting questions. I was about to take it back to the storage room, when you came in."

He leans closer. "I'm not sure if I remember this View from my collection …"

I say, "I really like this one in particular, the theme of the man staring at the mountain while battling a horrific sea. What do you think Takenoko is trying to say?"

He stares at it for several long moments. "Well, he's obviously so enraptured with the beautiful view of Mt. Fuji that even the storm means nothing."

"Ah," I say, as if Ichiro has shown me enlightenment. "That's very good."

Ichiro says, "Or it could be that in his suffering with the sea and his daily toil, he has at last achieved a concept of self. The mountain represents that achievement."

I nod slowly. "Could be that too."

Ichiro sits back in his chair and says, "My sister says you're becoming quite friendly with her daughter."

I smile nervously. "Oh, yes, well, she's, well, you-know-how-it-is. Oh, all part of my strategy. Yes, that's what it is, part of my strategy."

Ichiro taps his fingertips together.

Ichiro says, "My family has a long history in this area. We've been here for generations, and have had many trials and tribulations, as all families have to one degree or another. We've incurred debts, paid them back, incurred some more, paid them back. We survived the war, and other tragedies. We've had our share of successes and failures, as all families."

I say, "More successes than failures, I mean, you're all quite successful. You with Ono Robotics and now the Takenoko museum, your sister Akiko has a beautiful onsen ryokan, and Gun has ..."

Gun. I haven't told Ichiro about Gun's desire to control the museum.

As I try to decide what to say, the security guard says over my intercom: "There's a Gun Ono to see you."

Takenoko

The pale man in the dark blue kimono came to the charcoal shed where the boy and his father were stacking the logs. When his father saw the man he froze. The boy could feel the fear of his father. The pale man said, "You know why I'm here."

His father placed a log on top of the stack. The boy reached for another log to hand to him.

"Send the boy away," the pale man said.

His father nodded at him. The boy shook his head. His father said, "Go." The boy dropped the log and walked slowly out of the shed. He bumped into the pale man, who made a disgusted sound and brushed off his kimono.

The boy hid behind the shed, and peered through the slats. The man said to his father, "You haven't paid your debts."

Ichiro

The silence filled the room awkwardly. It had been almost a year since the war ended when Ichiro finally made it home. Gun sat against the wall, Akiko at the low table.

Ichiro said, "I'm sorry I haven't been home until now."

Akiko said, "We've nearly starved."

Gun said, "I'm leaving for Tokyo."

Ichiro picked at his trousers. "I've decided to start my own company. I learned a lot at the submarine factory."

Akiko said, "So you two are going to leave me here with her?"

Gun

Gun said, "I know an art dealer who can sell the paintings."

Akiko stared at the table.

To Ichiro, Gun said, "To be fair, we should divide the Views between us. We can keep some if we want, sell the others. It would be up to each of us."

Akiko said, "What about Mother?"

Ichiro said, "We'll have to do something about her first."

Akiko nodded then asked quietly, "How much can we get?"

Before Gun comes into my office, Ichiro says, "My meeting with Akiko yesterday is not to be mentioned to Gun, understand?"

"Yes. Of course." I start to tell Ichiro about Gun's offer when the security guard shows him into my office.

Gun says, "Ichiro, it's been a long time."

"Yes. A long time. What do you want?"

I smile awkwardly at them.

After a long moment of silence, Gun says, "Well, the Takenoko museum is nearly finished I see."

Ichiro glances at me and says, "There's a lot of finish work."

Gun says, "A beautiful building, no doubt about it. You've spared no expense."

Ichiro says, "Let's take you on a tour."

We walk through the main gallery spaces. As Gun looks around, I can tell what he's thinking: horribly institutional, the exact opposite of what he would have done.

Gun says, "Ichiro, what do you think of my proposal?"

232

Ichiro stops. "Proposal?"

Gun says, "Didn't you tell him, Yukawa?"

I say, "Well, um, we've had quite a busy schedule the past couple of days, and we just now had a chance to sit down and talk. I was just getting to it, when you arrived."

I say to Ichiro, "Gun met with me night before last and had a proposal that he wanted me to pass along. And, well, now that he's here, perhaps he should tell you in person."

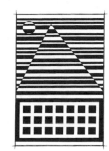

Gun doesn't look happy. He sighs and says to Ichiro, "I certainly expected your curator to pass along this most important proposal at the first opportunity. This puts me in an awkward position."

Both Gun and Ichiro stare at me.

Gun says, "As a preface to my proposal I need to be honest, and direct."

Ichiro stands in the middle of the great, empty gallery with his arms folded across his chest.

Gun goes on, his voice echoing, "I find your museum very sterile and predictable, much too uninspiring for Takenoko's genius found in the 365 Views of Mt. Fuji."

Ichiro doesn't move, doesn't say anything. I hold my breath. Ichiro finally says, "And?"

Gun says, "And I propose that I take over control of the museum. I can rescue this project from failure, from doom."

Ichiro says to me, "You didn't want to tell me this?"

"I did, really, I was just about to tell you, and we were quite busy yesterday, in—" I stop myself before I say "Heda."

Gun says, "Heda? You were talking with Akiko yesterday, weren't you?"

Ichiro glares at me as if I were a mosquito. Then he nods at Gun and says, "I thought it was appropriate to discuss her collection of Views."

Gun shakes his head. "So brother and sister gang up against brother."

Ichiro says, "If you want to look at it that way you can."

Gun says, "It's not going to happen."

I think I've held my breath for five minutes now.

Just then, the steer-headed contractor comes into the gallery with his blueprints unrolled. "There you are, boss." He comes over to me. He nods at Ichiro and Gun, then he wipes his red nose on his sleeve. "Got a problem here, boss. Can you come look at it?"

"Oh, yes. Excuse me," I say to the two brothers. "I don't want to hold up progress." I could kiss the steer-head of the contractor.

There is no substitute for a private office with a lock. After I've handled the contractor's problem, I go into mine and turn the lock. The quiet and privacy is paradise.

I sit at my desk. I wish I had someone to talk to. Junko had always listened to my complaints about the chief curator; at least for the first couple of years. Then my complaints started sounding like a broken record, boring even to me.

My whole world is crashing down on me.

The past is its own world, a world lost, a world of regrets, a world of shame.

Hope was there once, in Edo, but it evaporated like a drop of sweat on a roof tile in summer.

I pick up my phone and dial my old phone number in Tokyo. It rings a couple of times, but it's an odd, unfamiliar ring. A computer-generated voice answers, "This number has been disconnected and is no longer in service."

I've been cut off from my past. Totally.

The hopes of the past gave into the disappointments of the present. All he wanted was to paint—what happened? He was as good as the others, but he didn't have the approval of those who mattered.

All he wanted was to paint what he felt.

My door handle rattles. Then there's a knock. I jump up and open the door. It's Gun and Ichiro.

Ichiro says, "Locking us out?"

I force out a laugh. "Oh, no. No. The contractor just wanted to see if the locks are working. I guess they are."

Ichiro says, "My brother and I have agreed for the moment to disagree, but that's a good first step. We feel there's some ground for continued dialog."

"Ah, good," I say. "Excellent."

235

Gun said to Ichiro, "I've arranged the favor you requested. There are some details to be decided."

Ichiro nodded once.

Gun asked, "Is this person to be killed quickly?"

"Quickly ... no not quickly. He should understand why he's being killed. He should understand the suffering, shame, and pain he's put his former co-workers through. He must learn a lesson about loyalty."

Gun said, "It's too late for him to learn a lesson."

"For his next life, then."

Ichiro says, "Perhaps a creative partnership might work."

"Of course," I say. "A creative partnership. Why didn't I think of that?"

Ichiro gives me a funny look.

Gun says, "We'll work out the details later. After you finish cataloging our collections. When are you returning to Atami to finish mine?"

"Oh, let me see." I check my computer scheduler, which I haven't yet figured out how to work. "Um, tomorrow? Would that work?"

Gun nods. "Tomorrow's fine."

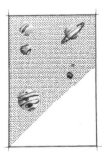 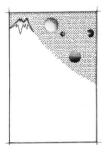

Ichiro says, "Gun and I are going out for lunch; would you care to accompany us?"

From the tone of his voice, I get the impression I'm not really invited. That's okay with me. "I'm sorry, but I better refuse. I've got a lot of work to do here."

The View on my desk has caught Gun's eye. He is about to say something when Ichiro says, "All right. Let's go, Gun."

When the Ono brothers are gone I lock my office door. I sit in the quiet. I wonder what they're going to talk about at their lunch. Me, no doubt.

I liked it better when the Ono clan were at odds with each other, arguing about the museum and the Views. I had some use. With their creative partnerships, whatever that means, I feel I'm in the way.

The quiet in my office turns oppressive. I'm all alone, no one can help me. What am I going to do?

I need to get to the cleaners.

Gun

Ichiro showed Gun into his office.

Gun accepted the cup of tea. He took a sip. The tea was tepid, weak. The atmosphere in the office was oppressive. He couldn't imagine anyone working in this environment.

Ichiro said, "Things went well?"

"Yes. He understood quite clearly the suffering he caused you and his former co-workers."

Ichiro exhaled slowly. "Good. Perhaps it would be better if we didn't see each other for awhile."

Cavorting
with Criminals

In the museum's storage room I try to catalog the Views, but my mind keeps wandering: what are Ichiro and Gun up to? I'm sure that I'm being discussed at their reunion luncheon. I want to know what they're saying. I know things haven't gone the smoothest, but I've tried my hardest, I think, so far. I'll do better as I get to know Ichiro and the others, won't I?

If Gun does become a partner in the museum, what will that mean for me? Undoubtedly, Gun has his own idea of the kind of curator best for the museum. I'm the traditional curator he despises.

And there's Akiko, another new member of this creative partnership. So far, she doesn't seem too impressed with my performance. I haven't done myself any favors sleeping with her daughter. She could convince Ichiro to dump me in a second.

I think I'm in trouble. Big trouble.

Takenoko

"You cheat!" one gambler shouted. He picked up the dice and inspected them.

"How can I cheat? You're watching me all the time. Just because you're losing—"

The accuser grabbed the other by the collar. His bony hand was covered in red splotches—a birth mark, or scars.

Takenoko sketched furiously.

239

Takenoko

Takenoko recalled the day his teacher broke his bamboo brush. It had been as if his own bones were breaking.

He looked at the sketch of the gambler's agony. It was good. He had sketched from feeling, not seeing.

He couldn't go back to his room in the brothel. Nothing there made him work with feeling.

He started walking, then running. Away from Edo.

Another topic at their lunch will be the View I left on my desk; both Gun and Ichiro seemed interested in it. They'll put two and two together, and when they return, they'll have me arrested for theft. I glance at my Seiko; they'll be back soon.

I realize that I've been staring at the same View and page of the Takenoko book without taking in a word, or writing down one word in my notes. I'm not doing any good here. I need to get away, take a break to clear my mind.

Takenoko

A knife appeared. The gambler accused of cheating slashed at the hand grasping his collar. The blade was sharp; it sliced through flesh and tendon as if nothing were there. Blood spurted, adding bright red to the purple-red splotches on his skin.

As the gambler howled and clasped his hand to this body, the man with the knife fled. Takenoko kept sketching the scene.

What I need to do is get organized. Start over. That's what I'll do. I'll go back to Numazu, before Ichiro and Gun return.

Let's see, first I need to find a cleaners, get all my clothes freshened. Nothing like clean clothes with sharp creases to give one a sense of worth. That will be a good start.

Then I'll find a new apartment. My own apartment, away from Ono Robotics. Where should I live? Near the

museum, or in Numazu? Maybe neither. Once the museum is up and running I'll be spending most of my time here, but on my free hours, I won't want to be anywhere near it.

I close up the storage room, and go back to my office. I throw my notes and the book into my briefcase, grab my raincoat and suit coat, and start out the door.

The steer-headed contractor is there. "Wish I had your hours. I wouldn't be a fifty-two-year-old man in the body of an eighty-year-old. I age two years for every one in this racket."

"Did you want something? I've got a very important appointment."

He sniffs and mumbles something I can't catch.

"What?" I say.

"Before your very important appointment, could you answer a couple of my stupid questions?"

I hold back a long impatient sigh. "Okay. Your questions?"

The steer-headed contractor unrolls his plans. "The other day, you said we should move this counter back to here." He points with a stub of a pencil. His fingernails have been chewed to nothing. "Well it blocks the electrical outlet."

"Move the outlet."

"Okay, boss, but we'll have to get the electrical contractor back in. They'll charge us for another move-in and move-out, plus the work is an extra. But if that's what you want, that's what you'll get."

"Just do it. Next question?"

The contractor unhooks a tape measure from his belt. He places it on my office floor. "The big boss said you want a closet. I can fit it in here."

The third gambler boxed Takenoko in the ear and threw his sketch pad out into the cold rain. "You worm. Sitting there drawing a man's misery."

Takenoko picked up his pad. Water had already soaked through it.

"Don't let me see you again, or I'll cut off your hands."

"Yes," said Richard. "It's the serious student."

Gun, staring out the window that overlooked the Seine River, asked, "Why him? He's so ..."

"I know. Serious. But that's why I'm ..."

"Attracted to him?"

Richard nodded. "He doesn't scare me. Like you do."

"Fine," said Gun. "I've been ready to go back to Japan for awhile. I need the contrasts there, in Japan."

Richard said nothing.

"You know," said Gun, "your serious student will kill himself one day."

I say, "I don't care where the closet goes, or even if I have a closet. I don't care about the closet at all. Do whatever you want with the closet."

"Well, okay boss, but don't blame—"

I grab my briefcase and run out of the office. In my car, I take a few deep breaths. I start the engine and drive out of the lot. Halfway down the hill toward Numazu, a car approaches that looks like Gun's. It is: Tabo's driving, and Gun and Ichiro are in the back seat. I hope they won't see me, but they get a good look at me as we pass.

Takenoko

With a sliver of charcoal, the boy drew the scene: his father kneeling in the dirt, the sword in the air, the samurai with the face of a devil. He showed it to his father.

The man yelped. He slapped the boy and tore the drawing into a hundred pieces. He forced the boy to throw the pieces into the charcoal kiln.

I speed all the way to Numazu, not worrying about the police stopping me. I don't care if they do. I've reached the point of not caring. But it's a dangerous point; you do rash things, like belching in the face of the chief curator.

I slow down when I'm near the Ono Robotics plant. The white Mark II is parked outside the main gate to the plant.

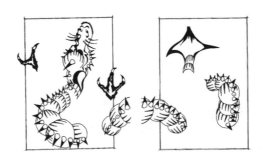

I don't wave at the Mark II as I drive past. I want to though. I sit on my hand.

I park near the entrance to the dormitory. In my side mirror I see the Mark II pull into the dorm parking lot. I get out of my car and walk to the entry. The Mark II pulls up to the curb and stops. I'm inside the dorm when two men get out of the Mark II.

I try to calm myself, ready to play innocent. What? I am innocent. I decide to face them now.

One of the men is Officer Tani. The other, a little older with an ordinary face, is dressed in a blue suit, nothing fancy. The kind that ninety-nine percent of male salary workers wear. And TV detectives.

"Hello, officer," I say.

Tani says, "This is Inspector Noguchi. We have a couple of questions for you. Is there someplace private we can talk?"

I look at my watch. "I'm running late for an appointment." My heart starts pounding with the lie. "My room is tiny, no place for visitors. And believe it or not, I don't think there's a private office in this whole plant. The only place with chairs is the cafeteria, hardly private. This lobby is probably as private as it gets around here." I'm rambling now, so I shut up.

Noguchi says, "I'll make it short then. You've been seen cavorting with known criminals, what do you have to say about that?"

"What?" I say, genuinely surprised.

Noguchi and Tani exchange a glance. Possibly a meaningful glance.

"Who?" I say.

Noguchi says, "Of course, you already know."

"What? How am I supposed to know? I have no idea what you're talking about."

Noguchi gazes at me like I'm a hamburger he's about to bite.

Takenoko rehearsed his apology as he trudged back into the studio.

243.

The boy had never seen anyone so angry. Not even the samurai. The pale man in the dark blue kimono screamed, his face turned blood-red, thick veins popped from his neck.

The pale man slapped his father over and over. His father stumbled out of the shed and crawled toward the street. The man followed, striking his father with fists and kicks.

The boy ran after them.

I stare at Noguchi. He stares at me. We stare at each other. Finally, I think I see a slight smile crossing his lips. The detective says, "Don't get angry."

"Angry? Who said I was angry? I'm not angry. But why shouldn't I get angry? You accuse me of being a criminal, without so much as a 'good afternoon.' I'm just a curator, trying to do my job. Trying to do things right."

Noguchi says, "No one's accusing you of being a criminal."

"Well, I beg to differ. What was the word you used—cavorting? Isn't cavorting with criminals the same as being one?"

Noguchi smiles.

Noguchi says, "In certain situations, yes, you're correct. Association with known criminals can itself be a criminal offense, though in reality it's never pursued unless the person has himself committed a criminal offense."

What?

Noguchi says, "Well, that's all. Officer Tani and I will check your story. From now on, watch out who you associate with."

"What do you mean, 'check my story?' I haven't given you any story."

Noguchi and Tani exchange another glance, then turn and leave without so much as a "good-bye."

What story?

I'm glad I didn't bring Tani and Noguchi up to my room—four (!) more packages have arrived. I drop my briefcase on the floor. I start to open the packages, then wonder if the cops might make a surprise appearance. Break down the door with their burly shoulders.

I leave the packages where they are. If the cops do come in, I could say I have no idea where they came from or what's inside them. But wouldn't that be suspicious as well? Wouldn't an innocent person (the person who doesn't cavort with known criminals) open the packages?

So I open one.

It's a View, and so are the others. I need a drink, that's what I need. I need to go to a comfortable place where no one knows me. A little peace and quiet and a drink. Someplace dark. Preferably not the hangout of known criminals.

I know a perfect place. The mama-san bar that serves omelets and sake and beer. Perfect.

I briskly walk the few blocks to the station. No cops follow, at least that I can see. Inside the bar, there's only one other customer; he looks like an out-of-work laborer, not a known criminal.

Just in case, though, I sit on the other end of the counter bar. The mama-san greets me as if I'm her favorite son, not as a person known to cavort with known criminals.

Takenoko

Outside the art studio, Takenoko took a few steps in the dusty street, then stopped.

Across the street, a laborer, bent under a load of plaster clay, struggled to keep his balance.

245

I order a large Sapporo lager. She serves me right away; she can tell I need a drink. I take a big swig and she refills my glass from the bottle. I munch on a boiled soybean.

"How's your day?" she asks.

"Fine," I say. What can I tell her that would make sense? "Very busy, I was up early. Got a lot done, so I figure I can take off early."

"It's nice to be the boss."

I take another long swig. I'm already relaxing. My appetite makes an appearance. "How about a mushroom omelet?"

"Coming right up."

As omelets go it's very delicious. The mama-san says, "Hear any more stories about the nekobaba?"

"Not one. How about you?"

"I know a bunch more. Want to hear some?"

"I'd rather hear something about the history of the Ono Robotics plant. It's built over a submarine factory, isn't it?"

She nods slowly. "Ah, yes, the submarine factory."

The mama-san says, "The factory was bombed a few times during the war. Most of the factory was underground, so they could keep working. Of course, the above-ground buildings had to be rebuilt more than once."

The worker at the other end of the bar says glumly, "We could use another war. At least we'd have jobs."

The mama-san berates him for his stupidity. When she finishes, I ask, "Did the sub factory—the underground part—survive the war? Is it still there?"

She shrugs and refills my beer.

I finish my omelet and start on another beer. The mama-san takes my plate away and wipes up the bar. I ask her, "What about the Ono family? Do you know anything about them? Like Ichiro's wife—how did she die?"

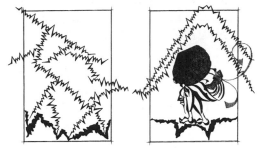

"Die?"

"She didn't die?"

The mama-san chuckles pleasantly. Not an old lady cackle. "No. Ichiro sent her back to her family in disgrace. Paid her off to never come back. At least that's what I heard."

I have two more beers in the mama-san's bar. Then I need some fresh air. I walk back toward the Ono plant, wondering what to do with the rest of the evening. For one thing, I'll avoid association with any known criminals. If I can find any to avoid.

Kumi—that's whom I want to see. Maybe she's the criminal … No.

Back in the plant, I first go into the museum where I study the old drawings of the submarine factory. I decide that when it gets late, I'll try to open the grates leading into the culvert.

I find Kumi at her computer terminal. She's concentrating on the screen. I clear my throat. She looks up.

"Hello," she says. It's actually a nice "hello."

Takenoko

In the street, the pale man rained blows on his father. The passers-by stared, and did nothing.

The boy jumped on the pale man's back, but the man wouldn't stop. Blood poured out of deep gashes on his father's head.

The boy sunk his teeth into the man's ear. The man screamed and flung the boy halfway across the street. The man roared and clutched at his ear. The boy spit out a chunk of bloody ear.

The pale man careened down the street.

The boy ran over to his father. He was dead.

Kumi

Father: "It would be nice if you could combine a true intelligence with a robotic mechanism. But why would you want to? You can teach a dog to fetch a ball, so you could also teach him to fetch a loose nuclear fuel rod. Of course, it would be his last act. What if you had a true intelligence in a robot? It wouldn't be satisfied to weld twenty-four hours a day."

But that's not an appropriate use of AI.

Father: "The AI-robot would never be intentionally programmed to suffer, therefore it would never truly be a self-perpetuating intelligence."

247.

Correction: adjust the learning algorithm.

<<small talk function [weather]>>

What role does curiosity play? Is curiosity an emotion? Or merely a reaction to cognitive dissonance? Is any reaction an emotion? Yes, a reaction is an emotion. Or can be an emotion?

<<small talk function [food]>>

We go into the company cafeteria. The early dinner rush is over, and we get a table to ourselves away from most of the others. She gets a carton of plain yogurt; I get a square of carrot cake and a cup of coffee.

We do the small talk thing for awhile: weather, food, work. Then she asks me, "I've been working on aesthetic algorithms. Do you have a few minutes so I can verify my theoretical assumptions?"

To be honest, I'm really not interested in aesthetics. I suppose there was a time in college when there was

 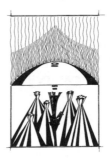

nothing I'd rather talk about. It made good bar talk, it made me a cultural philosopher (and attracted good-looking, or at least liberal, women).

But now, the subject bored me. There were no answers. Things without answers tire me out.

But I give it a try. "Okay, I'll try. But my mind is kind of shot right now, so if you pick at it too much it'll probably fall apart like stale carrot cake."

She thinks about my statement. At least I think she's thinking about my statement. It gives me time to think of something intelligent to say about aesthetics.

Finally she says, "Well, I'm in the middle of writing a pattern-recognition algorithm, one that applies the principles of symmetry and asymmetry."

"Symmetry, that's a good start," I say. "Have you tried reading the great philosophers for their views of aesthetics?" That would keep her busy.

"Yes," Kumi says. "I've read the major works by many of them. I find it difficult to put their thoughts into algorithms. No, what I'm more interested in is working aesthetics. Like what you do for my father at the museum. Evaluating the paintings, designing the displays."

I swallow a bite of the carrot cake. It's a perfectly serviceable carrot cake, neither too sweet nor not sweet enough, and has just the right amount of frosting. "Perhaps you should talk to your uncle Gun and your aunt Akiko. Both of them are more than willing to talk about their artistic vision. Gun has more eclectic tastes, especially compared to the traditional tastes of Akiko."

Kumi thinks about that while I take a sip of the precisely brewed coffee. Then she shakes her head. For some reason that gesture irritates me.

Kumi says, "I don't think I could talk to them about it. Besides, at this point in my work I'm looking for some basic, universal aesthetic principles."

"But there aren't any universal aesthetic principles! No one's ever said to me, 'Here are the 3 or 4 or 236 universal aesthetic principles.' I don't know what you want from me. I don't want to talk about this anymore!" I pick up my coffee cup and drain it. I set it back onto the saucer with a clatter.

Kumi blinks several times.

After my outburst, I don't know what to say. So I just sit, feeling stupid and ridiculous.

Kumi says, "So there aren't any universal aesthetic—"

"No! No!" I sputter madly. "And you know what? I heard today that your mother didn't die. Your father just sent her away. He paid her off to stay away, never to see him, or you, again! That's what I heard today. What about that?"

Kumi sits there. Doing nothing. Saying nothing.

The pilot announces, "And on the left side of the plane, we have a fine view of Mt. Fuji."

Blink. Blink. Conical shaped mountain created by volcanic eruption.

Swallowed up all.

Deeper, deeper.

Blink, blink.

Kumi

"It's me, Kumi. Ichiro, your father."
Words + syntax = language
Perception + action = intelligence
Non-polynomial complete ...

Kumi hasn't said a word or moved for several long moments. I stare at the crumb remains of the perfectly moist carrot cake. I can hear the coffee in my cup evaporating.

Now her silence grinds on me. "Did you hear what I said?"

She says nothing.

I soften a bit. "Look, I'm sorry. I didn't mean to just spring that on you. It's probably just some wild gossip I heard at a bar. This silly bar I went to that serves omelets and sake and beer. I had a mushroom omelet that was pretty good."

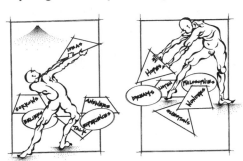

She finally moves her head, down to the right, maybe a millimeter or two.

I say, "That's what the mama-san in the bar said, anyway. About your mother. It can't be true, though. I mean, you did tell me she died. After all, you would know, wouldn't you?"

She tilts her head the other direction a quarter of an inch.

"Okay," I say, "I'll just forget about it. None of my business anyway, right? But there is something you can help me with." I pause, she actually looks into my eyes. "A couple of cops—a local police officer and an inspector—warned me that I've been seen cavorting with known criminals. The only people I've been cavorting with lately are members of your family. You wouldn't know if any of them are criminals, would you?"

Her expression is utterly blank.

I say, "Do you understand? The cops are following me around like I'm the criminal. All because someone in your family—at least I assume it's someone in your family—is a criminal. How can I do anything about it if I don't know who it is I'm not supposed to be cavorting with?"

Kumi actually opens her mouth. But then she closes it again.

"Please, Kumi, help me. Tell me something. Surely, you must know something that can help me."

Nothing.

I feel hot, like I've got a fever. I'm not going to let her get away so easily.

"And not only that, Kumi, but these packages keep getting delivered to me, to my room, left in my car, left with the guy down the hall. These packages just keep showing up. Do you know what's in these packages?"

I wait for an answer. And I wait some more. Nothing.

I try to control my anger. It's built up to the point of insanity. In a voice slurred with anger, I say, "In each of these packages is one of the 365 Views of Mt. Fuji by Takenoko. Do you know what would happen if I'm caught with them? I would probably be accused of embezzling. No telling how much they're worth. Millions of yen each. If I'm not thrown in jail, I'll be banned from working as a curator. I've been putting them in your father's collection, but he'll catch on sooner or later. I should have told him right away, but I didn't. I don't know why, I just wanted things to get off to a good start."

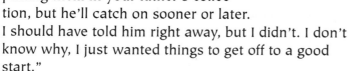

Takenoko

The end of the summer brought the hottest days of the season. Takenoko sweltered in the unending heat; flies buzzed around his salt-stained body. His arm drooped low. He had to force it to keep painting.

He caught a fever of chills, flashes of fire, and hallucinations. His body burned up, as if it was no longer attached to him. Only his arm and eyes were still connected. Eyes to see, arm to paint.

Then he would ache, his body heavy, dragging him down. Still he would paint, even when all he could imagine was death and darkness.

"What have I done?" Ichiro said.

<<Function: Pattern_Recognition
   [Language]>>

"I pushed you too hard, made you suffer too much."

Return: No matching pattern.

I squash the urge to shake her. "I'll get fired for one thing. Maybe that's what someone wants. 'Art Curator Found With Stash of Museum Treasures.' Or maybe your father is testing me; he does have a weird management style, from what I've seen."

Kumi's chin trembles. "Function."

What? "What?"

"Misunderstanding."

"It's a misunderstanding? Whose misunderstanding?"

"Function."

I repeat: "Function?"

Kumi stands up.

"Wait," I say. "What's wrong? Sit down. You've got to tell me what's going on."

She turns and starts to walk away.

"Thanks a lot," I shout at her. The few workers in the cafeteria stare at me. Yelling at the boss's daughter won't get me an invite to the company's summer outing.

In my depressing room, I flop onto my futon. I find the quarter-liter of Suntory whiskey, still three-quarters full. Well maybe two-thirds full. Whatever. Full enough.

I take a sip. The whiskey burns, but that's exactly what I want.

I try to empty my mind of thoughts, but they keep coming back to Kumi. I was pretty hard on her; I haven't been myself lately.

Another sip of whiskey burns at my self-pity.

The bottle of Suntory is less than half empty when I put the cap back on. Less than half full? Half full, half empty, who cares? Doesn't mean a thing.

The room has thoroughly depressed me now. I check out the window. It's dark. I check my watch: midnight. Time flies when you're wallowing.

So now what?

It's time to check out the culvert, get that grate open. It's something to do. Maybe I should start a club: The Culvert Explorers of Japan. I'd have a newsletter, and come up with classification categories based on accessibility, length, danger. The Culvert Adventure Rating Scale.

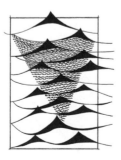

The mysterious sounds of the night became the marching footsteps of the fishermen, coming for him, because he painted Natsuko. They marched toward him.

He had to destroy the paintings of her before they got to him. But he couldn't remember where he put them, but ... he hadn't painted her, had he? No, he was sure he hadn't. He had been painting Mt. Fuji.

But he had been painting her, at least in his mind. Many times. He knew exactly how he'd paint her, when he was finished with the Fuji views.

Of course, there would have to be guidelines on how to safely explore the culverts. I wouldn't want anyone suing me for liability when they get stuck, or caught and arrested for trespassing. They'd have to sign a waiver. I'd have to include a disclaimer in all of the publications:

The Culvert Explorers of Japan publishes this information strictly for the use of members only. All information is checked as thoroughly as possible to be accurate and up-to-date; however, the Club can assume no liability for inappropriate use of this information or changes that may have occurred.

Or something like that.

I go down to my car to get my flashlight and tools. I don't see any cops around as I steal down to the culvert entrance.

I start with the first grate in the culvert. I feel between the grate openings, and find the bolt. I measure its width with my fingers. Then I find a wrench that will fit.

The bolt twists easily. When it's loose I do the same to the others.

The grate swings open.

I step inside with my toolbox and flashlight. I put the box just inside the tunnel, and close the grate. I flick on the flashlight and start up the tunnel.

The hum is low and rumbling.

The tunnel smells of moldy, damp concrete, like the bottom floor of an underground parking lot.

There are two rails, about a meter apart, on the bottom of the tunnel. I imagine a submarine sliding on the rails toward the sea. It would roar and shake the tunnel horribly.

It would flatten me as if I were a bug.

The humming gets louder the further I go. There isn't much to see in the tunnel, except the occasional shard of metal. I pick one up. I can't tell if it came from a submarine or not. Not that I know anything about submarines.

Just as I get to the end of the tunnel, which is blocked by a wall of concrete, my flashlight starts to go dim. Rule number one for culvert explorers: carry extra batteries. I shake the flashlight, then it goes out completely.

In an instant, the utter darkness closes in on me.

Absolutely,
Entirely Ordinary

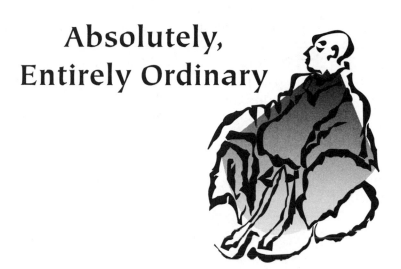

I sneak back into my room, and drop onto my futon.
The trip into the tunnel hadn't turned out entirely successful. Still it was an adventure. It certainly took my
mind off all that's been going on.

As a rule, I don't need adventure—the basics are
fine for me: a steady job with a sprinkle of stimulation;
a stable love life, not necessarily marriage or kids, at
least not yet. And that's about it.

Things sure have gotten off track.

In the dark of my room, I recall how my heart started
pounding when the flashlight went out. Like a kid on
his first roller coaster.

I should go about this exploring more methodically.
For one thing, I need a map, so I can keep track of
where I've been. The map from the museum would
work. There must be a way to make a copy of it. Or I
can sketch the parts of it I need.

Maybe I should get one of those hard hats with the
light on top that cave explorers or miners wear.

I take a sip from the nearly empty bottle of whiskey. Someday I'll be in a glossy magazine ad, posed in front of a culvert with my hard hat on and my map spread out in front of me. I'll be covered in filth, unshaven. I'll be holding a bottle of Suntory whiskey. The print will say, "Any self-respecting culvert explorer drinks Suntory Best."

Speaking of filthy and unshaven, that's what I am now. But I'm too tired to wash. And I didn't make it to the cleaners again.

Takenoko

Natsuko blew cool air onto Takenoko's feverish neck while he painted. She asked him, "Can't you take a rest?"

He shook his head.

The Ono woman was singing a song as she entered the hut. She stopped when she saw her daughter. She stamped her foot. Natsuko obediently came over to her. The woman grabbed her daughter's wrist and dragged her away.

Takenoko wanted to help, but he had to keep painting.

I take another sip of whiskey as I ponder my fate. ("All self-respecting fate ponderers drink Suntory Best.")

I really lost control with Kumi. But there's something about her that can be so irritating. She's got a one track mind. An artificial whatever-track mind.

She didn't help me figure out who is sending me the Views, or who the criminal I've been cavorting with might be.

I can guess who the criminal might be.

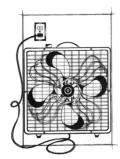

Gun must be the criminal. He seems shady enough, and he had made some vague reference to ex-partners who had to be kept happy. No, that doesn't automatically make him a criminal, but …

Gun. Sure. He was waiting for me the other night, he and Tabo, in the parking lot. The cops could've seen them. They would have seen me get into their car on our way to the hotel restaurant.

Gun.

I'll confront Gun. He won't mind me showing up this late, or this early. He never seems to sleep, just like his nieces.

I throw on my overcoat and go to the door. I stumble over the latest batch of Views I've accumulated. I need to do something about them, maybe sneak them into the museum. But Ichiro is getting suspicious. I should distribute them more evenly. Gun won't notice a few more in his storage room. I gather them up.

Outside, the night air is sultry, comforting. I get in my car and drive out of the lot.

A pair of headlights follows me out of town.

The headlights must belong to the unmarked police car.

I fool the pair of headlights following me by turning the direction opposite of Atami. I'm on the expressway, heading for Fuji City, according to a highway sign. I'll go the long way around Mt. Fuji if I have to.

No telling how long the headlights will follow me. But I can drive around all night if I have to. They'll give up.

Takenoko

Before she left, the Ono woman asked Takenoko if he had been stealing coins from the guests.

Coins? No, he hadn't.

She told him that a few guests had complained about missing coins. She told him that the village fishermen would take care of him if she caught him stealing.

A few hours later, Natsuko came into the hut with his supplies.

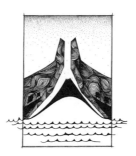

Takenoko

Takenoko painted as much at night as during the day. The night had different tensions and releases, both peace and fear. At night, the dark mountain loomed larger, its mass pressing on his chest.

Before dawn, the worst time always came, when he struggled to finish that day's work, before he had to start on the next. It was like dying. This life had been used up and the soul was ready to be reincarnated into the next.

259

This author speculates that much of the work on the Views must have been completed at night, in very dim light. Without a doubt there weren't gas lamps in tiny Heda at the time Takenoko was painting his Views. The only other light may have come from torches or firelight.

The reason for this speculation is that some of the more radical color combinations might actually be mistakes caused by such poor lighting.

I rummage through the glove box until I find my Handy Map of the Mt. Fuji area. As I pass under the yellow-orange street lights, I check the map for a route around Mt. Fuji. There definitely is one. It will probably take a good four hours to get all the way back to Atami.

The traffic on the expressway is mostly truck traffic, so the headlights of the car are easy enough to keep track of.

I wonder if it is the police following me. There must be a way to get close enough to see.

It does seem strange that Takenoko—primarily a figure artist—would undertake such an ambitious project with limited skill accumulated in landscape works. However, he had, by this time, been a working artist for almost twenty years (assuming his apprenticeship started in his early teens). He had achieved at least technical competence and (in this author's opinion) had much more creative imagination than his contemporaries.

And it's not uncommon for artists to switch themes successfully.

I slow down, and the headlights slow down as well. I speed up and they match me. Somehow I need to get them to pass me, so I can look inside the car to see who it is.

Surely the founding member of the Culvert Explorers of Japan can figure out how to do that. Actually

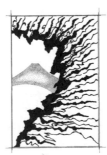

ditching the cops might be an important skill for culvert explorers. Not everyone would be happy having their culverts explored. Because of liability, privacy, security—those kinds of

issues.

The drive is quite enjoyable; it beats being cooped up in my dorm room. That reminds me, I was going to start looking for an apartment. And get to the cleaners. Oh well, I can do that tomorrow, or rather, later today. There's plenty of time for apartment hunting and the cleaners. I've got more exciting things to do.

I drive in the slow lane at the speed limit. The trucks inch past me in the fast lane. I can't see Mt. Fuji to my right. But I can feel it.

Just outside of Fuji City, I come up with a plan: I'll drive into Fuji City, and find a narrow street. When I get to the end of the street, I'll stop, turn off my lights, and wait for the car following me to come up the lane. They'll shoot out of the lane, to see which way I went. I should be able to see who's in the car.

I take the turnoff to Fuji City. The headlights follow.

The city is smaller than Numazu, judging by the low-rise downtown. Everything's dark. No nightlife here.

But there is a McDonald's.

I slam on my brakes and yank on the steering wheel. I spin into the parking lot, around the building, and park on the street, right near the lighted Golden Arches sign. I turn off my lights.

The car following me screeches out of the parking lot and flies past.

It isn't the white Mark II. It's a white Toyota Corolla. There're, probably, twenty million of them in Japan. I don't recognize the man driving.

At sunrise, Takenoko's fever broke. It was a clear, lucid moment, unlike any he'd felt for weeks. Overwhelmed, he took off all his clothes, and ran from his hut, through the bamboo grove until he reached the ridge. He stood with his arms outstretched above his head and his feet spread.

The sunlight and steam from the outdoor bath washed over him.

I wait for a few minutes by the Golden Arches. The white Corolla doesn't return. I'm quite pleased with myself. I drive off, through the dead streets of Fuji City. I get back on the expressway, continuing on my route circling Mt. Fuji.

The mountain doesn't say anything to me in the way of wisdom. It just sits there.

I get to Atami just as the dawn sky changes from gray to pinkish. The steam clouds from the onsen resorts rise about fifty feet in the air, then flatten out and disperse.

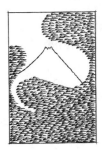

I park just off the road where I can watch the sunrise. I'm not sure why I want to watch the sunrise. I've never been romantic about the sunrise before. The sun comes up every day.

Maybe I'm just putting off seeing Gun. I feel kind of silly being here this early. My anger and frustration have vanished for the most part. Still I deserve some answers: Who's the criminal? Who's sending me the Views? What's the truth about their family? Gun has been the most open so far.

As soon as the sun peeks over the horizon, I drive to Gun's.

I stop in front of Gun's. Now I'm filled with doubt. Gun won't answer my questions.

I suddenly just want to sleep. Curl up in a nice bed. A bed all my own. I don't remember when I last had a good night's sleep. It hasn't been since Ichiro Ono called me for an interview for the museum curator position. I didn't sleep well worrying about the interview. And then when I got the job, I was worried about quitting my old job. And then after that, I was worried about leaving Junko.

And since I've been at the job, well, it's been one thing after another, that's for sure.

"You don't sleep much, do you?" Richard said.

Gun swirled the red wine in the glass. "You've noticed."

"Well, it would be hard not to. Do you ever sleep?"

Gun took a sip of wine. "Nice wine. Do I ever sleep? Well that's hard to say. Sometimes I feel like I'm asleep, I mean I close my eyes and sort of drift off. But it's probably not sleep like your sleep."

Richard lifted his empty wine glass and Gun filled it. "Strange."

Gun said, "It's a family affliction. We all have the problem."

"I wouldn't necessarily call it a problem."

Gun stared into his wine glass, and watched the red liquid swirl.

I leave my briefcase on the passenger seat. I drape my overcoat on top of the Views on the back seat. I get out and walk up to the door. I try the handle—the door's unlocked. I push it open and poke my head inside and say, "Hello?"

"Come in," says Gun, his voice coming from the sitting room just off the entryway.

I walk in. Gun, in a fluffy white robe, is hunched over several photos spread out on a table. Tabo is asleep on the sofa. He's naked.

"Yukawa. I knew you were going to come today, but at dawn?"

"Sorry," I say.

263

Gun said, "I feel ... well, I don't know how to describe it. I've felt this way at many points in my life. Each time it comes on slowly, but inevitably."

Richard asked, "What does it feel like?"

"I don't know. Like nothing matters. Or ever will. A great emptiness."

"Hell, I feel like that everyday. Hopeless."

Gun said, "It's deeper than how I've described it. I have to fight the feeling. If I don't, it will overwhelm me. To fight it, I have to do the opposite of what I'm doing now."

"The opposite?"

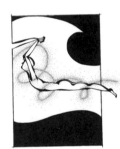

Gun gestures for me to sit opposite him on the floor. He says, "Don't worry about it, as you can see I'm quite awake. Looking at some photos."

"Yes. I see."

Gun gazes at me. "If you don't mind me saying so, you don't look too good."

"Well, I haven't had time to get to the cleaners."

"Not just your clothes, though they are wrinkled. Did you fall into a mud puddle?"

Dirt and grease speckle my shirt.

I say, "Oh, you know. From the construction at the museum."

Gun says, "You look like you could use a good night's sleep. Or a nice breakfast. I'll get Tabo to fix us something." He leans toward Tabo.

"No, that's all right." Too late. Gun jostles Tabo's shoulder.

"Tabo, how about fixing us some breakfast? Plenty of black coffee."

Tabo stretches out his sleek, smooth-skinned body. He nods at me. Yawning, he strolls off to the kitchen.

Gun pushes a few of the photos from one place to another, as if he's working on a jigsaw puzzle. His hands seem more misshapen than they had the first day I'd seen them in his office. He says, "Ichiro and I had a good discussion at lunch yesterday."

About me? "Good. I'm glad to hear it. I was beginning to get worried that the museum might not get off the ground. I mean, that's really what's needed in these kinds of situations, direct face-to-face discussions." My voice trails off.

Gun stops pushing the photos. "Situations?"

"Well, you know, situations where, um, where two parties are not quite in agreement, but then they aren't too far apart either." Perhaps I should shut up.

Gun leans back against the sofa and locks his hands behind his head. "Didn't Ichiro and I see you when we were driving back to the museum?"

"Yes, um, sorry I wasn't there when you returned from lunch. I had several errands to run. Business errands. Research, that sort of thing."

"Ichiro was a little upset that you were gone."

Great. "Thanks for telling me that. I'll have to make it up to him. So, tell me, what did you decide, exactly, at lunch?"

"Well, we still have many differences. But we have agreed to look at the other's point of view."

I say, "It's just good that you two have gotten together after so many years."

Gun says, "Not really. We don't have much in common."

I say, "I haven't seen my family for a few years myself. I do feel guilty about it, but I don't have much to say to them. And they certainly don't approve—or didn't—approve of my girlfriend. But your family has more to talk about anyway. You're all so involved in such diverse enterprises; I think you'd have very stimulating conversations. And with the tragedies that have unfortunately fallen on your family, well, they sometimes bring a family together, don't they?" There, I got it out in the open. Maybe not delicately, but out in the open.

Gun unlocks his hands and drops them to his side. "Tragedies?"

Gun held up his small, boy hands in front of his face. He cleared his mind of all thoughts, and just stared at his hands. If they were his hands, they would be able to do what was needed. Otherwise, they were no good.

He waited.

Then his hands started to move. They reached up to his face. The fingertips caressed his cheeks, then stroked his neck.

Gun said to his brother and sister, "So, this will be another family tragedy?"

Ichiro said, "This is not a tragedy."

Akiko nodded her head.

Gun said, "Then what shall we call it? An event? A mishap?"

Akiko said, "Let's not call it anything. It's no one's business but ours."

"Well," I say, "Haruna told me her father died at sea. Kumi said that her mother died when she was very young. Those tragedies."

Gun says, "Those aren't tragedies; those are events. Or perhaps circumstances is a better word."

"So, they're true?" I ask very quietly.

"True? Why wouldn't they be true?"

I don't know what to say. Before I can think of how to bring up the rumors, Gun says, "I'll tell you the truth."

Gun says, "The truth is, we are a unique family. I don't mean to sound as if I'm boasting we're better than any other family. Unique simply means different."

I nod.

"Our uniqueness lies in our creativity. Each of us has creative leanings in one direction or the other. Ichiro in his business and technological sense, Akiko in her traditional approach to running her ryokan, and you've seen what I do, with the club. Haruna and Kumi are still young; they're finding their own way. I do keep up with their progress, despite my lack of time with them.

"Of course, creativity and uniqueness, especially in Japan, can create negative feelings from society. These negative feelings further push the unique person into her or his own world, which in turn further fuels the creative fires."

Impatience tenses my hands into fists. "What does this have to do with truth?"

Gun flashes anger, then his expression softens, as if he feels sorry for me. He goes on in the same tone of voice—soft yet preachy: "What is truth to those with imagination often sounds like sheer fantasy to those without imagination."

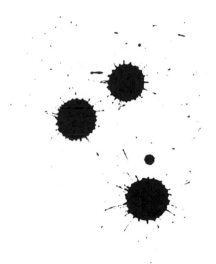

The gold ring flashed in the gangster's palm. "This will be a down payment on what he owes."

It was the scrawny man's wedding ring. Gun picked it off the gangster's palm and weighed it on his own by bouncing it a couple of times. "It isn't going to be worth much."

"That's why it's only a down payment." The gangster laughed and took back the ring. "He's lucky he doesn't have any gold teeth."

Tabo returns to the sitting room carrying a loaded tray. He's put on a robe, a match to Gun's. He puts out dishes of fried eggs with runny yolks, buttered toast, orange slices. He pours coffee—a very dark blend—from an ornate silver pot. Then he leaves.

Gun motions for me to start, while he leans back with his coffee. "Don't you remember what I told you about the line between genius and madness?"

I chase a bite of toast with a sip of coffee. "On which side of the line are you and your family members?"

Gun laughs. He exaggerates a shrug.

"And which one of you is a criminal?"

Gun

The U.S. Army doctor motioned toward Gun's hands. "They're broken. You speak any English?"

Gun nodded once, barely moving his head. He didn't understand much.

"I'm going to have to set the bones and put both hands in casts. You understand?"

No, but Gun nodded anyway.

"Okay. It'll hurt some, but I imagine they hurt already. They won't be good as new either. But they'll work. Okay?"

"Okay."

Gun laughs again. "Criminal? Who said anything about being a criminal?"

I tear off a corner of a toast slice and dip it in the egg. "The local police force has been following me around for days. Last night they confronted me, asked me weird questions, about why I've been cavorting—their word—with known criminals. The only people I've been cavorting with since I left Tokyo are members of your family." I hold the toast corner up, egg yolk and white drip back onto the plate.

I add confidently, "And don't tell me being a criminal is all in the eye of the beholder." I take a bite of the soggy toast.

Gun doesn't laugh.

I finish one whole egg before Gun says anything, "You must have done something to make the police suspicious."

Me? I didn't do anything, other than act suspiciously. "No."

"Why should the police care whom you're seen with? It's not like you're doing anything criminal your-

self, are you?"

I hesitate. "No."

Gun picks up a piece of toast and stares at it. "The past is past. When are they going to let go of it?"

Gun puts the slice of toast back on the plate without taking a bite. He says, "I'm the criminal."

I suddenly feel sorry I asked.

"Certainly anyone in my business—entertainment—has sometime or other had to deal with certain elements that wish to control it through largely illegitimate means. And when one is beginning such a business as mine, this criminal element can easily get its claws into it. Like a tiger finds it easier to hunt a young and vulnerable creature."

I say, "But why does that make you a criminal? It sounds more like you're the victim."

"If you don't want to become a meal, you have to become a tiger."

Gun says, "So, you see, I've survived. If that's a crime, then I'm the criminal."

I'm not sure what he's told me.

Gun says, "How about you? What are your crimes?"

Excuse me? My crimes? "But I'm not admitting to being a criminal. I've never broken the law, which is my definition of being a criminal. I'm not sure what your definition is."

Gun smiles. Sneers. "What about the crime of wasting a life?"

I say, "What do you mean by that?"

"Well," Gun starts, then he digs into his breakfast. He devours the eggs first, scooping them up expertly with a fork. Next, he starts on a piece of toast.

I say, "I don't think I've wasted my life. I went to a good university, got a job with the most prestigious public art museum in Tokyo. Now I've become the director of a private museum. That's not wasted."

Gun shrugs and starts on his orange slices with knife and fork. He deftly slices off the rind.

Gun

The gangster asked Gun, "How did you become such a connoisseur of violence? If you don't mind me saying so, it's very unusual. Personally, I'd rather do it than watch it."

Gun said, "I don't know, exactly. I suppose, we all have our tastes." But he did know: it kept him balanced, it chased away emptiness.

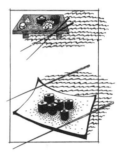

269

This curator, Yukawa, thought Gun, will never understand. He's doomed to exist in his structured cell of a life.

He has no promise of changing, no prospects for seeing anything other than his black-and-white existence. He's a colorblind artist, a tone deaf musician. A lover with no sex drive.

Without a word, Tabo clears away our breakfast and refills our cups with the last of the coffee from the pot.

When he's gone I start in: "Okay, okay. Maybe my life hasn't been as colorful as yours. So what? That doesn't mean mine is a waste."

Gun says, "I didn't say yours is a waste."

I want to scream.

Gun says, "That's for you to decide."

Very slowly, I say, "Will you just give me a straight answer—are you the criminal the police accuse me of associating with?"

"I don't know."

Gun says, "This is all I can tell you: my past hasn't been completely free from brushes with the law. For example, just after the war I ran an underground club that was raided and shut down. I spent a few days in jail for that. I've had run-ins with the police on lewdness and public decency charges, concerning my show. Nothing I'd personally categorize as criminal, of course.

"And as I've told you, I've had to deal with certain criminal elements to stay in business. That surely got the attention of the police." He pauses. "Does that answer your question?"

I don't know. I'm getting tired, despite the coffee rush. But I push on, bravely. "What exactly do you mean by having to 'deal' with criminal elements?"

Gun shakes his head. "That's not important, or relevant. The point is, if you aren't guilty of anything, why are you so worried about it?"

"Why am I worried about it? Why do you think?" I spout loudly. "Do you think I like having cops watching my every move, following me around, confronting me where I live? Huh?"

Gun locks his hands behind his head again.

I say, "Well? How should I react to cops harassing me like that?"

"I see your point."

A point? That's all I've got? A point?

Gun speaks again; his voice sounds like it's coming from far away. "I've had to do certain things to get what I wanted, I suppose we all do that to a certain degree. No one gets through life pure. I've incurred some debts, our family has incurred some debts."

It doesn't even sound like he's talking to me. Debts ... who's talking about debts?

I need to leave, or go crazy.

I try once more to get some specifics. "What exactly do you mean by doing certain things to get what you wanted? What kind of debts are you talking about? Specifically."

Gun says, "The specifics aren't important. If you want to blame me for the police intimidation, then go right ahead. Do you want me to talk to them? See if I can straighten out your problem?"

I sigh audibly.

271.

When I sigh, Gun's face flames red with anger. He says, "How dare you sigh at me. How insulting." He stands and tightens the sash of his robe.

He says, "You know I've always said that there is madness and genius in everyone. I was wrong. You're the first person I've met who has neither. You're perfectly ordinary. Absolutely and entirely ordinary."

He turns and walks out of the sitting room.

Off Balance

When I get bored of sitting in the sitting room by myself, I decide I might as well do my job while I'm here. Maybe I can finish cataloging Gun's collection of Views; then I won't have to come back. That's a pleasant thought.

Tabo walks into the sitting room and tells me that Gun is working in his office. And that if I need anything, he—Tabo—will be more than happy to help me. He yawns. I tell him I need to get into the storage room; he says he'll unlock it. I tell him I'm going to get my notes. He nods and shuffles off.

When I stand up, my legs tremble slightly, tingling from sitting cross-legged. I go outside to my car and get my briefcase. I also pick up the packages of Views wrapped in my raincoat.

Tabo isn't around as I walk back into the house and into the gallery. The storage room is unlocked. I close the door behind me. In the storage room, I put out my briefcase and the Views on the table.

In the intense quiet of the storage room, Gun's description of me rings in my ears—absolutely and entirely ordinary.

Is that worse than practically worthless?

Gun

Gun asked the gangster, "When you get violent, as part of the job I mean, do you get angry?"

The gangster lit a cigarette. "Angry? At the punk I'm beating up?"

"Yes."

He exhaled a long, thin cloud of smoke. "I used to. Now I try not to get too wrapped up in it."

I open the packages and spread out the Views I find inside. I don't take time to inspect them as I insert

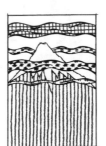

them into Gun's collection in the last file drawer. Then I fold up the wrapping paper and put it in my briefcase.

I try to catalog for awhile. I do a cursory job, allotting myself five minutes on each. Enough time to do a perfectly ordinary job.

Ordinary. There's no crime in being ordinary. At least I haven't had to associate with criminals to keep a club open. At least I don't treat my daughter like a servant, as Akiko does. At least I don't bully my employees, as Ichiro does.

The more I think about it the angrier I get. I want to know the truth. I want to expose their lies. I want to hurt them—Gun, Ichiro, Akiko. All of them.

Akiko

Akiko said, "I'm fighting the darkness, and she doesn't help me. She makes it worse because she's already given in. She's been seduced by it. She'll never come back out."

Gun said, "I understand."

Ichiro grunted.

Akiko said, "We must deal with her now."

Akiko must tell me the truth; she is hiding behind the most lies. But I need a stick to hold over her.

Haruna.

I can threaten Akiko that I'll tell Haruna about her father. That might work. Something will work, if only I can find out what it is.

Cataloging, planning the museum, that's all I should be doing. I should just do my job, my perfectly ordinary work. Nothing wrong with that.

But I can't, not until I know what's going on.

Akiko stroked Haruna's hair. "Nothing outside the ryokan can hurt you as much as what's inside you."

Haruna looked at her mother.

Akiko went on, "No, I'm not threatening to send you out again. You may stay home. But your biggest fight will be for your own soul. No one will be able to help you. You have to find your own way."

Haruna stroked her mother's hair.

Takenoko stood on the ridge. The light had changed suddenly from the hazy, muddle of summer colors to the crispness of autumn, when each color is sharply defined. He felt a sudden surge of energy. He sat down to sketch.

The topmost cone of Mt. Fuji had a dusting of snow. He sketched the snow line, where it disappeared and reappeared following the mountain's creases.

The energy left as suddenly as it came. The urge to give up overwhelmed him.

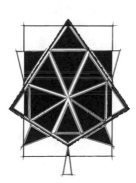

Haruna and I have something in common. We're both being taken advantage of, exploited. Haruna works every day, probably twelve hours a day, maybe more. It's hard work.

And here am I, slaving away for Ichiro, and getting insulted for it. And being told lies. Nearly getting arrested.

Haruna deserves the truth. I deserve it.

Gun believes he is a creative genius. What does he have to show for it? His tacky club. His ridiculous show. Who is he to call me ordinary, without a shred of genius or madness?

I'll show him. I'll show them. Two can play at the game.

I open all the file drawers of Gun's collection. From the middle of each drawer, I take one of the Views. When I have four, I carefully roll them up and put them into the packaging.

I wrap up the newly packaged Views in my raincoat, pick up my briefcase, and sneak out of the house. Neither Gun nor Tabo are around to see me to the door. In my car, I put the Views in the back seat and the briefcase on the passenger seat.

Driving away, I feel guilty and excited at the same time. I've just committed an act that's rather unordinary. It might even have a hint of genius, or madness.

I drive smoothly away from Atami, and turn onto the road toward Heda. A bath would be nice when I get there. But I have work to do.

Takenoko

The wave of emotions reached his fingers. The emotions took control of the brush.

Anger
  Hate
    Passion
      Shame
        Joy
          Fear
            Brush strokes

The drive is peaceful, hardly another car on the road. The drive gives me time to think. I think about what I'm going to say to Akiko. I think about what Gun told me.

Anger, and fear (of going too far?) and other unidentifiable emotions rise and ebb.

When I arrive in Heda, I feel spent. All my energy has been sapped by the tide of emotions. And also my lack of sleep. I stop at the coffee shop. Nothing like a cup of coffee, a slice of cheesecake, and a generous helping of gossip to get the blood flowing again.

The coffee shop owner recognizes me. She welcomes me several times, then asks if I want the usual. Now that's what I call professional service. I say, "Why not?" While she fixes my coffee and cheesecake, she chats about the weather. I nod and give her little words of encouragement.

When she serves me, she asks how things are going with my work for the Onos. I say, "Fine, but …"

"But what?"

I shrug. "Oh, nothing." I swallow a bite of cheesecake. It's on the dry side, so I take a sip of coffee. "Well, it's Akiko Ono, she's quite unusual."

The coffee shop owner grins. I grin too.

She says, "Yes, Akiko's unusual. Yes, strange. Has she told you more stories about her husband dying at sea?"

"No. You're sure there never was a husband?"

"Yes. Check at the family registrar's office, if you don't believe me."

I wave my fork. "Sorry, I didn't mean that. I believe you. What about Akiko's mother? Whatever happened to her?"

She refills my cup. "As far as we know they put her away somewhere, a home probably. This was many years ago, of course. No one knows if she's still alive. She'd be very old. She's probably dead."

The coffee shop owner points to my plate. "Something wrong with your cheesecake?"

"No, no. It's delicious." I dig in.

"You know," she says, "Akiko's mother used to entertain her guests quite, um, liberally."

I pause, my mouth full of cheesecake.

"That's who fathered Akiko, an anonymous guest. Ichiro and Gun, too. Fathered by other guests."

Akiko

Akiko said, "What I hate most are the smiles and the snickers when I'm in the village searching for her. They pretend to be helpful, saying, 'She went that way,' or, 'She's digging in the Yamada's flower bed.' Like a dog, they're thinking. Behind my back they smile. Behind their doors they laugh."

Ichiro said, "I can put a stop to the laughter."

Gun nodded.

Akiko said, "We need to do something about her. I can't handle her by myself."

Akiko

The sleek guest from Nagoya said to Akiko, "I enjoyed your show tonight."

Akiko thanked him.

He wrapped the flat of his hand around the warm teapot. He smiled at her. When his hand was warm, he slipped it down the front of her kimono.

277.

I ease down the cheesecake with a gulp of coffee. "Really? They don't know who their fathers are? Other than unnamed guests?"

She nods. "She probably doesn't know herself. Think about it. Night after night of entertaining guests. So many guests."

And Haruna? I wonder.

As if she can read my mind, she says, "Akiko took up right where her mother left off."

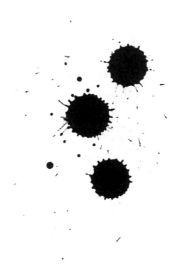

After my cheesecake and coffee, I drive up the hill toward the inn. The sun is bright, and lethargy drags me down. I pull over to the side of the road and turn off the engine. I recline my seat about forty-five degrees. The sun feels good. I close my eyes.

I wake up after only a few minutes; my neck has a painful crick, and I've managed to get a headache. I roll down the window and take a couple of breaths of fresh air. It doesn't help. I drive up to Heda Onsen. I park on the gravel and get out.

Inside the inn, it's quiet. I wander from room to room, until I hear Haruna humming. I peek around the corner and watch her at work with the feather duster.

After watching her for a few moments, I walk back through the inn. I don't see Akiko; she's probably doing the morning shopping. I go out to my car to get the Views and my briefcase.

Back in the inn, I find the storage room where Akiko keeps most of her collection. I put the packages of Views in the cabinet. Then I find the room where I saw Haruna.

"Hello," I say.

She smiles. "Hello."

"How are you?"

"Fine. And you?"

My headache's getting worse. "Can we talk for a few minutes?"

She says, "Talk?" She continues dusting.

"Can we get away from here to talk? Just for a few minutes?"

She hums. And dusts. Hums and dusts.

"What I have to say should be discussed in private. It's important."

She pauses her humming and dusting long enough to say, "I'm happy here."

"I know that." My voice trembles. "You've told me that many times. I'm only asking that we get away for a few minutes. It's not for the rest of your life."

She hums and dusts.

You were right.

Haruna sat up. The voice wasn't from one of the boys. It hadn't sounded like a person at all. The voice had a strange ... shape. Pointed. Sharp.

They were wrong.

The voice didn't seem to come from anywhere.

Yes. You'll see. They'll see.

She felt comfortable, safe.

Go home. You'll be fine there.

Haruna

At home, Haruna no longer heard the taunts of the kids. She no longer heard her teacher scolding her. The voice with the pointed shape had quieted. She would be fine.

Haruna's mother said, "I want you to be happy, but more importantly, I want you to find your own way."

Haruna thought for a moment. "How will I do that?"

"You'll know, someday. If you listen. If you watch."

I'm getting very irritated. "Don't you want to know the truth? The truth about your family?"

She dusts and hums.

"The truth about you, and your mother?"

She hums and dusts.

"What about your grandmother? Do you know anything about her?"

She pauses. "My grandmother?"

"Yes, Haruna, your grandmother. She never got married, you know?"

She dusts, without humming. A minor victory.

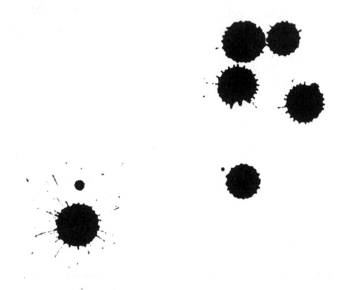

I say, "Your grandmother had sex with her guests. She likely didn't know who fathered your uncle Gun and your uncle Ichiro. They may have had different fathers. And your own mother—your grandmother may not have known who fathered her. Did you know your grandfather?"

Haruna dusts slowly.

"And, what about your own father? He didn't die at sea. Do you know that? Your mother was never married."

She hums loudly.

I grab Haruna's shoulders. She goes rigid, no longer humming or dusting.

"Don't you want to know the truth?"

She whimpers.

I turn her around gently. "The truth, Haruna." Haruna drops her duster. Her eyes are focused behind me. I turn.

I catch a glimpse of Akiko moving away from the door.

Haruna walked along the beach. The voice said, Walk slowly. She slowed. The moist sand and pebbles dampened her bare feet.

The boys came out of the cave. They hollered like wild animals as they descended on her. She stopped and faced them.

They surrounded her in a circle. She dropped her backpack. One boy picked it up and ran with it. The others followed.

They opened it up and started to spill the contents onto the beach. Then one screamed, "It bit me!"

The others screamed the same thing.

I run after Akiko. She enters the room just off the garden. I follow her. She sits at the table.

I say, "I've had enough of you spying on me."

"Oh? Spying?"

"Eavesdropping then."

She titters in a fake laugh I've heard her using for guests. "Eavesdropping in my own home? While you assault my daughter?"

"I wasn't assaulting your daughter."

Akiko

Akiko opened the door. There were two women from Heda.

One said, "Your daughter has been assaulting our sons. Biting them."

The other nodded.

Akiko said, "Haruna?"

The two looked at each other. One said, "Do you have another daughter?"

Akiko said, "They must have deserved it."

"She's dangerous. Keep her away from them."

"We're going to get her expelled from school."

Akiko slammed the door.

Akiko says, "You grabbed her, twisted her around, and berated her. Did it make you feel good?"

"I was only trying to get her to listen."

"Oh? I don't think she's deaf."

"I wanted her to listen to the truth."

She laughs. Heartily, not the fake titter. "Oh, the truth. Yes, of course, she must know the truth. And you know the truth? Did you have another talk with the old gossip at the coffee shop?"

"Yes," I say. "She told me some interesting things about you and your family. I believe her. It makes sense, from what I've seen."

Her voice quietly serious, Akiko says, "You can believe the version of the truth you want. It doesn't matter to me, or to Haruna." She pauses, glaring at me. "Don't ever touch her again."

The tone of her voice and her glare make me hesitate. I have no idea where I'm going with this, or what it's going to get me.

I don't care.

I'm not going to let her intimidate me. I have my stick. "Don't you think Haruna should know the truth about her father? About you?"

"Haruna knows the truth."

"Your version of the truth."

"Haruna knows the truth. Leave her alone." Akiko's voice remains controlled, deliberate.

Mine, however, raises a couple of notches. "If she knows the truth, why does she tell me her father died at sea? That he was a fisherman? That's a lie isn't it?"

Akiko says, "You don't know what you're doing. You're disturbing a peace, a balance, that's taken many years to reach."

"What?"

She shakes her head. "You'll never understand."

I cross my arms and shift my weight from one foot to the other and back. "Tell me, then. Tell me what I don't know."

"You'll never understand."

Because I'm ordinary, and practically worthless?

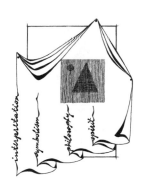

I try once again. "What peace? What balance?"

Akiko says in a low, spooky voice, as if she's talking to someone else, "The fight against darkness. It's seductive, but don't let it win. Fight it. It's a matter of balance, keeping your balance. Find your own way."

Akiko motions for me to sit down. I think maybe I should keep standing. It gives me an air of authority. A slight air, but an air all the same. But then if I do sit down, she might open up. My sitting would be a gesture of … I don't know … conciliation. Maybe that would be a good gesture to make.

I sit.

Akiko smiles. She must appreciate my gesture.

She says, "I'll tell you the truth. If you promise to stop assaulting Haruna."

Akiko

Akiko walked away from the school. She walked neither too slow nor too fast. She came to the home of one of the women who had accused her daughter. She looked straight ahead, even as the door opened.

"Your daughter is a vicious animal!"

Akiko kept walking.

"And you are nothing but a whore!"

Akiko stopped. The woman slammed the door.

Up the street, Haruna was watching.

My voice squeaks with desperation: "I wasn't assaulting Haruna. I was just talking with her."

"You violently and savagely shook her when she wouldn't listen to your vicious gossip."

"No, it wasn't like that at all. I just turned her around, gently. Ask her, she'll tell you."

Akiko says, "Promise me you won't assault her again."

"But—" There's no way to win this argument.

She's just twisting this whole thing around, I know she is, even though I'm getting fuzzy in the brain. "But, I didn't assault her. How can I promise I won't assault her again if I didn't assault her in the first place?"

Akiko is silent.

"Well, how can I?"

She smiles. "So, do you see my point?"

She made another point while I wasn't looking.

"Your point? No, I don't see your point."

Akiko waits a moment then says, "The point is quite obvious. What is assault to one person is a gentle touch to another person."

So?

She continues, "What is truth to one person is fantasy to another."

"Oh." That point. How did I miss that? "That's all fine and good," I say, not knowing what to say, "but what does all this have to do with Haruna?"

Through clenched teeth, Akiko says, "Everything I do is for Haruna."

I shake my head. "Everything Haruna does is for your benefit."

"No!" Akiko shouts. She looks like she could bite off my head.

"Yes," I shout back. "Haruna is your slave."

Akiko takes in a couple of deep breaths. "No, you don't know."

"Then tell me. You're keeping Haruna caged here. She's going crazy."

"No. You're the one driving her crazy. She stays balanced here, working in the onsen."

I jump on that. "This is the only life she knows. What she needs is to see the world, see there's more than dusting and scrubbing and doing stupid dances. She needs to get away from you."

Akiko says, "You'll push her off balance if you take her from the onsen."

"Balance? What are you talking about? What are any of you talking about? You're acting like you're in some bizarre movie. I'm just trying to do my job, and for that I get followed by the cops, who accuse me of cavorting with known criminals. And I'm being used as a dupe, a go-between in a ridiculous old family feud. You're all crazy!"

Akiko stands and points to the front door. "Go away. Never come back."

I've done it now. I leave her alone.

I have to show Akiko that she's wrong. That she's wrong about me, about what I'm trying to do. I'm trying to help Haruna, that's what I'm trying to do. Sure. That's what I'm trying to do.

I find Haruna in one of the rooms, dusting. I smile and say, "I'd like to show you a secret. Outside. In front. By my car."

She starts to say something, smiles, then puts down her duster and follows me out of the inn.

Haruna

As her mother pulled her away from the street, back to the onsen, Haruna felt a dark shape envelop her.

Haruna screamed and tried to pull away. Her mother held her tightly. Her mother was saying something in a voice that sounded so far away. "Don't listen, don't listen."

The shape was angular, evil. Haruna screamed again.

"What's the secret?" she says, standing by the car.

"It's inside." I open the passenger side door. I point to the floor. When she bends over to look, I push her

in. As gently as I can. I don't want to be accused of assault. Kidnapping is bad enough.

Haruna screams. I shut the door and run to the driver's side. Haruna has twisted around and is grabbing for the door handle. I get in and pull her toward me and hold her tightly with one arm. I manage to get the key into the starter.

She screams again as I put the car in gear. I spray gravel when I step on the gas.

Haruna

Haruna could barely hear her mother: "I'm sorry. I'll make it up to you. Let me help you fight it."

Haruna tried to think of soft shapes. But the angular shapes were strong, they gnawed her flesh, ripped her open to the bone.

Haruna cries with her head in her hands. I keep one hand on her shoulder, and one hand on the steering wheel. I drive as fast as I can. We get out of town in a few seconds.

"It's okay, Haruna. I just want to show you there's more to the world than your mother's ryokan."

Her shoulders shake and her chest heaves as she tries to get air into her lungs.

"I'm sorry," I say. "I'm not going to hurt you."

She sobs.

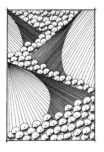

I pull into the first officially designated Scenic View I come to. It's rated a three. I park in the best spot to take in the panorama.

"There," I say. "See what I mean? Look at this incredible scenery."

"No," she says, still with her head in her hands.

"Please," I say, "just one look."

She moans.

I reach across her shoulders. I gently push her back into the seat. She keeps her hands up to her eyes.

I gently pry them away. She starts taking in sharp, little breaths, as if she's panting, hyperventilating. Her eyes are closed.

"Haruna," I say. "Just one look. See how green it is."

She opens her eyes. They look all black. No white. No iris.

"What?" I say.

She opens her mouth and bites my forearm. Bites hard. I yelp and yank my arm away from her. It feels like the bone is broken. I hold my arm and rub it; my eyes flood with tears of pain.

I blink back the tears, my ears are ringing with pain. I push up my sleeve. The teeth marks are red gashes in the skin.

When I look up, Haruna is gone.

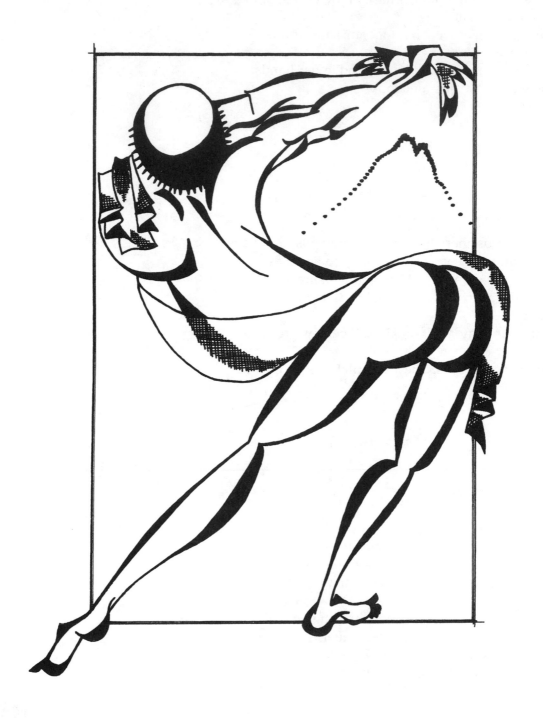

The Investigator's Report

I jump out of the car, saying, "Oh boy, oh boy, oh boy." I'm in trouble.

I look left and right, all around the car. I don't see Haruna. I squat down and check under the car. She's not there.

I look down the steep hillside. She could be hiding in the thick, green underbrush. What color kimono was she wearing?

Dark green.

Great.

I look in the woods near the car. No Haruna. She's just disappeared.

Back in the car, I check my arm. It throbs and has started to swell. I drive around the lot once, then slowly back toward Heda. I don't see her along the way.

She couldn't have gone far. When I get to the edge of the town, I double back to the Scenic View. I search the woods near the parking lot without finding a trace of her. The muggy air makes me sweat until I'm drenched. The bugs are big enough to devour me.

I drive back to Heda.

I have to tell Akiko what happened; I don't know if Haruna can find her own way back home.

As I start turning into the drive of the ryokan, I see Akiko pulling Haruna in the front door. I drive past the inn, and keep driving out of Heda.

I decide to drive straight to the museum. I need to get to Ichiro before Akiko has a chance to talk to him. I have to tell him my side of the story first.

I don't know why I did that to Haruna.

I'll beg Ichiro to give me a second chance. I'll get on my knees. I need to start over.

I don't know why I got so angry.

Besides explaining about Akiko and Haruna, I'll have to explain what happened with Gun. And with Kumi. I didn't leave on the best of terms with either of them. Funny, I don't remember exactly what happened at Gun's. And it was only this morning. I think. Yes, it was just a few hours ago. It seems so much longer ago. All I remember is that we had a disagreement. I wonder if Gun has talked to Ichiro yet.

And I can't remember what happened with Kumi. That seems even further in the past. Again, I don't remember the details. My mind is spinning.

I've got a lot of apologizing to do.

I'll make one big apology for everything I've said and done in the last twenty-four hours. That will make it easy. I'll plead temporary insanity.

Chalk it up to one extremely bad day. One day out of a lifetime. That's not such a bad record. Certainly less than one percent. Let's see, that's one day out of about … 1,000? No, 100,000. Er, 10,000. Kumi could figure it out.

Whatever. One big apology and start over.

Easy.

I drive past Numazu and continue on to the museum. My arm is numb, still swollen. At least the bleeding stopped almost immediately. My sleeve is dotted with blood spots.

I recall my suspicion that Ichiro is testing me by sending the Views. A thought: What if the whole family is part of the test?

I'm failing.

Ichiro gave me the job too easily. Did he actually give me the job? I can't recall exactly what he said. Perhaps this is still the interview process. But I've already quit my other job, with no way to get it back. I've already quit my other life.

This is my life. I can't fail before I even get started.

Yes, everyone is in on the test. Not just the Ono family: the chief curator, my colleagues, Junko. Ichiro could have convinced them to be part of the test. So if I fail, can I go back to my old life?

That doesn't seem likely. If I fail the test, I've failed completely. The test is more than part of the interview, it's a test of me and my life. If I fail the test, then my entire life is a failure.

If this is a test, then I need to start performing better. I need to recapture the professionalism I used to pride myself on.

I need to patch things up, starting with Ichiro. He has to see that I'm the professional curator he needs: a curator with confidence and professionalism. He did say he hires the best to make the best decisions.

As for the others—Kumi, Gun, Akiko, Haruna—I need to start by apologizing to Ichiro for my actions. I definitely have to personally apologize to each, maybe bring a gift. That would be a nice touch, a gift.

Start fresh. Apologize. Gifts.

Okay. A plan.

Akiko asked Ichiro, "Do you have someone in mind who will buy the Views?"

"I know an art collector with whom I have made preliminary inquiries."

Gun asked, "Who?"

"I must keep that information to myself. But he knows other collectors who might also be interested."

Akiko asked, "Are they art lovers or merely investors?"

Ichiro asked, "Does it matter?"

Gun said, "I see Akiko's point. Someday, when we've made our fortunes, we will want to get them back."

Ichiro said, "We can worry about that when the time comes."

The Views I've been receiving must be a test of my honesty and loyalty. Surely, Ichiro doesn't think I

would sell them and keep the money. They are valuable, each must be worth my year's salary. Maybe he thought that I would keep them for a private collection.

I try to remember what I did do with the Views … It takes me several minutes to remember that I put the first few into Ichiro's collection, then I put some into Gun's, then I took some from Gun's collection and put them into Akiko's collection.

I wonder if that is a passing score on Ichiro's test.

Akiko said, "We should each get a third. We can individually decide which ones to sell, which ones to keep."

Gun said, "I agree. Of course. One-third."

Ichiro nodded.

Akiko said, "We can draw stones. Three different colors, 120 each. Put them in a bag and draw one at a time."

Gun said, "There are certain Views I prefer for my share. Why don't we go through them one at a time? If a person wants it and the others don't then that person can have it. Up to a third share."

Ichiro said, "And if two or all of us wants a View, then we can draw Akiko's stones."

As part of my plan, I need to make a clean slate of everything, including the Views. I'll approach Ichiro

lightly, laughing: "Guess what? Ha. Ha. I've been getting these packages delivered to me … No, I don't know from whom … What's inside? Well, you'll never believe it—each package contains one of Takenoko's 365 Views of Mt. Fuji … I know, isn't it strange? … What have I been doing with them? Well, I didn't want to bother you with them, you know me—making decisions, that's what I get paid for—so I've been putting them back into the collection I thought appropriate … yes, I know, a great idea, thank you."

That's how it'll go.

That's it, my plan. The key is to treat Ichiro as an ally. Show ample respect for him, as he showed confidence in me. That's how I'll pass the test.

I'll show him that his confidence hasn't been wasted. I'll be aggressive, I'll make decisions, I'll hire staff, I'll set the opening date for the museum, I'll develop a marketing plan, I'll design informational brochures (four-color), I'll arrange ukiyo-e experts to speak.

I'll put a coat closet in my office.

When I get to the museum, I march up to the front door. Someone's reflection in the glass gawks at me. That someone has tousled hair, wild eyes, and an unshaven face. He's wearing a wrinkled and stained suit.

My confidence in my wonderful plan vanishes. My confidence in myself follows right behind.

The security guard opens the door. If he's disgusted by my appearance, he doesn't show it. What a professional.

I walk to my office through the unusually quiet museum. There are the power saws, no steer-headed contractor.

It's eerie.

I sit at my desk, trying to recall my plan. I know I had a list of actions, but not one of them comes to mind.

I take an inventory of stains on my suit: blood, grass, sweat, egg.

Surely by now Ichiro has heard from Gun and Akiko. He must be deciding what to do with me.

My plan … my plan. What was my plan?

Ichiro picked up the robot toy. He flipped the start switch, and the limbs began to swing. He put it on the table. The toy took a couple of steps then fell onto its side, its limbs still swinging.

To his employees, Ichiro said, "This is why I called you here." He raised a fist then brought it down onto the toy. The plastic splintered and cut the side of his hand.

A severed arm of the toy whirled on the desk.

I don't have to wait long. Ichiro comes into my office carrying a large, white envelope. He sits in the chair across from my desk. He doesn't say a word. He looks like he's mulling over how to start yelling at me. That's a bad sign—he's got a lot to say.

Hoping to stall him, I ask, "Um, where's the contractor today?"

Ichiro says, "He ran out of things to do. That is, he needs more decisions from you before he can go on. I said I'd call him when you put in an appearance."

Decisions—weren't they part of my plan?

That's right. Decisions are part of my plan. But that isn't the first step, no, I remember now. Apologize.

Here goes: "Um, I'm afraid I have to make certain apologies. To begin with, I've really been under a lot of stress lately, what with changing jobs, moving to a new city, and having so many responsibilities—not that I can't handle responsibilities, I assure you that I can. It's just that it all came at once. Anyway, I've recently made several bad choices in my actions; choices that I wouldn't consider normal for me, so I can only blame the recent situation."

I pause. Ichiro just stares at me.

Starting with a stutter, I go on: "It's-it's-it's important not to jump to any conclusions about my behavior; I must emphasize that it's totally uncharacteristic of me. Of course, I will make my apologies directly to the members of your family. But first I must apologize to you."

I stand up and perform a deep penitent bow. "I am very sorry."

I sit down. Ichiro taps his fingertips together. Why doesn't he say anything?

Tap, tap, tap. I say, "Strange things have been happening. For instance, some of Takenoko's Views have been delivered to me. I should have told you when the first one showed up, but I kind of panicked, you can understand why. My first day or so on the job and a very valuable painting shows up? One of the very paintings I'm entrusted with?"

I continue, "The Views showing up on my doorstep added to my stress, as you can imagine. And then, yes then, the police start following me. Yes! Can you believe it? Yesterday they confronted me, claimed I had been seen cavorting—their word—with known criminals. Me! I don't know any criminals. I'm a perfectly honest man, at least as honest as the next man. Maybe even too honest for my own good."

The noose tightens.

Ichiro finally speaks. "You seem very upset. Perhaps you should start over, concentrate on telling me the facts. Tell me everything that happened, from the beginning."

At last. I feel he might actually be on my side. I take a deep breath. "Well, first I must apologize for my appearance. I was up all night. I haven't had a chance to go to—"

Ichiro impatiently waves his hand. "From the beginning."

Ichiro

Ichiro Ono stood in front of the painting hanging in the tokonoma alcove. The painting showed a boy, near his own age, walking behind a man, probably the boy's father. An overflowing sack of charcoal on the man's back threatened to topple him over. The boy should have been helping steady the load and pick up pieces that fell out. Instead he was staring at Mt. Fuji.

Ichiro stood in front of the painting from sunrise to sunset. Toward the end of the day, his legs shook, and trembled, but he willed them not to collapse. He willed away his hunger and thirst.

I don't know where to start. Like a tangled rope, it's not easy to find the beginning or the end. But I try. I tell him about finding the View the morning after my first night in the dorm, then how the others showed up. I tell him about being followed, about not getting any sleep, about being confronted by the police, about my confronting Kumi, and Gun, and Akiko. It all comes out in a jumble.

Ichiro says, "You accused Gun of being a criminal?"

"Well, no, not really. I mean I asked if he had any idea who the police were talking about."

"The police didn't tell you who this criminal is supposed to be?"

"No."

"Then why would you accuse my brother?"

"No, I definitely didn't accuse your brother of being a criminal." But I think I did.

Ichiro says, "You did ask Kumi if she thought Gun, or any other member of our family, is the criminal referred to by the police. In fact, didn't you force her to talk about it, even when she didn't want to?"

"No," I say. "I didn't force anyone to do anything." But I think I did.

"Didn't you continue to berate her, even when she begged you to stop?"

"No, no. Certainly not." But I think I did.

Ichiro says, "And what about all these rumors you've been spreading about our family?"

"Rumors?'

Ichiro clenches and unclenches his jaw, like he's chewing gristle. "Rumors, gossip, whatever you want to call it. About our family's tragedies."

"I'm sorry. I really didn't mean to sound as if I were spreading rumors. Not me. I'm not a rumor and gossip person. It's just that, well, I heard them, and I was simply letting others know such rumors exist."

To that silly response, I'm sure that Ichiro will ask, "What's the difference?" Instead, he changes the subject. "I'll have you know the Numazu police have contacted me. They told me that a person named Yukawa who claims to be in my employ has been acting quite strangely."

"Oh?" That's all I can think of to say.

Ichiro says, "Can you imagine how embarrassing it is for me to say, 'Yes, the person to whom you refer is indeed in my employ'?"

"I'm sorry," I mumble.

Ichiro says, "Do you know what I had to say to this officer of the law?"

"No."

"I had to say, 'Yes, Yukawa is in my employ. I'm sorry he's acting strangely and disturbing the peace of the community. As his employer I'll assume all responsibilities for his actions.' That's what I had to say."

Oh.

"Now, if I can do that for my employees, what should I expect from them in return?"

"The same?" I try hopefully.

I don't know what else to say. I have to say something good, although I sense I'm losing grip on my plan. If I ever had a grip on it at all. "Yes, well, I have to thank you for dealing with the police. I'm sorry that you had to be embarrassed by my actions. It will never happen again."

Ichiro taps his fingertips together.

I say, "I just want you to know, I'm ready to start over. I feel I've gotten off course in the last few days. But I'm over that."

His fingertips silently tap, tap, tap.

Over the phone, Gun said, "You have the envelope?"

Ichiro said, "Yes."

Gun said, "Open it."

Inside was a list of the collectors of the Views. Over the years the paintings had dispersed over Japan. A few had ended up overseas.

Gun said, "Most of them are quite willing to sell us back their Views at our offering price. However ..."

Ichiro said, "A few might have to be encouraged?"

"Yes. Encouraged."

I say, "Things will be different. I'll apologize to everyone. I'll write down my plan of action and stick to it. I promise."

Ichiro says, "That's all fine and good, but ..."

But?

"But what other things have happened or could happen that I don't know about? How much risk should I take? In fact, what do I really know about you?"

"You have my résumé." That's a stupid thing to say.

Ichiro puts the envelope he's been holding onto my desk.

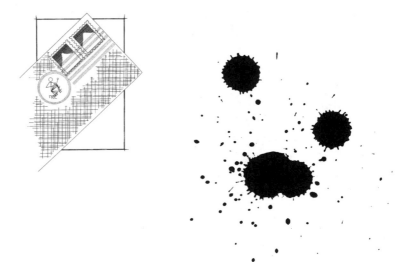

Ichiro stares at the envelope. I stare at the envelope. I'm afraid to ask what's in the envelope. He'll tell me sooner or later. Later would be fine with me.

Ichiro says, "I had a private investigation service recommended by Gun look into your background."

What? A chill courses through me as if I'm getting sick. I am getting sick.

Ichiro says, "They were very fast, very thorough."

Thorough?

Ichiro opens the envelope. There are several pages inside. "First," says Ichiro, reading the top page, "there is a Miss Junko Iwata, 29, a performance artist in Tokyo, also known as the Pink Doughnut Girl. She has known you for ten years, and claims she and you lived together, out-of-wedlock, for five."

He glances at me then continues: "Miss Iwata describes you as a hanger-on, with no friends of your own. You had no loyalty to her, or to your own family, whom you haven't seen for several years. She sums it up by saying you're, quote, practically worthless, unquote."

He reads on. "She says you've been harassing her since you left Tokyo. Calling her number and hanging up. She had to get an unlisted number."

Junko, why? Oh, Junko.

Ichiro turns the page over. "Next, there is a Nobuhiro Tanaka, the chief curator at the National Art Museum in Tokyo, your previous supervisor. He claims you were a listless employee, unmotivated, argumentative, and had no loyalty. He says you assaulted him with a noxious odor when giving your notice of termination. He also claims you've been making prank phone calls."

Ichiro clears his throat. "He lists several other instances to back up his claims. I won't go into them. Next, there are several of your ex-colleagues, who back up the chief curator's descriptions of your malcontent attitude. They've also been on the receiving end of your prank phone calls."

Oh. No. Oh.

Next, the report details the investigator's interviews with my neighbors in Tokyo, childhood and college friends, professors. All of them have nothing good to say about me. Nothing. And I've never so much as kicked a dog in my entire life.

Ichiro says, "The investigator says you've been roaming the streets at night asking strange questions at bars and coffee shops about the Ono family. And driving around the countryside at all hours of the night."

That must have been who followed me in the white Corolla.

Ichiro looks at me. "What do you have to say?"

"It's not true. Well, it's all exaggerated. It must have been the way he asked the questions. You can get people to say anything, if you ask the question the right way."

"So it is true?"

It can't be true. I have to fight back. "No, it isn't true. Everything has been taken out of context. For  instance, I didn't assault the chief curator. I just happened to have a very spicy lunch, with lots of garlic—oh, and a beer or two—and when I was giving my resignation speech, I got so excited, well, a belch just slipped out."

Ichiro looks bored.

"So you see," I say, "it was an accident. Nothing intentional. Certainly not an assault. And the same with those other incidents. They've all been exaggerated and put in the worst possible light. It's as if there's a conspiracy against me."

Ichiro raises an eyebrow.

Ichiro

Gun asked, "How do you want to handle it?"

Ichiro squeezed the phone. "What about the investigator who compiled the list, would he be willing to do the encouraging?"

"No. That's not his style. But there are the others, the ones who handled your other problem."

"Then use them. They handled it quite professionally."

"Yes," Gun said, "they are professionals."

I say, "The same thing happened today at your sister's ryokan." Ichiro leans forward. "You see, I was speaking with Haruna and I just happened to put my hands on her shoulders, affectionately, gently, just to emphasize a point, and I turned her a little, just a little, so I could see into her eyes as I talked.

"But Akiko accused me of manhandling—assaulting—her daughter, and you can see from what I just told you that I did no such thing, not even close. But there you have another example of how people's versions of the truth differ depending on their point of view."

I'm not making any sense; I'm digging my grave deeper.

Ichiro says, "But the pattern is clear. If so many people say the same thing about you, there must be some truth in it."

Oh no. I'm losing everything. I reach for the investigator's report. "Why don't I go through these charges one at a time and give you my side of the story?" I thumb through the report. My life has come down to a few pages of gross exaggeration and lies.

Ichiro reaches for the report and pulls it away. "That won't be necessary."

"But how can I undo the damage?"

Ichiro slowly shakes his head.

Ichiro folds the report back into the envelope. "It's largely out of your hands at this point."

What's that mean?

Ichiro starts to stand up. "For now, I want you to stay away from Kumi."

Kumi, oh Kumi. "Why?"

Ichiro is standing. Behind my desk, I feel small.

"Just do what I say. You're still in my employ. Do what I tell you."

I stand up and say, "Yes, sir. Stay away from Kumi. You're right. I'll just do my job. As you say, I'm still in your employ. I'll put together a plan of action. I'll get things moving around here."

Ichiro doesn't say a word as he walks out the door.

I slump into my chair. I could easily throw up.

That didn't go very well.

Some Inner Voice

Ichiro has been gone for a quarter hour. Exactly. I've watched the minute hand crawl over each one of the tick marks.

Watching time pass for a quarter hour is quite difficult. After only a few seconds my eyes wandered away from the watch face. I had to force myself to keep focused on it. Keeping focused on a single point for fifteen minutes is something of an achievement, I believe. It could also be considered torture. I don't know what else to do right now.

But I can't go on watching time crawl forever. I would go insane. Or am I already insane? No, if I'm asking myself that question I can't be, can I?

Takenoko

Just put down the brush.

Takenoko paused in his work. Where did the voice come from?

You can stop painting if you want.

Takenoko lowered his brush. Then a thousand voices screamed at once. Whispered. Cried.

He covered his ears. The voices got louder.

A voice inside my head says to me (whom else?): "Get away from the museum. Leave now."

I've never before heard a voice inside my head. This voice has quite a pleasant sound. A gentle yet firm voice. A voice that I trust. I wish I'd heard the voice before. I could get to like the voice.

I drive slowly away from the museum. I'm not sure where I should go. The voice inside my head keeps to itself.

I decide to drive back to my room. I can finally get to the cleaners.

I can still salvage this job. I can still salvage this life.

As I drive into the Ono Robotics plant, I realize that Ichiro didn't bring up my disagreement with Gun, or my recent problem with Haruna. Perhaps Gun and Akiko hadn't talked to Ichiro yet.

When they do, things will only get worse. I'll have to deal with that when it comes up. Should I have a plan, or worry about it when it happens?

I park in the dormitory lot. In my room, I see that no more Views have shown up. Maybe things are starting to turn around.

There's a knock on my door. I open it. It's the guy from down the hall. He has bits of food stuck between his teeth. He says, "I've got a bunch of packages delivered to my room for you." He walks away. I follow him.

He says, "They've been there since early yesterday, but I haven't seen you until now."

"I've been out."

"I guessed that," he says, opening his door. He points to a pile of tubes and flat packages.

There are six.

I gather up the packages and lug them back into my room. I put them on the floor, and sit next to them.

I think about opening them.

I think some more. Thinking kind of hurts.

I take a deep breath. That feels pretty good.

What I need is a shower, a nice hot meal, and then get to the cleaners. But first, just a little nap ...

When my little nap is over, the sun has set. My little nap lasted three hours. It's too late to go to the cleaners.

I'm feeling groggy, so I just lie there staring at the ceiling. My emotions are in turmoil, as if I've had a night of bad dreams.

Kumi, Gun, Haruna, Akiko, Ichiro: maybe they're just bad dreams.

Takenoko

Natsuko said, "You don't talk much anymore."

No?

"What do you see when you paint? Do you see everything before you start? Or do you have only an idea?"

Shapes

Colors

Dreams

Who are you?

Things really have gone wrong. Didn't I already have a plan? Yes, I remember, a plan to start over. But what was the plan? I should write down my plan this time, so I won't forget it.

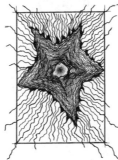

I get up and look around for my briefcase. It's not in my room. In my car? I can't remember if I left it there, or in my office at the museum, or ... or where was I before the office ...

My memory never failed me like this before. Not that I can remember.

Takenoko

The Ono woman asked, "You haven't missed a day?" She sat next to the stack of Views. "There must be 250 by now. No, closer to 300."

She looked at the top few paintings.

She laughed. Takenoko stopped his work.

She said, "What are you thinking? These are nothing like any paintings I've ever seen. How are you going to sell these? They're junk. You should have just painted me, like I told you."

I find the bottle of Suntory whiskey—now down to a few swallows—and take a sip. Things really have gone wrong.

The whiskey settles my nerves, calms my emotional turmoil. Okay, my plan. Apologies first. I will visit Kumi, Gun, Akiko, and Haruna. Then Ichiro. Gifts, that's right, I remember now. Gifts.

What kind of gifts? Fruit baskets? An expensive bottle of liquor? Flowers?

Whatever. First thing in the morning, I'll go shopping. No, first thing I'll go to the cleaners.

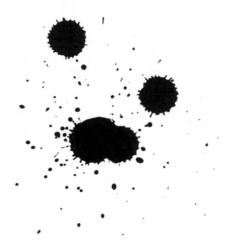

What I need to do is convince the people who were questioned by the private investigator to retract their statements. That's a great idea.

I'll ask them the same questions the investigator did, only put a more positive spin on them. For example, instead of asking, "What despicable things did Yukawa do in his job/schoolwork/relationship?" I'll ask, "What outstanding things did Yukawa do in his job/schoolwork/relationship?"

They'll answer, "Oh, he was quite steady as a worker/student/friend. He tried his best, and put up with a lot that would have driven others over the edge."

Yes, that's exactly how it will go.

I'm still groggy. But I need to continue working on my plan. I wish I had a pen and some paper to write this down. I feel it's very inspired. Surely there has to be a pen around here someplace.

I dig through all the drawers and cabinets. I find three golf balls, two soft porn comic books, assorted coins, a couple of pop music cassettes, and a pen from a bank. The end has been chewed on.

I tear a page out of the phone book, the blank "Important Phone Numbers" page. I write down my plan as I have it so far:

1. Suits to cleaners
2. Buy gifts
3. Apologize to Kumi, Gun, others
4. Interview Junko, co-workers, others

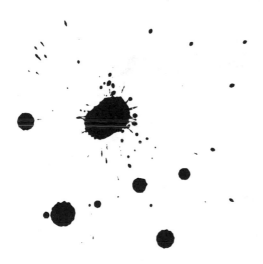

Okay, that's a good start. If all the steps go well, that might get me well on the way to a fresh start.

I'm set for tomorrow, then. If I work hard I might be able to get the list taken care of in one day. Just to have a written plan feels good.

I take a sip of whiskey to celebrate.

And another.

Might as well kill this bottle.

What happened over the year, this author speculates, is that Takenoko went through an entire lifetime of artistic evolution. In a typical artist's career, such changes usually come with a burst of production, during which the artist unconsciously abandons his or her rigid training and style. The artist comes to hear—and to trust—some inner voice.

To Takenoko, this happened several times, particularly during the end of the year, when his evolutionary process skipped ahead almost weekly.

The Suntory bottle is dead. Nothing left but vapor. The bottle's been a good friend. Maybe I should bury it.

I should get a good night's sleep for my full day tomorrow, but I'm awake now, full of energy. There was something else I needed to do … Oh, yes, the culvert and tunnels below the factory. I might as well continue exploring.

I can't remember exactly why I'm so interested in the tunnels. But I don't have anything else to do.

  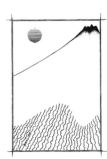 

I stand up quickly and almost step on the packages of Views. I'd forgotten about them. They should fit into my plan, somehow.

What I shouldn't do is make the same mistake I'd been making. I should take them to Ichiro.

To my plan, I add Step 5: Bring Ichiro results of my interviews and the packages of Views.

I really shouldn't leave the Views in my room though, in case anybody drops in, like that investigator. I need to keep them in a safe place until I've finished the first four steps. Each step must be followed in order.

The voice inside my head says, "Tunnels."

Great idea, voice. I'll keep them in the tunnels. I was going to explore them anyway.

Okay, let's see ... batteries. That's right, my flashlight batteries went dead in the culvert.

Okay, first step: buy new batteries.

I bundle up the six packages in my raincoat and take them out to the car. Then I drive to the nearest Seven-Eleven. I buy some batteries. I drive back to the plant.

I remember from my last trip down the tunnels that a map is vital. I run back into the plant and into the museum. I find the old plans of the sub factory and sketch the tunnel locations on my "Important Phone Numbers" page.

On my sketch, I draw an X through the first tunnel. The one with the dead end. Four other tunnels wait to be explored.

Back in my car, I sit for a few minutes. It seems no one is watching me—the white Mark II or white Corolla isn't lurking. I get out of my car.

I bring my map, the flashlight, the wrench, and the Views to the culvert entrance. I put everything down where the concrete is dry.

The grate to tunnel No. 2 opens as easily as the first one. I swing it aside, then I put the Views inside and close the grate. On my map I mark the place where I put them. No use doing something unless you do it right.

I feel good. Excited.

I start down the tunnel. It's the same as the first, so far, except the hum is slightly different. I don't know why, exactly; it's louder or has a different pitch.

It's warmer, too. Or maybe I'm warmer.

Several steps into the tunnel, I see something glitter on the floor.

It's a Fuji film box, with a picture of Mt. Fuji on it. The box is green.

Green as Haruna's kimono.

I put the film box down where I had found it. For some reason I want to note its location on my map. As founding member of the Culvert Explorers of Japan I should set certain standards.

I walk back to the tunnel entrance and pace back to the Fuji film box. Fourteen steps. I make a note on my map.

I resume walking, this time counting my paces as I go. Along the way, I note other treasures I find: shards of metal; a squashed, unmarked tin can; a light bulb (60 watt).

At 164 paces, the tunnel widens, then comes to a dead end. I note the location, guessing at the distance on the map. I've come about twice as far as I did in the first tunnel.

The hum is quite loud, and I swing my flashlight beam toward the sound. Along one wall, I can see another grate, the size of a ventilation duct.

As I get close to the duct the hum also gets louder.

Through the slats of the grate, I can see part of the robotic assembly line. Tubes span the length of the room. A conveyor line transports materials.

I watch the plant at work. No workers are on the assembly line, just robotic arms.

Air is blowing onto the top of my head. I shine the light up. There is a circular opening in the tunnel. I make a note on my map, and then reach up. There's a lip I can grasp to pull myself up.

I put my flashlight and map in my pockets, and I hoist myself up. With my foot on the ventilation grate, I push up as high as I can.

I reach around and find another duct taking off at right angles. This newer duct is smaller than the other, and is lined with smooth sheet-metal. There's just enough space for me to crawl in it.

After making a note on my map, I start to crawl forward.

After what would be 30 paces, I estimate, the duct makes a right angle. A continual breeze of warm air rushes past me. I can hear the "whoosh, whoosh" of a large fan rotating somewhere.

After another twenty paces, the duct turns upward. I stand up. From here I can see through another ventilation grate. This one leads directly into the main floor of the plant. I can see out one of the modular control boxes.

I think I see Kumi's computer work station. Yes, it is.

I check the ventilation grate to see if it will open; it holds solidly. I shine the flashlight around the grate and find four corner screws holding it in place. I loosen them with the wrench, put them into my pocket, and pull out the grate.

I stick my head into the plant.

The opening is large enough for me to squeeze through. But I don't want to go inside the plant.

I put the grate back in place—replacing the screws, but leaving them loose enough to unscrew with just fingers. I mark the location on my map.

I backtrack through tunnel No. 2. I open the main grate, close it behind me, and go to tunnel No. 3. The grate opens like the first two, and I'm soon pacing down the tunnel.

This tunnel seems much the same as the others, at least for the first hundred paces. Then I come across a knee-high pile of trash. I bend down to get a closer look.

The conical pile consists of strips of foil, empty cartons of instant noodles, crumpled handbills and flyers, cigarette packages. That kind of stuff. Typical gutter trash.

Typical nekobaba trash.

It's a neat pile of trash, the bits placed quite precisely. I touch it softly, on the tip. It's quite solidly constructed as well. I wonder if I've found the work of the nekobaba.

Well, anyway, it's a nice tidy pile of trash. I note its location on my map.

After admiring the pile once more, I walk ahead. The pile of trash has lightened my mood. I feel almost giddy, like I know a secret.

The pile of trash must have a purpose. Perhaps I should go back and make more notes. I could approach it like an archeological dig. Take exact measurements. Deconstruct it, noting the precise placement of each object.

That's a good idea. But first I'll go on ahead. Maybe there's more.

The hum isn't quite so loud in this tunnel, compared with No. 2. But the air seems fresher, tinged with pleasant odors to it. Cooking odors, I believe.

At 87 paces I find another pile of trash. It's a little larger than the first, rising to just over my knee. The bits of trash are pretty much the same sort of things.

The piles could be location markers, showing the way to some treasure. Or maybe they draw unwary visitors into a trap.

I make a note of my speculations on my map.

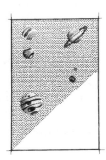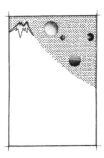

Takenoko

Takenoko hadn't eaten. For how long, he had no idea. He walked from the ridge back to the hut. There he found some tea and a few strips of dried squid.

He sipped the tasteless tea. He chewed on the leathery squid. He felt a rush of energy.

Yes, he can finish. He could finally paint Natsuko.

Then the energy became eclipsed with fear. He couldn't finish. He'd never paint Natsuko.

He ran from his hut, back to the ridge.

The construction engineer asked Ichiro, "What did you decide to do about the underground tunnels?"

Ichiro said, "It's much too expensive to fill them with concrete, or demolish them and backfill. And, as you tell me, they are structurally adequate—"

"More than adequate."

"Then we'll use them as material supply tunnels and ventilation shafts."

The engineer nodded. "It should work."

"One thing, I want an extensive map of the tunnels."

"I'll get the survey crews right on it."

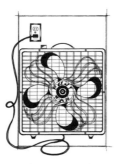

At exactly 200 paces the tunnel begins to widen as it had in No. 2. There, I find several of the trash pyramids. To be exact, there are 1, 2, 3 … 8. They range in size from a few inches, to one that comes up to my waist.

The trash piles remind me of a miniature representation of some ancient ruins. The monolithic ruins of the Trash People who disappeared mysteriously from the face of the earth.

There's also a strong odor coming from the area. I shine my light ahead of me. The tunnel ends a few feet away at a wall. I swing my light down the other side of the tunnel.

Running several feet is a rectangular ventilation grate. At about midpoint is an opening; a section of the grate has been removed and left on the tunnel floor.

Through the opening I can see the clear plastic supply chutes for the robotic company cafeteria. The foodstuff travels along the chutes to the appropriate access points in the cafeteria.

To get a meal, all you have to do is reach in, lift up the plastic cover, and grab what you want. To prove my own point, I reach in and pull out an apple.

After the discoveries of tunnels Nos. 2 and 3, I feel like I've done a good bit of exploring. A satisfying night of culvert exploration.

I should stop now. I need to get some sleep for my big day of putting my plan in action. I close up tunnel No. 3, and then I go back to tunnel No. 2. I open the grate and go inside. I gather up the Views and take them down to the end of the tunnel.

I push the packages into the metal-lined ventilation shaft. The Views should be safe there.

I close up the grate to tunnel No. 2 and leave my wrench and flashlight just inside the tunnel where I can reach them.

Outside of the culvert, the air is much fresher. I stand in the middle of the grounds and gulp in the sweet air. I could just lie down here to sleep. But that's probably not appropriate. I vow to act only in a socially appropriate manner from this moment forward.

But I'm not sure I trust myself to judge socially appropriate behavior, at least not by my recent actions. I wonder if there are books I can read on social appropriateness. I'm sure there are; books have been written about everything.

But it's probably just common sense, social appropriateness is, that is. And I should have plenty of common sense, being the perfectly ordinary person that I am.

On the way up to my room, I sneak back through the parking lot. Can't be too careful. I don't see anyone watching me.

A couple of steps inside the dormitory, a hand grabs my shoulder and spins me around.

There are two of them. I recognize both. They are two of Gun's friends, from the night we went club-hopping in Tokyo.

"Hello," I say.

They don't respond. They just push me ahead.

"Hey, take it easy."

One of them slugs me in the stomach. My lungs empty of air, and I drop to my knees. I can't breathe.

The two drag me off, one on each arm.

I'd like to ask them what's going on, but my lungs won't inflate. The pain is intense. I'm probably dying.

My legs are limp. They're dragging me toward my room. They didn't have to hit me. I would have gone peacefully. I was going there anyway.

When we get in front of my door, one of them knocks. I finally get a short breath of air back into my lungs. It tingles like when a foot falls asleep. But at least I'm going to live.

The door to my room opens. Ichiro is standing beside it. The two goons drag me into the room and throw me down onto a chair. I'm still gasping for air.

Besides Ichiro, Gun and Akiko are also there. The three of them stare at me without a shred of sympathy.

Dementia

I'm sitting in the chair, bent over at the waist. That position helps my breath come back. I gradually sit up straight. Ichiro is pacing in front of me. Gun and Akiko are seated not far from me. The two goons stand against the wall; both look quite smug. They're dressed in nice suits, but I can't identify which designer.

Ichiro says, "You've had a taste of what will happen if you don't cooperate."

Of course I'll cooperate. I nod.

Ichiro says, "We have several things to clear up. We don't want to resort to violence in our efforts, but we won't hesitate either."

In a voice still shaky from fright and the lung-collapsing blow to my stomach, I say, "There's no need for any kind of violence, of course. Absolutely, no need. I want to get things cleared up myself. So it's good you're all here. I've been thinking about a lot of things tonight, in fact that's where I was, out walking and thinking—"

Ichiro interrupts me, "Be quiet or I'll have them quiet you."

I nod. "Sorry." I smile at "them" the two goons. Then I smile at Gun and Akiko. She scowls. Gun has a wild look in his eyes.

Ichiro says, "First, we want to know why you have treated Haruna and Kumi so poorly."

I say, "That's one of the things I want to get cleared up myself. So I'm glad you brought it up." I squirm in my chair. In the light of my room, I can see I'm rather filthy, covered in dirt and sweat. I smell rather rank, too.

Ichiro says, "Well?"

"Oh, yes, well, um, let's see. First I have to apologize. I'm sorry, for anything that caused any problems. I didn't mean to harm anyone." I wish I had gotten the gifts; I could have handed them out.

I continue: "I was going to make my formal apologies tomorrow. I really was."

No one seems to care.

Akiko says, "An apology doesn't explain why you tortured Haruna and Kumi."

I don't think I tortured anyone. If anything, they'd been torturing me. But, I decide to save myself from another fist exploring my internal organs. "I'm sorry. Truly sorry. I didn't mean to torture them. I've been very stressed lately, and, well, I just went too far. You see, I was really trying to help them. They'd both been quite nice to me, and I was trying to return the favor."

Akiko huffs and rolls her eyes.

Ichiro stops right in front of me. "What are you talking about?"

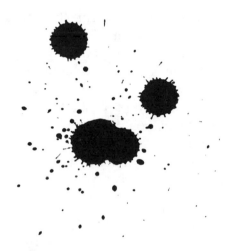

Of course, I don't know what I'm talking about. I have no idea why I did whatever I did. Maybe that's what I should say. Maybe I shouldn't say anymore. No, that's not a good idea. "To tell you the truth, I don't know what happened. I just snapped. I really have been under a lot of pressure lately. I haven't been myself. Not at all. I can assure you, nothing even remotely like what happened will happen again."

Gun says, "You've caused many problems for my nieces."

Ichiro says, "He's right."

"What kind of problems?" I ask tentatively.

Gun said, "So we meet again." He raised his glass.

Ichiro raised his drink off the table an inch or so, then put it down.

Gun said, "What's the matter? That's Napoleon brandy, aged twenty-five years."

Akiko said, "We aren't here to celebrate."

"We need consensus," Ichiro said. "On Yukawa."

"And on the Views," Akiko said.

"Yes," Gun said. "The two issues aren't separate."

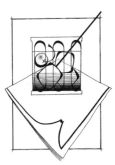

Ichiro says, "You've brought up many old issues that had no reason being brought up."

Akiko says, "You've upset the balance."

Gun says, "You've hurt these girls, maybe irreparably."

I plead, "But I don't know what I've done."

Ichiro says, "We'll show you."

Ichiro and Akiko leave the room. Gun takes over the pacing duties from his brother.

"So, Yukawa, you really went over the edge. I have to admit, I didn't think you had anything like this in your boring personality."

"It just happened. I didn't plan it."

"Right. Tell me why you did it, and don't give me that ridiculous line about stress."

Which "it" is he talking about? "I don't know."

Gun shakes his white locks.

Akiko and Ichiro return with Kumi and Haruna. Neither one looks at me. Haruna is dressed in her green kimono; her head hangs down, until her chin rests on her collarbone. Kumi is dressed in orange coveralls. She stares ahead blankly. They don't look so good.

Akiko and Ichiro help their two daughters into the chairs. The parents stand beside them.

Ichiro says, "Can you see what you've done now?"

Akiko says, "You pushed them into their unbalanced worlds. The worlds of darkness."

I want to sigh, but I remember that Gun didn't appreciate my last sigh. I also want a drink, but no one is offering. I try to speak rationally, even though I want to scream. "I'm sorry, I don't understand. What exactly do you mean?"

Akiko says, "Each of us had to struggle against the darkness. Haruna and Kumi are still in the early stage of their struggle."

Gun says, "By each, she means each of the Ono family members assembled in this room."

I ask, "What do you mean by darkness?"

Haruna starts to moan.

Akiko holds Haruna's head against her breast.

Ichiro trembles. He points at me, "You see what you've done?"

"No! I don't!"

Gun rubs his forehead, as he paces in front of me, taking two or three quick steps in each direction. "The darkness my sister refers to affects us in different ways. It isn't easy to explain. It's like a darkness to Akiko, so that's how she explains it. To me, it's an utter hopelessness."

Ichiro says, "To me, it's like a constant buzzing of electricity flowing through my brain."

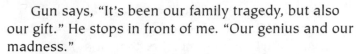

"I agree," Gun said. "It's time we got back the Views. They've been gone too long. I feel as if something is missing in my life."

Akiko nodded. "Yes. I still have a few, but they hardly seem complete without the others."

"We agree," Ichiro said. "The Views are more than gifts from our ancestors. They are part of our struggle."

Gun says, "It's been our family tragedy, but also our gift." He stops in front of me. "Our genius and our madness."

His words grip my spine and squeeze.

"I had no idea," I say.

Ichiro says, "He had no idea? If he had merely acted in a civil and sociable manner, nothing like this would have happened."

Akiko hisses, "He kidnapped and assaulted Haruna. No telling what else he did."

"Nothing, I swear. Nothing. I, I didn't mean to hurt her. I didn't know. I'm sorry, I'm sorry. I'll say it a thousand times. I'll leave town and never come back."

Gun says, "Stop groveling."

Okay, okay. Get hold of yourself.

Ichiro bends close to my ear. "Apologize and leave town? That's not enough."

I need to do something in my own defense. Things are out of control. Think, think, what to do. I should stick to my plan as much as possible. I want to take out my list—it's in my shirt pocket—but it's got my tunnel map on it. I don't want them to know about my culvert explorations.

What was the first step of my plan? Apologize? No, the cleaners. I don't think they will let me go to the cleaners. Next step, apologize? No, buy gifts. I don't think that's possible right now—excuse me folks, do you mind if I go shopping before we continue?

Next was apologizing. I twist in my seat to face Kumi. I'll start with her. "Kumi. Kumi, please. I'm sorry. I'm very sorry for treating you badly. I didn't mean to do anything wrong."

Kumi turns her head toward me. Her eyes focus on me.

In a weird sing-song voice, she says, "Apology function. Social factor. Male-female interaction."

Huh?

Ichiro stares at his daughter while she speaks. Then he glares at me with hate. "She's trying to regain a concept of her self. She's suffering."

Akiko and Gun go to her side. "Kumi, Kumi," they purr.

I didn't do much good with Kumi. I should try Haruna. She's sitting so still, she could be dead. Her eyes—are they still completely black?—are shut tight and her head dangles as if her neck has lost all strength.

I call out softly, "Haruna, Haruna. Look at me. I'm sorry."

She shivers, then buries her head in her hands. She starts to sob.

Akiko steps over to me, raises her hand, and cuffs my ear.

Akiko cuddles Haruna. I say, "I was only trying to help."

Gun says, "Your attempts to help have done more harm than good."

"No," I cry out. "Please, just let me apologize. Let me speak to them. I think I can help them. I want them to know I didn't mean any harm."

Ichiro stands next to Gun. He asks his brother, "What should we do with him?"

That doesn't sound good. I've got to show them they don't have to do anything. I've got to show them I meant no harm.

I try to make eye contact with Kumi. Her eyes are glassy, unfocused. Haruna's face is still buried in her hands, and she is pressed against her mother.

Somebody has to help me. The cops—why aren't they following me now? That makes me think: now I know the identity of the "known criminals." Gun and his friends.

Gun turns to his two friends. He asks them something about "techniques." As in the techniques to use on me? Oh man, oh man, what's going on here? I'm starting to get very concerned.

I've got to work harder. I've got to apologize with more force. How can I get through to Kumi and Haruna? Maybe if I were closer, maybe if I could hold their hands.

I stand up and take half a step toward them.

Both the goons rush at me with such quickness I don't stand a chance. They hit me at the same time, one blow each on my chest. I fly backward, onto the chair. But it doesn't stop my fall. The chair and I flip over and crash to the floor. My skull cracks on the floor.

I must have blacked out for a second or two. The goons are helping me and the chair back upright. My head lolls back and forth, and a moan escapes from deep inside me. My head throbs and I feel dizzy.

No one seems too concerned about my health. In fact, they seem quite happy about my accident. The two brothers and sister form a triangle across the room. They're discussing something.

I've got to get out of here. I need a plan. A new plan.

The Last Ukiyo-e Artist

Toward the end of the year, at the beginning of winter, Takenoko's techniques take a sudden turn. The strokes are almost tortured, sometimes cramped, sometimes they scream out as if he were in constant pain. His themes also take a turn to the darker side: a giant fish, gasping for oxygen, rests on the slope of Mt. Fuji; a man runs toward the mountain, clearly trying to escape the mob chasing him.

The mountain's shape itself becomes twisted and distorted, almost to the point of perversion.

They're talking about me, what to do with me. They talk in oblique terms: chastise, distress, mistreat, damage. It doesn't sound good, whatever they mean. I hear Ichiro mention the private investigator's report. I hear Akiko mention the "malicious rumors." Gun mentions my pathological ordinariness.

I don't know what to say to convince them that I'm harmless. I am harmless—things just got out of control. I got out of control. I've never been out of control before.

I hear Akiko say that Ichiro should take care of the "problem." That must mean me. I'm the problem. I never in my life thought that I'd be considered a problem.

Ichiro admits to having some primary responsibility to handle the problem, as he hired me in the first place. He says that he can handle the problem. Akiko says something about the way he handled the "other problem."

I don't want to be "handled." I'm not a problem to be handled. "I'm not a problem!" My shout echoes in my room. Or maybe just in my head.

Everyone is staring at me. Except Haruna and Kumi.

I say, "Please, just let me go. I'll leave and never come back."

Ichiro says, "No. It's too late for that."

"No, it's not too late," I plead. "Just open the door, and I'll be out of your lives forever. I've tried to apologize; what else can I do?"

Gun says, "You want to run away? Haven't you already tried that? Face up to your crimes; don't be a coward."

But I am. I'm a perfectly ordinary, practically worthless coward. I admit it.

They go back to discussing me—the "problem." It's clear they aren't just going to let me go. I don't want to find out how they're going to make me face up to my crimes. I've got to come up with a plan. The goal of the plan is to escape.

Let's see … to escape I need to get out the door. If only the goon wasn't standing beside me, I could make a dash for it. Okay, where's the voice in my head?

The voice says: Cops.

I say loudly, "You know, the cops are still watching me. They're out there right now. Probably wondering what's going on in here with all the lights on. They might even know you're in here."

Gun says to Ichiro. "I thought you took care of the police."

"I did. I don't know if they believed me. You never can tell."

Gun motions for the goon standing next to me to check at the window. When he's peering out the blinds, I focus on the doorknob. Here's what I'll do: I'll burst up, lunge for the knob, fling open the door, get out in the hall, slam the door behind me, then sprint down the hall. I'll make for the plant; it'll be easy to get lost in the maze of modules.

I tense all my muscles.

I explode out of my seat. My hand reaches the knob and turns it. The door opens and I'm out in the hall. I slam the door behind me. I start sprinting down the hallway.

So far so good. I turn down the corridor leading to the plant. I slow just a little, so I won't burn out. I can't hear anyone following me, but the blood rushing in my ears and my labored breathing drowns out all other sounds.

But they have to be there.

I reach the end of the dormitory. A double, swinging door blocks the corridor. I burst through it. The door swings shut behind me.

I'm running out of gas. I take a turn into the company museum. It's pitch black, but I know my way around. I slide along the exhibits, then duck under the exhibit with the old maps. I take several deep breaths, then slowly and quietly take shallow breaths.

I can make out footsteps, voices. Someone, no, two people come into the museum. Near the entrance, they fumble for the lights. They can't find any; the lights must be automatically controlled.

One set of footsteps runs into the museum. I hold my breath. The footsteps run out of the museum.

I crawl along the floor to the museum entrance. I peer around the door and down the hall. There's no one in sight. I can hear voices coming from the cafeteria.

I dart into the hall, and run the other direction. I slip into the entrance of the main area. No workers are on the floor this time of night.

I run between the modules, looking for the one across from Kumi's computer work station.

There it is. I duck inside.

Takenoko

Takenoko's lungs filled completely, emptied completely, filled completely. His legs pumped up and down. The soles of his feet gripped the ground and pushed off.

But he never moved from the ridge.

He was always running. And if he stopped ...

327.

After I've caught my breath, I crawl to the end of the module, to the ventilation grate I had found in the tunnel.

Footsteps pound through the plant. With trembling fingers, I turn the screws holding the grate in place. One, two, three, four. I put them in my pocket.

I ease the grate from its frame. The footsteps get closer.

My heart is racing. I put the grate next to the hole.

Feet first and on my stomach, I push myself down. My feet touch the bottom of the shaft. I reach for the grate, and pull it back.

I fit the grate in place. Holding it still, I squat as low as I can.

The footsteps stop at the module.

I hold my breath.

The footsteps start and fade away.

I wait a few more seconds. Then I put the screws back into the corners of the grate. My hands are still shaking.

When I finish, I lie down in the ventilation shaft.

I don't move for several minutes. Or several seconds. Or an hour. I don't know; it doesn't matter.

What does matter now? Nothing. My life is over.

The footsteps of my searchers return, I hold my breath. They hurry off.

I wait awhile, then I start to crawl down the ventilation shaft toward the tunnels.

328

I follow the shaft to the main tunnel. The darkness is complete, a pure black. I need to get my flashlight and wrench. I feel my way down the tunnel, being careful not to trip over the rails or any trash lying about.

Wait a minute … hadn't I left the packages of Views at the end of the ventilation shaft? Surely I would have tripped over them crawling along the shaft.

I go back and check the shaft. There aren't any packages. Maybe I left them in another tunnel.

I need to get my flashlight and make a thorough search. Then I remember my map. My wonderful map! I touch my pocket and the piece of paper crinkles comfortingly. It's like running into an old friend. If I had any old friends.

When I retrieve the flashlight I can check my map. My wonderful map!

I make my way back down the shaft, then into the tunnel. I find the darkness comforting, safe. I can stay down here forever if I have to. They won't think of chasing me here.

They'll think I made it outside the plant. They'll check the grounds, the neighborhood. Maybe even ask the police to help. I'll be safe in the tunnels.

Then I hear a noise.

The noise sounds like an aluminum can dropped a few inches. I strain to listen for another sound, and the direction it came from.

For a long time, there's no sound. Then there's a clatter that makes me jump. It's ahead of me in the tunnel. I walk ahead slowly, being careful not to make any noise myself.

The clatter stops. I stop and listen.

The clatter starts again.

In marathon running, the athletes can "hit the wall," which makes every step agony. It is not inconceivable that Takenoko experienced the same phenomenon with his Views. This might explain his tortured technique. Just the strain of the year of painting would be enough to produce a stress-related dementia. What drove him on from this point is an unknown that will never be discovered.

Still, he persevered, through the dark phase, and emerged into a state of euphoria. This euphoria has also been described by marathon runners who break through the "wall."

As I make my way down the tunnel, the clattering noise begins to sound familiar.

Before I get to the end of the tunnel, I catch up with the noise.

It's the nekobaba, pushing her shopping cart.

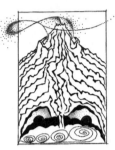

An Emotional Act

I creep up to the nekobaba as she pushes her cart. One of the wheels slides next to the rails; that's where most of the noise is coming from.

I slip ahead of her. There's a sliver of light near the tunnel entrance. I don't think she sees me. I know she's not blind, maybe she's deep in her own thoughts. I doubt it would matter if she did see me. She's not the type to run to the police complaining about a strange man fol-

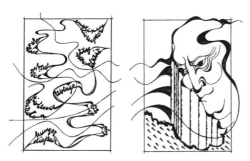

lowing her in a culvert. No one would listen to her.

I pick up my flashlight and the wrench. I put the wrench in my back pocket, and flick the switch of the light. I shine the beam over the shopping cart.

On top of the pile are the packages of Views.

There's no way she could've climbed up the venti-lation shaft to get the Views. Then I remember she used a coat hanger to fish some trash out of a drain. She could have used her coat hanger to drag the Views down from the shaft. But I can't figure out how she knew they were there.

She couldn't have known the packages were there unless she'd seen me put them there. That's possible, but if she could see me then, why can't she see me now? I shine the light on her. She doesn't seem to notice. Could be that she regularly checks the shafts for treasure.

When she bends down to pick up something, I step over the rails to the cart. I quickly gather up the pack-ages of Views and step away. She doesn't notice that either.

Or doesn't care.

When we get to the end of the tunnel she stops. She walks to the grate, pushes on the side. The grate swings open.

She pushes the cart out of the tunnel, then pulls on the grate. It swings shut with a clang. She turns down the main culvert.

I shine the beam of my flashlight along the grate. There's a latch recessed into the side of the grate. It's almost invisible. I pull on it and the grate swings away easily.

Sure is easier than unscrewing the bolts. What else does she know about these tunnels? If I'm going to stay down here for awhile, I could use all the secrets she can show me.

I run back to the ventilation shaft and put the Views inside, far enough so she can't reach them with her coat hanger. Then I run back to the end of the tunnel and out the grate. I close it behind me and head down the culvert.

I shine the light into the next tunnel. The nekobaba is already several yards down the tunnel. I feel along the side of the grate. I find the recessed latch and pull it. The grate swings open.

I shut the grate behind me and walk behind the nekobaba, counting paces as I go.

Tunnel No. 4 starts out much the same as the other three I've been in. There are a few scraps of trash scattered about. Some of them interest the nekobaba, most of them don't. On my map I describe and locate the things she does pick up. I find I can get as close as I want to her without disturbing her.

The nekobaba stops at a trash pyramid. From her shopping cart, she takes a soy milk box—complete with straw sticking out the hole—and inserts it onto the pyramid. I pause to look at her latest addition, while she clatters down the tunnel.

Although I can't explain exactly why, the soy milk box seems somehow to fit right where she put it. The feeling is … I don't know … right?

She leads me through the tunnel, placing items here and there, picking up others. She doesn't seem to like drab bits. The brighter the color the better. But how can she see colors in the darkness of the tunnels? She apparently can't even see me.

She might be blind.

Akiko watched her mother stare at the painting—one of the Mt. Fuji paintings. What did she see in it?

Akiko sat behind her and stared.

Gradually, the colors and shapes began to move. They became alive. They told a story. They talked to her.

Her mother picked at a corner and started to tear the paper. Akiko pushed her, then chased her away.

The tunnel starts to widen as had No. 2 and No. 3. I shine my light around. There are hundreds of the trash pyramids. It's a forest of pyramids. They go on forever. Some grow out of another pyramid. The highest comes up to my chest.

The nekobaba spends a long time here. She adds new pieces of trash, rearranges the old. Entranced, amazed, I watch her work.

After a long time—I no longer care—the nekobaba starts to move deeper into the tunnel. The humming gets louder. We must be getting closer to the robotic assembly line.

We make our way through the maze of pyramids. I feel a growing excitement at finding out what lies ahead.

We come to a wall. I shine my light up and down. It's an immense wall, rising way above our heads. In the center is a huge square door, made of iron. It has rusted away in a few spots.

The nekobaba crawls though a ragged hole in the lower corner. She has to leave the shopping cart outside.

I crawl in after her, and almost run into her on the other side of the iron door. I step aside, as she reaches back through the hole and pulls the cart close.

The space is high enough for a two-story, maybe three-story building. It's equally as wide, and long enough for a soccer field. Along both sides are tiers of concrete, connected by metal scaffolding and stairs. The tiers and scaffolding form a semi-cylindrical shape.

A submarine would fit perfectly into the shape. This must be one of the rooms where they actually built them.

Only instead of a submarine there's a towering pyramid of trash, filling most of the space under the scaffolding.

The trash pile is so immense the beam of my flashlight gets swallowed up in it. The myriad of colors, the intricate patterns, the hugeness of it ... I have to sit down.

The humming noise pulsates through the wall to my right. It must be adjacent to the robotics plant. Ventilation grates dot the far wall. I shut off my flashlight. Through the grates, light filters down onto the scene. It's not much light, but enough to see shapes.

And the shape I see now in the massive trash pyramid, is the shape of Mt. Fuji.

Mt. Fuji!

All of the nekobaba's trash pyramids represent Mt. Fuji.

I can only sit and stare at her Mt. Fuji. How long did it take her to construct it?

Years, no doubt. Decades probably. A lifetime.

What craziness.

The nekobaba slowly walks past me, carrying a handful of trash. She's bent over at the waist, until her upper body is nearly parallel with the floor. She takes small, steady, oddly graceful steps.

She walks along the concrete platform to the middle of the mountain, where she places a piece of her trash. Or is it treasure? Post-modern artists would call it "found-object art." Whatever, it's no longer trash.

She's no longer merely a crazy old nekobaba.

The Ono woman asked, "If you were to sell these Mt. Fuji paintings of yours how much would you make?"

Takenoko shook his head. "I don't know. I've never sold such works."

"You never sold anything before? I thought you said you were an artist."

"I've been hired to do illustrations. I've never sold my own paintings."

The Ono woman dropped the painting onto the stack. "So they're worthless, then."

Ichiro unlocked the storage room. Inside, he removed a stack of Views. He took a deep breath and began to study the top painting. His gaze followed each line; he soaked in each color as if it were a hot bath.

After going through the stack, he put them away and went to find his mother.

In the garden, he found her staring at a moss-covered rock. She reached out and picked up a small pebble. She placed it on top of the rock.

Ichiro said softly, "Are you ready to go, Mother?"

The nekobaba is an avant-garde, multimedia, found-object, collage artist. She could be the darling of the Tokyo art scene. She could get nationwide—worldwide—press coverage. She could make a fortune.

She slowly climbs the metal stairs. Very slowly. One step a minute. She keeps one hand on the railing.

At the top of the stairs, she walks along a concrete tier until she reaches a precise point where she places another of her found objects.

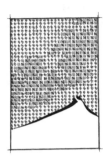

She repeats the process several times, until she runs out of objects to place, or none that she's collected satisfy her.

She climbs out of the hole in the metal door, and pushes the cart back down the tunnel. I stay with her Mt. Fuji. I just want to sit and take it all in.

Gazing at the mountain is the most restful, stimulating, enjoyable thing I've done in a long time. Perhaps ever.

After a long while, the nekobaba returns with more objects. She places them on her masterpiece. This time I follow her closely.

She seems to have a method (to her madness?) but I can't figure it out yet.

The white hamburger wrapper goes between the yellow plastic beer cup and the blue candy box.

The scrap of pink towel goes on top of the calendar photo of a sailboat.

Days go by. The nekobaba comes and goes, never seeming to rest, never sleeping. I seem to have lost the need to sleep myself, although I may doze off and not know it. I've lost connection with my consciousness.

I suddenly want something to eat and drink, but it's a different feeling from hunger or thirst. It's more like a phantom memory, déjà vu.

I pull out my map. The cafeteria supply chutes are there at the end of tunnel No. 3.

The cafeteria supply chutes offer whatever I want to eat or drink. I select apple juice, a ham sandwich, corn chips, a small salad. It tastes all right, though I would have thought it would be really delicious after so long without food.

But all I want to do is stare at the nekobaba's Mt. Fuji.

Gun said, "It's decided. We'll all be better off. Including her. So let's not be glum." He went into the bar and returned with a bottle of the best sake and three cups. He poured a round and set down the bottle.

He raised his cup. "To Mother."

Akiko and Ichiro raised their cups. "To Mother."

After I've eaten, I explore the last tunnel. It's similar to No. 1, not much there, and it quickly comes to a dead end. I return to tunnel No. 2 and check to see if the Views are still there. They are. I crawl through the ventilation shaft.

At the grate inside the control module, I peer into the plant. I can see Kumi's work station, but she's not there.

I wonder briefly how she is doing. Even more briefly, I feel a pang of regret, but I don't know exactly why I should. I don't dwell on it. It's too late to do anything about it.

It's too late to worry about anything.

I spend the next several days watching the neko-baba work on her Mt. Fuji. For awhile I keep notes of what she puts where, but I quickly run out of room on my page. So now I just watch.

I try not to think about what she's doing. I try to absorb.

The urge occasionally comes over me to find a piece of trash and place it where I think it works. Then I could see if she agrees or not. But I don't want to disturb her.

Her use of colors, I find, is especially intriguing. When up close, the colors seem quite randomly placed, even garish, or clashing. But from a few steps back, it's obvious the mix works.

On a grand scale, it's a giant water color, painted on a three-dimensional canvas.

The colors form patterns that swirl and move. Stare at one place long enough and the mountain dances.

Her artistic themes are becoming clear to me, although I still wouldn't know how to emulate her. She definitely is applying a set of aesthetics.

Aesthetics—the word brings up another dimming memory. I hope Kumi is all right. She's better off without me around. I don't really miss her. In fact, I haven't missed the outside world. No one misses me, I'm sure. They're all better off. I'm certainly better off.

In every moment, I exist at a sustained level of excitement, of joy. I can barely stand to be away from the mountain to forage for food.

As time passes, I try to anticipate where the nekobaba will place each object. Often I'm wrong, but when I'm right a thrill races through me.

I find I'm most successful when I don't think about it, but rely totally on feeling.

Does the nekobaba paint on pure emotion?

In appreciation for the nekobaba showing me her work, I decide to give her a gift. I go to tunnel No. 2 and climb into the ventilation shaft. While I'm inside I think about looking through the grate to see if Kumi is back at work. But that wouldn't mean anything to me—either she is or she isn't. Either she's back to normal or she isn't. Either way doesn't change things for me.

So I don't look into the plant. I crawl back down the shaft with the six packages of Views.

Back at the giant Mt. Fuji room, I open the packages. The Views inside bring back memories of cataloging them at the museum. And at Gun's club and Akiko's ryokan. But the memories no longer have emotions attached.

The six Views themselves, however, give me a little spark of emotion. Nothing as powerful as when I'm gazing at the nekobaba's mountain, but a tremor all the same.

I use my flashlight (which I hardly ever have to use anymore) to examine the Views closely.

I see something that makes me jump.

The patterns of colors in Takenoko's Views have the same feel as the nekobaba's.

There's the same clash that works.

The same animation.

The same emotion.

I'd like to ask the nekobaba how she arrived at her style, her aesthetics. And to ask if Takenoko's Views influenced her. But our relationship isn't verbal. I have to find out some other way.

I take the Views outside the main room while she is working on the mountain. I place the Views on top of her piled-high shopping cart.

Then I wait.

She eventually returns to her shopping cart. She pokes around, picking out objects and putting them back. Then she feels higher, and stops at the stack of Views.

She pulls the top one down and holds it in front of her.

She makes a small sound. I've never heard her make a sound before. The sound isn't much of a sound. It's not much more than a murmur.

It might be a murmur of recognition. Or of loss. It's hard to tell one murmur from another.

She holds a painting in front of her, as if she's looking at it, though I still have no idea if she can see. She holds it for a long time, as time goes in the tunnels. Then she reaches up and feels the others. She brings them down one at a time and holds them in front of her.

She returns all the Views, except one, onto the pile. Then she begins to tear the painting.

I don't stop her. I'm enthralled, thrilled. It's such an emotional act, one that goes against all my training as a curator, as an art historian.

She isn't tearing at random. She selects very specific areas to tear away. Areas of particular colors, of certain patterns, get her attention.

It's a slow deliberate process. But everything she does is that way.

As I watch her, I realize she's become ancient since I've been in the tunnels. She no longer has a body.

She's merely dust.

Takenoko

Standing above the praying mantis, Takenoko inhaled sharply. It was as if he suddenly recognized a long-lost friend in a crowd. He began to sketch.

The insect's two antennae poking out of its head formed a perfect, inverted Mt. Fuji.

The Last Ukiyo-e Artist

To say that the last seven or so of the 365 Views of Mt. Fuji—indeed, the last known works by Takenoko—reveal the artist's brilliance would be a subjective opinion at best. However, this author must express such an opinion. Their construction portrays a range of emotion from utter despair to a fervor of exhilaration. They are embodied with pure emotion.

What was happening to the artist at this time? Was he going mad? Indeed, the dramatic emotional contrasts in the Views might be explained by psychologists as the work of someone undergoing violent mood swings. Contrary to normal pathology when such mood swings occur over the course of days or weeks, Takenoko's were occurring on a daily (perhaps hour-by-hour) periodicity.

When she's torn away several bits of the View, she puts what's left on top of the other Views. She crawls back through the hole into the main room. I follow her.

She adds the bits on her work. I nod to myself at each brilliant placement. I anticipate each of her moves—well, nearly all of them.

My excitement reaches a new high. Her genius fills me up.

Or am I just going mad?

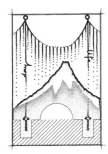

Genius. Madness.
Gun!
Genius and madness. The blurry line between them.
If there's a line at all.

The nekobaba works steadily on tearing the Views into bits of color and patterns. I watch with glowing confidence in my own ability to place the trash using my emotions. The nekobaba is training me to give up thinking. I'm her apprentice. Now I want to graduate to assistant. I want to help her more directly.

Without much effort, I think of an idea.

I walk out of the culvert and into the night air. The openness is frightening; I want to run back into the comfort of the tunnels, but I force myself ahead.

I hurry across the grounds of the Ono Robotics plant, and to the dormitory parking lot. My car is where I left it. I get in, take a deep breath, and let it out slowly.

I put the key in the ignition, the engine starts right up. I look into the rearview mirror.

I don't recognize the reflection. The person's hair is matted, wild. The person's face is bearded, smudged with dirt and grease.

I'm glad it's not a full-length mirror. I never did make it to the cleaners.

Fine
with Me

My muscles have lost much of their coordination for driving. The car feels alien, as if it's in control, not me.

After a few minutes, though, my muscles respond automatically to the car and the road. Similarly, I suppose, I could reintegrate myself into society without much effort. All it would take is a shower and a shave. Update my résumé, get a job, get an apartment. One trip to the cleaners.

But all that would be too much effort for me.

I turn onto the road leading to Hakone.

With my headlights off, I turn into the museum parking lot. I pull up near the front, but away from the front entrance. I don't know if the security guard is on duty. I'll deal with him if I have to. I just hope my card key works.

I peer through the front door. I don't see anyone prowling around. I try my key. It still works. I open the door and step inside.

I stride toward the Views storage room. My legs are stiff, not used to walking so fast. I start to trot; I need to get in and out quickly.

I think I hear a noise. I stop and listen, but don't hear anything. It might be my own footsteps echoing in the stark museum corridor.

I open the storage room, flick on the lights, and begin pulling out the Views from their file drawers. I pile them up on the table behind me.

I make them into a neat stack and pick it up. The stack is heavy, but I think I can handle it.

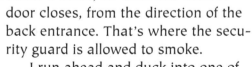

Ichiro

"Nothing matters," Ichiro said. He stroked Kumi's hair as she trembled. "Nothing matters except that you get better. I'm sorry that things didn't go well. I thought you were stronger. You seemed to be doing very well."

Kumi pulled at her hair.

Ichiro noticed she had her mother's perfectly proportioned fingers.

I close the storage room door, and walk quickly toward the front. I hear a noise, for sure this time. A door closes, from the direction of the back entrance. That's where the security guard is allowed to smoke.

I run ahead and duck into one of the gallery spaces. I flatten myself against the wall and listen. The guard's shoes clip-clap down the corridor toward me.

My arms start to ache, then tremble under the weight of the Views.

The guard walks past the gallery.

I wait until the footsteps stop. From the distance he's gone he's probably in the administrative offices. Maybe settling in for a nap.

I wait as long as my arms will let me. Then I head out of the gallery.

Before I leave the gallery, I notice I'm in the room with the view of Mt. Fuji.

I turn and take one last look.

Kumi

<<aaplgy:f c ti ti o>>

UNREADABLE FILE-
DO YOU WISH TO RESTART-

<<,sy m, =,,.. i fneht.fi l.... /so/ci/>>

-Y/N?-
-Y/N?-

 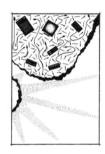

I slip out of the museum undetected. I open the trunk and lay the Views flat. I close the lid quietly.

I slip the car out of gear and coast down the sloping parking lot until I reach the road. I start the engine.

Then, at last, I take a breath.

The gangster's son asked, "Did it turn out like you planned?"

Gun thought about the question. "That's difficult to answer. For one thing, it wasn't my plan so much as my brother's. But I suppose in the long run it will work."

The gangster's son lit a cigarette. He nodded and said, "The long run."

Gun said, "I need a fix. Do you have any recalcitrant clients who need your special treatment?"

The gangster's son exhaled smoke from his mouth and nose. "Always plenty of them around. Let's go."

During the drive to Atami, I recall some of the conversations I shared with Gun. At times he was quite interesting, at others he was irritating. Thinking back on it now, I had been blind to the dangerous edge to all his conversations.

My memories of the Onos and the museum are coming back now that I'm out of the tunnels. It makes me want to get back as quickly as possible.

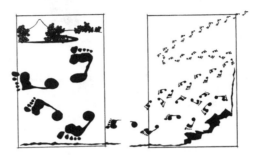

I arrive in front of Gun's club, around midnight, according to my dependable car clock. The show should just be under way; Gun should be busy for another two hours. I park in front of the door to Gun's residence.

I get out and unlock the trunk, but leave the lid down. I walk up to the door and try the handle. It's unlocked, as it had been the last time I was here. I open the door and go inside.

I tiptoe in, leaving the door ajar. I peek around the corner into the sitting room. Tabo is there.

He's asleep on the couch, his naked backside to me. His robe is pinched between his legs. He's snoring loudly.

I sneak past him, and into Gun's private gallery. The door opens. I go in, then try the door handle to the storage room. It's locked.

I go back to the sitting room, where I steal up to Tabo. I reach down to his robe and find the pocket. His keys are inside. I grasp them firmly so they won't jangle when I pull them out.

I get the keys and creep away from Tabo. He doesn't twitch a muscle.

Back in the gallery, I close the door behind me, unlock the storage room, and turn on the lights. I leave the keys on a table behind a vase of flowers out in the hall. Then I empty the Views out of the storage files. I also take the Views out of the moveable frames in the gallery.

Before I gather them up, I turn off the lights and peek into the sitting room.

Tabo is still asleep. I carry the Views out of the gallery, and quietly shut the door. I walk out of the house, and put the Views in the trunk. I go back and shut the door silently.

Then I get back in the car and roll down the slope until I'm well out of sight.

I drive down the Izu coast. Moonlight reflects off the water. I'm feeling good, successful. But getting the Views out of Akiko's ryokan might not be so easy.

The drive to Heda is tiring. The road winds constantly, without giving me a chance to relax. Tension builds up.

I decide I can get inside the ryokan easily enough, and get the Views from the storage room and the ones from the rooms with no guests.

That would be the majority of Akiko's collection, but I want them all. I hope there aren't many guests. I'll have to sneak into their rooms. Guests at a ryokan usually sleep soundly, what with the food and drinks and hot bath, not to mention sex.

The most difficult Views to get will be the ones in Akiko's and Haruna's rooms. From what I remember, they never sleep at all.

When I get to the inn, I see another problem I hadn't thought of: the gravel drive. It would be noisy driving on it, so I park off the side of the road. I walk up to the inn.

I go around the main entrance and enter the garden off the guest wing. I can smell the warm mineral waters of the onsen. It's tempting, but I don't have time for a bath.

The sliding door off the garden is unlocked and I go inside. The inn is quiet. I look into the first room off the garden. It's empty. I take the View from the tokonoma alcove.

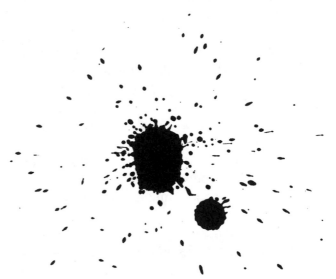

I quickly gather the Views from the empty rooms. Only three of the rooms have guests—a fairly slow night. Next, I gather the Views from the storage room. I take these outside into the garden and put them on a rock bench.

Back inside the inn, I sneak into the first room with guests. They don't stir as I slip the View from the tokonoma and slide out. The other two rooms go just as smoothly.

I put these three Views with the others. Now, I have to get the last two Views.

I creep through the ryokan, until I come to Haruna's room. It's dark, and I peer inside. The room is empty. I hurry in, take the View, and put it with the others.

Then I edge down the hall. A light comes from the door, which is ajar slightly. I peer inside the room.

Akiko and Haruna are sitting across from each other, at a low table. A teapot and two cups are on the table. Akiko is speaking in a very quiet voice. I can't make out any of her words.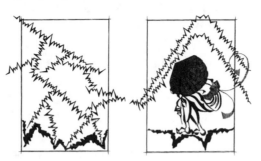

The last View is hanging in Akiko's tokonoma.

I back away from the room, and go back into the garden. I gather up the Views and take them down to my car.

I put the Views in my trunk and stand beside the car looking up to Heda Onsen. I can't leave it; there's something important about having all of them.

I rummage through my glove box and find a couple of boxes of matches. I walk back to the inn, along the outside porch until I come to Akiko's room. A few feet away from her window, I gather some dry twigs and pile them up. I strike a match, and use the flame to ignite the box. I toss it into the pile of twigs, then throw the other box on top. The matches flare up with a loud hiss.

I run around the inn to the garden entrance. I wait in the darkness.

Akiko runs past the garden window, toward the front door.

Akiko

Akiko said to Haruna, "You'll never have to leave again. I promise. It's over."

They sat together, huddled as if against the fury of a storm.

Akiko said, "You have to be strong. To help me when I can no longer fight."

Haruna stared ahead blankly.

Akiko said, "You'll be a wonderful mother. I'll help you."

351

Haruna

Shapes out of focus
  Whorls of light
  Tortured shadows

I bolt out of the garden, down the hall, and into Akiko's room. Haruna is lying on the tatami floor, staring up at the View. I don't say anything to her. I don't know what I could say.

I rip the View off the wall. Haruna reaches a hand up toward the painting. She doesn't seem to notice me, all of her focus is on the View. I hesitate. For a moment I think I should give it to her.

I turn away and run back into the garden. From there, I climb the steps that lead past the outdoor bath. I head for the ridge clearing.

On top of the ridge, I look back to the inn. I don't see a conflagration, so I assume Akiko has put out my little fire.

I take one last look at the dark outline of Mt. Fuji from the ridge before I climb down to the road.

Back at the Ono Robotics plant, I drive as close as I can to the culvert. I unload the Views into tunnel No. 1, then I drive my car back to the same parking place. I turn off the engine, and leave the keys in the ignition.

I tell my Toyota Sprinter Marino good-bye.

Takenoko

Takenoko waited on the ridge for the sun to rise. He shivered in the cold. He shivered in fear. He shivered in anticipation. One last painting.

He could barely raise his hand; his fingers were stiff as crab claws. His brushes were worn to nubs. He had to scrape his paint jars for colors.

Back in the tunnels, I transfer the Views to the great Mt. Fuji room. I spend hours (days? weeks?) looking at them. Even in the dim light I can see their beauty, their genius, their madness.

In fact, I see them completely differently now from when I first started the curator's job. They reach deep inside me, pluck at my emotions.

The outside world had seemed different as well. No longer real, it was cold, artificial.

Practically worthless.

As I finish looking at the Views I stack them near the hole to the great Mt. Fuji room, where the nekobaba can find them. And find them she does. She begins tearing them into color swatches.

I continue to watch her methods and learn more. Just when I think I've learned all I can from her, she uses a slight variation that astounds me.

Perhaps her own style is evolving as she works. I'll never catch up with her.

I come to the last View. It's different from the others. The scene is mostly taken up with the face of a young woman. She's gazing toward the viewer, slightly off to one side. Her eyes are sad, tired.

The corners of her mouth are slightly upturned, a hint of a smile. She has a dimple on one cheek, but not the other.

There's a very blurred image of Mt. Fuji far in the distance. Almost as if it were an afterthought.

The Last Ukiyo-e Artist

Did Takenoko suffer from a psychological pathology such as cyclothymia disorder, which could have propelled him to perform such a prodigious feat as the 365 Views of Mt. Fuji? It has been shown that many artists suffer from violent mood swings that launch them into periods of high productivity, or into periods of severe depression that inhibit them from working at all. No works have appeared that post-date the Views.

The final mystery is the young woman in the last View. Who is she? Is she real at all?

I keep this View to myself for several days. I look at it often, staring at it for hours at a time. Almost as much as I stare at the nekobaba's grand Mt. Fuji. There's something about the woman in the last View … do I recognize her?

Who knows how long this goes on? Days, weeks, months.

Then, the nekobaba dies.

353.

Takenoko

"So," the Ono woman said. "You've actually done it. A painting a day for a year. Let's see the last one."

She picked it off the top of the stack. She gasped. "I told you not to paint her." She started to tear it in half.

Takenoko used his last dying bit of energy and grabbed her hands. They struggled against each other, until Takenoko took back the painting. The Ono woman ran from the hut.

Takenoko bundled up the 365 Views, and hauled them to Natsuko's room in the inn. Then he stumbled back to his hut.

She hadn't come back to the great Mt. Fuji room for a long time. I go in search of her and find her in the tunnel.

I kneel next to her. She's in the fetal position beside her cart. It was as if she leaned over to pick up a piece of trash and just died.

I touch her arm; it's light as a handful of ash. It's as if she's been dead for centuries.

What should I do with her?

Her face is caked with dirt. I try to brush some away. But its hard to tell dirt from skin.

I just sit beside her.

I wonder who she was—where she was born, how old she was, how she came to her life in a culvert.

It doesn't matter. What matters is what she's accomplished, what she's built. A magnificent piece of art.

But no one would have seen it, if I hadn't stumbled into the tunnels. If I hadn't screwed up my life.

It doesn't matter who she is. Even if she does have some family somewhere, they likely wouldn't want to know she died. They wouldn't want to know how she lived. Her family would be the uninspired people who only stop at officially designated Scenic Views.

They wouldn't care what their eccentric granny did with the litter of the outside world. They wouldn't see her genius. They'd only see her madness and be ashamed.

I owe the nekobaba more than I can repay. That's a heavy burden. She's shown me her genius. I can only do one thing.

Keep her genius alive.

First I bury the nekobaba. I place her in a clean spot of the tunnel, near her forest of smaller Mt. Fuji monoliths. Then I carefully place several of them around her. Then I place more on top of her, until she's completely covered.

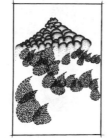

Good bye, nekobaba.

After I've put the finishing touches on the nekobaba's grave, I go on my first scavenging expedition. Just outside the main culvert, I come across a box of trash. Inside are
envelopes stuffed with photos,
design magazines,
several pieces of sports equipment (a tennis racket, a squash racket, skates, jogging shoes), and
a few videos, mostly French film noir.
Someone's discarded life.

When I return, I feel I'm ready to take over for the nekobaba. I tear off a piece of a View—a bit of red from a sunset. The paper rips easily.

I take the scrap into the great Mt. Fuji room. I walk up the stairs and down the scaffolding.

I place it in precisely the right spot.

Takenoko

The blows from the fishermen were heavy. Takenoko couldn't fend them off. They rained down continuously, until he could feel nothing.

The Ono woman was screaming.

When they stopped, Takenoko couldn't move, couldn't breathe. It was as if the weight of Mt. Fuji was on his chest. Then the flames of the volcano surrounded him.

The praying mantis skittered across his face.

Junko

Has anyone ever really died from a broken heart?

Junko doubted it.

Of course, many have committed suicide out of rejection.

But that's an ego problem, not a broken heart.

Ichiro

Of course, thought Ichiro, the tunnels of the old submarine factory were the right spot for her. She could roam without hurting anything. Perhaps she would find herself.

Ichiro gathered his mother out of the car.

355

It takes me a very long time to place all the bits of color from the Views. A very long time.

But eventually I run out of colors to place on the Fuji. It's time for me to go out into the world and gather new objects. New colors.

I push the cart down the tunnel. I open the latch and swing open the grate. I push the cart out into the culvert.

I close it, and push the cart down the culvert.

Out of the culvert, I push the cart down the street.

A mother with two children cross the street in front of me. The youngest says, "Mommie, look at that dirty man."

The other says, "He smells."

The mother drags away her kids.

Another woman hurries past without looking at me. It's as if I'm invisible.

Fine with me.

Ichiro, Gun, Akiko

The three siblings stood in the great Mt. Fuji room. Akiko spoke first: "It's beautiful, isn't it?"

Gun said, "Pure genius."

Ichiro said, "It turned out much better than I had dreamed."

OTHER FICTION AND POETRY TITLES
ABOUT JAPAN FROM STONE BRIDGE PRESS

One Hot Summer in Kyoto by John Haylock

Death March on Mount Hakkoda by Jiro Nitta

Wind and Stone by Masaaki Tachihara

Still Life and Other Stories by Junzo Shono

Right under the big sky, I don't wear a hat by Hosai Ozaki

The Name of the Flower by Kuniko Mukoda

CONTEMPORARY JAPANESE WOMEN'S POETRY
A Long Rainy Season: Haiku and Tanka
Other Side River: Free Verse
edited by Leza Lowitz, Miyuki Aoyama, and Akemi Tomioka

Basho's Narrow Road: Spring and Autumn Passages
by Matsuo Basho, with commentary by Hiroaki Sato

Naked: Poems by Shuntaro Tanikawa

Hojoki by Kamo-no-Chomei

Milky Way Railroad by Kenji Miyazawa

Ravine and Other Stories by Yoshikichi Furui

The Broken Bridge: Fiction from Expatriates in Literary Japan
edited by Suzanne Kamata

ABOUT THE AUTHOR AND ILLUSTRATOR

TODD SHIMODA is a third-generation Japanese American born in Colorado, and has lived in California, Texas, and Nevada. He also lived and worked in Japan with his wife Linda (L.J.C. Shimoda). He has

worked as an engineer, a technical writer, and has published fiction in small-press venues. When not writing he is working on a Ph.D. at the University of California at Berkeley, studying artificial intelligence applications in education. He strongly believes in the saying that everyone should climb Mt. Fuji once, but only a fool climbs it twice.

L.J.C. (LINDA) SHIMODA was born in Texas and has lived in California, Colorado, Oklahoma, New Mexico, and London, England. She is an artist working in media ranging from pen-and-ink to photography, digital to brush, oil to found-objects. She has shown her work through Asylum Gallery, the Women's Caucus for Art, other juried shows, and several books and magazines. The illustrations in *365 Views of Mt. Fuji* were first conceived while she lived in a small town at the foot of Mt. Fuji. She never felt the need to climb the mountain.